MOONSET

MOONSET

THE LEGACY OF MOONSET: BOOK ONE

SCOTT TRACEY

Woodbury, Minnesota

First Edition
First Printing, 2013

Book design by Bob Gaul
Cover design by Kevin R. Brown
Cover images: Antique padlock © iStockphoto.com/DNY59
          Highlight © iStockphoto.com/Amanda Rohde
          Rusty chains © iStockphoto.com/Brian Carpenter
          Antique blank book © iStockphoto.com/Joe Cicak
          Orange vintage background © iStockphoto.com/ShutterWorx

Flux, an imprint of Llewellyn Worldwide Ltd.

This is a work of fiction. Names, characters, places, and incidents are either the product of the author's imagination or are used fictitiously, and any resemblance to actual persons, living or dead, business establishments, events, or locales is entirely coincidental. Cover models used for illustrative purposes only and may not endorse or represent the book's subject.

Library of Congress Cataloging-in-Publication Data
Tracey, Scott, 1979–
  Moonset/Scott Tracey.
      pages cm.—(The Legacy of Moonset; book 1)
  Summary: Five orphaned teenagers, the offspring of a terrorist witch coven known as Moonset, struggle against the destructive legacy left by their parents.
  ISBN 978-0-7387-3529-0
  [1. Witches—Fiction. 2. Magic—Fiction. 3. Terrorism—Fiction. 4. Orphans—Fiction.] I. Title.
  PZ7.T6815Mo 2013
  [Fic]—dc23
                                                    2012033956

Flux
Llewellyn Worldwide Ltd.
2143 Wooddale Drive
Woodbury, MN 55125-2989
www.fluxnow.com

Printed in the United States of America

ONE

"Moonset, a coven of such promise. Until they turned to the darkness. Their acts of terrorism fueled by dark magic nearly destroyed us. But we fought back. And we won."

....

Illana Bryer (C: Fallingbrook)
From a speech given the
night Moonset was captured

There were two hundred forty-five students involved in the riot. What had started as a minor altercation between the basketball and track teams had devolved into a literal kind of class warfare. Freshmen against juniors, girls against boys, art kids versus burnouts, 4Hers against everyone.

The town's entire full-time police force, all three of them, had been trying for the better part of an hour to reestablish control. Reinforcements had been called, the rest of the school had been evacuated, and I found myself in the principal's office with my sister, only two days shy of winter break. We'd been so close this time.

We sat in silence: Jenna examining her nails and touching up her makeup and me leaning against the window, afraid to peek between the blinds. The view overlooked the front quad, and today it offered a glimpse of madness. I don't know how she'd managed it, but the entire school had lost it an hour ago.

These things tended to happen when Jenna got bored.

She favored me with a sullen, annoyed look. I didn't have to say anything, didn't have to sift through old frustrations and new accusations until I knew the words I wanted to use. One look, and Jenna saw it all on my face. She always did.

"Calm down, Justin," she said after I'd closed my eyes. "It's no big deal."

"Getting kicked out of school is a big deal, Jen."

"The first time, maybe," she mused, "but you've had enough practice by now. You're a pro." This was school number seven, and I definitely should have seen this coming.

Jenna and I were unaffectionately known as "the twins." It was how people introduced us, talked about us, traded stories about us. Like we were really a single person split between two bodies. It never failed that the minute Jenna crossed the line and got hauled in to a principal's office, I was right behind her. Our fates had been super-glued together for our entire lives.

Especially in situations that involved buzzwords like "vandalism of school property," "suspicious fires," and "criminal charges."

Seven schools in three years. We'd almost made it through an entire semester, and I'd gotten lazy. I forgot what Jenna could do with just a few whispered words. Riots were the tip of the iceberg. Fitting, since Jenna's rap sheet was the size of Antarctica.

To be fair, not all of the expulsions were her fault. One of them was our brother Malcolm's, and a few others were for reasons we didn't fully understand.

Our lives were just a tad complicated.

I looked around the room, but the precarious stacks of paperwork on the desk were definitely a theme in this office. Every available surface had something on it. Even the lampshade was littered with blue Post-its.

"Bailey's going to be crushed," I pointed out absently. How does anyone find anything in here? There's too much paperwork—and too much bureaucracy—for one small-town principal. I couldn't even think of his name. It wasn't Reynolds, that was the last school. Jeffries, maybe?

"She'll get over it," Jenna said, keeping her words light. Bailey always got her heart crushed when we moved. She threw herself into every new school as if it would be the last. It never was.

"Don't you think we're running out of schools?" I said wearily. This was an argument we'd had a thousand times.

"We haven't even tried Europe," she fired back. Her fingers tapped restlessly against the wooden arm of the chair. "I hate waiting. Where is he?"

"I apologize if cleaning up your mess has inconvenienced you in any way," the principal said from behind us. I turned just in time to see him pushing a wiry blonde boy into the room and then closing the door. "I can only imagine the kinds of delinquency I'm keeping you from, Miss Bellamont," he continued.

The blond boy was the last of our siblings, Cole, and his arrival with the principal meant nothing good. Cole tried to saunter in, only to nearly trip over himself. He ended up lunging for the back of my chair, trying to keep himself upright.

Somewhere after Seattle, he'd finally grown into his ears. When we were kids, Cole was the kid with giant Dumbo ears dwarfing the sides of his head. Now they were barely notable. Although he still hadn't hit a decent growth spurt. He was the shortest boy in the school.

What'd he do now? was quickly followed by how could he possibly make a riot any worse? "What'd you do, Cole?" I asked, already wishing I didn't have to ask. Things went from bad to worse so quickly around us I should have been expecting it.

Jenna was more acerbic. "You got caught?"

Cole had the decency to look ashamed. I pretended it was because he'd helped start a riot and not because he'd gotten caught. "I just wanted a good seat." A few seconds of silence went by, and he continued. "And maybe I was egging some of the football jerks on."

"You were shouting out quotes from *Gladiator* and trying to tear your shirt off," the principal said dryly. He was a red-haired, mustached man who I hadn't talked to since we'd enrolled four months ago.

"I just wanted to know if they were entertained," Cole said, blushing a little, before he caught a glimpse of Jenna's waspish look and his voice died.

She and I traded a look. "Can we get on with this? I'd like to deface my locker before the last bell," she said, as though she were on a schedule.

The principal sucked in a deep breath, and held it. I wondered who he was praying to. Buddha? Jesus? St. Jude, the patron saint of lost causes? Whatever god he was praying to, it wouldn't help. Jenna defied the power of prayer.

"I have put up with enough from you and your lot," he said.

Your lot. I could practically hear Jenna preening next to me. There was nothing she liked better than someone who tried to put her in her place. Especially when it was an adult.

I could see it all laid out in front of me, even before it happened. It wouldn't be enough for Jenna to embarrass the principal by making him look like an incompetent, she'd want a hand in embarrassing him personally. I chanced a look to my left. The anticipation was nearly killing her. There was more to come. What did she have on him? Alcoholism? Mistress?

"Now then," the principal said, exhaling. I could almost see The Speech building up strength, rising from his gut as he worked through the preliminaries. The part about not quite understanding how things had gone so wrong. A whole subconversation about how we clearly needed things that Byron High could not provide. Principals, no surprise, rather enjoyed The Speech. The one that ended with the word "expelled."

But his joy was to be short-lived. An insistent knock cut off what he was about to say. "I told you I wasn't to be disturbed," he shouted.

There was silence on the other side. And then a slower, insolent series of raps on the door. Jenna covered her mouth with her hand, but it didn't stifle the giggle. Not that she wanted it too.

The principal muttered something under his breath, and got up to open the door. "Marjorie—" he cut off, because the woman on the other side definitely wasn't the part-time receptionist that he expected. The woman on the other side was all business. She wore a pantsuit paired with an emerald-green blouse and a charcoal gray overcoat. Her thick, unnatural red hair hung down loose, almost as curly as Jenna's.

Cole's eyes about fell out of his head. Jenna and I exchanged a look, and without missing a beat she grabbed the fabric of his shirt, pulling him closer towards us.

"Jeffries?" the woman asked in a deep, smoky tone.

I could tell that Jeffries wanted to hitch up his pants and start blustering. This woman—though she was only in her twenties—had him sized up in a second, and strode into the room, heels staccato against the floor.

Who is she? Jenna mouthed. I shrugged.

"If you'll step outside," the woman said to him, while her eyes slid over us imperiously.

Jenna sat up, even more alert than she'd been before.

Neither of us had missed the dismissive curl of the redhead's lips as she looked us over. Whoever she was, she knew who we were.

Without as much as a please, the woman turned and headed back out into the front office. Through the gap in the door, I saw another man waiting near the receptionist's desk, in the same kind of business casual as the redhead. Jeffries gaped for a moment, then all of a sudden he lurched forward, like an automaton brought to life.

Jenna was muttering under her breath when the principal grabbed the door handle on his way out. The door swung closed, but didn't catch all the way. I crossed the room, nudged it open just a crack, and waited.

The three of us were absolutely still, our ears straining for what was going on out there.

" … taking them immediately."

Principal Jeffries cleared his throat. "I'm sorry, I don't understand what you're telling me."

"As long as they remain here, your students, as well as your faculty, are in danger," the woman said, obviously annoyed at having to repeat herself.

"I'm aware of that," the principal said in a huff. "Those students started a riot. Or didn't you notice when you stormed in?"

"Your naiveté is nearly precious," the woman murmured.

"And who are you exactly?" the principal continued. "You're not one of their guardians."

"My name is Miss Virago," she said, sounding like some sort of crossbreed between stuffy boarding school matron and prissy coed. "And giving you any details about what is coming here, now, is a waste of my time. You won't remember—or believe—me anyway. The only thing that will help is to get them out of your quaint little farming community as soon as possible."

"What the hell's going on?" I whispered. Next to me, Jenna looked pensive.

"Now you're going to leave with this gentleman," Virago continued, her voice suddenly cheerful and disarming. "And when he's done talking with you, the troubles these children caused will be little more than a dream."

"What?"

There were sounds of movement hidden by the door. "I'll handle the children's transport," Virago said, all business once again. "Clean up the girl's mess, and make sure the principal ... " Her voice dropped, and I missed the rest.

A man's voice. "What about the rest of the school? The riot?"

The woman exhaled slowly. "I don't care," she snapped. "These people aren't our concern. Let them sort out their own problems."

They were going to make us disappear. Take every trace of us and make it vanish: yearbook photos, our houses and things, everything. This wasn't the first time. This was just a little more thorough, and that made me wonder. How bad was it really?

"Someone's coming after us?" Cole whispered, looking even smaller than normal. "Again?"

"We don't know what's going on," I said, patting him

on the back. "Maybe that's just what they're telling people. Y'know, like a cover story."

The three of us jumped when the door swung open again. The redhead, Miss Virago, came in alone. As usual, Jenna beat me to the punch. "What's going on? And who the hell are you?"

Virago ignored the questions. She pointed at us with the first two fingers, then pointed to the door. "Take your things. There's a van waiting on the south side of the building. Don't stop to talk to anyone, don't leave anything behind."

Jenna stood up. Even though the woman was in heels, Jenna's Amazonian height gave her the advantage. She looked down on the adult. "We're not going anywhere until you tell us what's going on."

"Get your things, Moonset," the woman spat, making the word into a curse. "And go to the van. You're being evacuated."

If the woman knew anything about us, and she knew enough to call us by that name, she should have known not to engage Jenna's stubbornness. The two of them engaged in a stare-off that lasted almost a minute before the woman rolled her eyes. "You were listening just now. Which part was unclear?"

"The part where something's on its way to Farmville? And all you care about is pulling us out of town? What about the people here?"

"Your concern for your fellow man is touching," the woman said dryly. "Especially the half-dozen already en route to the hospital because of your little riot."

"Better the hospital than the morgue," Jenna retorted, refusing to give an inch.

The woman's expression toward us was cool. Maybe a bit mocking. "All the more reason to get your unworthy asses out of town as quickly as possible."

This would go on for hours unless I did something. "What about the others? Where are they?" Malcolm and Bailey weren't with us, and that made me nervous. I didn't like not knowing where the two of them were. Rule number one: always take care of each other.

There were five of us altogether. Jenna and I were the only two actually related, but I considered all of them my family. My brothers and sisters. Bailey was the youngest, a freshman this year, pixie haired and as light and blonde as Jenna and I were dark-eyed and serious. Then came Cole, almost a year older but still a freshman, who tried too hard and was far too earnest for his own good. Jenna and I were both seventeen, though she was just a few hours older even if she never acted like it. And finally there was Malcolm, the pretty boy who would have left by now, if it had been possible.

"Already evacuated," Virago said, eyes flicking to me.

"Let's go, Jen," I said quietly. She blinked at me, caught by surprise. I shook my head and shot a meaningful glance at Cole, who was watching the goings on with a rapt expression. Fire flashed behind Jenna's dark eyes for a moment, but eventually she nodded.

We walked out of the office, trapped somewhere between the kind of privilege that required an armed escort and the kind of infamy that required armed guards.

Miss Virago had called us by name. Moonset. The name we'd inherited from our parents, now a slur as bad as any other four-letter word. Even fifteen years after their death, people didn't use the word Moonset lightly.

Because of it, we had people like Miss Virago following us around. Waiting for the mistake that would push us over the edge from "innocent" to "dangerous."

Waiting for the day they could kill us, too.

TWO

*"Before magic, we were victims before the wraiths
and princes, the fallen and the blighted."*

....

The Book of Hours

I was nine years old when I learned what it meant when
someone called me Moonset. Malcolm had to be the one
to tell me. He was only a year older than Jenna and me, but
he told us about our parents the same way he'd broken the
news about Santa and the Easter Bunny.

Witches were supposed to work in secret. Secrecy was
the first lesson any of us ever learned. There were thousands
of us spread out across the world, enough that we even had
our own shadow government, a ruling council made up of
the most powerful covens and solitary witches.

All of that was threatened, nearly destroyed, because of Moonset.

They'd been an ordinary coven, nothing special. But something set them on the path to dark magic, and soon there was nothing dark enough, no power too forbidden.

Moonset's first strike was the most brutal—the equivalent of a nuclear assault that decimated the heart of the Congress, the ruling body that kept order. The papers called the Manchester bombing an accident, citing a gas leak that stank of a cover-up. Even with the threat of war on the horizon, keeping magic secret was still the first priority.

Hundreds died—specifically, the hundreds who were strong enough and smart enough to end the Moonset threat. Weeks went by, with no one stepping forward—until our parents did. Even as the acts of terrorism continued, they released statements and appeals. A cult began to form, worshiping the charismatic leader of Moonset, drawn to the movement that fought back for the disenfranchised and the ignored.

At first, it wasn't even a war. It was slaughter. Moonset engaged in terrorist acts all over the globe, destroying covens, libraries, anything and everything that could have risen up as a threat to them. The magical world had to fight a war on two fronts—fighting against Moonset while also fighting to keep the rest of the world ignorant of what was really going on behind the scenes.

Moonset was winning, but then they surrendered. No one really knew why. Theorists suggested they had a moment of clarity, momentarily freed from the dark powers that had overtaken them. But no one knew for sure, because though they were tried and executed quickly, they never spoke a word about the war and no record of their plans was ever recovered.

We were the only things they left behind.

"I don't like this," Jenna said under her breath at my side.

"You're crazy!" The principal's strident, nasal voice carried all the way down the hall. "I'm not just going to go off with you. In case you haven't been paying attention, there is *a riot going on.* I don't have time for this."

"Sir," his escort tried. And then again. "Sir." But the principal kept going on in a rant that devolved into references to tailgating and a lack of school pride. The principal's escort glanced back, as if looking for aid, but Virago ignored him.

She sighed, shaking her head in irritation. Then she froze, staring straight ahead at a man who I would have sworn wasn't there a moment ago. With his arms folded and head down, he could have been sleeping. "I've got this," Virago snapped, eyes narrowing to little slits.

"You should have *had* this a week ago when you first heard something was coming," the man said, lifting only his eyes, "instead of waiting until one of them broke the rules. Your boss still denying everything, huh?"

They'd known there was a threat, and they'd been waiting? Unbelievable.

Virago's gaze swept over the three of us, hardening like this was somehow our fault. Even if we didn't know what *this* was. I decided to hang back to wait and see how things were going to proceed. Virago wasn't acting like we were in danger, but the man before us definitely gave off a vibe of *dangerous.*

"Who are *you?*" Cole asked, suddenly belligerent with his chest puffed out. I gestured to Jenna, and she grabbed him by the back of the shirt. He tried to squirm away, but she kept a hand on his shoulder, her fingers digging into the shirt's fabric.

"I'm Quinn," the man offered, pushing himself up off the wall. Quinn was like a black-and-white film brought to life: dark black hair and pale white skin. Bela Lugosi with a Bowflex, and he moved like someone who had been in the military.

"Hello, hotness," Jenna muttered under her breath, eyes alight and mouth curved. *Oh, fantastic,* I thought to myself.

Because Cole never met a situation he didn't like to make more awkward, he looked away from Jenna and Quinn, and decided to *bark.* Even worse, he barked like one those tiny dogs, the ones that yiff instead of ruff.

Jenna increased the pressure on his shoulder until Cole started to drop. "Ow, ow, sorry, ow!" She held him for a few seconds longer, then released her grip. Cole rotated his shoulder, glaring up at her. "Bully."

"Enough," I said quietly. I took over Cole duty from Jenna, coming up behind him and resting one hand on his shoulder close to the neck. Prime strangling position, if I needed it.

"I know, kids," Quinn said sympathetically. "It's awkward when Mom and Dad fight in front of you. Don't worry, it'll be over soon." He probably wasn't much older than Virago, but I instantly liked him better, even though my instincts were still on edge.

"You're here to evacuate us?" I asked.

Quinn gave me a brief once-over. "Justin, right?" I nodded, and he smiled in a way that was probably supposed to be charming. Rule number two: never trust adults. And never, *never* trust anyone from the government.

"I'm here to make sure everything goes off without a hitch," he continued. "Malcolm and Bailey are already secure; now we just need to get the three of you."

Hearing it from Quinn put me a little more at ease. I wasn't so much worried about Mal—he could take care of himself—but Bailey was the youngest. Leaving would already be hard enough on her.

"We don't have time for this," Virago said with a roll of her eyes. "Move," she huffed at us, setting a brisk pace down the hall towards where the principal was *still* arguing with the other government mook.

The principal's office wasn't far from the front of the building, and that was the way that Virago decided to take us. The school was a hodgepodge of new additions tacked onto a side and renovations to make it look seamless on the outside. The only way to the south side of the building was to walk all the way down the length of the building and turn at the end. Otherwise, the school was a mess of aborted hallways and layouts that folded in on themselves.

I shook off the twinge running up and down my back, like there were strings sunk into my skin and someone was pulling them for the first time I could remember. I looked at Jenna, then Cole, but neither of them seemed to notice anything.

At first.

Jenna slowed, touching my arm. "Do you hear that?"

Nothing jumped out at me right away, so after a few more steps I stopped entirely, pulling Cole to a stop with me. Jenna had her head cocked to the side, and she was still. So very still. But she was right. There was something. A hissing. Faint.

"What is that?" she asked, lowering her voice. Cole's nose was wrinkled up, but he stayed between us.

"Stop stalling," Virago said briskly, turning to glare us down again.

It sounded familiar, like the hiss a of a snake, only softer—but I just couldn't place it. The hall had grown still around us, without even the sounds of the riot leaking in. Like we were the only six people for miles.

The sound was getting louder, or rather it was coming from several directions at once now. "Gas leak?" I asked.

Jenna considered that, then shook her head. "I swear I've heard that somewhere before."

"When you said there was stuff coming," Cole piped up suddenly, turning back to Quinn. "Did you mean *some-one*? Or some*thing*?"

Quinn hesitated just long enough for Cole's eyes to whiten all around.

Miss Virago snapped. "Enough of this! This day is enough of an embarrassment already."

"Jamie Sim told me that there's monsters who hide in

mirrors and glass, and if you look at them, they can steal your thoughts," Cole fretted. "And the ones that look like dead wood, who can make your life just puddle out of you like blood. And the ones—"

"Relax," Quinn said, even as Jenna ruffled Cole's hair. "You've got an armed escort, remember?"

Quinn, maybe. But the redheaded Virago looked like she'd push us in front of any incoming threat just to be rid of us. Again, not something we're unfamiliar with.

The hissing got a little louder, broken up by tiny tinkling noises. Something struck my shoe and I looked down, only to follow it back towards the source.

"Jenna," I said quietly, "look at the walls."

The entire front half of the building was built out of brick, the original school from sometime back in the forties. That's where the hissing sound was coming from. More accurately, from the bricks themselves.

Jenna's forehead knitted up in confusion and she took a step forward. "What ... ?"

The mortar between the bricks was crumbling down into sand, spilling out from between the stones like a broken hourglass. In places, larger chunks were breaking free, no bigger than pebbles, and bouncing off the tiled floor where they struck.

Something swept over me, a feeling, or a warning, and I grabbed Cole and pulled him closer.

"Honestly, there's nothing to be scared of," Miss Virago said, her mouth barely able to express such an incredible amount of contempt. "You're all being ridiculous."

The front of the school exploded inward, just to prove her wrong.

Bricks were falling. Bricks and ... something else cracking and splattering against the tile floor. Crack. Whoomf. Crack. Crack. Whoomf. I opened my eyes, choking back a cough. The dust was already passing, swept away by a rapid surge of rancid air from outside.

There was a hole in the school. The long wall of brick was exposed like a renovation gone wrong, jagged spots where stones had simply fallen away, and others where they were snapped in half. A few bricks littered the ground, but most had smashed apart like snowballs, a pile of terra cotta ash the only evidence of what they'd been.

I pulled myself up on hands and knees, and crawled the short distance to Jenna and Cole. We'd been thrown back by the blast, but except for a few moments of disorientation, I was fine. Jenna and Cole were already starting to stir as well, but there was a nasty gash on Cole's jaw, and his face was paler than normal.

The principal and his escort weren't so lucky. They caught almost the full force of the blast, having been much closer than we were. Both of them were slumped and still on the far side of the hole.

"Justin," Jenna said in a warning.

I looked up, and that's when I saw it. The creature that had caused the explosion.

The *thing* that climbed into the school—and it was clearly inhuman—moved with unnatural grace. No matter where it stepped, on sharp edges or exposed wiring, its balance was never threatened. It crept through the wreckage, moving like a spider. Erratic and quick, skittering like this was just a game. It was tall, gaunt, wrapped in strips of cloth and weighted down by dozens of chains wrapping from wrist to torso and neck to ankle.

"What *is that?*" Cole asked, his voice rising into a high-pitched squeak.

The thing looked at him, exposed a mouth of black, crumbling teeth, and *smiled.*

The chains should have made it obvious. The way its flesh was rotted and rictus and *wrong* should have made it obvious. A pallor like spoiled milk, creaking bones, and the *chains.* Chains that rattled and vibrated so loud my jaw started to hurt, and all other sounds were drowned out underneath it.

The thing was a wraith. And we were so incredibly fucked.

Wraiths were ghosts in need of anger management. Their deaths had twisted them, sharpened them into predators, and they were so consumed by memories of the living that they would ravage anything, kill anyone, in order to claw their way back. Though they all had a certain anorexic zombie quality to them, the last thing they were was frail.

Case in point: the gaping hole where the front of the school had been.

Quinn was already on his feet. "*Pyr toom,*" he snapped,

holding his hand out. The air above his palm caught fire, collected and writhed against the sides.

"*Siths torak*," the creature hissed. It had a voice like bones breaking, full of crackles and sibilant like a tire leaking air. The spell—and it had to be a spell—swept forward, the air rippling as a sudden displacement of heat blew out the fireball like a birthday candle.

At its core, magic was a language. Spells were verbal, the right combination of consonants and vowels could summon up a projectile of fire, but just as easily extinguish it. But magic had a cadence and common tonal qualities to it— even if you only knew a few spells, you could recognize the language being spoken.

The clicks and dips in the spell the wraith used were something foreign, like a dialect I'd never heard before.

Virago had taken the hardest hit, slumped over against one of the walls, but even she was managing to get back onto her feet.

"*Lex divok*," Quinn spat, thrusting his open palm forward. The creature went flying back suddenly, hit by a wave of invisible force. It tumbled head over foot, an animated skeleton trying to somersault. Every time one of the chains slapped against the tile, I winced, feeling the vibration of it tearing through my skin.

The moment the creature landed, sprawled in a broken heap of limbs and iron at the farthest end of the hall, Quinn looked up to the ceiling. "*Lexic vok*," he shouted, bringing his fist down. The ceiling, the walls, all of it came tumbling down in a shuddering mass above the wraith, drowning it underneath a tonnage of bricks, stone, and at least fifty years of accumulated dirt.

The collapse lasted for at least a minute before it started to die off. Unlike the wraith's explosion, Quinn's was perfectly controlled, a circular hole that was both sharp and precise.

"Still happy you sat around doing nothing?" Quinn demanded, helping Virago to her feet.

"Orders were orders," she muttered, a tangle of hair in her face.

"We have to get them out of here, now," Quinn said. "Can you walk?"

"I—I think so," she said, pulling away from him to test her balance.

"Go," he said. "Chris and I can hold it off."

From the far end of the hall, a reverberating crunch interrupted. The wraith was already vertical, standing above a pair of dark-shaped lumps that I didn't recognize at first.

"Oh, God," Jenna whispered.

The creature's hand was a canvas of red, and something crimson and splintered dropped from his grip. The principal, now missing his esophagus, which lay about a foot and a half to his right, stared at the ceiling unblinking. The man in a suit—Chris—was just as much of a bloody mess, though he was still gurgling. Until he, too, shuddered and stopped.

A black tongue licked at decayed lips as the wraith looked at the five of us. "Moonset," the thing whispered, fighting a smile. "*Mine.*"

The sound of the chains, which were now moving on

their own like prehensile limbs, drowned out anything else the wraith whispered.

I saw Quinn's mouth move, felt the spell shudder into existence around him, but there was nothing but the chains. Hideous ringing, clanging sounds a thousand times more intense than they should have been. The sound was worse now, piercing through me, and at my side I saw Cole and Jenna struggling, too.

Cole was the first to drop, falling to his knees with hands pressed against his ears. His face flushed as he screamed, howled, but I couldn't hear it. Jenna dropped next, and then me, until the three of us were huddled together. Jenna and I grabbed Cole, shielding him as best we could and trying to help cover his ears with one of our own.

"*Vex dunn*," I shouted. "*Vexic dunn. Vexa dunn.*" I screamed out every variation of the only muffling spell that I knew, but though the magic ignited around me, the chains penetrated through.

There was movement—lots of it—around us, but it was everything we could do to stay together. I felt, rather than heard, Jenna continuing to shout spells into existence, but nothing did any good.

My muscles screamed, and I tried to shift only to find they wouldn't respond. It was like being hit with a stun gun, my body was no longer my own, tucked and frozen in place like an abandoned marionette.

They're going to die. And it's all my fault. Keeping Cole and the others safe was my job, my only job. And I'd failed.

I should have done something, should have been smarter, or stronger.

I'm sorry, I mouthed.

The silence was so sudden it *hurt.* Agony replaced by an empty void so vast I thought it might drive me mad. A pounding sound that resolved itself into my heartbeat, a rattle that became my breath.

Quinn towered above the three of us, a little bloodier for the trouble, and had a knife in his hands.

The echo of what he'd done still hung in the air, creating a poster bed-sized space of safety where sound was normal and even.

"Keep them safe," Quinn shouted at the redhead before he started his advance on the wraith.

The wraith held out his hand, whispered a word, and a wave of gray rushed out from him. It caught up to Quinn and Virago before either of them could deflect or cast a counterspell, and I couldn't help but watch in terror. They were all that was standing between us and the wraith.

Quinn *aged* in seconds, his body shifting, changing, stooping forty years in less time than it took me to realize what I was seeing. His skin became sallow, his posture hunched, his hair went platinum, then full on white, then wisps. Pock marks and liver spots lined his skin. Virago had her back to us, but I could see the color draining from her hair until it was a sterling silver.

The spell spread across his body, and Quinn's arm trembled before he defiantly slashed down with the knife. "*Aret!*"

The effects of the spell dissipated at once, severed somehow by both the knife and the spell, the aging reversing almost as fast as it had started. Quinn straightened immediately, but Virago dropped to her knees, winded or worse.

"*Witchers*," the wraith sneered. "Vermin."

"Learn how to use a verb, douchebag," Cole muttered.

I clamped my hand down over his mouth, eyes darting fearfully towards the wraith, who appeared not to have heard, thankfully.

Part of me had known what Quinn and Virago were as soon as they arrived. Witchers. Witchers were Navy Seals, Green Berets, and Chuck Norris combined in one. They were trained, heavily, in offensive spells and in counteracting supernatural threats. A single Witcher was about as deadly as the average coven. A group of Witchers, on the other hand, could take down almost anyone. Or anything.

"We need to get away," Jenna said out of the corner of her mouth, lips barely moving.

"Tell that to the wraith," I said.

"Justin, Jenna, go," Quinn said over his shoulder, though he didn't look away from the creature.

"Stay," the wraith countered, its rheumy, cataract-colored eyes trained on us.

"Who sent you?" Quinn demanded.

The wraith laughed, releasing a cloud of dust from somewhere deep in its chest. "Bridger," it answered, shaping the word like a caress.

If possible, my panic intensified. *Cullen* Bridger? *He's supposed to be a myth!*

No one knew who he really was, where he came from.

The stories say he appeared on Moonset's door, and they took him in. Indoctrinated him. Trained him. During the war, people called him the Disciple. Bridger was the name he created to suit his new role.

When Moonset was captured, Bridger had escaped. He'd been working in secret for over twenty years, and no one had any idea where he was or what he wanted. He was the only living link to Moonset's dark agenda. Not a single sighting in all those years.

The three of us took a step backward simultaneously, and the wraith's frozen mouth snarled. "*Ess debok ssen,*" it hissed, pointing a hand at us.

Quinn threw himself into the path of the spell even before the wraith had finished speaking. "No!" I gasped, waiting for the effect, the fall.

But the spell sailed over him, around him, and past us until it caught the far end of the hall, and repeated in seconds what it had done to the wall it had entered from.

Entropy swept out and around, and the hallway simply started to fall apart. But unlike before, when even the bricks had decomposed down to ash, this time everything stayed solid. Walls fell in, the ceiling collapsed, sparks of electricity flared against the sudden darkness of lost light, and the hallway was swallowed up in ruin.

We threw ourselves to the ground, trying to get out and away from the collapse, but for the first time our synchronicity failed. Jenna and I both hurtled to the left, but Cole broke for the right.

It took me a second to get my bearings, in between

coughing through all the new smoke, pulling myself back upright, and figuring out where Cole had landed. A standoff had developed between Quinn and the wraith, and he'd pivoted around until he could safely back up to Cole without losing ground.

"Enough," the wraith rasped. The chains, which had only writhed around him like serpents until this point, began to shoot forward, striking for Quinn, and behind him, Cole.

Quinn didn't even hesitate. "*Da lum*," he said calmly, making a tiny slicing movement with the knife. One of the broken electric lines, abandoned and voided of energy, surged up into the air, and struck at the chain. Iron links sparked electric blue as a surge of electricity caught the chain, and traveled back up the line to the wraith, who stumbled back.

Quinn used the opportunity to reach down and help Cole to his feet. He murmured something I couldn't hear, and at first Cole looked at him in utter confusion, but then something clicked, and he smiled and nodded. Looked almost eager.

Another chain flew forward, and another burst of electricity stopped it short. The creature didn't look slowed by the energy charging through it, but Quinn didn't look any worse for the wear, either.

"Am I supposed to be scared of you?" Cole laughed— laughed!—at the wraith. "You should see Jenna without makeup. *That's* scary."

"Cole, shut up!" Jenna and I shouted as one.

The wraith growled, the next chain flying a little sloppier, a little less fierce.

"You look like Betty White's grandmother," Cole called. "And you smell like a Kardashian."

"I can do this all day," Quinn added, twisting the knife in his grasp.

Cole's ability to irritate even the undead was going to his head. "I mean, really? You know this guy's a virgin, right?" Quinn's mouth tightened. "And he's kicking your ass all over the place. All the other ghouls are gonna laugh at you."

Another volley, another electric shock. But this time, Quinn stepped around Cole, behind him. Using him as a shield. Quinn ducked his head, whispering something. Cole's face hardened, and he nodded.

The wraiths' chains were flailing now, rising anger at the impasse channeling out through the metal limbs.

"You throw like my grandma," Cole snickered, holding out his arms and posing. Making himself a target.

"What the fuck are you doing?" Jenna screamed.

"Cole!" I started running, and things started happening so fast.

Quinn pushed Cole down and then threw himself against the wall, dropping the knife and shouting a spell I didn't catch. Cole went sliding across the floor, straight towards Jenna.

The wraith snarled, his targets suddenly not where they'd been a moment before.

I was already in motion, and I couldn't stop myself in time. I heard another spell, and I was thrown into the air, pulled towards Quinn just as the chain lashed out.

It caught me around the arm, burning through my shirt

until it decayed and collapsed into ash. The metal was *cold*, burning brands into my skin and even reverberating through my bones.

"Justin!"

"Justin!"

Twin shouts, seconds apart.

I could feel the wraith's power ripping through me. It tore at me, at the part of me that wasn't skin and blood and bone. Draining me. A vortex pulling away the part of me that was living, the spark that kept my heart pumping and my fear rising.

A switch flipped.

Polarity reversed. Life became death became life again.

The vortex became a geyser, and everything that was mine returned in a flash flood of light and life.

"No," the wraith hissed. "No!"

A dark pall burst into murky light around me, like an aura made from shadowed half-truths and eclipse light. It wasn't magic, not exactly. Parts were, scraps that felt like something I should recognize, but they were threads in a much larger tapestry.

"Justin! Grab the chain!" Quinn gestured to my arm, and the iron that was already trying to unravel itself from my skin.

I twisted my forearm, grabbed the chain, and refused to let go. The chain shook, contorted, and tried to break free, but I wouldn't let go.

The aura grew darker, like storm clouds summoned above my head. I could feel *something*, an invisible pressure that settled against my skin like a shirt that was too tight.

It swept around me, a presence and a power that dwarfed anything I'd ever seen.

The wraiths' eyes had looked like they were incapable of emotion, but there was one there now: fear. "You were to be rescued," it hissed at me.

The aura swept forward from me, slicing through the air like a scythe, and cut the wraith down like it was the first-born son, and this was a plague.

Shadows swallowed up the wraith, until there was a portal of tangible darkness where it had once stood.

I squinted, feeling the pressure around me ease. The light in the room was more intense than it had been a moment ago.

"What's going on?" Cole asked, worried.

"Just relax," Quinn directed. "Close your eyes."

Close our ey—oh. The light continued to intensify, coupled with a ringing sound that sounded exactly like electronic feedback, a high-pitched whining that was just as intense as the corona of light that blurred everything.

The light grew too intense, the sounds too loud. The humming got so loud, but after our experience with the chains, it was very nearly nothing.

When it faded, the wraith was gone.

THREE

"There is a presence over them. Some call it a binding, some a curse. Those that threaten them, or try to separate them ... "

....

Simon Meers
Case Report, *The Moonset Legacy*

When Virago walked through the motel room door two days later, the reaction was incendiary, to say the least.

Jenna lunged for her immediately, murder in her eyes. "That thing could have killed us, you stupid bitch!"

We were god-only-knew where, dropped off in the middle of the night, and forty-eight hours cooped up in one small room was enough for cabin fever to set in. I spent the majority of my time mediating between Cole's hyper need for attention and Jenna's restless irritation.

We hadn't been able to take anything with us when we fled the city. It wasn't until sometime the next morning that we stopped long enough for Quinn to pick up new outfits for us at the nearest Walmart. He'd taken the clothes we'd been wearing when we arrived and disappeared, most likely taking them to be burnt.

Leaving town wasn't normally this intense, but there was a lot of extra crazy to go around because of the wraith. Virago's reappearance, with Malcolm and Bailey in tow, was just the excuse Jenna needed to put that irritation to bad use.

I grabbed Jenna, even as Malcolm darted around Virago to catch our sister from the other side and prevent a catastrophe.

"Jenna, think!" I pulled on her arm, but fury had her adrenaline flowing and it was more of a struggle than it should have been.

"So predictable," Virago yawned, feigning boredom. But I could see her eyes darting around, the nervous tightening of her fist.

"I'm *thinking* I'll break her nose," Jenna snarled.

Between Malcolm and I, we were able to hold her back. Well, mostly Malcolm. He was the one built like a pro wrestler.

It was hard not to live in Mal's shadow since he towered over all of us. Jenna and I were neck and neck, but Mal had at least four or five inches on me. I stopped comparing when I realized I'd never catch up.

Mal was the "-est" sibling. Oldest. Tallest. Calmest. Biggest. We couldn't exactly join sports teams when we arrived in a new school, but that didn't stop him from working out like it was his job. Football and wrestling coaches started salivating the moment Mal walked into a new school, but he always turned them down. Everyone probably would have held him up as the perfect child but for being the spawn of terrorists.

It helped that he was gay. It kept me from having the world's largest inferiority complex.

"Told you Jenna'd stay out of trouble," Mal called over his shoulder, casual as can be.

Bailey hesitated in the doorway, dwarfed in a white faux fur jacket she must have insisted on. Bailey, in contrast to Mal, was the youngest and tiniest.

Jenna lunged forward again, and this time Malcolm caught her fully, grabbing her by the waist and scooping her up off the ground like she weighed nothing. To him, she probably did.

"She's a Witcher," Mal said. "Just let it go."

Virago's childish, snide expression only lasted a moment.

"Meghan!" Quinn said sharply, speaking to Virago, "Let's go. Give them some privacy."

The added tension left with the two adults, so even with the five of us crammed in a two-bed motel room, it didn't seem as bad as it had before.

"We saw a wraith," Cole announced happily to Bailey, who didn't look as thrilled.

"Figures she's a Meghan," Jenna muttered, once Mal put her down. "I've never met one that wasn't a raging bitch."

Bailey shrugged out of her coat, folded it carefully, and

set it over the motel room chair. "You guys are okay, right? Miss Virago said that Cole got hurt."

Cole turned his head and pointed to the side of his jaw. But the only remnant of the cut he'd suffered was a penciled red line. "Quinn used his athame on me; it was cool. All the blood went *slurp* right back inside!"

Jenna rolled her shoulders, and just like that, her mood changed. "Thank god you're here," she said to Bailey, claiming one of the beds. "I'm so bored."

Malcolm eyed the pair of them, then walked over to me while Cole went back to playing with the television remote. "A wraith? We knew something happened, but they wouldn't tell us anything."

"A wraith," I confirmed. "We're lucky to be alive. Or...here, I guess." The wraith hadn't been there to kill us; it had come to *collect* us. The wraith said it had come to rescue us. What was the plan? Bring us to Cullen Bridger?

But I couldn't tell Malcolm that. Not with four other pairs of eager ears in the room. Information had to be compartmentalized. I trusted the four of them more than anyone in this world, but I also *knew* them. Knew Cole's tendency to blab, Jenna's ways of making trouble, and even how Bailey got attached to things she shouldn't.

It was dangerous for them to know everything all the time.

"So what happened? I heard Quinn's a badass blah blah blah," Malcolm said.

I shook my head. "It was the curse."

The room instantly quieted.

The truth was that none of us knew what the curse was. Only that it was chained around all of our necks, an invisible albatross that protected us.

It hadn't been enough to just be the children of Moonset. We had to be freaks, too. Before they surrendered, our parents had *done* things to us. Something beyond simple magic. When we were threatened, or when we were separated for too long, Bad Things started to happen.

I'd never seen it in action (that I could remember) until the other day.

I recited the story for Mal, well aware that everyone else was listening just as intently. Jenna and Cole were *there*, and yet they were still hanging on every word. I explained it the way I understood it in hindsight—the way Quinn had used Cole to antagonize the wraith, knowing full well that one of us would jump to his defense. Quinn had apologized, but as much as I wanted to be mad, he *had* saved us.

"What'd it feel like?" Jenna asked, once I was done. We'd made a point of *not talking* for the last two days. At least not about anything important.

I had to think for a few minutes. "Heavy. It felt heavy. Like there was this *thing* around me all the time, but I just couldn't feel it before."

"Can you still feel it now?" Mal asked.

I shook my head. "But I remember it. You know how you go to the dentist, and even a few days later, you remember how it felt? It's like that. Kind of claustrophobic, knowing that there's a room full of dark magic around me all the time."

"You're sure it's dark?" Jenna asked pensively.

I shrugged. "What else would it be?"

She stared up at the ceiling, but didn't share whatever she was thinking. Jenna could read my thoughts at a glance, but the connection wasn't two sided. Most of the time I had no idea what was going through her head. Especially now.

"I'm glad you guys are okay," Mal said, but I could hear something in his tone, like the rumblings of train tracks before the inevitable collision. Bailey bit down on her lip, and Cole stared through his sneakers. "But what the hell were you thinking, Jenna? You're lucky no one died."

"They were going to take us away regardless," Jenna said dismissively. "Does it really matter?"

"What if Bailey got caught in the crossfire? Or Cole? He was throwing himself right in the thick of it."

Jenna pushed herself up. "That's what you're there for, Mal. Ride in and be the white knight," she said sweetly. "How else can you feel superior to us mere mortals?"

Somehow nearly dying at the hands of a wraith had become about Malcolm and Jenna's long-standing issues. As everything did, given enough time.

I did my best to cut it off at the pass. I really did. "I think what Mal's trying to say—"

Jenna didn't let me finish. "I *know* what he's trying to say. So how about you actually let *him* say it."

"How about you drop the rebel badass act for five minutes?" Mal fired back. "You're not the one that has to pick up the pieces. Do you have any idea what this has been like for Bailey the last couple of days? She *liked* that school."

Bailey's stained cheeks and pursed lips were her only

response. She stared straight ahead, like she was trying to ignore it all. More likely, she was trying to keep from crying.

Jenna's eyes flicked across the room, long enough to see for herself, and she sighed. "Look—"

"No, you look," Mal snapped. "It's not like they can just split us up and send us to wherever we want. One of us goes, we all do. The curse, remember?" None of us were exactly certain how that worked, either. They could move us separately, ten or twenty miles apart on the journey, and things were fine. But if anyone tried to separate us, like take one and leave the rest, it was bad. Dark clouds and explosions bad.

"At least we won't have to take midterms," Cole said brightly.

"Unless they make us start homeschooling," I pointed out.

"I heard they've got a detention center somewhere," Mal added, "for kids that can't keep it together. They call it the Priory, but it's more like jail. No contact with *anyone*."

"They wouldn't really do that, would they?" Bailey asked softly.

"Sooner or later they will," Mal said, "especially when they have to keep moving us to a new school."

"For the last time, they were going to move us anyway," Jenna shouted, hands grabbing at the duvet and squeezing for all she was worth. "They knew the wraith was coming and they sat on their hands waiting. Probably hoping it would have killed us."

"Actually, Quinn said they were waiting on you. They

knew we were up to something," Cole, ever helpful, pointed out.

"Waiting for you to make us all look bad again," Mal added.

Jenna wouldn't make eye contact. "Look, the spells just got a little out of hand. I didn't mean for it to get that intense."

But Malcolm wasn't buying it. "You can't just throw out a half-assed apology and think that makes everything all right again!"

"Hey, come on," I jumped in, turning on Mal. "Calm down."

But Jenna didn't need anyone to take her side. "Then what do you want from me? Sorry I'm not perfect like you, afraid to learn any magic because, God forbid, you find a spell to grow a personality!"

Within thirty seconds, Jenna and Mal were shouting over one another, and even Bailey and Cole were jumping into the fray. I couldn't even hear what *one* of them was saying, let alone all four of them.

"ENOUGH!" I shouted at the top of my lungs.

Four pairs of eyes turned on me, instantly quiet.

"This isn't getting us anywhere," I pointed out, "and I don't want to spend the rest of the day with a headache."

"You can't keep letting her off the hook, Justin," Mal chided. "It's getting out of hand."

"I know that. There's no one in this room who *doesn't* know that." I took a deep breath, exhaling slowly before I continued. "But ganging up on her isn't helping."

"So what?" he challenged, "We all back away and stick our heads in the sand? We did that the last time, and the time before that."

"I didn't notice an intervention the time Malcolm got us thrown out," Jenna chimed in spitefully. "But I suppose the golden boy gets a pass, right?"

That started the furor up all over again. Mal started to go red in the face, and even Bailey and Cole were jumping in, getting angry and animated in turn. Jenna was the only one who looked composed, but then again, she was used to this.

"Hey! Hey!" But no matter how loud I yelled, I couldn't make a dent in the chaos. I'd have to do something else.

"*Cen fal la*," I whispered, eyeing the wall sconce on the far side of the room. It wasn't a sanctioned spell, but a hodgepodge of words I'd glued together when I was still in grade school. It had only one real effect.

The light bulbs in the sconce popped—loud enough to cut through the noise—one after another, a tiny fizzle of sparks accompanying each tiny explosion.

"Jesus, Justin," Mal cried, swatting at the back of his head. He wasn't close enough to actually get burned, but that didn't stop him from overreacting. "What the hell?"

"Mal, can you guys give us a minute?" I asked. Maybe I would have a better chance at getting through to Jenna if it was just one on one.

There was some grumbling, and some dirty looks, but eventually Mal and the kids went outside. Either to one of the other motel rooms the Witchers had rented—because they could shove three of us into one room, but god forbid any of *them* have to share—or to go harass the vending machines.

"I'm not the only one you should be mad at," Jenna started immediately. "We almost *died* there. That thing started wagging his chains all over the place, and I thought for sure that we ... "

"But we didn't," I pointed out as gently as I could. "Quinn was there."

"But he didn't have to be," she insisted, looking me full in the face. "We don't know how to protect ourselves. We *can't* protect ourselves. And you saw the way Virago was. She was basically useless. The other one died before he could even do anything. If Quinn didn't have half a brain, that thing would have taken us."

There was something she wasn't saying. Her words cut off too quickly, and I could *feel* the unfinished thought in the air. "And ... ?" I asked, pushing her.

Jenna looked back up at the ceiling. "And maybe it should have. If it was really working for Bridger, maybe he would have taught us. Showed us the things we need to know."

I came close to throwing my hand over her mouth. As it was, my eyes flew to the closed door, even as I was whispering every anti-eavesdropping spell we knew.

They taught us simple magic like that in spades. Spells that would never really be useful except in random situations. Nothing that would ever save our lives. Jenna was right in that regard.

"You can't say things like that," I whispered furiously. "What if someone was listening?" Any minute, I expected the

Witchers to come rushing through the door and haul us off to wherever they took warlocks and warlock sympathizers.

"What if they were? I'm not saying we follow the family business, Justin, I'm just saying… maybe it's the smart move. Maybe he knows why we're like *this*," she said, gesturing around her in a circular motion. "And what they did to us."

"And then what? He teaches us and tells us things and bakes us cookies? He's a *terrorist*, Jen. Come on."

No one had seen Bridger since the fall of Moonset, but his name kept coming up, like a cockroach burrowed into the foundation. He, or someone using his name, claimed credit for a variety of terroristic acts. Like the mass hysteria unleashed at a Paris art gallery, when a secret spell had become an airborne virus that spread from person to person, compelling each one to tell every secret they *knew* they shouldn't. Not devastating in the small scale, but within a day, government secrets were at risk, as were secrets of the Parisian covens.

It was said that he'd inspired even more horrific acts of violence, like being a muse for the Spokane Ridge killer, who'd killed seven teenagers in the last four years until being caught last summer. The stories we heard said that the killer had thought of his spree as an audition, trying to make Bridger take notice.

There was one thing we had in common with him, though. Bridger, like us, was a reminder of a war that most wanted to forget.

"What if we're just like them?" Jenna asked.

"We're not."

"We *could* be."

"No, we couldn't." I could be just as stubborn as Jenna when the mood struck me.

They say the blood of warlocks is black as pitch. I've grown up staring at the veins in my arms and the ones trapped beneath my wrist, tapping them at times in restless fear, waiting for the day they changed. But they never did.

That wasn't to say they never would, no matter what lies I told.

FOUR

*"Our government is overseen by the Congress.
The leaders of the seven Great Covens—so named
because of their contributions to magical society—
and five Solitaires chosen by general election
act as the stewards of our future."*

....

Coventry in the 21st Century

Just as quickly as we were reunited, they split us up again. The vans that had brought us to the motel were gone, replaced by a trio of hybrid SUVs.

"The environment, really?" Jenna asked, quirking a brow at Quinn.

"It's our planet, too," he replied with a grin.

There was no sign of Virago—Meghan—anymore.

Instead, a clean-cut pair of college kids had showed up, looking like the poster children for the Greek system.

"Malcolm, you'll be going with Nick," Quinn said, pointing to the frat boy. "Cole and Bailey, you guys are going to be with Kelly."

Cole didn't hesitate for a second. "We're good with that," he said, speaking for the both of them. Bailey gave him a cross look, but she didn't argue.

I did the math. "So that means we're—"

"With me," Quinn confirmed.

Jenna perked up. "So you're our permanent guardian now?"

"That's the plan," Quinn said absently, barely paying attention to her. "For now."

I looked between the two of them, considering my next move. Jenna had never thought one of our guardians was hot before. They changed with every new city we moved to, as if a change in babysitters would somehow change the behavior that led to us being kicked out of school.

I tried to predict all the ways that this could turn out badly. The disasters that would come if something *did* happen between them. The disasters that would come if something *didn't* happen. The disasters that could come along the way.

Malcolm edged his way towards me. "So?"

When he wasn't angry and running on emotion, Mal would and could boil down his every thought into as few words as possible. Right now, his "so" contained so many different questions and demands that I could barely handle them all at once.

"I don't know," I said honestly. It covered as many of them as I could. I didn't know how to get through to Jenna, I didn't know if I even could. I looked around, desperate to change the subject. "Do you even know where we are? I was asleep when we pulled in a few days ago, and we haven't left the room since."

"No television? They make these things called news channels that could narrow it down for you." Mal smirked.

"Tried that," I said automatically, "but they all keep referring to the tri-state area. Nothing that narrows it down."

He shrugged. "We're in New York, I know that much. Upstate somewhere, I think."

"Any idea where they're taking us?"

"No clue," he said. "Maine, maybe? Canada?"

Either was a possibility. I overheard Cole and Bailey's excited chatter, discussing the exact same thing. Bailey was hoping for New York City (which would never happen), and Cole was hoping for a ski lodge, even though he'd never skied a day in his life. As it turned out, Mal was right, *and* we were closer to our destination that any of us expected.

Half an hour in the car with Jenna and Quinn played out in relative silence. We were definitely in New York: signs heading back the way we came promised arrival in Syracuse, Buffalo, and even New York City.

We alternated between highways that skirted Lake Ontario and back roads that probably hadn't seen real traffic in a year or more. But eventually, the back roads led to an actual city, and ten minutes after *that,* a sign appeared, welcoming us to Carrow Mill.

The town doubled as a Hallmark movie set. Small town, lots of churches. Even a Main Street with an ancient green-tinged light pole in the center of a roundabout. Everything moved at a snail's pace, but at least it could properly be called a town. Byron was a whole lot of farmland with a few houses in between. Carrow Mill was what they meant when they said "small town America."

"So this must be a nice change of pace," I said to Quinn while we waited at one of the traffic lights. "Big change from D.C."

The supernatural America, much like the natural one, had headquartered itself in the capital. When it came time for the Witchers to be trained, programs had been quietly set up right in the political world's backyard. The political covens wanted to prevent another Moonset, and many of them oversaw the training personally.

Normally, our guardians were a little older—rarely old enough to pass as our parents, but still old enough that they weren't so immature themselves. But we'd never had a Witcher for a guardian.

I wanted to get him talking, maybe get some insight on what we could expect. But all Quinn did was give a little half-shrug.

"Did we ever thank you for saving us?" I tried. Jenna, who was checking her makeup in the passenger mirror, met my glance and pointedly rolled her eyes.

"That's the job," Quinn said noncommittally. "See the world, fight monsters."

"Throw your charge into the line of fire?" I supplied.

"I figured better you than Jenna or Cole," he said. "Your psych profile made you the best option. Plus, chivalry and all that."

"I don't think chivalry covers the undead," Jenna interjected frostily. "I wouldn't have pegged you for a Neanderthal."

I could hear the smirk in Quinn's voice, even if I couldn't see it. "You don't really know enough about anything to pin me down."

"Wait, there's a psych profile on me? I want to know what it says." The idea that they'd been studying me, taking notes about my behavior without my knowledge ran across my skin like a steady stream of spiders.

Having a Witcher down the hall made me uncomfortable. Having a Witcher down the hall who had been studying our psyches made it even worse. *What did he know about us? Did they know something we don't?*

"I'm sure you do," Quinn said, "but now's not the time."

"Why not?"

"Because we're here," he said cheerfully.

We turned down onto a closed street, pulling into a driveway just short of a cul-de-sac.

"Welcome to student housing," Quinn continued, getting an odd level of enjoyment out of this. "The Congress owns all the houses on the street, so we're splitting you all up like normal. We're on this side of the street, and the other three on the other."

Keeping five kids in the same house stopped being healthy back before all of us had reached double digits. Cole was too hyper, Mal too easily annoyed, Bailey too needy. No one ever really questioned it, because aside from our guardians and the witches who knew who we were, we never talked about it. Didn't invite people over to our houses, never brought it up. It was one of the many things about our lives that was just too hard for normal kids to understand.

"They own the whole street?" Jenna asked, her nose wrinkling up. "How many kids do they have here?"

"Doesn't matter to me. I'm just in charge of you two."

I eyed Quinn, who was still all smiley. "You don't like answering questions, do you?"

"Don't I?"

Before I could reply, I got a look at *our* house.

"There's been some sort of mistake," Jenna said faintly. We couldn't look away. Our house was basically the flaming wreckage of a freeway pileup. Well, it wasn't on fire, but it probably should have been.

"No mistake," Quinn said, hopping out of the driver's seat. "Welcome home."

"It's some sort of practical joke," I said weakly. "Right?"

Christmas had come to Carrow Mill, and it had vomited all over our house. I'd seen outside decorations for the holidays before, but never this many. And I definitely hadn't seen them all in one place.

Not one, but two giant pine trees were decked out with strings of lights stretched taller than the house itself. I counted five different Santas perched around the property, competing with two nativity scenes (although the scene itself was life-sized with its own fully decorated stables), reindeer, wreaths, and a giant sleigh on the roof. And about fifteen miles of Christmas lights decking out every surface they could find.

"Do you think it all lights up?" she whispered.

I could only stare. "Bright enough to be seen from space."

Quinn unlocked the front door. "Nice, right?" His enthusiasm didn't hide the mockery underneath. The bastard was enjoying this.

"This is a joke, right?" Jenna asked as we walked up to the front door.

"Just think of it as a little welcome gift," Quinn said. "In honor of all the hard work that landed you here." Without another word, or any more mockery, he vanished inside the house, leaving the door open.

"Oh," Jenna said.

The part of me that wanted to snicker was strangled by the overwhelming embarrassment at having to live in a house that looked like a Christmas village.

She covered her mouth with a hand. "We're being punished."

"You're being punished. I'm being punished by proxy."

Jenna took a moment, studying the street we were now calling home. "We're the only house with decorations," she pointed out.

Most people didn't know how to deal with Jenna. Sure she was stubborn, occasionally hostile, and had a sixth sense for finding trouble, but she didn't deal well with embarrassment.

I was pretty sure that Quinn had already picked up on

that. And that he was the one responsible for the holiday decorations.

At least the inside of the house was Christmas free. *For now,* I figured. The furnishings were sparse but livable—all of our homes and apartments over the years had a certain "long-term housing" quality. All the basics were there—tables, chairs, couches, TVs. But there weren't any personal touches anywhere. No pictures, no collectible figurines, no wacky color palettes.

The house could be filled and vacated with a minimum of effort, ready for the next inhabitant. That was how it worked for most of us.

Witch children weren't like most kids. Minor enchantments are taught to kids who aren't even old enough to attend school. It isn't until later, in the early teen years, that aptitudes and talents start to emerge. At that point, most witches are moved from their homes to places where they can hone their particular gifts. Thus the need for temporary housing like this.

It wasn't an entirely infallible system, though. The five of us were the exception—grouped together in one backwoods town after another, trying to keep us out of sight and out of mind.

If we went strictly based on skills, Cole would be down South learning illusions, Bailey would be in the Midwest learning evocations, and Jenna and I would be in D.C. Supposedly, we both had the kind of qualities that would have made us logical choices to join the Witchers. And

Malcolm...well if he had his way, he'd be going to a normal high school, dealing with normal teen stuff.

"I'm taking the master bedroom," Jenna's voice floated down from the second floor. We were claiming bedrooms already? I tore up the stairs, only to find that Quinn had beat me, too. He was standing in front of what I assumed was the back bedroom, shaking his head at Jenna.

"You can fight over one of the others," he said. "I don't care who goes where." He cocked his head to the side. "But you might prefer the one down the hall."

She rolled her eyes, a hand on her hip. "And why would I want that one?"

I worked it out faster than she did and started to laugh, remembering the two giant trees outside the house. Both of them turned to look at me. "The trees," I said to her. "He heard about Birmingham." Jenna had managed to make two of the trees grow enough that she could sneak in and out easily, climbing the limbs almost like a ladder.

"Oh, this is going to be fantastic," Jenna grumbled, spinning around and striding into her new room. She was too classy to slam the door, but there was a definite emphasis to the way the lock clicked into place a few seconds later.

FIVE

"No one knows why a coven bond forms.
Sherrod, Diana, Cyrus, and Emily—they were
the beginning. Within days, Brandon Sutter had
moved to town, and the bus carrying the runaway
Haley Spencer broke down just outside the city
limits. Then they were six. Complete."

Moonset: A Dark Legacy

The next few days were a mess of activity: clothes shopping,
bickering, new cell phones, more bickering, toiletries, at
least one sob session, and school supplies. Usually when we
left a place, we were allowed to keep *some* things, but with
the way we left Byron, we'd had to leave it all behind.

It wasn't that difficult for me, because there was nothing I'd had that I'd been particularly attached to, but the girls and Cole were a little harder hit.

"My PS3," he'd wailed.

Kelly, Bailey's guardian, had gone with her and Jenna for an entire day. "Outlet shopping," Jenna said with only a touch of her usual acerbic flair.

After everything had finally calmed down, we all fell into usual routines.

Monday, Mal and I ended up in the kitchen first thing in the morning. The shower was running upstairs, but I couldn't figure out if it was Jenna or Quinn who'd woken before noon. Some days it was a toss-up.

We weren't starting school until after the first of the year, which meant there were two weeks of relative peace before Jenna's next campaign started. Every school was a little different—sometimes, she wanted out immediately; other times she didn't mind a little patience. Only time would tell which one Carrow Mill would be.

"Nick says there's a gym somewhere in town; I was thinking about checking it out. You want to go?" Mal asked from his spot at the table. I sat across the room from him on one of the barstools set alongside the counter like a breakfast nook. He'd pulled a bowl of grapes out of the fridge and kept playing games, tossing them in the air and catching them in his mouth. Every time he missed, he looked at me pointedly, like I was the one that was supposed to dig under the oven for the lost grape.

There was coffee brewing, but it wasn't brewing nearly fast enough.

I shook my head. "It's too early for working out."

Mal snorted. There was no such thing in his world. He drummed a steady rhythm against the counter. *Rat-a-tat-tat. Rat-a-tat-tat.* "So what's he like? The new guardian?"

What was Quinn like? I still didn't know. "Hard to say. What about yours?"

"Nick's all right," Mal admitted. "I think he's got a thing going on with Cole's guardian. Kelly, right?"

I nodded.

"But they've gotta keep it quiet. Can't be fraternizing with your co-workers, and all that. But anyway, he said you guys getting Quinn is pretty lucky. Apparently, he's a big deal."

"He didn't freak out about the wraith," I admitted. "Not like Virago."

"Yeah, but Nick made it sound like he's a big deal. More than just 'I killed a wraith and I liked it.'"

"Who?" Quinn asked, striding into the kitchen.

"You," Mal admitted shamelessly, popping another grape into his mouth.

"Then I need coffee," Quinn grunted. "Don't you guys have anything better to do than gossip about the well-mannered gentleman down the hall?"

"The same well-mannered gentleman torturing Jenna with the Christmas house?" Mal asked, raising an eyebrow. "I heard she came home from shopping and you put a mini tree in her room."

Quinn's face was impassive, save for a crinkle at the corners of his eyes. "I have no idea what you mean."

"Anyway, Justin made the coffee," Mal warned.

Quinn winced in reply, dropping the hand that had been reaching for the coffee pot.

"Screw you guys, I make good coffee!" I protested.

"No," Mal said patiently, "you make a perfect vessel for your milk and sugar. That's not coffee."

Quinn grunted a quiet agreement.

"Justin and I were heading into town. You can tag along," Mal offered, suppressing a grin. "Maybe even help little Justin find a girlfriend this time."

I punched him in the arm, but the problem was that Mal's arms were the size of tree trunks and about as hard. I walked away wincing.

"Justin's never had a girlfriend?"

Great, now even Quinn was getting in on it.

"I've had girlfriends," I protested. I . . . had. It was just difficult.

"None of them pass the Jenna test," Mal admitted.

Quinn looked confused. "The Jenna test? What? She has to approve?"

"She has a tendency to destroy the kinds of girls who also happen to like Justin."

"That was one time!" I argued. There'd been a girl when we lived near the Chesapeake Bay. Her name was Amanda, and she was a cheerleader. That was her first strike. The second was that she was blonde. And the third was that she dared to be more than a stereotype: an airhead that wouldn't understand when Jenna was mocking her.

Amanda stood up to her at first, but Jenna played dirty,

and by the time we left at the end of the month, Amanda wouldn't even meet my eyes in the hallway.

"There's a diner," Quinn said abruptly, changing the subject. "I'm in the mood for breakfast." He glanced at me. "One thing I *will* miss about D.C.? Starbucks."

"There's a coffee shop on Main Street," Mal said, stretching up and out of his chair.

"And there's a coffee pot right there," Quinn said, pointing. "Doesn't mean anything. I happen to like paying nine dollars for a coffee."

Half an hour later, Mal and I walked into Shortway's Diner while Quinn stayed outside taking a phone call.

"You feel bad about leaving Cole behind?" Mal asked as he pushed the door open and we were greeted by a blast of humid air. The diner was straight out of the fifties. Black and white checkered floor tiles, red booths, waitresses in poodle skirts.

"He'll go bother Jenna, it'll be fine," I said with a grin.

"If she doesn't kill him first," Mal said.

I laughed. "It's a rite of passage that big sisters torment their little brothers."

"Jenna never tormented *you*."

I leveled a stare at Mal. "Really?" I asked, voice flat.

He scoffed. "You've always been too sensitive." We walked up to the counter and sat down at the bar rather than wait for a table. "Hey, check it out," he said, nudging me and pointing back at the entrance.

Through the glass door that led outside, and the picture windows on either side, there was a man stumbling through the parking lot. He wore a jumpsuit like a mechanic, stained from something more than just dirt—thick, dripping streaks that were splashed across his middle. His long hair hung down limp and scraggly around a face that hadn't seen a razor in weeks, and a shower in twice that.

I couldn't decide if he looked more like a serial killer or a homeless person. *All those stains could be blood...*

"Shit, stop staring," Mal said, nudging me. I focused, realizing that the man was looking through the glass now, and striding purposefully towards the door.

"What'd you have to stare at him for?" Mal whispered furiously.

"Me? You were the one who pointed him out!"

"I can't take you anywhere," Mal said, spinning away from me on his barstool, leaving me to look at his back. *Brothers are overrated*, I thought, and not for the first time in my life, though usually it was Cole who was driving me insane.

The jingling chime over the door rattled through an awkward lull in diner conversation, somehow louder than it should have been. I didn't even dare look up into the mirror behind the bar to see if it was really the man from outside coming to find out why people were staring at him.

"I'm starving," I said, a little louder than I intended. "Do you think they have those giant omelets that come with the side of pancakes?"

"This isn't IHOP," Mal said, shifting only slightly in my direction. He broke off sharply, but I didn't have to ask why. I could feel it—a presence far to my right, at the tail end of the bar where a waitress ran the cash register. He was a dark blob in the corner of my eye, but it was definitely him.

After that, neither of us said anything. The waitress asked the man something, but her voice was too raspy and low to make it out. He didn't say anything at all, but I could feel him there. Like the quieter he got, the more *present* he became, until it was all I could think about.

I chanced a look up, trying for casual and my reflection showing panic instead. My eyes slid to the mirror's right, and I saw the man, all right.

I saw him staring at the two of us.

"Mal," I said out of the corner of my mouth. "Mal," I repeated, when he didn't respond. Then I hit him with my elbow.

"You're him," the man said, and it was hard to tell if the jumble of words spilling out of his mouth was an alcoholic slur or something else. "The dark light in the sky. The sun."

"The sun?" Mal rose off the barstool.

But the man ignored him. "Oh, I've been hearing the signs. The voices whispering in my head, chirping little voices, tick-tock, tock-tick, *wait for him*. The sun that will usher in the never-ending eclipse. The daughter."

"Time to go," I said tightly, scrambling up off my own seat and backing up into Mal. The sun? The daughter? Of course. "He's one of *them*," I said to Mal significantly. I looked back at the man. "You're a Harbinger, aren't you?"

When Moonset had revealed themselves, their impassioned speeches had reached the ears of the weak and hurting. A cult of followers, people who literally *worshipped* them, swelled their ranks. They became known as the Harbingers—the ones who spread the word. In lessons, we were taught that Moonset preyed on the broken, feeding into their delusions and their weaknesses. Breaking them, and reshaping something more loyal out of the pieces. And so the cult of Moonset was born.

"You've got the wrong people," I said slowly. I shot Mal a dirty look; this was all his fault. If he hadn't started staring in the first place, I'd be halfway to my breakfast by now.

"You don't know us," Mal said, like talking to the mentally disturbed was something he did all the time.

"I always knew they'd bring you back, Daggett. Many things I was, but never a fool. They tried to put worms inside," he tapped at his head, "to steal all your secrets, but I wouldn't let them. Ground them up and fed them to the angels."

"That's…good," I said, still trying to keep as much distance between us as possible, for the smell, if nothing else. I was definitely right about the not showering thing—the man smelled like a rest stop urinal.

My first instinct was that the man was totally crazy, but I wasn't stupid. I had to wonder if there were tiny grains of truth underneath the crazy haystack. If this man was a believer, if he knew *my parents…*

"You can't be here," Mal said, interrupting my thoughts. "C'mon, Jus, we shouldn't even be talking to him."

We weren't allowed to have contact with cultists, for obvious reasons, so I wasn't sure how this mistake was even happening right now. Didn't they do security checks before they brought us somewhere? What if he tried to kidnap us just like the wraith had?

"Just because many lost faith doesn't mean we all did," the man said, his voice tobacco thick. He pointed his finger at Mal, his hand trembling. "The Denton boy. Of course you're thick as thieves, just like your daddies."

"We're nothing like them," Mal said tightly. I wondered when his tune had changed from *don't engage with the crazy*. Mal normally wasn't known for having a hair-trigger reaction to our parents. He was usually the one who let it affect him the least.

"It's one of the signs," the man insisted. "Can you hear it? They whisper and plot, and they'll grind up my bones to make their bread. They promised!"

Whatever sign the man was seeing, or hearing as the case may be, it didn't look like a good one. No Exit, maybe. Or Beware of Avalanche. We were starting to attract an audience, as people found their morning chat far less interesting than the crazy, ranting homeless man at the counter. I cleared my throat. "Look, we're not—"

"—that's enough." It was almost a mirage, the way Quinn suddenly popped up like a bodyguard. Or an enforcer. He had his hand around the mechanic's forearm before I even realized he'd moved, and it slowly started to drop. "Justin, Malcolm, go wait outside."

"Quinn?"

His dark eyes flashed. "I said wait outside, Justin."

"Come on," Mal said, still focused on the mechanic, grabbing my shoulder.

"Witcher, witcher, witcher," the man singsonged.

"Hello, Johnny," Quinn said with a sad smile. "It's been awhile, hasn't it?"

"Do they know? I bet they can feel it in the air, can't they?" The mechanic closed his eyes, looking euphoric, as if the very air was the greatest smell ever. He took on a pleading tone. "Just tell me they know. Please."

I turned back, and heard Quinn mutter *something,* but I couldn't decipher it. The tingle in the air confirmed it was magic. The man was caught off guard; his jaw worked but no sound came out.

"C'mon," Mal urged, pulling me away. I wasn't sure, but it looked like Quinn had used some kind of silence spell on the Harbinger.

Since most magic required a voice, anything that affected the ability to speak was a highly coveted ability. But as far as I knew, as far as *any* of us knew, there was no such spell. They drilled it into our heads year after year. You can't steal someone's voice, you can't drown it out, you can't take it away.

If they were lying about that, then what else had they lied about?

"What the hell is going on?" I breathed, once we were outside. Mal opened his mouth, then abruptly closed it and shook his head. He had a hand in his hair, his expression unreadable.

That threw me. Mal had seventeen different early morning grunts for "hello." I knew them all. But I couldn't tell what he was thinking—maybe for the first time ever.

No one else in the diner seemed to notice anything out

of the ordinary. Quinn had his hand on the other man's shoulder, and whatever conversation they were having, it wasn't going so well. Mechanic was shrinking in place. Another man walked in from the back, taking off a white apron and joining them. Quinn nodded to him, saying something emphatic while gesturing with his hand.

"What was all that?" I demanded. It wasn't like I expected Malcolm to have the answers, but I had to ask *someone*. Now the two men were facing the mechanic, and the new guy had his arms crossed in front of him. I still couldn't tell what Mal was thinking, but his attention was on the exchange inside as much as mine was. "I don't think we're in Kansas anymore, Toto."

SIX

"Humility is for people who cower before storms instead of causing them. Power is there to be taken. If you can't stand the heat, then get away from the person with the fire."

....

Diana Bellamont (C: Moonset)
Unknown Date

I didn't get a chance to tell Jenna about the Harbinger, or about pretty much anything, because the minute the three of us walked in the front door, she was lying in wait with Cole at her side.

We were lucky Quinn even let us stop at a drive-thru on the way home for something. None for Mal, of course—he looked at the greasy bag with a horrified expression. I could imagine just what he was thinking: exactly how many hours on the treadmill or how many sit-ups it would take to burn off my instant breakfast.

I didn't care, though.

But generic fast food coffee and soggy bagel sandwiches were no fortification against Jenna on a mission. "Good, you're finally back," she began, a speech that I was sure she'd practiced more than once. "Now that we're all settled in, I think we need to talk about training."

"We do?" Quinn asked, sounding almost amused. He moved past us into the kitchen and leaned against one of the counters, a paper coffee cup held lightly in his hand.

"We do," she said firmly. "We were almost killed, Quinn. Because we couldn't defend ourselves. The only reason that we're standing here right now is because you were there. So what happens the next time, when you're not?"

"Lucky for you, I'm right down the hall."

Mal opened his mouth, but I held out my hand. I wanted to see where Jenna was going with this. She almost sounded reasonable. Maybe the wraith had been a wake-up call.

Jenna's lips compressed, and she shifted her stance. I don't think that was the answer she was looking for. "But even you couldn't beat it. You had to use one of us to stop it, and even then, you got lucky. Next time, you might not be that lucky."

Quinn's smile was wide. "You'll find I'm a *very* lucky guy. Relax, you're in good hands."

"And that's it? We should just trust you?" Her earlier composure was starting to slip, and the acerbic cut of her normal tone crept in around the edges.

"That's it," Quinn said magnanimously. "I'm on your side, kids."

"We're not kids," Cole muttered, speaking for the first time.

"So we've got your assurance for what ... three months? What happens after that, when we never see you again?" Jenna asked pointedly. "When it comes to us, no one's on our side. At least not for long. And you can't guarantee that the next one will be competent."

It didn't seem like Quinn let very much get to him. This was no different. "So what are you expecting? That you're going to demand to be taught some spells that will arguably be useful in self-defense? Spells that a girl with your track record could easily abuse in a plethora of creative ways. Now why would I do that?"

"Jenna has a point, though," I interjected. This was about thirty seconds from getting ugly—anyone could see that Quinn wasn't about to give Jenna what she wanted, and that was always dangerous. "Isn't there some kind of appeal system? I mean, no offense to Jenna, but she abuses the spells she knows anyway, and we don't get taught something without at least a dozen people signing off on it first."

It was more than a little annoying that I'd agree with Jenna on that. There was so much fear and nervousness that we were the Second Coming, that everything we were to be taught was checked and double-checked. I wouldn't be surprised if the Congress had entire think tanks established just to predict what kinds of chaos Jenna could do with a spell that turned glass opaque or one that could change an article of clothing into a primary color.

After all, this was the girl who had cobbled together a couple of eavesdropping spells, a rumor-spreading spell, and one that made the caster seem incredibly trustworthy, and somehow turned that into a riot.

"Jenna's not going to change—" I started.

"—and you're always going to be there to cover her ass," Quinn interrupted. "I get it. But you guys have to realize that everyone else is doing the same thing. Every time Jenna abuses what power she *does* have, it makes them question your progress all over again. There are some people advocating that you stop training entirely."

"They can't do that!" Jenna shouted at once. She started to pace, very quickly and without looking where she was going. Cole fluttered in her wake, looking unsure if he was supposed to pace with her or get out of the way. As a result, she nearly barreled into him at least three times.

"They can do a lot worse than that," Quinn replied matter-of-factly. "That's the way the system works. If you abuse your power, you don't get any more."

"And if we get killed because a bunch of old cowards are scared of us?" she demanded.

"Then they'll think that the problem worked itself out." Quinn raised his shoulders in a halfhearted shrug. "The Council may take care of you, giving you all the things you need to be comfortable, like your phones and a healthy allowance, but it's not a luxury. You're not the political darlings you seem to think you are. They teach you as little as possible because they're scared, and you give them every reason to be even *more* scared. So you can't be surprised that they're not looking out for your best interests."

"And what," Jenna scoffed, "you are?"

"I'm looking out for your survival," Quinn replied. "I'm a Witcher. That's part of my job."

Part of his job. The unspoken other part hung in the air, and the four of us who weren't Witchers each absorbed it differently. Cole shuffled his feet, Jenna's expression grew taut, Malcolm rolled his eyes, and me? My heart thudded in my chest.

Because there were two jobs that any Witcher around us would be expected to perform. To protect us from threats. And to eliminate us in the event that we *became* the threats.

———

Jenna still hadn't moved on by the next day. She was sulking, barely speaking to any of us unless it was a snide remark. Quinn's refusal to break the rules and teach us new spells hadn't sat well with her. For some reason, she was particularly hostile to *me*, as if I had something to do with it.

Trying to figure out girls, especially ones I was related to, was definitely not one of my superpowers.

It was another day of shopping. Jenna and Bailey were both complaining about not having enough clothes. Our wardrobe from Kentucky still hadn't arrived, if it ever would. After the wraith had showed up, I think we all wrote our stuff off as a lost cause. They wouldn't want to send anything to us on the off chance that it had been tampered with. So that meant a lot of shopping.

"Again?" Mal had groused first thing in the morning, when everyone had collected in his kitchen. I didn't really want to go, either, but the other three were all about it. And I figured it would be better to keep an eye on Jenna rather than let her unleash her temper on an unsuspecting population.

"Just because everything looks good on you is no reason for the rest of us to suffer," Jenna said crossly. "Besides, a girl needs options."

"Our guardian said it gets cold here, and there's lots of snow," Bailey added. "I need a couple different coats if she's right."

"I guess I could use a new pair of cross-trainers," Mal sighed.

The whole conversation made me think of what Quinn had been saying the night before. That the Council made sure we had allowances and credit cards just to keep us quiet. If we were taken care of, we were less likely to complain. I listened to Jenna and Bailey discussing things they'd seen in store windows, and Cole jumping in to talk about some video game he wanted, and I realized that he was right.

I'd never thought about it like that before. Just how far did they go to manipulate us? Were our moves always necessary, or were they trying to accomplish something else?

Carrow Mill didn't have a "mall" by the strictest definition, but Malcolm had found the closest alternative. There was a suburb where the trendy rich lived, and they had a little outdoor shopping plaza that screamed Old Time, America. Cobblestone streets lined with park benches gave off the perfect downtown vibe, even though it was all an elaborate ruse. The outdoor mall, Americana style. All the buildings stood at least three stories, the bottom floor filled with chains like Express, Forever 21, and even a Barnes & Noble. The girls were in heaven. The guys were there to carry bags.

"I missed my morning workout for this? I'd rather be sleeping," Mal groaned, throwing himself down on one of the benches on the street. The girls were inside with Cole, who'd been surprisingly quick to tag along with them. It made sense when he tried to tag along at Victoria's Secret, but less so when it was just a clothing boutique.

"You're the driver," I said, leaning over the back of the chair and watching across the street. More and more people were starting to crowd the streets. "Besides, how can you hate shopping? Stop ruining a perfectly good stereotype."

"Shopping with *them*?" Mal shuddered. "And I'm not a magic clothing genie. I don't care *what* they buy."

"I think you're just supposed to tell them it looks great," I said with an absent shrug. "That's what I always do, at least."

"Always playing peacemaker," he said with a fluid wave, like a conductor controlling the orchestra.

I followed the movement, reading the intent behind it. "It's not like that. I'm not manipulating them."

"Sure you're not."

"Who cares what you think, anyway?" I snapped. "You're the one with the Victoria's Secret bag in your lap."

He didn't need to look up to give me the finger. Then

again, by doing so he missed the group of girls crossing the street right in front of him.

The girl in front knew she was gorgeous. She owned it. Her brunette hair was pinned up with chopsticks, and her dark coat was the kind of fur that probably wasn't faux. She had what Jenna would have called "permanent bitch face"— a smirk that looked like it never left her face. She took one look at Mal with his middle finger in the air, turned right to her friend, and started whispering something. Almost the entire flock of girls burst into giggles as they passed us.

"Great first impression," I said, and Mal finally lifted his head.

He saw the girls and rolled his eyes. "I'm heartbroken. If it's so important, why don't *you* go apologize. You could use the practice talking to girls you're not related to."

"Dick."

Mal laughed. "Go talk to the girls, coward."

I watched them go, half wanting to. They were part-way down the street when one of the girls in back turned around. She was the only one with short hair, some sort of reddish auburn that stood out against her white jacket. Despite the snow and ice on the ground, she moved easily, and grinned in my direction.

"They're just girls," Mal said, like that made any sense whatsoever. "They're not going to hurt you. I mean, unless you want them to."

"I've had enough things trying to hurt me for one lifetime," I muttered. "You know this is why I let Cole do bad things to your reputation, right?"

Mal lifted himself upright like he was doing crunches at the gym. "Better hurry, before Jenna decides which one you like before you do," he said, nodding to the store the girls were in. Jenna and Bailey were at the cash register, and Cole stood mystified staring at a rack of jewelry.

"I'm going for a walk," I announced, and started off down the street. I might have hustled a little, but I couldn't say for sure whether I was trying to catch up to the girls or get away from my siblings.

It was probably an even stretch of both.

———

Half an hour later, I didn't have a clue where I was. Despite what I'd said to Mal, I wasn't about to go stalk a bunch of girls that I'd have to spend a few months at school with. Bad first impressions weren't my thing.

The downside to small-town Americana was that every street looked the same. I got lost quickly and managed to walk in a circle at least three different times. By a stroke of luck, I finally managed to find my way back to the bookstore, only to open the door just as the girls from earlier were walking out. The brunette leader sailed passed without even a thank you. The rest of the girls followed her lead, a few giggles escaping here or there. And then there was the girl in the back.

She held the inner door open, just as I held the outer. After a momentary stare down between us, she cocked her shoulders as if to say, "Well?" We stood like two gunslingers the Old West, waiting to see who'd flinch first. Who'd release their door and let the other walk through?

I glanced down the street, desperately trying to think of something cool to say. This girl didn't look like she'd fall for one of Malcolm's stupid lines or be drawn in by Cole's sometimes adorable nature.

"Your friends are leaving." Immediately I wanted to kick myself. That was how I opened a conversation?

Her smile widened. "Maybe they're not my friends." She ran a hand through her hair, and I ... forgot what I was going to say. The cold didn't matter, the people coming in and out around us weren't important.

"My name's Justin," I finally called out, during a particular rush through the doors.

She touched a little old lady in a tan coat on the shoulder and laughed. Then she looked back at me, shaking her head. "I didn't ask."

Right about now, Malcolm would be sliding in with some completely inappropriate line. Or Cole would be too busy staring at her butt to really pay attention. I just ... kept holding the door. I'd used up all my know-how with girls right off the bat. My brain couldn't form words. Make talky hard.

"You're gawking." She had a tinkling kind of laugh, like someone running fingers down the piano.

I shook myself, and shifted so I was holding the door with my foot. "Am not." Great. I'd regressed to kindergarten, thirty seconds away from kicking her in the shins and running away.

The last of the line finally dissipated. She gestured again, this time a flourishing move with her arm. My feet remained rooted in place. She smiled again, her eyes searching mine. Then she finally let go of her door and started walking towards mine. After a second's hesitation, she opened the other half of the double doors and exited through that one.

"Come on, puppy," she said with a backwards glance at me. "I'm going to let you buy my coffee."

I remained where I was. "Puppy?"

"Could've called you kitten," she said over her shoulder. "Keep it up, and maybe we'll work our way up to ducky."

"I have a name," I replied. But before I knew it, I was following her.

I could practically hear the amusement dripping from her words. "Still didn't ask."

"You know I'm a stranger, right? You always go around asking strangers to coffee?"

She walked into the street and nearly into a car as it drove past. A moment later, as I started to lunge forward, I realized she was in no danger. The car passed, and she moved behind it easily, her movements timed perfectly.

"This is Carrow Mill, porcupine," she said, and then grimaced. "No, definitely not porcupine."

I shouldn't have been surprised when our trip for "coffee" led us instead to a smoothie shop. "Do they even have coffee?" I asked skeptically.

"You know that was just an expression, right?" Her eyes said I should have. Small children in Botswana probably knew it was just a euphemism. "If I'd said 'Hey, let's go have a couple of Green Giant smoothies with extra ginseng and wheat grass,' you'd have looked at me like I was some sort of crazy person."

"That's still on the table." It was honest, but probably the stupidest thing I'd said so far. I tried to open the door for her, but she opened her own for the second time.

"Lucky for you, your opinion is invalid." She sauntered over to the counter, smiling at the guy dressed head to toe in orange. He couldn't have been much older than either of us, but he was a little taller and rounder than I was.

"Hey, Cal."

Cal looked at the girl, then glanced over at me. "Hey," he said tersely. "Who's this?"

"Stray I picked up." She leaned on the counter, whispering conspiratorially, "Would you believe he was selling his body for concert tickets."

Cal didn't look fazed. "What kind of concert?"

"Something boring. European clog dancers?" she replied. "I'm saving the boy from a life less tragic."

I snorted. Did I look like someone who needed to be saved?

Finally Cal started to smile. "So you want the usual?" She nodded. "And him?"

She turned to me. "What are you in the mood for? Lunch smoothie? Vitamin blaster? Post-Workout Indulgence?" She recited smoothies off the menu board faster than I could read the ingredients. "Or maybe the Just For Boys smoothie with a little extra gingko?"

"Uhm," I said, drawing it out and trying to read the

board. Didn't they just have like...strawberry smoothies? Or how about coffee? I would have settled for actual coffee.

"He'll have the Lunch smoothie with a shot of whey and a double of gingko," she said, ending my hesitation. And then she stage whispered, "I think he needs the brain fuel."

Cal pulled two cups off the stack and grabbed a magic marker. "Name?"

I looked to her first, but Cal sighed. "I already know her. What's *your* name?"

"Justin." I waited, wondering if he wanted a last name too. But the first name seemed to cover it, and after he'd scrawled a totally illegible version of my name on the cup, he set them both down and started to press buttons on the register.

"Eleven ninety."

I pulled out a twenty, which Cal nearly snatched out of my hand.

"Don't worry, it's worth it," she said.

"Oh, thank god. For a minute I thought I was wasting all my money on a bunch of fruit and milk tossed in a blender."

She tilted her head to the side and looked up at me thoughtfully. "Yeah, no. Sarcasm's not a good look on you. You're definitely more of a winter. Smolder in silence."

"Are you always this bizarre?"

She ruffled her hair and smiled slowly, offering no response.

"So when do I get to know your name?"

"Patience is a virtue, my little mango."

"Mango?"

She shifted her weight from one foot to the other. "Couldn't think of another animal," she admitted. Her eyes strayed over the counter to the piles of fruit on display. They'd been selected for their coloring and possibility their alliteration: kumquats and kiwi were arranged together, along with sliced cantaloupes and carrots.

"How about Pissed-off Panda Bear?"

She didn't laugh. In fact, that got no reaction at all. She looked me over. "You'd think the new boy would be a little more genial. Not quite so..." she mused over it for a minute. "Cantankerous." Her smile brightened. "SAT word."

"I'm not..." I hesitated. "How'd you know I'm new?"

"You think you're living in the big city? Everyone knows everyone around here. Besides, Maddy said you were. And she knows all."

"Maddy?"

"The brunette with the Mean Girl complex?"

Cal finally came back with the drinks, setting the pair of medium-sized smoothies down in front of us and moving on to the next person in line. The girl called out a cheerful, "Thanks, Cal," before walking off. I followed. I wasn't sure what else to do. This girl clearly lacked sanity. But there was something fun about her, drama free and exciting. I was fascinated.

We stepped out onto the street, and I strained to decipher the scrawl of her name on the cup. My concentration was broken by a very loud, very angry scream. "Where the fuck have you been?"

Jenna. Of course. Her "Justin was having a good time without me" senses must have been tingling. I turned back, followed the sound of her voice and found her standing at the corner across the street with a hand on her hip. She didn't move, just stood there and waited. Expected me to run right over. I almost wanted to turn around and walk away with my mystery girl, just to see how Jenna would react.

"I've gotta..." I wasn't sure how to make the excuse. Deal with my potentially psychotic sister? Fix whatever problem she'd managed to get into in the last half hour? Talk her down off a ledge that would lead to another move? Stave off the inevitable explosion? Waiting would only serve to piss Jenna off more than she already was.

"Wow, your girlfriend is pissed."

That caught me off guard. Jenna? My girlfriend? "Now who's digging for information?" I said, trying to sound teasing but a little afraid it just came across as desperate.

The girl snickered, shaking her head and looking away. "So far off, cowboy. Besides, most sisters I know don't yell at their brothers like that."

"You haven't met my sister," I muttered.

"Love to," she announced as if that had been an invitation. Then she hopped off the sidewalk and made a beeline for Jenna.

SEVEN

"Everyone knew Sherrod was the leader. But Cy Denton and I grew up together. He controlled the school. Everyone wanted to know him. He was the star of every play, the one who threw the best parties, and the funniest guy I've ever met."

Sara Bexington (S)
Personal Interview

"Who is this?" Jenna demanded, once I caught up. The girl just stood there while Jenna's glare homed in on me. Jenna would rip out her spine and dangle it out of reach like a cat toy if I didn't interject.

"What happened?" I countered.

"I asked you—"

I cut her off. "What. Happened?"

"Bailey's ... *upset*," was all she said. Her eyes flicked to my mystery girl (when did she become *my* mystery girl?), and I realized that there was a whole undercurrent to the situation that she wasn't going to reveal in front of a stranger. *That's what you get for thinking you could have an afternoon free*, I thought, actually able to *feel* my blood pressure rising.

"What did you do?" It didn't take a rocket scientist to figure out that Jenna's bad mood was her way of overcompensating.

"I didn't do anything," she said, her voice growing more shrill. In other words, she had GUILTY written across her forehead in big black letters.

"Fine, then Bailey took something you said out of context. Just tell me what happened."

"I don't know what happened," she snapped. "We were in the store trying things on, and Mal and I had this tiny little disagreement, and when I walked out of the dressing room, Bailey had taken off."

"Taken off?" My stomach sank.

"Yeah, like gone. Ran away, planning on never coming back."

"Well it's good to see you're not being overdramatic about it," the girl suddenly chimed in.

Jenna whirled on her. "And who the hell are you?"

"Jen—" I tried to grab her arm, but she threw me off. "Leave her—"

"My name's Ash," the girl said. I probably looked like Cletus the Slack-Jawed Yokel, the way I gaped. After struggling for half an hour, she offered her name up to Jenna in the first thirty seconds? As casual as can be?

Jenna didn't understand the significance. "Better question, why are you butting into our conversation?"

"Because you're making a scene," Ash said. At some point during the conversation, she'd pulled out her phone and was texting casually, her eyes barely glancing over the screen. "I figured if you stop yelling at your brother for a minute, maybe you'd realize that."

Jen whirled on me. "Who the hell is this girl?"

"We met at the bookstore," I said. "And then we went out for coffee."

"You're drinking a milkshake." Jenna made it an accusation.

"Going for coffee is a euphemism," I explained patiently, carefully avoiding Ash's eyes. "There's a smoothie shop across the street."

Jenna's hand flexed into a fist and then relaxed. "This wouldn't be a problem if they'd show us—" There were spells that could track the coven bond. Spells we weren't allowed to know. Truth be told, there were a lot of things we weren't allowed to know.

I cut her off. "I know."

"It's ridiculous," Jenna snapped.

"I'll help you look," Ash volunteered. She slid the phone back into the pocket of her coat, looking between us expectantly.

"Thanks," Jenna said as snidely as she could manage. "But this is a family thing." And just like that, I knew that

Jenna and Ash would never be friends. Ash wasn't the type of girl who backed down to Jenna's attitude, and as a result, Jenna would never see her as anything more than a bitch.

"I know the area, and you don't," Ash smiled, a saccharine look that didn't hold an ounce of sweetness. "I'm also an extra pair of eyes, and in case you haven't noticed, there's a lot of places to hide around here."

"Justin," my sister growled, "get rid of her." Watching the two of them was like watching a pair of wolves circling each other.

"You'll need all the help you can get," Ash added, looking up at me.

"Ash can help me look. You should go find Mal and Cole," I said, pointing back the way Jenna had come from. "The last thing I need is Cole doing something stupid, too."

Jenna and I shared one last look, hers promising a conversation I wouldn't want to have, before we both went in different directions.

"How old is she? Your sister?" Ash asked, while we waited for a gap in cars so we could cross the street.

"Bailey? She's fifteen."

Ash hmmed. "And what does she like?"

What does she like? "I don't know," I said, struggling. "Girly stuff? Makeup? Clothes?"

"Girly stuff," she repeated, her lips twitching. "All right then, c'mon," she linked her arm through mine, attaching us at the elbow.

"Where are we going?" I asked, essentially letting her drag me down the block.

"You have a lot to learn about girls," she grinned, "whether or not you're related to them."

Bailey running away wasn't what I was afraid of, not even close. Her particular talent was evocations, literally bringing things out in people and affecting their judgment. She still hadn't learned that magic couldn't solve everything. And her magic, much like Cole's, had a tendency to take on a life of its own.

Like the time she stopped a fighting couple, pulling out their feelings of love and attraction for each other. A spell that quickly spread, enveloping everyone for a full city block who dropped what they were doing and hooked up with the nearest person. That had been ... awkward. I'd never had to pair a "safe magic" lecture with a "safe sex" lecture at the same time.

When people talked about which of us had the most destructive potential, they always looked at Jenna, sometimes at me. My vote was Bailey—there was nothing scarier than the ability to change how everyone around you felt. What was worse was that she didn't understand exactly how bad that was.

"It's not far," she promised as we headed back in the direction of the bookstore. We crossed onto one of the side streets, and tucked in between an art gallery and a Banana Republic, we came to the pet store, Unleashed Boutique.

"Seriously?" I asked, pointing up to the sign.

Ash sighed, shaking her head at me. She had her phone in hand and was typing something out as we talked. "Not a pet lover, nice." Once again, I tried to open the door for her and she opened the other door instead.

"I like pets just fine," I said, already canvassing the store for my sister. The puppies lined one whole side of the store. An older couple moved to the other side of the aisle, and revealed Bailey.

"Bailey gets attached to things she shouldn't," I said quietly over my shoulder. "I'm probably going to have to pull her out of here kicking and screaming."

Bailey looked up, the splotchiness in her face already starting to fade. "It wasn't my fault," she said preemptively.

I held up my hands. "Not here to judge. What's with the running away?"

Bailey sighed. "I just needed to get away. Then I found the pet store, and the puppies were so cute and floppy and..." She didn't need to say anymore. One of the many flaws in Bailey's life was that no one would ever let her have a pet. She wanted a dog more than anything.

"Aww, he's so cute," Ash said, crouching down next to her. "You've got good taste."

"Thanks. Who are you?"

Ash grinned and looked up at me. "Come on, don't be rude. Make the introductions." So I did. Bailey's eyebrows raised as she looked up at me. I could only imagine the sorts of questions she was building up to.

"We should get going, Bails. You know you can't run away."

"Why not? You did." She didn't say it with any malice, just honest curiosity.

"I didn't run away," I said carefully, "I just wanted some time to myself."

"So did I," Bailey said.

Ash started laughing softly to herself. "Well, as fantastic as this has been," she said, "it's after midnight and my pumpkin's turning into a carriage."

I blinked. "What?"

Ash sauntered backwards towards the door with a rueful smile. "I have a prior engagement." She pivoted just as the brunette from earlier appeared in the doorway, wearing sunglasses.

"Where'd you run off too?" Maddy demanded, pulling off her sunglasses.

Ash turned to look at me, her smile widening. "I found a distraction."

"You know, I thought about leaving you," Maddy announced. She didn't look at me at first, focusing her attention on the girl who was too busy twisting my insides up to pay attention. "I thought we had plans and you run off with some…" She turned to me, and her lip curled, "guy."

"Don't be like that," Ash said with a smirk, "you know I still love you best."

"Whatever," the brunette sniffed. "We're going to lunch. Are you coming?"

Ash looked up at me, her auburn hair gleaming in the sunlight. "Sorry," she said to me. "I have plans with my friends."

"It's fine," I said casually. *You should ask for her number. Or give her yours.* I could feel her friend's stare even through her sunglasses, and it was putting me on edge. *Just ask for her number; otherwise Mal's never going to let you hear the end of it.*

"C'mon, we're leaving." Maddy had already started moving away, phone in one hand. She looked at me one last time, cool and contemptuous.

"So wait," I said. She turned and looked up at me expectantly. "I...uhm." How in the hell were you supposed to ask a girl for her number? Without looking like a tool.

Ash seemed to read my thoughts. My nerves made her eyes sparkle even more. "Don't worry, big guy. It's a small town. I'll find you again."

"That's not what..."

"Ash!"

"Run on home, practice, and we'll try again next time." She flipped around and bounced out the door just behind Maddy, who was texting furiously.

I followed behind Bailey, glancing at a cage full of puppies struggling over a chew toy and falling over themselves. Bailey grabbed the door and held it open. I was about to step through, and then I saw the guy across the street.

He was standing in line at the pretzel kiosk, dressed in khakis and flannel. But the last time I'd seen him, he'd been Quinn's backup at the diner. I hadn't thought much about him at the time, assuming he was another Witcher or something. But now he was watching us? There were people watching us when we went out now? I hesitated in the doorway.

"Come on, Justin," Bailey said, pulling on my arm. "I want to go get some coffee before we have to deal with

Jenna." She saw me staring across the street and turned that way. "What are you looking at?"

I shook my head and faked a grin. "Come on, I found this shop you'll like," I said, hoisting my smoothie. That was all it took to distract Bailey, who started telling me all about what kind of dog she wanted to get someday.

At the corner, I glanced back, but he was gone.

———————

The mood in the SUV on the way home was somber. Bailey was still embarrassed and blushing, Jenna wasn't pointedly *not talking* to any of us, and the guys didn't feel the need for small talk. Maybe Cole did, but for once he picked up on the context clues and kept his hyper thought process to himself.

Once we were in the driveway and the tension had exited the car along with us, Cole nudged Malcolm. "Hey, why's Justin smiling?"

I looked up. "Huh?"

Malcolm stared at me, even narrowing his eyes a bit. "Why *are* you smiling?"

"What?" I felt my forehead crinkle in my confusion. "What are you talking about?"

"Justin met a *girl*," Bailey announced with glee. "Isn't it obvious?"

"You met a girl?" Malcolm's smirk was obnoxious. Not only was he going to take credit, but he was going to be a dick about the whole thing.

"Maybe if you get laid you won't be such a pain in the

ass," Cole announced, loud enough that people three streets over probably heard.

I moved to hit him, but Mal got there first, cuffing him on the back of his head. "Seriously?"

"Dude!" Cole started rubbing his head, looking all flustered. "Jenna says that all the time!"

We all turned to find Jenna, but she was already disappearing across the street and into Bailey and Cole's house with Bailey in tow.

Malcolm came up beside me. "She's still pissed off?"

I nodded. Bailey was back and everything was fine, but that didn't mean that Jenna was going to let it go. "Just give her some space. Maybe Bailey will calm her down. Or maybe she'll just be pissed for days like usual."

"Well yeah," Cole wormed his way in between us, like this was some sort of "guy talk" moment. "She's totally embarrassed. She caused a scene, and Bailey got upset. Bailey still hasn't forgiven her for making us move again. Jenna might act like she doesn't care what most people think, but we're not most people, right?"

I opened my mouth to argue with Cole out of principle (I mean, I can't remember the last time the boy got something right), and then I stopped.

"Insight into the devil's mind," Malcolm murmured. "Powerful stuff."

Cole seemed to shrink. "You're making fun of me again," he complained.

"Actually, he's not," I said, ruffling his hair. "Besides, who cares if Mal makes fun of you? He still sleeps with a teddy bear, remember?"

That was all it took to make Cole start laughing. "Oh yeah!"

Mal glowered, but that was to be expected. A couple of years ago, boredom had set in and Cole and I came up with a plan. We'd found a stuffed bear that had been left in our hotel room. We waited until Malcolm fell asleep, and tucked it in the crook of his arm. For an hour we'd mess with him, until he shifted position. Each time snapping a photograph of him with the bear.

Once someone finally told, he'd tried deleting all the pictures. Cole, being the genius he was, had sent copies to his email account. He'd promised to delete them, but he never did. Jenna had too much influence on Cole, and she knew good blackmail when she saw it.

"Cole, if those pictures turn up as posters in the girls' restrooms again, I'm going to staple you to the ceiling," Mal threatened, pointing his finger in the much smaller boy's face. "I'm serious."

I almost pointed out that the posters hadn't been nearly as bad as the Facebook group that one of them had started. We never ended up at a school with more than a thousand kids, but after the first week the group had almost five times that many followers. Another week and that number had almost tripled, but by that time Mal found out the password and shut it down.

Now Cole was nearly bent over, he was laughing so

hard. "I can't make any promises," he said, and then yelped, as Mal lunged for him.

"In only a pair of tighty-whiteys," Mal added as he started chasing after him.

The horseplay continued on for a few minutes in the yard as Mal went after someone half his size and twice as agile. To Cole's detriment, though, was the fact that he kept slipping and sliding every time he hit one of the ice patches on the concrete. Malcolm just plowed forward like some sort of unstoppable monster.

"Maybe the one where you suck your thumb?" Cole giggled, dodging under Mal's arm and running for the backyard.

Not a minute later, Cole came sailing around from the other side of the house, but Mal's pursuit had stopped being so intense. "Screw this," he said, coming to a stop. "If I'm going to work up a sweat, I might as well go to the gym."

He looked at us expectantly, and Cole and I both immediately dropped our heads. "Is Quinn calling me?" I wondered, moving for the front door.

"Yeah, I think he is," Cole said from just behind me.

Mal snorted, but didn't push it.

We walked through the front door to hear raised voices. I instinctively wrapped my hand around Cole's mouth. His first instinct to being told "be quiet!" was to talk all about how quiet he would be.

"...of course they don't know anything," Quinn was saying from the kitchen. I left the front door cracked open and eased the two of us into the stairwell, out of his line of sight if he should cross to the hall.

"And I told you that was a mistake," Quinn continued a moment later. There were no other voices, so he must be on the phone. *What was a mistake?*

"They don't know why they're here yet," he continued. "But they're not stupid. They'll figure it out. Then what are you going to do?" He waited only a moment, but when he spoke again, his voice had changed. "Are you sure?"

Cole was squirming against my arm, looking up at me. I held my finger over my lips, then nodded back towards the front door. Just before we slipped back outside, I heard one last comment.

"No, of course I don't believe the rumors. But Jenna's right. They deserve to protect themselves, especially since we're not."

Once we got outside, I let go of Cole so that I could carefully ease the door closed again. My heart was pounding. On some level, I think all of us knew that after Byron, things were different. In our own ways, we were all on edge.

But to hear it confirmed like that, to hear things I didn't understand stated so casually. It just reaffirmed that we couldn't trust the adults. Any of them.

"C'mon," I said, before Cole could start in on his thousand questions. "I think we all need to have a talk."

EIGHT

*"Brandon was always the trickster. They turned
the school into their playground: a continuous
back and forth war of trickery and pranks.
All the boys participated, of course. And even
Diana, when a good humor struck her."*

....

Elizabeth Holden-Carmichael
Carrow Mill, New York:
From a written account
about Moonset's development

"What do you think he meant?" Cole asked as we bounded
up the stairs. There'd been no sign of Kelly, Cole's guardian, when we walked in, but that didn't mean she wasn't
lingering around somewhere.

"I don't know."

"Do you think another wraith's going to come after us?"

"I don't know." The house was a mirror image of ours, I realized. Instead of the hallway going right, it went left.

"Do you think we'll have to blow it up with another curse bomb?"

"I don't know, Cole!" Snapping at him didn't help anything, but there were already too many questions bubbling up in my head. "Which one's Bailey's?" I asked, nodding to the bedroom doors, all of which were closed.

"This one," Cole said, knocking on the door right next to us.

"Come in," Bailey called out from inside.

I let Cole go in first, and then I followed, shutting the door behind me. Bailey was on her bed, leaning against the wall with her feet tucked underneath her. Jenna, on the other hand, sat in the window seat, body flush against the glass. She favored us with a momentary look of irritation before she went back to her cloud gazing.

"We have a problem," I said quietly.

There were only two years that separated Jenna and I from Cole and Bailey, but those two years were the difference between childhood and adult. Mal was older than us, and by unspoken agreement the three of us looked after the other two like they were our kids. We let them *be* kids, even though we didn't have the luxury ourselves.

So in a situation like this, normally I wouldn't go to all of them at once. The three of us would discuss it (or Mal and I would discuss it first before bringing in Jenna) before we told them. When we were younger, and we didn't know who Moonset was or what terrorism meant, we'd tried to keep the truth from Bailey and Cole almost as soon as we found out. But the problem with being infamous is that if we didn't tell them, someone else would.

And did.

"Text Mal," I said, looking to Bailey, the only one with her phone out. "Ask him to grab me a sports drink on his way back."

Bailey's eyebrows lifted, but she did as she was told.

Cole sat at Bailey's desk, and I stood by the door. By unspoken agreement, none of us said a word. Less than five minutes went by before Mal's heavy footsteps thudded up the stairs. I opened the door for him, and closed it again after he passed through.

The lock hadn't even engaged when Jenna started whispering spells under her breath. Of the five of us, she had the best memory, and the litany of muffling spells rolled off her tongue. It didn't escape my attention that the last time we'd used these spells, we'd been under attack. And now, it seemed like we were again.

"Grab me a sports drink" was code. Utterly innocent, it had been Cole's idea. In the event that we needed to get together, but we didn't want to raise suspicion, we would ask the others to pick up a sports drink. Cole liked all those spy movies about double agents and infiltrations. Maybe it wasn't much of a surprise that he thought of something so paranoid.

"What's wrong?" Mal asked, kicking off his shoes and sitting next to Bailey on the bed. Either he was too tall, or her bed was too short, because his legs hung off the end.

Once Jenna gave me the nod that she was finished, I repeated what I knew. Cole tried to jump in a few times to embellish—"And then he got all snarly talking about how we deserved it!"—before I got through the whole, brief piece.

"That's it?" Mal asked, once I dropped my hands.

"That's it," I confirmed. "But if there's a specific reason why we're here, we should probably know what it is, right? Especially if it's going to be dangerous for us."

"Maybe they're not thrilled with security?" Jenna mused. "The wraith found us somehow. Could be that they'll find us again just as easily. It's not like people make any real effort to hide us. Social media's a bitch."

"That's why we're supposed to fly under the radar," Mal said tightly. "Stay away from things that are going to draw a lot of unwanted attention."

On a certain level, no one made much of an effort to conceal us. In every town we moved to, all the witches knew who we were. Our names never changed, and the fact that there were five of us moving together was always a rather obvious sign.

But the truth was that magic had a lot to do with it. I didn't know the particulars—none of us did—but there were wards and bindings in place to keep us hidden. The spells weren't on *us* because no one knew if that kind of magic would stir up the curse or not. It targeted the attempts to find us. When someone set out to look for the children of Moonset, they triggered the spells, which worked like viruses. Information was corrupted, spells were deflected to the wrong hemisphere. So far, until Kentucky, no one had ever managed to find us.

The truth was that we'd never had to worry about it before. But now we did. *I* did. "They brought us here for a reason, and it's not just to give us a place to start over. And then that guy that Mal and I saw at the diner, the crazy one?"

"The Harbinger," Mal nodded.

"So what are you thinking?" Jenna asked. She didn't look like she was taking any of this very seriously, her attention more on her nails than any of us, but that was just the way she was.

"We figure out what's really going on. Why they brought us here. What they want."

Cole scribbled on a piece of paper, having been still for too long. "Why don't we just ask him?"

"He'd just lie to us," Jenna responded with a snort. "And then he'd know that we know."

"Are you sure we can't trust them?" Bailey asked, with a weary attempt at hope. We all knew that there were only a small number of people we could trust, and they were in this room right now. Adults lied. Adults held grudges. They held you back and treated you like garbage, and taught other people to treat you like garbage.

"Quinn said he agreed that we should be able to defend ourselves," I admitted, "but it didn't sound like who he was talking to did. I think it's stupid if we don't confront him, though. He seems at least a little sympathetic."

"I agree," Jenna said casually. "And I think Justin's the person for the job."

Four sets of eyes turned on me.

Well, eff. "Fine, I'll go," I said, succumbing to peer pressure. "But we still need to keep an eye out. There's a reason why they brought us here, and I think it has more to do with Carrow Mill than with us."

———————

"I heard you on the phone earlier."

If I thought my announcement would disrupt the flurry of chopping going on in the kitchen, I was mistaken. Quinn had a variety of vegetables spread out in front of him, and an oversized kitchen knife in his hand. I kept a healthy distance, even though I was pretty sure he could still kill me at a distance.

"I'm not new at this," Quinn responded after a moment, his movements continuing to be precise and even. "I know when someone walks into the house."

That caught me off guard a little. I expected him to lie, to deny it. "You knew I was there?"

Quinn didn't reply. He moved to the next pile, a pile of green peppers. With one hand on the handle and the other on the dull end of the blade, he rocked his arms back and forth, dicing through them confidently.

"If you knew, then why were you saying all that stuff? Why didn't you just tell us what's going on?"

It was like talking to a brick wall. Quinn continued slicing and dicing, and with every thwack against the cutting board, I got more and more angry.

"Do you think this is funny? What's going on, Quinn? Why are we really here? What aren't you guys telling us? I know it's got to be something big."

"I've seen a wraith before. I probably wasn't much older than you," he looked up, waving the knife in my direction for a moment before he went back to what he was doing. "Took two full covens to take it down. Wraiths are nasty creatures. You can't kill something that's already dead."

What the hell was with story time? "What's your point?"

"That wraith was nothing. I was nearly a match for it all by my lonesome," he said, without any hint of arrogance. Just another fact. "What'd it do? Destroy a few walls? Knock us around a bit?"

"Killed two people," I pointed out.

"Two," Quinn agreed. "Not two hundred. It destroyed a building, not a village. Wraiths can control the dead, summon up an army of spirits, and kill you just as soon as breathe on you. This one didn't. It was only interested in one thing."

"Collecting us. We know this already."

"Collecting you. But did you ever think about the big picture? How did the wraith know where to find you? How did it know when, exactly, it should strike? There were a dozen Witchers in town that day, and all but three of them were busy trying to clean up your messes. There wasn't a better time to move."

I tried to see what he was saying, putting the pieces together in my head. "Someone told?" I knew we weren't the most popular kids in the world, but the idea that someone would turn us in like that? For as much as the Congress acted like we were this huge burden, they were always protecting us, keeping us safe. If that wasn't the case anymore, then what were we supposed to do? If there was a mole in the Congress, and they were feeding information to Cullen Bridger, then how would we be safe anywhere?

"Someone told," he confirmed. "And now there are more eyes on you. Some concerned, some afraid. But all of them are going to want something from you. Do you know what kind of weapon you could be, Justin? A warlock like Bridger could bring you along and use you like a shield, and everything in his path would be decimated. The same goes for any of you. Even the members of the Congress that fear you recognize that."

"But why are we *here*? You made it sound like there was something more specific than a mole, or the fact that we can be weaponized."

Quinn swore suddenly, and the brisk-necked chopping came to a stop as he dropped the knife. A thick line of red ran along the pad of his thumb. The knife clattered towards the edge of the counter and dropped to the ground just as Quinn jumped back a step, narrowly missing toe damage as well.

"Are you okay?" A lifetime of bandaging wounds kicked into gear as I went to the sink and grabbed a handful of paper towels and a wet cloth. I handed him a stack of towels and used the rest to wipe off the counter while he cleaned himself. Then, after handing him the wet cloth to hold over the cut, I went looking for everything else I'd need.

It took awhile to find what I was looking for—the

cleaning supplies were in the basement, for some reason, and the bandages in a first-aid kit under the bathroom sink.

I handed him one while I used the other on the counter. We didn't speak until the only traces of red left were the diced tomatoes. "You have people watching out for you," Quinn finally interjected. "I know it may not always seem like that, but there are. You're in good hands."

I scrubbed even harder at the counter, wondering if the finish would last. I didn't respond until I was done, and the damp paper towels were in the garbage. "Is he going to be coming after us again? Do we need to be on our guard?"

The smile on Quinn's face didn't cross into his eyes. "You should always be on your guard, Justin."

I started putting everything away, then looked at the bottle in one hand, and the box in the other. It was disturbing how many of my nights ended in bandages and bleach.

NINE

"I knew they were trouble from the very first
day. None of that 'they were quiet children;
good children' namby-pamby nonsense.
Those kids were spoiled, powerful, and reckless.
Someone shoulda seen Moonset coming
a mile away. But people are idiots."

....

Jack Wyatt (S)
Carrow Mill, New York:
From *Moonset: A Dark Legacy*

"I saw something the other day when I went to the gym,"
Mal said a few days later. I was waiting in his kitchen for
the coffee to brew when he dropped this little bomb on me.
"The kind of thing you were talking about, remember?"

The problem with the coffee maker at home was that it

hated me. Every time I tried to use it, the thing grunted and hissed at me like it was some kind of demonic creature. Possessed, no doubt. But Mal had no trouble with his, and so nearly every morning I made the frigid walk across the street for coffee.

I did my best imitation of a Mal morning grunt, one that said, "Really, I'm fascinated. Please, tell me more, and take as long as you need. Use big words."

He chuckled quietly, then looked pointedly at the T-shirt I'd come over in. "Go grab a jacket or something. We can stop and get coffee after."

Well, he did use the magic word. I went upstairs, grabbing one of the hooded sweaters that was fitted on Mal, but loose and roomy on me. I didn't need a jacket to run across the street, and none of us ever really locked the door, so there was never any fear of getting stuck outside. Until Mal decided on a field trip.

I figured wherever we were going would be near either the gym or the coffee shop, since those were the only two places that Mal went with any regularity. "One of the guys at the gym was talking the other day, telling me about this house," Mal confided as we got into the car. He was behind the wheel, of course, because he was the only one that the adults trusted to drive, and because I was still barely conscious.

"What house?"

"Well, it's not a *house*. It was some kind of city building. Like a rec center or something? Anyway, there was a fire a few weeks ago."

Mal started taking side streets at random, first zigging

then zagging in a vaguely nauseating manner. I kept getting jostled around the passenger seat, and while it helped wake me up a bit more, it did nothing for my mood.

"And why do we care?"

"You'll see," he said, glancing at me from the other side of the car. "It's hard to explain."

A few blocks later, Mal pulled over to the side of the road. We weren't *that* far from the downtown area—I could see the big clock tower that was Carrow Mill's pride and joy in the distance. I had no idea where we were other than that, though. There were almost as many side streets as houses in this town, making it a veritable maze of suburbia.

"I was curious, so I went looking for it," Mal continued as he got out. I did the same. "It's one more creepy thing to add to this town's résumé, though."

The building had been gutted by fire, a white finish that in the best spots was now a sooty gray, but the entire second floor had been consumed by flames. It looked like a house, but it was more of a duplex or triplex.

It wasn't just that there'd been a fire that had basically destroyed the house, though. I saw now why Mal was so interested in it. There was something in the air, a sense of foulness that made the house and everything around it seem a hundred degrees colder.

Mal crossed into the front yard, and I followed, feeling a pressure bearing down on me like we'd crossed an altitude threshold. My ears twinged, threatening to pop at any second.

But there was more. Mal vaulted up the porch steps, stopping at the center unit's front door.

"I know I've seen this before somewhere," he said. "Do you know what it is?"

There was fire and smoke damage everywhere I looked, but the burns on the door were...different. There was a pattern in the char. It looked like there had been *two* fires. The one that had swept over the entire building, and caused serious damage to the door, and one even older than that, one that had gouged a pattern into the wood.

At first I couldn't see it for what it was, but after a moment it snapped together, like eyesight suddenly going from blurry to clear. There was a circle, almost completely shaded in, and waves trailing off of the side, like when Cole was really young and drew his suns with wavy rays instead of straight and all his teachers kept trying to correct him.

It *did* kind of look like a strange sun, but the rays coming out from the sides were more like tentacles, writhing away from the center. The entire image was scarred deep into the wood, except for the sliver at the center that still hadn't been touched. Originally, the front door had been painted white, and there was a strip that still gleamed against the darkness next to it—a strip that was shaped like a crescent moon.

I reached out and brushed my fingers against it. The wood was still hot, burning against my fingers. As the feelings of *heat* and *damp* registered in my brain, my eyes saw the impossible. The tentacle *moved*. It strained forward, shifting clockwise as if it could somehow break free. The wood was still hot, burning, against my fingers. "What the hell!" I snatched my hand away, backing up several feet. "Did you see that?"

I understood what Mal was talking about now. There was a weird vibe to the building. Almost like déjà vu. But this was something else. There was a memory of words in my head, a memory that I was sure hadn't been there before. A voice, broken and tattered, that was pressed against the side of my mind from the outside. Like a stamp, or a scar.

"*We only need one.*"

"You heard it, right?" Mal wasn't looking at the door at all, in fact he had his back to it entirely.

"I heard … something."

"What do you think it is?"

I shook my head. More mysteries. "Who'd you say told you about this?"

"Some guy at the gym," he shrugged. "He looked like a gym teacher or something. You know, sweats and stained T-shirts, hair that tries to convince everyone isn't thinning, and all that."

Was the house haunted? Was that what this was? Maybe some kind of psychic imprint or something? I didn't know much about ghosts or residual energy, but there was definitely *something* going on here.

Mal interrupted my reverie. "You sure you haven't seen this before? I *know* I've seen it somewhere."

I might have seen the symbol somewhere before, but it didn't ring any bells. "I'm more concerned with the voice. And why did someone tell you about it in the first place?" *We only need one?* One what? And who needed it?

"I don't think he was a witch. They always give you that 'yeah, I know who you are' creepy look, and then they move as far away as they can," Mal said darkly.

"Next time you go, see if you can find that guy again. Find out if he knows anything else about the house."

"And the symbol?" Mal asked, as we walked back to the car. I turned back to the front door, remembering the way the tentacle had *shifted* like it was alive.

"We'll have to look for that, too." Magic was a language, and that meant there was a written component, too. Maybe the symbol on the door was some kind of spell, and it had been carved there by whoever's voice had been in my head. Written magic could be just as devastating as the verbal kind—it definitely could have burned down the house.

The question was why.

———

We headed towards Main Street and the coffee shop, just as he'd promised. Mal turned the radio up the moment I got in, and we left the discussion of the fire and the symbol back at the house. Carrow Mill didn't have a Starbucks or a fancy coffee place, but it had the mom-and-pop equivalent, and that was good enough for me.

"Told you we'd meet again, big guy," an amused voice called out before I'd even finished climbing out of the SUV.

It was her. Ash. Sitting on a sidewalk bench not twenty feet from us, completely oblivious to the way my heart dropped into my stomach. She had her phone between her hands, thumbs still texting away even though her eyes were on me.

"Who's this?" Mal said as he stuffed his hands into the pockets of his gray sweatshirt, eyes already crinkling and a smirk on his lips. Ugh. He was going to be a dick about it, I could already tell.

"This," she said, "is Ash." She stood up, a Styrofoam cup in hand. Like she was a model on display. And I mean, I didn't exactly mind. She was wearing a leather jacket over a purple top and jeans tucked into her boots. She looked like she was about to kick someone's ass. I just hoped she'd let me watch.

"Of course you are," Mal said slowly, giving me the side eye. "So *you're* the girl he met."

If you swallow me up right now, I promise I won't mind, I prayed to the earth. *Actually, on second thought, take him instead.* I waited, hoping that the sudden cave in that swallowed up my brother wouldn't do too much damage. But nothing happened.

Ash looped her arm through Mal's. "Obviously. I'm guessing you're the big brother?"

"Unfortunately."

The pair of them went inside, as though I wasn't even a factor anymore. Wait, what the hell? How had that happened? I hurried in after them, nearly tripping over my feet. Inside, the coffee shop was all blacks and somber greens, which actually fit my mood perfectly. A girl showing more interest in Mal than me wasn't unusual, but the fact that Mal was encouraging it was.

Love seats and couches were spread out into tiny little

nooks, broken up by dust-covered plastic plants trying to feign the illusion of privacy.

"I like this one," Mal said as he craned his neck over one shoulder to look back at me. "How'd you find a girl this fun, anyway?"

I glared in response.

"She found him, of course," Ash said, stepping up to the counter and flashing that devil-may-care grin my way. "Come on, Ponyboy, let's figure out what you're drinking."

Even though I didn't want to, I stepped forward like a dog being beckoned. Eager, even. "Coffee."

She tsked. "Not even going to try a bold new flavor?" I could hear Malcolm chuckling behind us. "Don't worry," she said without looking back at him, "we'll deal with your drink next." She stared up at the menus, hand written on tiny little blackboards. "I think you'd like the Turtle Mocha."

I looked at the list of ingredients. "Definitely not. It's more syrup than coffee!"

"Spiced Apple?"

"I'm not a big fan of apples."

She snorted. "I don't think that's really possible. No one hates apples."

Mal laughed. "He didn't say—"

She held up a finger. "Tut tut, bigger brother. You'll have your turn. Grown-ups are talking."

I don't think a girl had ever talked to Malcolm like that in our entire lives. We exchanged a look, both shocked into silence. Girls flocked around Malcolm like he was the second coming of swiveling hips and rock and roll. Maybe this wasn't going to be so bad after all.

Ash snapped her fingers a few times, still focused on the menu. "Come on, Captain No-Fun, don't be boring and ask for French Vanilla."

"I like French Vanilla!"

"Where's your sense of adventure?"

"You've met Jenna, remember? Rule number one, you never upstage the star."

Her head tipped and her smile widened. "Good point."

Malcolm coughed. "Better hope she didn't hear that." Ash glanced backwards, and Mal added, "They have that whole twin-brain thing."

I turned, placing my hands on the railing. "You should finish your errands," I said. "We'll be fine."

"Oh, but I like the brother. He can stay," Ash decided.

Malcolm, traitor that he was, didn't help matters. "Errands can wait. "

There had to be a spell that caused an acne outbreak. Maybe pair it with something to make his hair fall out. Jenna would probably know, I mused. I'd have to ask her.

Mal deserved it.

"So Justin got a bowl cut, all because his sister and I told him it was the coolest haircut ever." The three of us sat down by a small, round end table.

"So he just ... let you cut his hair?" Ash had her hand

over her mouth, trying to hold in the laughs. Malcolm was a decent storyteller, lots of arm motions and animated reenactments.

"I didn't *let* them cut my hair," I said, trying not to sound testy. But seriously, why this story? Why? "They kept harassing me until I finally gave in. I just wanted them to shut up."

"It's the power of peer pressure," Malcolm agreed. "I think that's the last time he listened to the two of us."

"And," I added, "I was seven. Who doesn't make stupid hair decisions when they're seven?"

"I didn't," Malcolm volunteered.

Ash chimed in too. "My mother wanted me to get my hair permed, but I said no."

"Well, you're both a pair of geniuses then," I snapped.

Ash giggled, holding her hands over her cup. "Maybe I should have let him get the French Vanilla."

Malcolm nodded. "Or decaf."

"So there's five of you?" Ash sat up, looking between the two of us before centering on me. "And you're the middle child."

I nodded. "Guilty."

"Not to be weird or anything, but you guys don't look at all alike. You sure you're related?"

Mal slid in smoothly, the way he always did. "Adopted. Kind of a long story, but Justin and Jenna are the only two who are actually blood related. The rest of us are just siblings by choice."

"Huh," she said, mulling that over. "Five kids, all the

same age? That's a little weird. Your house must be insane in the morning."

"With two sisters? Obviously," Mal said with a laugh. He was the best liar out of all of us, so I let him take the lead. Wherever we went, we never really talked about our living arrangements. Most people assumed we lived together, and we let them think what they wanted. We didn't have friends over or anything like that. "Especially Jenna. She's a little high maintenance."

"Yeah, I've met Jenna. 'High maintenance' is being nice. So which one haven't I met?"

"Cole," I said, jumping in. I didn't want Mal *completely* dominating the conversation. The fact that he was still here was already annoying enough. But he didn't need to completely hog the spotlight, either. "He's the next oldest after me. And Bailey's the baby."

"So Jenna's older than you?" she asked. I nodded. "She probably never lets you forget it either."

Mal snickered. I set my cup down and grinned. "Something like that."

"Justin's used to getting bossed around by girls," Mal said. "Just in case you were wondering."

"Candidates with that quality move to the front of the line," she grinned. "I'll have to make a note on your application."

"I don't like this," I said, waving my hand between the two of them. "The two of you together... nothing good will come of it. You're both too evil."

Ash laughed. "Relax, Justin," she said. Hearing my

name on her lips was strange—I almost forgot she knew it. I'd gotten used to her strange nicknames. "Besides, Malcolm wouldn't be nearly as much fun to torment."

"So Ash," Mal began, his tone abruptly serious. "What's the deal with that house that burned down."

"Seriously, Mal?" I snapped.

He shrugged, unapologetic. "I'm just curious."

Ash was literally the last person I'd want to get involved in any of this. She was a bit off, and she took too much pleasure in teasing, but I would have liked to wait a bit longer before dropping the "my family is insane" bomb. Not that Jenna hadn't already spoiled that a bit already.

She looked between the two of us, her lips curving slowly into a smirk. "Something I should know?"

"Justin thought it was a little freaky, that's all," Mal said, rolling his eyes. "He has nightmares."

"Wow, really? You're the one who was obsessed," I said, crossing my arms in front of me.

"Oh, is that all?" She pulled her legs up onto her chair and watched us, half hidden by her knees. "You're talking about the rec center, right? Not much to tell, I think. Some kids broke in one night, and one of them left a cigarette burning. My dad's trying to raise money to rebuild, but it's going to cost a lot, I guess."

"That's all?" I could have punched Mal for sounding so obviously disappointed. Like Ash didn't think we were weird enough. I was surprised she hadn't edged her way out the door already. Or asked us if we were some kind of weirdo homeschoolers.

"Is there supposed to be something else?"

He shrugged. "It just looked like there was some graffiti on the door. I was just wondering."

"Okay, seriously, that's enough," I snapped. "Sorry," I apologized to Ash, "he gets a little intense about fires. I think he wants to be a volunteer fireman or something."

"Or a pyromaniac," Ash said. It took me a second to realize that she was kidding. "I hadn't heard about any graffiti, but it's possible, I guess. My dad might know. I could ask?"

"No, that's fine," I replied, just as Mal chimed in with, "Would you?"

I'm going to kill you later. I don't know if Mal could read my thoughts or not, but he avoided looking at me and focused on Ash.

"Anyway," she said, turning to me. "You should give me your sister's number. I figure I can introduce her to a few girls before school starts. Might make her feel better about moving in the middle of the year."

"Jenna?" I asked, completely caught off guard. Why would Ash want to hang out with Jenna? *Jenna* wouldn't even want to hang out with Jenna.

"The other sister," she laughed. "Bailey? She who loves the puppies?"

Oh. Of course. "I mean, yeah, that sounds nice. I'm sure Bailey would love it." I tried not to sound too disappointed.

But Ash saw through me anyway. "Relax, big brother. No need to go into another pout." She climbed to her feet, and I leapt up to mirror her. "It was good to see you again, boy wonder, but I have places to go and minions to pester."

Should I walk her to the door? Or stay standing and really look like some kind of freak? What the hell was the matter with me?

Ash wagged her empty coffee cup at me, and I took it automatically. She clasped her hand around mine, so cool and amused. "You can take care of that for me, right?"

I nodded automatically, a warm rush running through my body at the touch of her hand on mine.

Mal waited until she left to laugh. "You're so whipped."

"And you're a dick." I waited long enough for Ash to get to her car or whatever, even though all I wanted to do was storm out of the coffee shop and go home. But I didn't want her to see me all pissed off.

Mal decided not to press the issue and waited with me in silence, breaking it only after we were on our way to the door and I was in the middle of tossing our coffee cups. "You're not seriously going to throw that out, are you?"

What the hell? "I'm not saving her cup just because she drank out of it. I'm not really the mouth breather you tried to make me out as."

I got the annoyed older-brother look that I hated. Usually, that look was reserved for Cole and Bailey when they acted out.

"No, you idiot," he said, pulling Ash's cup out of my hand and twisting it around. At some point during our conversation, she'd written her name and number along the side.

"Oh," I said.

Maybe Mal wasn't a total buzzkill after all.

TEN

*"Moonset may have been led by Sherrod,
but each member had their strengths.
They were smart. They collaborated.
And their bond was unbreakable.
They wanted to change the world.
They succeeded."*

....

Moonset: A Dark Legacy

Quinn was downstairs by himself when Mal and I walked in a little later.

"Where's Jenna?" I asked, crossing into the kitchen.

Quinn stood by the back door, staring out at only God knew what. Maybe the neighbor's swing set was some kind of latent threat? Or he thought the single mom a few doors away was some kind of sympathizer.

"She'll be down in a moment." Quinn looked over his shoulder. "You should get home, Mal."

Quinn never cared if Mal was here. Or any of us. As far as guardians went, he was a little lax in that department. I took a seat at the table. "What's going on?"

"Incoming," Jenna announced as she strode into the kitchen. "It's the Witch of Skankbird Pond again," she said under her breath before she began checking her reflection in one of the hanging pots.

Heavy footfalls started down the stairs as Meghan Virago swept into the kitchen. She was still wrapped up in a dark-green overcoat, her hair pulled back from her face. "The Congress has some questions for the two of you." Her eyes skimmed over Mal. "You can see yourself out."

"Or I can stay," he countered.

"I thought we finished this already," Quinn said in an icy tone. "They've been through enough already."

"Is this some kind of good cop, bad dye job thing?" Jenna asked. "Because honestly, I'd rather stick my head in the oven than deal with her again."

"The feeling's mutual, darling." Virago's pinched face was a mask of smug superiority. "But does a trailer park even have ovens?"

"Hey, back off," I snapped, moving to stand in front of Jenna. More for Virago's protection than Jenna's, obviously. Jenna would tear her apart with one hand.

"I'd be defensive, too," the redhead cooed, "if I was the spitting image of a sociopath."

"That's enough," Quinn said firmly. He crossed the room

and stood near the two of us. "If you have questions, ask them. But you're not waltzing in here and poking them with sticks for the hell of it."

Jenna took one look around the room, and spun around on her heel. "Screw this," she tossed over her shoulder.

But she didn't get more than one or two steps before Meghan's voice clearly rang out. "Diana Bellamont." Jenna's mother's name was like a talisman. Once invoked, Jenna's feet were leaden on the floor.

"Doesn't it bother you?" Meghan asked, pulling open one of the cutlery drawers and letting her fingers drift over the tools inside. "You act like twins. Tell people you are. But you're not. Not *really.*" Her lips quirked up into another insolent smile.

Even though I knew exactly what was coming, I didn't interrupt. None of us did. There were a thousand different ways to wrap up Moonset's crimes—a hundred different sins to tie up in a bow. We'd heard them all. Yet every time, it was as shameful as the first. Loathing held our tongues, kept our eyes lowered, and our shoulders stooped.

As if a world full of crimes and horrors hadn't been enough, there was the story of Jenna and me. She'd been born first, only a few hours before me. Both of us the children of Sherrod Daggett, the leader of Moonset. But only I, the legitimate child, bore his name.

Jenna's mother had been Sherrod's mistress. He might have loved my mother—every account confirmed this as fact—but Diana Bellamont had been his dark soul mate. She matched him, sin for sin—the co-conspirator for all of

Moonset's darkest acts. In the end, I guess he couldn't resist the temptation.

"How galling do you think it was," Meghan followed up, "when Diana gave birth before his wife?"

Most people looked down on us because we were the children of Moonset. But some took special care to demean Jenna and me in particular. As if it mattered to any of them that my father had cheated on my mother. That we cared when they called us the "white trash twins" as if that was somehow worse than our bloodline.

We bore the worst of it. Jenna and I were cut from the same cloth—thick dark hair, eyes so brown they were nearly black, and each the spitting image of our parents. In my case, Sherrod, and in hers a mix of the two. When we stood side by side, the resemblance was too strong to deny. It was obvious we were related.

There'd been confusion back when we were first recovered. We looked too similar, and we were so close, that they assumed we really *were* twins. My mother had been tall and pale, blond-haired and green-eyed. I didn't look a thing like her.

As we got older, the resemblances grew more pronounced. It wasn't as though I was Sherrod's mirror image, but the resemblance was so strong it made people nervous. Another thing about my past I couldn't help.

"Is that everything?" Jenna said, emphasizing the boredom in her tone. "Everyone's heard about Moonset's dirty laundry." But the words bothered her, I knew they did. They always bothered us.

It was hard, knowing what my parents had been capable of. What they'd done. The legacy that had been left for the others and me. But still, on some level, I wanted to separate them. To split the Moonset side from the side that would have been Mom and Dad. Monsters can't love, and everyone was agreed that the members of Moonset were monsters.

At least that's how I felt sometimes.

"And then my mom was a terrible person who did lots of terrible things," Jenna continued, exhaling. "She was weak, and she got killed. Gosh, doesn't it bother me to know my mom was a weakling?" She straightened, and her voice turned harsh. "You can't push my buttons, you twit."

Meghan raised an eyebrow. No matter what we did, or how we reacted, she always seemed pleased. Like we were giving her exactly what she wanted.

"How has no one shoved a stake through your heart by now?" Jenna wondered.

Quinn's lips twitched, betraying his feelings on the matter. "Ask your questions. Then politely get back on your broom and get the hell out of my house."

Meghan tsked. "Language, darling." She looked down at her tablet, and her pen started tapping out a rhythm all over again. "The pair of you need to be debriefed about what happened in Kentucky."

I exhaled. "You're kidding, right? You waited like two weeks to find out what happened?"

"Be fair, Justin," Jenna said, "she spent most of that afternoon flat on her back. She probably needed all the time she could get to recover."

Jenna was just as good at baiting as Meghan seemed to be. Maybe even better. Meghan's hand clenched into a fist and disappeared under the sleeve of her coat. "Was that the first time you've come across a wraith?"

"Have you read our files?" Mal countered calmly.

"I'm the one asking the questions."

"A question you already know the answer to." Mal's eyebrow rose slightly in challenge. "Next."

Surprisingly, she moved on. "Did the wraith tell you why he'd come after you? What he wanted? Where he was planning to take you?"

Mal looked pointedly at me. Oh, right. I should probably answer since he hadn't been there. "He didn't say a whole lot. Called us Moonset, said Bridger sent—"

"—We have no proof that Cullen Bridger is even still alive, let alone plotting kidnappings or assassinations," Meghan broke in immediately, talking over me. "At best, it's hearsay. At worst, suggesting it is dangerously close to treason."

My jaw dropped. "You're kidding me, right?"

Meghan's mask of indifference said that no, she wasn't kidding. "The Congress is investigating the wraith as an isolated incident. One most likely engineered, accidentally of course, by someone on the scene."

"Someone on the scene?" I asked. "You mean one of us? You think one of *us* called the wraith there? But you were there. You heard it! Both of you did! It said that Bridger sent it."

Meghan's voice became sharp. "There is no conspiracy of

Moonset sympathizers. There is no underground rebellion. Cullen Bridger has most likely been dead for twenty years."

"'Most likely?'" I said.

"So you're just going to pretend nothing happened?" Mal demanded.

Jenna summed it up perfectly. "Are you fucking insane?"

Quinn, on the far side of the room, hadn't moved since Meghan arrived, but now he reached up and scrubbed at his face. Unlike the three of us, he hadn't shown any reaction at the insanity Meghan was spouting.

"You knew about this, didn't you?" I asked him. It wasn't like I trusted him—we barely knew each other so far. But it grated at me, having *proof* that he couldn't be trusted.

"Justin..." Quinn had that tone that adults used, when Jenna was being exasperating, or Cole ridiculous.

"I much prefer children when they are barely seen and never heard," a new voice interrupted, neatly slicing through the mood of the room. The woman appeared almost out of nowhere, as though she'd pulled herself out of a secret door in the shadows.

"Me too," Meghan jumped in, suddenly eager and cheerful.

The woman was tall and bone thin, her dark hair swept away from a gaunt face. She was old, but it was hard to pinpoint her age. Her face was lined from years of living, but the sheer intensity of her eyes suggested a woman in the prime of her life.

Oh shit. Oh *shit*.

"Yes," she drawled, nodding her head as she looked

down at me. A moment of understanding passed between us, and then her thin lips twisted, almost in a smile. She was amused. *I* was amusing.

Because I knew this woman. A woman who shouldn't—couldn't—be here right now. I took a step back, and then sank weakly down onto a chair.

Quinn cleared his throat. "This is Mrs. Bryer."

Illana Bryer. She was the leader of the Fallingbrook Coven, one of the few Great Covens that had survived the Moonset war. But it hadn't been without a cost: she'd lost a husband, a child, and both of her siblings to the conflict. Before Moonset, she had been a powerful witch, but in their wake she had become one of the most famous and influential witches alive.

She'd executed most of our parents herself.

And this was not our first meeting.

"I'd say it's nice to see you again, Mr. Daggett, but we mustn't sugarcoat things," she said, with faint traces of an accent nearly cut from her words. Something European, or maybe Russian. "I believe we had a deal, did we not?"

Jenna stiffened at the introduction. She knew who Illana Bryer was. We all did. The classroom lessons about Moonset we'd had growing up featured her in a starring role. But even worse was the look on her face at Illana's greeting. I'd never told any of them about my encounter with Illana, nor the threats she'd laid out so casually. "Justin?" There were so many demands and questions laced in my name, but I didn't know what to say. She whirled on the older woman. "How do you know my brother?" she demanded.

"You don't speak to her like that," Meghan snapped, moving to come between them.

"Oh good, dramatics," Illana sighed. "Quinn, be so kind as to escort Miss Virago and the boy to the door. I'd like to speak to the twins in private."

Quinn looked like he wanted to argue, but he nodded his head stiffly and gestured to the others. Meghan spun on her heel and went without protest, but Mal was gearing up for a fight.

"We'll be fine," I said, and he eventually nodded.

Illana waited until the room cleared out and the front door closed before she answered Jenna's question. "Everyone knows your brother," she said, as pleasantly as a woman was called a "battle ax" as a compliment, could. "Just as they know you."

Not everyone has the pleasure of having their family threatened by Illana Bryer, though. It had been almost a year since I'd seen her. I'd come home from school one day, Jenna staying late for detention or vandalism or the usual sort of thing that kept her after school.

Illana had been there waiting, alone. Waiting for me. I made it easy for her, once I realized who she was. One didn't spend time in her presence without ending up drenched in sweat, brain sufficiently poked and prodded, and completely vulnerable and off balance. The woman was terrifying. And she had no problem telling me, in detail, about many of the warlocks she'd put to death.

She didn't do small talk. She never stopped by for a quick chat over tea. Illana Bryer only interrogated. Only threatened and promised and brought all the horrifying parts of her legend to life.

I'd never told any of the others about her visit. I wasn't sure why—fear? Shame? Maybe something else entirely. All I knew was that I showered as soon as she was gone and left the house rather than face any of the others. I'd ended up at the school, where I preceded to run the track around the football field until I literally dropped. Being so tired I could barely walk home had made it easier to push down, to repress.

But never fully forgotten. Illana's return was proof of that.

"What's going on, Justin?" Jenna demanded.

I could see her wheels spinning. I knew the places Jenna's thoughts would take her, all the stories and lies that would spring up like seedlings in the garden of insecurities. I shook my head, finally mustering up a response. "No," I said. No, I hadn't betrayed the rest of them. No, I wasn't secretly working for the leader of Fallingbrook. No, I hadn't turned on her.

"Then what?" she snapped.

Illana smiled at me indulgently. For a woman of rages, she could do graceful as well as any politician. "Go on. Tell her."

Was this fun for her? Coming in and tormenting people just to watch their reactions? I wouldn't be surprised. "Remember how Mal was talking about the detention center thing?" Jenna nodded, and I continued. "It's real. Illana said that if I can't set some boundaries, and you keep . . . well, doing what you do, then they're going to send us there."

"So she's had you spying on me?" Jenna spat.

"I'm not *spying* on you, you idiot!" How was it that Jenna could take a perfectly simple math problem like 2+2 and wind up with an answer equalling the square root of paranoid?

"Why you?" she continued, expression darkening in a way it only ever did when she fought with Mal. "I can't believe you'd do this to me."

"It's not about you!" I'd almost forgotten my voice could *get* that loud. Red hazed in at the edges of my vision, and all the anger I'd bottled up over the year—whole shelves full of bottles—started to spill out. Too much had already happened today. "It's about all of us, and what's going to happen to *us* if you keep doing what you're doing. So maybe stop being so damned self-absorbed for five minutes and *think* for once!"

Jenna took a step back like she'd been slapped. "Who do you think you are?" she asked. I wasn't sure if the hurt look and tone were real, or a show for Illana. "No one elected you the boss of us all."

"Someone has to be, Jenna. Didn't you hear what I said? They want to ship us off to the middle of nowhere!"

"You should have told me. You should have told *all of us.*"

"All right, enough," Illana said, hand pressed against her temple. "No one's going to the Priory today. We realize that what happened in Kentucky wasn't your fault."

"Do you? Maybe you should have gotten here five minutes earlier, because Meghan never got that memo," Jenna said. She stalked to the far side of the kitchen, putting as much room between the two of us as she could.

"There are different factions in the Congress," Illana said carefully as Quinn walked back into the room, "and they rarely agree on what to order for lunch, let alone something as critical as a wraith attack."

"So you believe in us and want to help protect us and everything is wonderful?" Jenna rolled her eyes. "I've heard all this before. Just because you're famous for Diana and the others doesn't impress me."

"My world shall never recover," Illana replied blithely, as if Jenna's moods were something she dealt with every day.

I cleared my throat. "So if you're not here to ship us off to juvenile detention, then why are you here?"

"I thought it was time we all met." Illana took a seat at the table, carefully arranging the skirt of her dress.

The tightness in my chest was still unraveling, but Jenna looked unaffected. Stay, go, it made no difference to her. "What's really going on here? And why are *you* here?" The leader of one of the Great Covens didn't just pop in for a social call.

"Curiosity. Concern. Take your pick."

I turned to Quinn. "She was the one on the phone, wasn't she?"

Illana laughed, responding before Quinn could. "Of course. I expect my grandchildren to check in with me regularly."

That bomb took awhile to clear. I kept looking between the two of them, Quinn and Illana, trying to find some similarity. Jenna just shook her head and smirked. Whatever she was thinking, it wasn't good. She was probably already plotting her next expulsion-worthy event. It made me wonder, could you get expelled even before you were enrolled?

"Really?" Quinn asked. "Did you come here just to keep poking them with sticks? Because irritating or not, Meghan had that covered before you arrived."

"She's your grandmother. Illana Bryer. You're *related* to her." I was trying to put it into reference. If Quinn was her grandson, then that meant he was almost as infamous as the rest of us. Illana Bryer, the head of Fallingbrook, had married Robert Cooper, the head of Eventide, joining their two families twenty years ago. It was like the Kennedys marrying into the Vanderbilts.

"Don't be ridiculous. I wanted to see them for myself. Remind the younger Daggett that I meant what I said, all those months ago."

"And to terrorize them," Quinn supplied.

Illana didn't dignify that with a response. But the corner of her mouth definitely moved.

She was the only one who was amused though. Jenna crossed her arms in front of her. "I asked you a question. Either of you ready to stop lying and tell us what we're doing here?"

The adults shared a look. The *family*. It was weird to think of Quinn being related to her. Was that why he was here? Not just to keep an eye on us, but to watch us for *her*?

"One of the more recent developments," Illana began,

"has suggested that we need to pay more attention to the lives you children are living."

"'We' meaning the Congress, right?" Jenna questioned. "Have they decided to stop being cowards and start teaching us something useful?"

"Jenna!" There was a time and a place for airing your grievances, but in front of the world's deadliest grandma wasn't it.

Illana, however, didn't look particularly offended, except by the decor in the kitchen. She turned up her nose at some of the "family"-themed wall hangings that had been put up before we arrived. "Quinn told me you've been...unhappy."

"I was *unhappy* getting stuck in the middle of nowhere." Jenna's words were sharp, and her expression as dark as I'd ever seen it. "I'm *pissed* that we almost died, no thanks to any of you."

Quinn cleared his throat.

"Not you, Quinn," she said, rolling her eyes. "You're perfection."

His chest puffed out and he smirked a little. Clearly he was ignoring the sarcastic drip of Jenna's words.

"When you can prove that you deserve to learn more, I'll happily teach you myself," Illana said. It was clear she thought that day would never come. None of us were under any illusions about that.

"So you'll risk our lives in the meantime? Just to prove some stupid point about responsibility?" Jenna demanded. "You're insane."

"So you'll risk their lives just to prove you don't care to *be* responsible?" Illana fired back.

"So what does that mean?" I interrupted, hoping to stave off the Jenna rant that would eliminate any hope of good will on Illana's part. "You said something about paying more attention to us?"

"It means exactly what I said. We need to pay more attention. So we will. I'll be staying on in Carrow Mill, as will a few others."

"You're leaving D.C.?" Quinn asked, clearly surprised by this news. So maybe the family didn't tell each other *everything*.

"Oh, great. More babysitters," Jenna snapped.

"Just hear her out," I tried.

"Are you kidding me, Justin? She's one of *them*. We can't trust her. We can't trust either of them." She brushed the hair out of her eyes, regarding me with something like genuine emotion. "You used to know whose side you were on."

"I'm on the same side I've always been on," I said.

"Yeah," she said, dropping her eyes from mine. "I'm just starting to realize it's not mine." She stormed out of the room.

Illana waited, then rose to her feet. "Justin will see me out. Quinn, start looking into those theories for me. I want to know how many other surprises have been buried in the soil here."

Buried in the soil? What? I looked at Quinn, who breezed past me. "He's been a mechanic here for thirty years; it's not like he ever went into hiding. The only reason we know anything is because he approached Justin and Mal."

"I don't care if he's selling used cars on the side of the road," Illana said harshly. "Someone didn't do their homework. Especially during a time like this—that's inexcusable."

Illana headed for the door, and I followed in her wake. She must be used to it, I figured. People scurrying after her, letting her set the current and forcing their direction. Jenna had been right about that much, at least. Illana was here for a reason, and it wasn't what she was telling us. It wasn't anything like what they were telling us.

"We're still in danger, aren't we?"

Illana didn't pause. The door opened, then the screen door, and she stepped through into the afternoon sun. "There's always danger. But danger and opportunity are fast friends. So take your opportunity, and show me who you're going to be. A child of Moonset, or a child of the Congress."

ELEVEN

"Sutter and Denton, seniors, first brought the incidents to the school's attention. Initial speculation was confirmed after a Coven was dispatched to Carrow Mill. Someone was altering the junior class: they had been made docile; their passions extinguished. At the time, no one wondered why Moonset had been immune..."

....

Council Investigation Report
Eyes Only

When I came back into the kitchen, Quinn was waiting for me. I bypassed him, went to the fridge, and grabbed a bottle of water. Why were the adults so hell bent on keeping us in the dark? They weren't making it any secret that something else was going on in Carrow Mill, but they refused to tell us *what*.

"You should go check on her," Quinn suggested, glancing towards the ceiling.

"Are you new?" He must be. Either new, or crazy. I grabbed my coat out of the front hallway closet. "I'm keeping my distance until she calms down. I'll be over at Mal's."

"School tomorrow," he said, almost sounding like a parent.

"You've met Mal, right? He loves a curfew almost as much as he loves school," I called, already halfway out the door.

We hadn't talked much about school. Or at all. The fact that it was tomorrow, and I'd forgotten, only proved how off kilter things were here. The weirdness of Carrow Mill trumped any attempt at normalcy. Sure, we'd done the normal kinds of school shopping—buying supplies, backpacks, the usual, but it hadn't been any sort of priority.

Until now.

"Did you know school starts tomorrow?" I asked Mal as I walked into his room.

He didn't even really need to answer. His bag was already packed and sitting next to his computer desk. "Is that a trick question?" he asked, looking up from whatever he was doing.

"You could have at least reminded me."

Mal arched an eyebrow at me and closed the laptop. "Are we really going to talk about school right now? What'd she want?"

I shrugged. "We're not 'supervised' enough. Supposedly, that's why she's moving to town."

"She's moving here? Can she even do that?"

"Is anyone really stupid enough to tell her she can't? I

have the feeling that the sun doesn't even rise unless she wants it to."

Mal crossed the room and closed the door. "I don't think Nick's home, but it doesn't hurt to be careful," he admitted. "I've been trying to look up that thing from the other day. The symbol?"

I perked up at that. "Any luck?"

"Not yet," he said. "But I know I've seen it somewhere before."

"While we're talking about it, what was that crap with Ash?" Mal looked confused, so I continued. "Interrogating her about the fire? Having her ask her dad? Aren't you the one always preaching that we should blend in? That we shouldn't call attention to ourselves?"

He snorted. "You're just mad I wouldn't leave you alone with your little girlfriend."

"She's not my girlfriend."

"Maybe I'm not the one that needs to remember that," he said, suddenly serious. "I get that you like this girl and all, but you need to remember the situation we're in. Odds are we won't be here come prom night."

"I'm not Bailey," I snapped. "I know what I'm getting myself into."

"Do you?" he asked. "You should have seen your face after the mall the other day. And then at the coffee shop? You're all blissed out on this girl."

Where the hell was this coming from? Mal was the one who always had my back, and suddenly he was acting like a dick? "Are you jealous? What the hell, man?"

"Right, because I'd have to be jealous to think it's a bad idea," he snorted. "Get over yourself."

"Then what is this? She's just a girl."

Mal laughed to himself. He crossed over to his closet, and began flipping through the clothes on hangers. Looking for something. Like our conversation wasn't that important.

Something crashed downstairs.

In the aftermath, there was an audible silence. Both of us waited, listening, but there was nothing. "I thought you said Nick wasn't home?" I whispered.

"I didn't think he was."

One of the doors downstairs creaked, a faint sound that we wouldn't have heard if we hadn't been straining for it. "It's probably him, right?" I said.

"Of course."

But neither one of us called out to check. Together, we crept out of the room and down the stairs. In hindsight, probably not the smartest move. It could have been another wraith. Or something else sent after us. Aside from the faint sound of our feet against the carpet, and hesitant groans in response to careful steps, the house was totally quiet.

As we reached the bottom landing, I tapped Mal on the shoulders and pointed down the hall. Lights were on in the study, the door closed. But when I'd come into the house just a few minutes before, the door had been open and the room dark.

"Can you tell who it is?" Mal asked, glancing between the study to his right, and the path to the front door, to his left.

"You know all the same spells I do," I said, trying to

figure out if *anything* I knew would be useful here. *Etheric maanu* would tell me how many people were in the house. That wouldn't help. *Ethera maan* could tell how far away they were. But nothing I could use to identify them.

"Yeah, but I don't pay attention in class," Mal responded, sounding aggravated. It probably annoyed him that he even had to ask. Magic was always his last resort. "If it was a wraith, it would have just blown up the house, right? Picked us up out of the debris?"

"Maybe," I hedged.

He squared his shoulders and chose his direction. The study, then. I followed behind, grabbing the only thing handy that I could find. In a perfect world it would have been a baseball bat or a golf club. I had to settle for one of those blue-fringed Swiffer dusters.

I hefted the weight of it in my hands, already regretting the decision. Mal looked over his shoulder at me, smirked, and then pushed open the doors to the study.

The two of us went rushing into the room, me with feathered blue justice in my hands. Mal didn't need a weapon of his own—he pretty much *was* the weapon.

"What the hell are you doing here?" Mal snapped.

I had to step around him to realize who he was talking to. Jenna, half crouched behind the study's desk, stacks of files and papers cleared out of the drawers and scattered across the top. She dropped a hand to her hip, rose even as her eyebrow arched at the Swiffer in my hands like a weapon. "What are you planning to do? Dust me to death?"

"What are you doing here, Jenna?" he repeated.

"Breaking and entering, completely ruining Nick's attempts at organization, and general crimes against the crown, obviously," she said blandly. "So either close the door and help, Dumb and Dumber, or go back to talking first downs and engines. Or whatever you boys talk about."

"You can't just go through all his stuff," I said in shock.

"Well, I'd go through Quinn's stuff, but they're both over there right now," she said reasonably. "It's harder to snoop through someone's things when they're in the room."

Mal sighed, then turned around and closed the door behind us. It was as good as giving Jenna permission to continue. The moment the lock clicked into place, she went back to skimming through the files. "So you decided to break into my house? Why?"

"I'm done letting them make me a victim," she said, moving from one drawer to the one below it. "They won't teach us new spells? Then I'll find them on my own. I'll teach myself if that's what it takes. But what happened back there will *never* happen again."

"You're looking for grimoires?" I don't know what surprised me more. That Jenna would steal another witch's book of spells, or that she hadn't already done it before.

Grimoires, or spellbooks, were basically journals that most witches kept all of their magic in. Because there were so many spells, and so many variations, most people needed a written record. It was difficult work—because magic was a language, written spells had power just as much as spoken ones. Spells had to be broken down into the lines, spaced apart like diagrams on how to copy a Chinese symbol.

Mal shook his head. "You can't do this."

"I knew *you* weren't going to help," she replied scornfully. "Come on, Justin, you know I'm right. We need to be able to protect ourselves. You're the one who keeps saying that they brought us here for a reason. If we're in danger, can we really trust them to make sure Bailey and Cole are safe? Or what about Mal? He refuses to defend himself."

"I don't need to use magic to defend myself," Mal snapped. "And quit trying to spin this into a good idea. It's pretty much one of the stupidest you've ever come up with. Going through the Witchers' things? Illana Bryer hasn't even *unpacked* yet, and you're already trying to get us in trouble."

"And what are you doing? Sneaking around looking at weird fires and making the locals think you're a freak?" Jenna's lips curled dangerously. "You're stirring up just as much as I am. But if Saint Malcolm wants to solve a mystery and get a treat from his owners, that's okay."

I looked over the mess Jenna had made, and the pair of them bickering with each other. "Put it all back, Jenna."

"You can't seriously be siding with him," she snapped. "You know I'm right."

I tapped out a rhythm like a heartbeat against the floor. "One minute, or I'm calling Quinn and turning you in."

She gaped at me. This wasn't done. It was one thing to side with Jenna, or against her. It was another to side with the adults. Even if Mal disagreed with her, argued that she should have stopped, if we got caught, he'd have her back.

So for her to stare at me like we'd never met before wasn't entirely unexpected. But she put everything back, if not exactly where she'd found it, then close enough. The tension in the room could have compressed coal into diamonds.

Just before she closed the last drawer, she looked up at me. "I don't know who you think you are all of a sudden," she snapped, "but whoever he is, he's a dick."

TWELVE

*"The Covens are not gods, and the Solitaires
are not the working class. We are all fragile,
simple creatures. When faced with tyrants,
what can we do but tear them down?"*

....

Sherrod Daggett (C: Moonset)
Unknown Date

I came downstairs the next morning to some sort of weird,
Opposite World version of the Brady Bunch. Mal and Cole
were at the table, already half hidden behind huge towers of
breakfast foods. Quinn was behind the stove and he was putting together something that could only be qualified as a feast.

There was a tray of cut-up fruit, scrambled eggs, French
toast, sausage, and an entire pot of coffee set on a warmer.

"Uhm…someone should go check on me," I said,

pointing back the way I came. "Because I must have cracked my head open in the shower. And this is my coma dream."

"No coma," Mal said.

Cole nodded vigorously. "Quinn's my new god," he said, shoving another sausage link in his mouth, "except not in a gay way."

Mal lifted a hand to smack him, but Cole jumped out of his chair first and bounded out of reach. "Okay, okay. Maybe in a gay way, too. Whatever. All I know is that his French toast is kick ass, Jay."

"Jay?" Mal and I spoke as one.

Cole shrugged. "Whatever. It's part of your name, right?"

"My name's *Justin*," I said, settling down at the table across from Mal. Quinn was even wearing one of those dorky aprons with a slogan on it. My eyebrows raised. "'May the forks be with you?'" I read.

He pointed with the spatula. "Shut up and eat."

"Where's Bailey?" Jenna half asked, half demanded as she breezed into the kitchen.

"She changed her outfit, so then she said her makeup had to be redone." Cole sounded mystified, but Jenna took it in stride, and sat down next to me with one leg propped on the chair. Last night's argument hadn't been forgotten though, which I realized as she angled her body away from me and towards the kitchen. She plucked out a cube of melon and popped it in her mouth. "Breakfast is yummy, Quinn," she announced after swallowing.

"So explain this to me again," Cole said. "They've already got schedules and everything for us?"

Quinn turned around, still half watching the things on the griddle. "They're adjusting your schedules based on what you took in Kentucky. Since midterms are coming up in a few weeks, the school is coordinating your tests with what you were studying down south. So you're not totally screwed for your exams."

Groans from around the table. There wasn't any getting out of test-taking, which sucked but wasn't surprising.

"Don't all thank me at once," Quinn commented. "It took a lot of effort to get your old school to agree to this."

"Thanks, Quinn," Jenna said sweetly.

Cole followed it up with, "What about magic lessons? Are they in-school here, or do we have to go somewhere afterwards?" He looked to my left, and I saw the look he exchanged with Jenna. She'd prompted him to ask, I was sure. But why?

"They'll be last period, but there's some adjustments that have to be made. So for now you'll go to a last period study hall." When there were enough witches in the school, our lessons were factored into a kind of independent study class, right down the hall from where kids were learning about Napoleon and Pythagoras.

What kind of adjustments had to be made? "Maybe they listened to you after all," I said under my breath, carrying just enough for Jenna to hear me. It was meant to be a conciliatory gesture, to make up for the argument last night, but she ignored me.

Bailey came in a few minutes later, still tugging one of her boots off. She and Jenna both had gone for trendy rather than practical. I couldn't understand why boots needed heels in the first place, but it was their choice.

"Pass me a yogurt," Jenna added, as Bailey pulled up a spot at the table. She leaned over the table and tossed one at her, and then sat down next to Cole and studied the table. The meal passed in relative silence, except for the frequent comments about how amazing everything was and demands for things to be passed one way or the other. For just a few minutes, it was like we were some sort of normal family.

I could almost relax and enjoy it. Except I knew that school was going to be its own kind of hell. It always was.

Eventually, everyone started packing it in, rummaging around to find coats, shoes, and book bags. By the time all five of us were out the door and into the SUV, we had less than twenty minutes until the school day started.

"You know how to get there?" I asked. As the one riding shotgun, I had to play navigator if Malcolm got lost. It didn't happen that often, but I didn't want today to be one of those rare days.

"Relax, Justin," he said absently.

The high school wasn't in the immediate downtown like most of the schools we went to. We drove through the center of Carrow Mill and down to the far side of town, where the school was located. Mal knew exactly where he was going.

Even eight schools later, there's some stress about starting somewhere new. *What's everyone wearing in New York? Are they going to treat us like freaks? How long until I get called into the principal's office? Is my sister going to protest animal dissection for the hell of it?*

Nervous energy was responsible for the way Cole kept tapping out a rhythm on his knees, and the way Bailey kept squirming in her seat.

"Everyone knows not to use magic in public, right? And if you slip up, find an adult that can clean up the mess." Slips always happened—the wrong spell at the wrong time. The witches who worked at the school were trained to cover up those issues—either by altering memories, undoing whatever effects were still ongoing, or providing a good cover story. It was even rougher being a magical teacher than a regular one.

I shifted around, trying to catch all of their eyes while the seatbelt strap cut into my neck. "Cole?"

The tapping stopped. "I'm not going to do anything." He sounded guilty already. Force of habit.

"We're all going to be on our best behavior, little brother," Jenna said, with absolute syrup in her voice. "No need to go turning anyone in to the authorities."

I looked at the console's clock. We still had about ten minutes. Plenty of time, I figured, as we pulled into the parking lot of . . . the most elaborate high school I'd ever seen.

"Wow," Bailey breathed from behind me.

Carrow Mill High wasn't some thirty-year-old structure built with only function in mind. This was a building that someone had taken great care to design. The curving walls of the buildings were sand-colored bricks, and everywhere I looked it seemed like there was something moving. Buildings sloped to one side, towered up into a clock tower, or circled around. It looked more like the kind of building you'd see in a movie, not a high school.

Malcolm finally found a spot in the side lot, where it looked like a lot of other students were parking as well. That made it a bit of a hike to get into the school, since we had to walk all the way back down alongside the buildings and then around to the front.

"We ready to do this?" I looked around, at the four other members of my family. Eighth school in three years. This was getting so old. But by this point I'd done it so many times I was used to being the new kid.

"Last school we went to got blown up," Jenna mused.

I looked at the school and wondered. How would this one fare? Would we walk away in six months, no harm done? Or would the school year end more actively: in fire or flood?

THIRTEEN

"Carrow Mill is holy. A true sacred space. It's where they came together. Where they left their hearts. Where they sacrificed themselves."

....

Lucinda Dale (S)
Former disciple of Moonset, interview

Once we walked into the school, it was like a whirlwind. Someone must have held a drill to practice because as soon as we stepped into the office, a trio of counselors appeared to shoo us back into the hallway. Malcolm and I were together, Jenna and Bailey were together, and Cole was off by himself.

They hustled us down the hallways, giving a rapid-fire summary of what we could expect as new students at Carrow Mill High. I gripped my orientation folder, and tried to make sense of the school map. Our first classes were helpfully marked with a big red X, but everything else was horribly smudged.

I tried asking questions, but the woman was on a mission. The hallways and everything in them had an entirely "new" look to them, and they were all decorated in shades of silver and blue, which must have been the school colors. The school was pristine, looking none the worse for wear despite housing almost a thousand kids a day—nine hundred of whom stared at us like we were the new sideshow freaks in town.

The bell rang, and the halls emptied out as everyone who knew where they were going slipped into their classrooms.

"The science building is through the walkway there," the guidance counselor pointed to the rear of the building. "Mr. Daggett, you'll be in SC 201. Mr. Denton, you're in 114. Show the teacher your copy of your schedules and you should be fine."

Even though the woman had barely introduced herself before hustling us off, and hadn't bothered to really greet us at all, I still smiled at her. "Thanks."

She turned to go, but then hesitated and turned back, looking concerned. "Try and stay out of trouble, boys."

Our reputation preceded us.

We compared our schedules as we headed out the doors and into the science building. Both of us were on a "B Schedule," whatever that was. It was also confusing since we didn't start the day with homeroom like most of the other schools I'd been to. We started out with our science labs, then homeroom, another couple of classes and then lunch together.

That's as far as we compared before Malcolm found his class-room.

"Catch you later," he said, setting off with a wave.

I headed up the stairs and through a curtain of blue and silver streamers that hung down from the second floor. Another school with too much spirit. I sighed. *Fantastic.* Jenna hated spirit. My morning passed quickly, each class just as awkward and uncomfortable as I remember. The first days were almost always the worst. Almost, because with Jenna around, the last days were *also* the worst.

I sat through the forty-two minutes of Anatomy and Physiology relieved to realize they'd picked up where my A&P class at Byron had left off. I also tried to familiarize myself with the school and my schedule. Independent Study was the official name for our magic lessons. It was hardly independent, since they gathered up all the magical kids in one room. But they had to call it *something* so the regular people didn't get suspicious.

On my way to try to find my locker, I passed a poster of a yellow brick road with a green-faced woman in the background. "AUDITIONS SOON" was scrawled in white along the bottom. Of course, the school play was *The Wizard of Oz*. Everyone loved dead witches.

My locker number, along with the combination to the actual lock, was printed at the top of my schedule. I followed the line of lockers down, getting lost twice before I found my locker.

"You've got to be kidding me," I said under my breath.

I looked back the way I'd come, and then further up

ahead in the hallway. Every locker I could see was the same blue color, and there were bits of paper and things taped to a few here or there, but none of them were *defaced*. Only mine.

They'd assigned me a locker with a hideous tan splotch over the front, where the blue paint had been scratched off and revealed the color underneath. *This almost looks familiar,* I thought, and then I twitched. A circle, almost completely shaded in, with rays wavering around the sides. I'd seen this symbol before, at the house Mal and I had gone to. The symbol had been scratched into the door.

"I figured that was yours," Mal said, nodding to the front of my locker. "I met one of the other kids in our independent study group. Someone here has a sick sense of humor."

I cleared my throat, nervous and unsure why. "What?"

He tapped the graffiti design. "It's not random. It's *theirs*. It's how you knew Moonset took credit for something. Like their signature."

"And someone scratched it on my locker. Why?"

"I'm not the one with the devious mind," Mal said nonchalantly. "But if I had to guess, I'd say one of the other kids here isn't happy to see us."

I found my homeroom with an extra thirty seconds to spare before the bell rang. Once again, I had to do an awkward pause at the door until I could find out where there were open seats. In homeroom, though, the teacher barely seemed interested in what was going on. She was flipping through a ledger when I handed her my class schedule.

"Over there, all the way in the back," she said, waving me away after looking at my schedule. "Over there" was probably the least helpful direction she could have given me, but I just went to the row closest to the windows and sat in the seat furthest back.

Several minutes passed, and then the announcements began over the loudspeaker at the head of the room. It was basically permission to zone out for the next fifteen minutes, as nobody else in the class seemed to be paying much attention.

Then she walked into the room, and suddenly my day wasn't quite so bad anymore.

Ash swept into the room like every eye was on her, and once people started to realize she was there, it was. She wore a skirt over leggings, heels that clacked with every confident step, and a mauve long-sleeved shirt. In essence, she looked amazing. She waggled her fingers at the teacher as she passed the desk and headed down the aisle next to mine until she could take the free seat across from me.

"*You* are an overly ambitious boy," she said, leaning across the aisle towards me. Her fingers tangled into the chain she wore around her neck, that ended with a cross at the bottom.

She thought we were getting close? That almost made my brain sputter into to a halt. "I'm what?"

She ran a hand through her hair, watching me with a teasing smile. "You're the talk of the school, didn't you know?" Ash waved a hand. "My own little celebrity."

I squirmed in my chair. "I'm not," I muttered. It was bad enough when I was around witches who *did* know who I was. I didn't want to be a celebrity among the regular kids.

Her smile widened. "Don't worry, I'll protect you from the paparazzi."

"Ashen Farrer, you aren't even *in* this homeroom," the teacher announced, looking up from her bookkeeping.

"I'm Justin's student advisor, Miss G. I'm supposed to make sure he gets to his classes all day."

They had student advisors? And Ash and I were spending the day together? Suddenly my day, and my life, were looking up. Maybe this school wouldn't be so bad after all.

Someone further up in my row started giggling. Miss G, or whatever her name really was, was frowning in our direction. "You know we don't have student advisors, Ashen. Now don't you have a homeroom full of classmates that miss you terribly?"

"Ashen?" I asked.

She grinned. "If you knew the alternative, you'd be pleasantly surprised with Ashen. Why do you think I go by Ash? Ashen sounds so morbid, don't you think?" She made no move to get up and leave the room, and the teacher didn't seem to want to push the issue.

The voices over the loudspeaker were still going strong. Every few minutes they changed, as the next person stepped up to deliver their announcements. "...for the spring play will be held in the auditorium Monday and Tuesday after school..."

"Being the new kid doesn't bother me so much." I don't know why I was confiding in her, but maybe the revelation of her real first name was a sign. "I'm more of the 'stay quiet and keep my head down' type, though."

Her perfectly sculpted eyebrow lifted. "A few more days, and girls will be lining up to date you," she said, brushing off any concern about what her friend was doing. "Secrets make you more interesting."

I don't want to date other girls. "I guess," I said noncommittally. The bell rang and we both climbed to our feet. Ash followed me into the hall. She plucked the map out of my hands the moment I had tugged it free from my bag. "Hey!" I grabbed for it, but she darted out of the way.

"Come on, you don't want to be late for your class," she announced before sprinting down the hall.

Somehow in a matter of seconds, Ash had managed to worm her way through the crowd, leaving me a half-dozen heads behind her. Every time I tried to move around someone, or gain some ground, I got more dirty looks.

I finally caught up with her at the end of the hallway. "You're heading down this way," Ash said, turning to her left and starting off again.

"What are you doing?" I followed her. What choice did I have?

Once we were in front of my next class, she stopped and handed me back the map. "I told you, I'm your student advisor. Now go be brilliant!" As she started to walk away, she reached up and ruffled her hand in my hair, totally messing it up. Just like that, she wandered back the way she'd come like nothing had happened.

FOURTEEN

"They disappeared for a few years after high school. All of them had bright futures, but they didn't pursue them right away. No one knows what happened—why they left so suddenly. Until they turned up in London, enrolled in school and petitioning for working internships with the government."

....

Adele Roman
Moonset Historian: From a college
lecture series about Moonset

The rest of the morning was a blur.

My last class before lunch was Economics, and thankfully I walked into the room to see Malcolm already in a seat near the back. A class with someone I knew. There wasn't much chance of sharing a class with either Bailey or Cole, but I was a little shocked that the three of us hadn't shared more classes together. There'd been a few times where we all had nearly identical schedules.

"How's your day been going?" Mal asked as I slid in behind him.

"Not bad," I said, thinking of Ash showing up as my advisor.

His eyebrow raised. "Are you blushing?"

I turned away immediately, dropping my bag on the desk and resting my head on it. Mal didn't press the issue.

On my lunch break, I went to the office to find out about switching lockers. The secretary first tried to assure me that I was over exaggerating about how big the mark on my locker was until I pulled out my phone and showed her a picture of it.

"And this happened today?" she asked, looking at me with a hint of suspicion.

"I didn't mark up my new locker," I said, trying to suppress my annoyance. Finally she agreed to have someone from the maintenance staff look at it.

As I walked out of the office, I caught sight of Jenna coming towards me.

"And this is my brother Justin," she announced, looking from her companion to me and back again.

I recognized the girl. "You're Ash's friend," I said.

"Maddy," the girl replied, a little frosty. "I remember you."

"Yeah," I said, "I remember you, too."

Jenna looked between the two of us, a hint of a smile in place. Jenna found a friend on the first day? That was weird enough in itself.

"Listen, you guys should come hang out with us after school," Maddy said, glancing down at her phone. "It's this little hole-in-the-wall place that almost no one knows about. Ash'll be there. I know she'd like to see you."

"Yeah," I said, nodding. "I think we can do that."

"Cool," Maddy replied. "It's called Mark's. You know where the coffee shop is on Main Street? It's right by there, like a block away."

"Okay," I nodded. "We'll try to stop by."

———————

"Well, this is an interesting place to bring me," Mal said a half hour after we'd gotten out of school, squinting up at the building. "Is this part of some life lesson to make me appreciate all I have?"

I glared at Malcolm, but really, I was glaring at Maddy. Of *course* it had been a trick. She'd been too nice, and too helpful. *And* she'd taken to Jenna like a duck to evil, which only proved that she shouldn't be trusted.

Mark's, the hangout that she'd suggested we check out, turned out to be *Saint Mark's*. A homeless shelter.

"I'd give her some points for moxie, but the prank itself is pretty lame," he added.

"Shut up," I said. "No one says 'moxie' anymore."

"You're just mad that no one says you've got moxie."

"Stop saying moxie!"

It was like a spell of its own. I knew he was going to say it again. So I did the mature, responsible thing, and ran into the first store I could find just to put some distance between us. I knew Malcolm would never act like the embarrassment he was in front of an audience.

But the store I had chosen was so much more. The moment I crossed the threshold, it was stifling. The walls were simply drenched in hangings—paintings, art, objects, and garbage. Shelves were crammed with knickknacks and weird bookends, one holding nothing but a series of bronzed elephants. Another table was weighted down by an elaborate crystal chess set. When I picked up one of the pieces, not only did the table rock alarmingly, but I didn't recognize the design in my hand. And the board was strange, tri-colored instead of dual.

It was nearly impossible to walk down the aisles because they were so narrow. Each step, I was afraid I'd bump into something and start a chain reaction that would topple everything in the building.

Mal had no similar feelings. He moved at ease through the store, occasionally picking up something that caught his eye and studying it from all angles.

"Welcome, boys!" A man literally popped up from behind a glass countertop in the corner. As we approached, I saw the sliding glass panel was open, and he was carefully removing everything from inside. From here it just looked like a lot of ugly, tarnished jewelry. "What can I do for you today?"

"We're just looking," Mal said. "But thanks."

"Sure, sure," he said, straightening one of the trays full of rings.

Mal and I continued browsing, but I couldn't help but keep turning for the door. "Maybe I just got the name wrong, and the place she was talking about is right around here and we missed it."

He saw right through me. "You have Ash's number, right? Just call her."

"I can't *just call her*. And say what? 'Your best friend sent me to the homeless shelter?' Yeah, real nice."

"You need to relax, man. She's just a girl."

"You've met her. She's not exactly a normal girl."

He held up a trio of books that were wrapped up in a ribbon. One of them was a copy of *Wuthering Heights*. "She's a girl. Get used to not understanding half of what she does. That's how they rope in precious little boys like you." He ruffled my hair and I jerked back, nearly bumping into a display full of postcards.

The man behind the counter piped up again. "Looking for a present for your girlfriend?"

I turned back to him, really seeing him for the first time. He was older, with thinning gray hair and dressed in plaid. He looked more like a librarian than a shop owner. "No, thanks. She's not my girlfriend!" I said a little too quickly.

"Ahh," he replied, "but you want her to be?" His eyes focused shrewdly on me. "I've got just the thing."

He crouched down and started rummaging through the shelves he had been working on, eventually pulling out a tray filled with necklaces. "I'm sure she'll love one of these," he said. "You're lucky; I've been cleaning out the stock all week, weeding out the things that aren't selling."

I wanted to tell him that it looked like most of the stuff here wasn't selling, but I didn't want to be rude. Curious more than anything else, I walked to the counter. There was a hallway opened up behind the counter, leading into a kitchen badly lit with fluorescent lighting. That and the yellowing wallpaper made it look like some tragic seventies parlor.

"Ethan Alexander," a raspy voice bellowed from somewhere beyond that kitchen, "where the hell is my *TV Guide?*"

"Oh, hell," the man muttered quietly. "Be right back," he said, although I noticed he pulled the tray back and slid it back under the glass before he turned. "Coming, Dad!"

He didn't need to bother. A much older man hobbled his way into the kitchen and from there into the hallway, moving with a determined gait. He favored one hip and kept a hand on one of the walls as he walked. "I told you not to touch my *TV Guide*," he bellowed louder.

"Dad, I'm with a customer," the man pleaded. I saw a moment of fear in his eyes—being embarrassed in front of a total stranger by his father.

"Always with a customer," his father growled, finally halting in the doorway. "Where'd you put my—oh my sweet Jesus."

I didn't want to watch the man get tongue-lashed by a father who clearly needed medication, so I'd knelt down and started looking at the jewelry through the glass. But at the man's gasp, I looked up again—to find him staring right at me.

"Can't be, can't be," he muttered, suddenly wringing his hands in front of him. "Dead and buried, Sherrod Daggett is. Always knew he'd come back from the dead. Back for me!"

The old man swiveled back to his son, as though all his hip problems were nonexistent. "I told you he'd come back for me! He always said he would!"

I stiffened, looking to Malcolm, but he'd heard it as well and was walking up right behind me.

"Dad, it's just a customer," his son said, holding his hands out. He turned to the left to catch my eye. "Sorry about this," he murmured. "Come on, Dad. Let's go find your *TV Guide*."

The man voice got thicker the more worked up he became. "You don't never listen, boy! Sherrod Daggett! I told you he'd come! I told you." The man stared holes into me. "You won't get it back! You know it's mine."

Malcolm's hand settled on my shoulder. "Now we know what they were hiding," he said quietly.

"Dad!" Ethan started shuffling him back into the hallway.

"He said he'd come back for it, don't you remember? I told you!" There was a sudden plea, a need for his son to understand him.

"You gave it back to him," the son said gently. "Come on, your shows are about to be on."

"My shows," the man said, suddenly melting down. "I gave it back?" he asked, sounding completely lost and uncertain.

The two of them disappeared back into the kitchen. "Everyone knows you look just like him," Mal said quietly from behind me.

"But he *recognized* me," I said. "He knew Sherrod's name. He knew he was trouble." That shouldn't have been the case if the man wasn't a witch, but neither he nor his son had shown any sign that they knew anything about magic. If nothing else, the son would have recognized us the moment we walked into the store, and that hadn't been the case.

"I am *so* sorry about that boys," Ethan came back into the shop with false cheer. There were beads of sweat on his forehead, and his smile was just a bit too wide. "My dad doesn't always remember to take his pills."

"It's no problem," Malcolm said, taking point. I don't think I could have lied very effectively at the moment. The man's accusation was like a sucker punch to the stomach.

"He's been getting so confused lately," he confided. "He's convinced all the people he used to know have turned into monsters. Half his stories are about evil children who want him dead." He laughed a false, overcompensated laugh. "Can you imagine?"

"So whoever he was talking about was some kind of student here?" Mal asked. The question was laced with casual interest.

Ethan shrugged. "How would I know? Dad was the head of the history department for near on thirty years. Didn't make much sense, he *hated* kids." He picked up where he'd left off, pulling the tray of necklaces back out of the cabinet. "So ... how about that girlfriend of yours."

"We've actually got to be going," Mal said, clapping his hand on my shoulder again. "Justin here has a lot to do before school in the morning." His grip on my shoulder tightened, and I half walked, and was half pushed back the way we'd come.

The shopkeep's eyes squinted, but he didn't argue. A silver chain dangled between his fingers. Mal led me to the door.

My father had been here? And people in town knew him? Had he gone to school here?

Was this where Moonset began?

FIFTEEN

*"There was a growing unrest between the classes
of witches. The Covens had held power for so long,
they expected to hold it forever. They were
nearly untouchable. All that changed on
Dark Monday, with the London bombing."*

Moonset: A Dark Legacy

Mal and I agreed not to say anything to the others for the time being. At least until we could start to figure out what was really going on in Carrow Mill. Jenna and Cole were loose cannons on the best of days, and knowing that our parents might have had history here would not have ended well for anyone.

The next day at school wouldn't have been so bad, except

that Jenna had fully embraced the dark side. Or encouraged Maddy and her entourage to become her disciples.

"So you never told me how Mark's was yesterday," Jenna said, appearing at the side of my locker like a vampire emerging after sunset. She grabbed one of the belt loops of my jeans, her smile twisting dangerously. "Was it everything that memories are made of?"

I pulled away from her, and slammed the locker door. Someone had come by and sanded the symbol off my locker door, but now there was an ugly tan stain where the original color was exposed. Tan-colored lockers? Who'd ever thought that was a good color?

"Was that your idea?"

Jenna covered her mouth with her hand, but her eyes were confirmation enough.

"Are we really doing this, Jenna? We've got more important things to worry about then whatever grudge you're carrying. You're pissed at me, I get it."

"Relax," she said, with her hand still covering her mouth. Whatever she said next was so low and garbled I couldn't make it out. Her hand dropped, and she rolled her eyes. "I'm not the one who's *pissed*," she said.

It's not until a couple of minutes later that I realized what she meant. The color of my jeans suddenly faded, significantly, turning from dark to pale blue as though the color simply dribbled out the bottom. All except the crotch, which was still the same dark color. It looked like I'd pissed myself.

Jenna 1, Justin 0.

"Nice shorts," Ash announced, sliding into the desk next to me during homeroom.

None of the counterspells I knew had worked on the jeans, and even trying to enlist Cole to cast an illusion to make them look normal hadn't worked out. "I'm not getting Jenna pissed on me," he'd said, wide eyed and nervous. "Pissed *off,* I mean." Mal had refused to drive me home to change, but had offered up the change of clothes in his gym bag. I had to cinch the waist twice to keep the pants up, but they were better than nothing.

I rattled my fingers against my desk and ducked my head away. It was bad enough that I had to deal with Jenna's wrath. Did Ash know what had happened? Was it spreading around school that I'd supposedly wet my pants? The fact that I was in shorts stood out a little, since it was January in New York and all.

"Oh, no witty retort? Come on, Mercutio. You have to have a thicker skin than that."

I didn't even blink at the name. Shakespeare was the new theme obviously. "If you're looking for witty retorts, you want one of the older, more sarcastic siblings," I pointed out. "Though I'd stay away from Jenna today if you value all your limbs staying attached to your body."

"Ooh, snarky," Ash responded, eyes sparkling. "Getting me all hot and bothered," she said, fanning herself. "Tell me more about these severed limbs."

I laughed.

"There we go," she said, ducking her head down so that our eyes met. "Glad to know a wardrobe malfunction didn't completely kill your sense of humor."

"It wasn't a malfunction," I started, and then stopped, because how was I supposed to explain Jenna's spell?

"What was it then? Sartorial assassination?" Ash leaned across her desk. "Relax. Jenna dumped water all over you, big deal. Don't get all emo on me again."

That was the story they were going with? I exhaled, feeling a tiny bit of my stress fade. "It's not that. Not *just* that," I amended. "I found out some stuff about my family yesterday that's... stressful."

"Family stress? If you found out you've got another sister like Jenna, that might be a deal breaker," Ash said. "One queen bee is enough, thanks."

"Nothing like that," I said, trying to hold my smile.

"Then what?"

She said it like that was so simple. Like I could lay my problems out and she'd sympathize, we'd have a moment, and both of us would move on. But the reality of the situation was living under Moonset's shadow was a complicated life—one that no one outside the five of us could really understand. Especially not a normal person who thought magic was nothing more than card tricks and sleight of hand.

I shook my head, conjuring up my own sleight of hand to hide my thoughts behind a smile. "Nothing major. Nothing that should ruin the day anyway."

She settled back, looking pleased with herself. "Excellent. Then as a reward, I'm going to let you buy me coffee."

I looked at the clock on the wall. "Are we even in the same lunch period?"

"I mean later, Lysander. Tonight."

Like a date? Instantly the cool and calm conversation was gone, and in its place was something heavy and terrifying. My heart became an overwhelming cadence. *Tonight* implied a date. Didn't it? My mouth dried out, all the moisture in my body rushing to my hands, which were clammy and gross.

"Sure," I said, looking away again. Hoping for indifferent, praying for casual, but my voice cracked right in the middle. I coughed, cleared my throat, and prayed for death. It was the only solution now.

Ash didn't laugh, like I expected. Not that I expected her to mock me or take huge amounts of enjoyment in my suffering, but I expected at least a little tinkling of laughter. But there was nothing. No reaction at all. I looked up, saw her tucking a book back into her bag. "Great. I'll see you at the coffee shop after school? Six or so?"

"Uhm, yeah. Sure. Six sounds good." I could go home with the others and figure out a way to ditch them all by then.

Suddenly, everything was looking up.

It was easier sneaking away from everyone than I thought. Mal was watching a football game on our TV for some reason, and who knew where the others were. I left a half hour early, figuring the walk would do me some good.

By the time I finally walked into the coffee shop, it was

almost dark already. That was my least favorite part about winter—the fact that the sun set so early. It was just barely past six when I walked inside, but the sky was already overcast and nearing black.

"Running late, Caliban?" Ash was set up near the front corner, framed by glass windows on one side and green and black walls on the other. It started to snow a little bit as I sat down across from her. There were already two coffee cups on the table, both still steaming. She hadn't been here for very long.

Caliban? That was a name I didn't recognize. "Shakespeare?" Because it would be just like Ash to shift conventions without a word.

"*The Tempest*," she smiled. "You should know that."

"If we don't read it in English, I don't know it," I admitted.

"Heathen." But she smiled as she said it. "So how was the rest of your day? I see you found pants. Always an improvement."

I looked down, and then focused on the cup in front of me. "Do I even want to ask?"

Her eyes twinkled.

"Is there even any caffeine in this? Or is it all sugar and syrup?"

She lifted her cup to her mouth and took a sip, but her eyes never left mine. It took a minute before I realized I was being prompted yet again. She glanced down at my cup, and her eyebrow quirked in challenge.

It wasn't until I'd taken a sip of something that was a

little bit pumpkin and a little bit spicy (and better than I will ever admit out loud) that Ash cleared her throat. "So what did you do that made Her Highness so angry?"

I eyed her warily. "Don't let Jenna hear you call her that. She's already amassing a hit list around school."

Ash leaned back in her chair, the very picture of composure. "I'm not scared of your sister, Justin."

"You should be," I muttered. All I needed was a war between Jenna and Ash.

"You've met Maddy, right?" Ash asked. "She's like Jenna-on-training-wheels. Trust me, I know exactly how to deal with girls like Jenna. She'll crush anyone she thinks she *can* crush, and never look back." As if realizing that sounded a bit harsher than she planned, she added, "I get it. Having to start over at new schools, build a new reputation. It's got to be tough. Everyone copes differently."

"That's just Jenna," I laughed. "It's not about school or anything like that. She has to be the star, and if she's not, she has to destroy whoever's in her light." I realized how that sounded, and I shook my head. "Sorry, I don't know why I said that."

Ash leaned forward, tucking her hand under her ear. "People need to vent sometimes. It's okay. I can't imagine it's easy to live with a sister like that."

"It's not so bad, most of the time. It's just that she tends to go out of control, and I'm supposed to be there to pick up the pieces. It gets annoying."

"It's not your job to clean up after her," Ash said quietly. "You're not her parent, Justin."

"Yeah, but I kind of am. I mean, we're all we've got." After a moment, I rushed in to cover. "I mean, we've got our foster family and everything, but it's been the five of us for so long that we're really...close."

"Yeah, but it seems like all you do is cover for her. Even now, you're venting about how hard it is to live with Jenna, and you're making excuses for how she acts," Ash pointed out. "You're allowed to have a life of your own. It doesn't have to be all about Jenna—even if she expects it to be."

The truth was that I wouldn't have the first clue about how to do what Ash was suggesting. I'd spent so much time running behind Jenna that I never had much time to think about my own life. Everything I did involved the others. Covering for them. Helping them. Keeping them out of trouble.

A few minutes passed, and I didn't say anything else. I was too busy thinking, wrapped up in seventeen years of thoughts. Who was I, if I wasn't Sherrod Daggett's son? Or Jenna's twin, or Mal's little brother?

"I didn't mean to make it all maudlin," Ash said, trying to force a laugh. "Come on, Lady Macbeth, let's have a smile." She looked down at my cup. "Did you want extra whipped cream? I could do that, if you like."

I didn't reply right away, and before I knew it, Ash was gone from the other side of the table, only returning a minute later with an industrial-sized can of whipped cream. "The best weapon in a girl's arsenal," she smirked before spraying an absolute tower of topping onto my coffee.

The moment the tower started to bend under its own weight and toppled off the side, I laughed. I couldn't help it. "You're the strangest girl I've ever met," I told her, and that was the truth.

"I'm an enigma," she admitted. "I don't like being predictable."

"See, I prefer predictable. I just don't get too much of it."

Ash grinned, but there was a moment where the smile faded, where something else floated to the surface. It was only a moment, then the smile was back in full force. "You never did tell me what you did that pissed your sister off."

I shrugged. What I'd done to Jenna was too wrapped up in Moonset and magic. "We...had a disagreement," I said carefully. "A very big one. Jenna wanted me to side with her, and I agreed with Malcolm instead."

"Wow. And you're still breathing?" Ash looked impressed.

"It doesn't happen very often," I admitted. "But Jenna's had a hard time letting it go."

"Still making excuses," she chided. "Tell me how you really feel. Doesn't it suck, sometimes, having to pick up after her? Don't you wish you could just do your own thing and let her handle her own messes?"

Before I could answer, there was a commotion outside. Several people hurried past the window, at least one of them shouting. A few seconds later, several more people did the same. They were all heading towards the town square.

"Is there something going on tonight?"

Ash had half risen out of her chair, her forehead wrinkled. "I didn't think so," she said slowly.

We both stood awkwardly around our table as yet *another* group of people hurried past the coffee shop, their eyes locked on something in the distance. When the police car, sirens blaring, flew past a few seconds later, we both went for the door. Even the barista trailed behind us, unable to escape the curiosity of the moment.

A crowd was forming in the square, surrounding and beneath the picturesque clock tower that defined the city square. Streetlights designed like lanterns lit the streets, and strings of lights in the trees brought the quaint and homey vibe. But there was nothing quaint or homey about the gathering crowd.

"What do you think it is?" I asked, as we approached.

Ash's expression was grim. "Nothing good."

"Can't you hear them! They're screaming," a man shouted from somewhere beyond the crowd. I followed the eyes and craned necks of the crowd, and found the man somewhere near the top of the clock tower. Though it's only a few stories high—four if I had to guess—he's still a tiny figure in comparison. But his voice carries throughout the square, and cuts through the buzzing voices of the fascinated townsfolk.

"I saw him once. The sun! He fizzled and faltered, and then they locked the door on his cage of blood."

"Come on," Ash said, wrapping her hand around my arm. "They'll talk him down. But we shouldn't watch. It's not right. He's obviously sick."

I would have left right then, except that the man shifted on his ledge, leaned forward like he was teasing the sky's edge, and I recognized him. It was the man from the diner. The Harbinger.

"I know him," I said without thinking.

Ash looked surprised. "You do?"

"Well, not *know him* exactly. He got drunk and harassed Mal and I when we first came to town."

Now was no different. "I see you," he called, and I could swear he was staring right at me.

"Come on, Justin," Ash said, a little more urgently.

One of the lantern lights on the street corner exploded with a paff, releasing a sprinkling of sparks. Like a collective unit, the crowd shrieked and panted and screamed. But they were used to it when a second pop followed, and then the third. Three streetlamps in as many seconds.

I felt *something* in the air. Like a current of air that I couldn't quite feel, but I knew was there somehow. It sailed over us, and I was reminded of the wraith. Of the way I'd felt moments before the wall had exploded inwards, and innocent men had died because of me.

I suddenly didn't feel so good.

"Can you hear them yet? They bite and they whisper, and it never ends." His body spasmed, his left arm jerking suddenly behind his back. The crowd gasped, fearing that this would be the last moments before he tumbled forth.

My body grew cold.

"Traitor, caller of spirits, warlock! Following you down, laying out the signs." the man howled. "They want you to know. They *need you to know.*"

Any witch who turned to the black arts was considered a warlock. There was truth to the legends that some witches made pacts with the Devil. Warlocks were the common term, but I'd heard the others before, too. Warlock supposedly *meant* traitor, once, and before that, it had meant a caller of the dark spirits.

Ash tugged on my arm again, but I took a step forward. Then another. My eyes never left his.

"Can't you hear it? The dark things are coming, and *they only need one.*" The man's arm straightened, his posture smoothed. "They only need one." Once the words crossed his lips, he couldn't stop them. He was like a skipping CD. "They only need one. Only need one. Need one."

"Oh god," Ash said, a moment before the man let go of the ledge.

By now the man's voice was hoarse and starting to falter, but he still continued to proclaim his strange message. "I can hear the litany. They're here."

The man's lips kept moving, but the sound finally died. Even at this distance, I could see that one little detail. He looked scared and resigned—like an addict who was helpless in the face of his habit. The words continued to crawl out of his mouth as if invisible hands pulled them forth, even though there was no sound. *They only need one. They only need one.*

Then the man tumbled forward, suddenly so relaxed that his fall from the roof was graceful and smooth. There was silence around me, and I wondered if I was the only one who saw this sudden change. But then the gasps started, and I realized I wasn't alone. I turned away, wincing even before the impact. Ash buried her head against my chest, and that moment of comfort sparked a lifetime of habits.

I stroked her head, whispered comforting things, even as there were screams and tears in the crowd. People surged forth around us, either out of some misguided attempt to help, or because they wanted to be the first to see the body.

When Ash pulled away, I expected to see tears, or at least the effects of the man's suicide. But her face was eerily calm, slack of any emotion at all. Over the top of her head, across the open space between the crests of the crowd, there was a woman staring at me. She had the kind of stern, hard gaze as Illana Bryer, and for a second I thought it *was* her, but the two women couldn't have looked any different.

Her hair was long and dark, her expression pinched and plucked like it was the victim of an overzealous surgeon. She glared at me with the kind of recognition that made it clear she knew who I was—knew whose child I was.

I went to say, "Who is that?" to Ash, to see if she knew the woman, but when I looked down and then back up, the woman was already gone, absorbed into the crowd. I caught a momentary glimpse of almost-familiar green eyes brushing past us, but there was a gasp in the crowd and my eyes went towards the body.

The last thing I wanted to do was to see the Harbinger now. It was something I'd never be able to unsee. I could still picture the way the Witcher had looked, ravaged and bloody after the wraith had torn through him.

Seeing the Harbinger would be another.

But something made me look anyway, and it was another sucker punch.

His body had cracked the sidewalk in a single line, arcing from his right shoulder down past his left hip. The police officer on the scene was crouched in front of the body, his posture slumped. Dead then. The officer got up, and started herding people back away from the scene. Ash and I took a step back, and something in the way the light reflected off the concrete made me stop. Blood began spreading out from the body like a water balloon with a tiny leak.

It pooled out from some hidden wound beneath the body, sliding forward like it was the concrete that was bleeding, and not the man. The blood trailed out in several directions at once, one at the crown of his head, one along the lines of each of his shoulders, one from either hip. The lines bent and curved, and it wasn't until I saw them all at once, saw the *pattern* that I realized.

Ash sucked in a breath.

A circle of blood spread underneath his chest, and tentacles stretched away from his limbs. I'd seen this symbol before. If we pulled him up, I knew what we'd see. A dry spot in the shape of a crescent moon, a circle, and six wavy rays. The same symbol Mal and I had seen on the burnt-out house and on my locker.

Moonset's symbol.

SIXTEEN

"Reports from the scene suggest that the explosions started just before noon, when the Invisible Congress would have adjourned for lunch. At this time, we don't know if there are any survivors. Feared dead are the Covens of Devon, the Sisters of Air, Iron Rose, Moonset, and Calmingbrook."

Released Reports
On the Dark Monday attack

There wasn't much time to put my thoughts together, or mourn, or whatever it was you did in situations like this. The adults took over almost immediately. Reinforcement police, two of them, appeared from either end of the crowd, herding people back. I pulled Ash out of the street and away from the body. As we walked away, the officers were putting up police tape and had brought out a sheet to cover over the man.

"All right people, move along. It's time to go home," a strident voice called out. My heart sunk. I knew that voice. I *hated* that voice. Miss Virago appeared on the scene and took control. There was a small group with her—men and women no older than her. The Witchers were on the scene. The coffee I'd drunk started burning a hole through my stomach lining. It shouldn't be possible, but the situation just got worse and worse.

Was she pretending to be an actual government official, now? As far as I knew, working for the Congress was not the same as working for the FBI. Witches continued to survive by living a life of secrecy—all our laws, our crimes, our prosecutions had to happen under the radar. We didn't have any actual authority to the rest of the world.

But never underestimate the power of a bitchy woman in a business suit and heels. It helped to have magic, of course, to stop people from asking questions.

At my side, Ash looked nauseous. "I need to call my dad," she said. She untangled herself from my arm, leaving me only with phantom pain as she dipped and ducked through the crowd.

"Time to get off the street, Mr. Daggett," Meghan said, taking her place on my other side, and grabbing the arm that Ash hadn't just been clinging to. She dragged me back the way we'd come, towards the coffee shop, and all I could do was panic. What if Ash saw something? What if she heard something?

But no, the Witchers were supposed to be good at containment, at making sure normal people don't remember anything about magic.

"What's going on?" I asked, because the Witchers she'd brought with her had rounded up some of the onlookers in groups of four or five. Each of the Witchers was talking, but the people they were talking to were ... wrong. Slack-faced, wide-eyed. Vacant. It took me a second to realize they were being fascinated.

Fascination is a highly regulated branch of magic. The ability to control a person's thoughts, to bewitch them so thoroughly that they'll believe anything you tell them, was widely coveted and easily abused. It was almost exclusively the purview of the Witchers themselves, along with whoever the Congress decided to allow to learn the basics. Even those who were good at it—normal witches—could barely work more than five or six at a time—fascination had its limits.

My stomach twisted again. *Normal.* If there was one thing the five of us were, it wasn't that. But those were secrets I'd sworn never to tell. I covered my nerves up with curiosity. "You're making them forget?"

Meghan didn't *actually* smile, but the muscles in her mouth unpinched for just a moment. It looked like the closest she ever came. "First, we're finding out what they remember. Then we're making them forget."

She said it so easily. Like stripping away people's memories meant nothing to her. Who knew, maybe it didn't. The only comfort to me was that spells of fascination didn't normally work on witches. Again, normal.

I knew an interrogation was coming, and I had to prepare. I had the entire length of the street before the coffee
shop to pull myself together. To wipe away any trace of
what the Harbinger's words had done to me, the truths he'd
revealed.

Meghan didn't take us to the coffee shop, though. We
walked one building further—an empty storefront with
dust-coated windows and Going Out of Business flyers,
faded and grimy, taped to the glass.

The door was unlocked, and she gestured me inside. I
followed, at least grateful that Ash wouldn't stumble in on
whatever interrogation this was going to be. The idea that
she'd find out what I was on a night like tonight... that was
unconscionable.

"How did you find out there was going to be an... *incident* tonight?" Virago asked, feigning a sweet tongue as if I'd
forget the callous shrew she really was.

"I didn't. I went out for coffee with a friend, and we saw
people running for the clock tower." I shrugged. "We went
outside to see what was going on."

"And that's when you saw the man. The sympathizer."

I nodded.

"He was very sick," she confided, like we were friends.
"Did you know that?"

"He harassed Malcolm and me before," I said, because
I knew that *she* knew. Everything that happened to us
ended up in a report somewhere.

"And what did he say to you tonight?"

"He was up in the clock tower," I said. "I never saw him tonight. I mean, other than that."

A benevolent, charming smile. "You don't expect me to believe that, do you Justin? Now, what did he say to you? We need to know what he was planning."

What he was planning? "What are you talking about?" I asked. Maybe if I knew how Virago and the other Witchers were planning to spin this, I could figure out . . . something. Some idea of what they wanted.

Some of her patience wore away, smooth like an ocean wearing away at a rock. "We know he was shouting things. Preaching, proselytizing, whatever. What we need to know is what he said. That's the only way we can stop whatever he's set into motion."

But it didn't sound like the Harbinger had set *anything* into motion. He'd been scared, and his mind wasn't all there, but he'd been more a victim than a villain. He'd said there was a warlock, and after the streetlight explosions and the Moonset symbol pooling beneath him, I was convinced.

What I needed was to talk this over with Jenna. She saw through things easier than I did—maybe she was just better at reading people, or maybe the fact that she inherently distrusted *everyone* made her see things I couldn't. But she'd know what to do with what I'd heard.

"Nothing that made any sense," I said, looking down at the floor. There were several different sets of footprints, some of them starting to dust over, and others as fresh as ours. Were the Witchers using this as some sort of hideout?

"It might not make sense to you," she said, her tone getting more brittle. She knew I wasn't interested in cooperating. "But it's important that you tell all the same."

"Tell her what she wants to know, Justin," Quinn said, coming into the storefront. He was dressed in a pea coat and a sweater that looked like they could have both been the same shade of gray. They could have given the grime on the floors a run for their money.

"You heard what happened?" I asked. Quinn nodded his head, actually looking sad, where Virago just pretended. "I don't know what he was talking about," I said honestly. "He kept talking about hearing things. Voices. I mean, I knew crazy people were supposed to hear voices, but I didn't expect him to *talk* about it, y'know? I think they told him to jump."

Quinn's expression was curious. "Why would you say that?"

"Because he didn't want to. I couldn't really hear what he was saying most of the time; he was screaming and the crowd was too loud, but he looked scared. Not like someone that wanted to kill himself."

"Anything else?" Quinn asked. He had taken the lead, and Meghan had relinquished it silently. She stood behind him, pulling out her tablet computer and punching away while we talked.

There's a warlock in Carrow Mill, but I don't know what it means. I'm being haunted by the symbol my parents used to take credit for their darkest acts. He may have been crazy, but I think the Harbinger was trying to warn me, but I don't know why. I don't trust you. I don't trust anyone.

But I didn't say any of that. "Not that I can think of,"

I said, biting down on my lip. I wasn't as good a liar as Jenna, and I couldn't talk so fast and in so many circles that you lost the point like Cole, but I could withhold information like no one's business.

Except Quinn didn't seem to believe me. "You're sure," he said, catching my eye. "This is important, Justin. All we want is to keep you safe."

Is that all? Are you sure? "No," I said, exhaling slow. "Like I said, it was all kind of crazy. He said some stuff, but it was nonsense. It was like his brain got scrambled."

Quinn stared at me for a long minute. "Okay," he said finally. "Let's get you home."

———

Quinn didn't come inside when we got back to the house. "Ask your sister not to sneak out tonight? Please? We've had enough drama for one day."

"Where will you be?"

He looked in the rearview mirror, scrubbed at his eyes. There were dark circles there that stood out severely on his pale skin. I hadn't noticed in the store because the only lights had come from the street, but with the car door open, his exhaustion was on display. "There's still some coordination that needs to take place tonight. To make sure everything's okay."

"But the guy killed himself. It's not like suicide is contagious."

Quinn wouldn't look at me. "I'm not sure it *was* a suicide," he said quietly.

It was an opening, albeit a small one. "Then what was it?" I pressed. "What's going on, Quinn?"

But just as quickly as the wall went down, it came back up stronger than ever. "You should get inside. School tomorrow."

Of course he wasn't going to tell me anything. He was just like the rest. I unbuckled my seatbelt and hopped out into the driveway. "Justin," he called, just before I slammed the door. I bent down, looking at him in the driver's seat. I waited, but he seemed to be wrestling with something. "There's a guard inside," he said finally, resisting whatever he'd wanted to say, "so don't freak out."

A guard. And there was nothing that we needed to know. I bit down on my irritation and nodded, slamming the door shut with a little more force than necessary. Once inside the house, I took the stairs two at a time and skipped past my room to head straight for Jenna. I knocked, and barely waited for the annoyed "What?" before I turned the knob and slipped inside.

She was curled up on her bed, applying a coat of nail polish to her toes. It was hard to tell if it was black, or just a really dark purple. Not that it mattered much. She raised an eyebrow at me, and in lieu of greeting, I raised my index finger over my lips.

My phone was in my pocket and I fumbled for it before pulling it out and into my left hand. I nodded at her, then at the phone next to her on the bedspread. The eyebrow rose even higher, but Jenna's toenails were forgotten as she slipped off the bed and picked up her phone. She crossed the room to her laptop, and clicked on the music player, pressing the button until the volume went almost as high as it could go. Then she walked back to me with her phone. Hers went into her left hand, too. We both raised our right hands, palms out.

Jenna had traded another girl for the spell a few years ago. It was a communication spell that the girl had managed to tweak to work with her cell phone. It had become invaluable ever since. We whispered the spell in stereo, and the screens of our phones lit up.

Something happened tonight, I thought, and the words lit up on her screen.

Jenna's eyes went to her phone, her lips pursed. My screen remained blank. She was waiting for more.

The Harbinger we met; he killed himself. He said there's a warlock here.

You said he was crazy, she thought-texted.

I thought he was. But there was something there. Something in the air.

Jenna frowned. *What else did he say?*

It was weird, I thought, shaking my head. *He said they were coming. And something about only needing one.*

One what?

I shrugged helplessly. *Oh, and I saw the symbol again. Only this time it was made out of his blood.*

Symbol? And then I remembered that I hadn't told Jenna about the Moonset symbol, or how many times I'd seen it lately.

I let my empty hand fall, and went over to her desk. Quick as I could, I drew the circle, shading all but the crescent moon on its side, and the six tentacles sprouting from it, three at the top, and three at the bottom.

I held it up to Jenna, then raised my hands to return to the spell. *It's theirs. Moonset's. And it keeps showing up.* As quickly as I could, I told her about how Mal had found the first symbol and about the fire that had burned down the building.

Every time my cell drops service, Jenna thought, and then there was a pause. She chewed on her lower lip, eyes leaving her phone to meet mine. She was worried. Words on the screen appeared as she completed the thought, but it took me a moment to look away. *Every time my cell drops service, that picture flashes on the screen.*

But why is it showing up now?

Jenna was still, and I wondered at the furious spin of the thoughts I couldn't see. You had to concentrate on the spell to make your thoughts appear, but you could just as easily concentrate on having them *not* appear.

Why did they bring us to Carrow Mill, Jenna?

What else did he say about the warlock?

He said something about signs, I thought.

Jenna nodded pointedly at the drawing I'd done. *Signs? Like Moonset's symbol?*

Yeah, maybe.

You're not the only one who's seen that symbol. And I bet they've been showing up for a while.

What are you saying?

Jenna's screen was blank for so long I thought that the spell had dropped. *If there really is a warlock, I don't think it's an accident the Congress brought us here. Or that Illana Bryer is relocating.*

??

Justin, I think we're supposed to be bait.

SEVENTEEN

*"In the span of a single day, one hundred
of the most powerful witches in the world were
killed. They were the ones trained to combat
warlocks, to use magic as a weapon.
Without them, there was no defense."*

Moonset: A Dark Legacy

Monday started out strange. I kept staring at Quinn over
breakfast. Jenna's theory made sense—it *fit* the weirdness that
had been going on ever since we'd gotten here. Quinn's phone
call, talking about how we'd figure out why we were really
here.

They'd brought us here to be bait. To smoke out a warlock. *Was it Cullen Bridger? Was he closer than anyone thought?*

"Magic classes start today," Quinn said, interrupting the

silence. Jenna still hadn't come down yet, and everyone else was eating at home. Thank god, I didn't think I could stand an overly sugared Cole bouncing around the room.

"About time," I replied noncommittally.

Quinn narrowed his eyes at me. "There were a lot of things to consider," he said, almost chiding. "How are you holding up after last night?"

"Justin's fine," Jenna said, "but who cares about that. You said they finally agreed to teach us?"

"I said magic class starts today," Quinn said, getting up to refill his coffee.

But Jenna's good mood wasn't deflated by his response, even though we both knew what it meant. More classes about the theory of magic, probably. Not so much in the spells department. As usual.

"So lots of theory, then. Got it." Jenna blowing off the chance to learn new magic? I knew why—at the moment we were both more concerned with what was going on here—but she was taking it a little far. I glared at her across the table, then nodded towards Quinn's back. *Don't be so obvious,* I tried to telegraph.

She rolled her eyes at me. "So what's the Congress's master plan?" Quinn stilled at the coffee pot until Jenna continued. "The next time a wraith or some other monster comes crashing through the wall, we should nag them with the theory behind what makes a good illusion? If we could *do* better illusions, we might get out of town without destroying the whole school next time."

"There's not going to be a next time," Quinn said. It's

not like I believed him, or like I even would have believed him a week ago, but now the lie was so blatant and obnoxious that it soured my stomach. I got up and dumped the rest of my breakfast in the trash.

"Not hungry?" he asked, only sounding half interested.

"Performance anxiety," Jenna stage whispered.

I huffed in irritation, but it wasn't at Jenna.

I spent the day swamped in review materials, as the school geared up for midterms. It helped a lot, because it laid out in neat little columns all the things I already knew right next to all the things I didn't.

It was kind of like the rest of my life, only there were no worksheets that could tell me how a warlock was being allowed to run around Carrow Mill, and why they'd brought us here if they knew that. The guardians watching us had always been abusively careful in making sure we never came close to anyone who had been a Moonset sympathizer before, and now we'd not only met one, but there was a warlock in town, which was infinitely worse.

"Hey," Ash said, appearing in the halls just as I was looking for my Independent Study classroom. Independent Study was what all our magic classes were filed under—easier for us to blend in, I supposed.

"Hey, how are you?" I asked.

"I'm okay," she said with a nod, and while she looked a little on the exhausted side, the same strength I'd seen last night was there. What happened to the Harbinger hadn't been eating her up. "Where are you off to?"

"Independent Study," I lied with a grimace. "So much fun, right?"

Ash made a face. "Better than Pre-Calculus. I'll see you later," she said, brushing my arm as she passed. I watched her go, still trying to wrap my head around the mystery of the girl. Up until now, she'd been like a force of nature, inexplicable and ever-changing. But something was different, and it had been ever since last night.

It wasn't the Harbinger's death, I didn't think. It had been something else. Had I said something? Done something?

A boy came up at my side. "You know Ash?" I turned to my left and had to do a double take. For a second, it was almost like looking at Mal. A younger, less-perfect version of Mal, but Mal nonetheless.

It was the eyes, I decided. They had the same hazel-green eyes. And maybe something of the height, once this kid finished growing. He was younger than me, but it was hard to say whether he was a freshman or a sophomore.

"Sort of," I said, half to him, and half to myself. Who was this kid? By the time I went to ask him his name, he was already rushing down the hall, weighed down by an extremely full backpack. He disappeared into a classroom at the end of the hall.

I paced the hallway, waiting on the others. *Where are they?* The clock ticked down, but there was no sign of Jenna or Mal, Cole or Bailey. They should be here—we always had

Independent Study together, but I was seriously independent at the moment.

I followed the hall to the end, somehow not surprised that the Mal-lookalike was in the same room as my magic lesson. *What's going on here? Is this some kind of prank?* There were other kids in the room, a couple that I didn't recognize, and one that I did—Maddy. Maddy was a witch?

One of the first things that had come after Moonset was the understanding that magic had to adapt. Every student needed to be taught, and a central organization needed to make sure that happened. "No witch left behind" became a serious movement. Magic met bureaucracy and since then magic has been considered a privilege, not a right. Magic was taught in classrooms, and the curriculum was controlled.

"Come along, Mr. Daggett," a woman called as she swept up the steps at the hallway's end. She had raven-dark hair and an ankle-length skirt, and I recognized her. The woman in the crowd, the one who'd glared at me. In the daylight, she looked even more severe. Definitely an Illana Bryer clone. "I'll not hold up my class so you can loiter in the hallways," she said in a crisp British accent.

I was rooted in place, unable to move even if I wanted to. "I'm waiting on my sister and the others. They should be here any second," I promised.

She laid a hand on the door frame. "Not unless they plan to skip their own lesson. I dare say I barely have the grace to handle even one of your little brood in my classroom. All five?" She shook her head and tsked. "I think not." "Wait...what?" They were splitting us up? That had never happened before. Who was going to keep Cole from trying spells he couldn't handle or console Bailey if she didn't get the pronunciation right the first time?

She walked into the room and I was left stuttering. It was only the sound of the bell that spurred me into action and into the classroom ... and the last person to see the giant drawing that dominated the chalkboard at the front of the room. Someone had taken the time to get all the details just exactly right—the circle was shaded in perfectly, no gaps forgotten.

The woman had stopped just inside of the door, once she saw what dominated the room. At the sound of my footsteps behind her, she spun around, her skirt spinning almost like a top. "Do you think this is funny?" she hissed.

"What is it, Mrs. Crawford?" Maddy asked, eyeing the two of us.

"It's Moonset's symbol," the blonde jock next to her said. "So you didn't draw it for the lesson, Mrs. C?"

"No, I most certainly did not," the woman muttered, still staring me down. "It seems our new student has a sense of humor. A sick one, but can we really be surprised?"

"This is the first time I've even been in this room," I protested.

"It was here when we got here," the jock admitted, nodding to him and Maddy.

"So he came in earlier, and left us a little welcoming present," the teacher said, her breathing growing shallow even as her face reddened. "That's all it means, Kevin."

"I didn't *do* this!" I said. "That thing was scratched into my locker last week before I even got here. You can ask the principal's office. They had to fix it."

Of course Maddy, who had proved she doesn't like me, didn't seem convinced. But it was the voice at the back of the room that defended me. "It was here this morning before school started," the kid from the hallway—the one with Malcolm's eyes—said. "Someone must have done it over the weekend or after school on Friday."

"I will not be mocked in my own classroom," Mrs. Crawford said.

"It's probably someone who just wanted to stir up some drama," Kevin said. He shrugged off his backpack and went up to the board, doing the thing that everyone else had avoided so far. Erasing it. "There," he said, once it was done. "Problem solved."

"The problem is *not* solved," Mrs. Crawford snapped.

I wasn't going to help this situation any. Instead, I walked over to the back of the room and dropped my bag next to the kid who'd spoken up in my defense. "I'm Justin."

He licked his lips and looked down. "Luca," he said nervously. His eyes lifted towards mine. "Luca Denton."

Denton? Denton was Mal's last name. "How—" But I wasn't given a chance to finish.

"Cyrus Denton had a brother, of course. And that brother had a son," said Mrs. Campbell, acting like she hadn't been losing her cool only a few minutes ago. "Isn't it obvious? The Denton boys have always had a certain look. Easy pickings in a crowd."

"I'm sorry," I said, still trying to wrap my head around it. "We were told there wasn't any family. That we didn't *have*—"

"You don't," she said shortly. "Luca's father, all the other Dentons, even the ones that weren't Denton by name turned their back on Cyrus. There might be some Daggetts or Owens lurking out there somewhere, but they'll never come looking for you."

"That's not the same thing as not having a family," I said. I don't know why, but finding out that there was even more that the Congress had lied to us about got under my skin. They told us we were orphans. That there was no one! We grew up thinking Moonset had existed in a vacuum, and all the while there were blood relatives with their heads down, pretending that they'd never heard of us before.

"Malcolm's father chose to become a warlock. The word itself means 'traitor'—blood is just one of the many things he betrayed," Crawford said.

The rest of the room was quiet. My skin was burning. It wasn't enough that the teacher clearly despised every second I was invading her classroom, but the way she talked was somehow even worse than Miss Virago. The redheaded Congress operative was contemptuous and dismissive, but Crawford acted like she actually hated me, and the fact that she had to speak to me at all was completely unacceptable.

"Very well," she said suddenly. "Let's have a little lesson for Mister Daggett, since he's so oblivious to the history he comes from. Kevin, what separates a witch who rebels from the Congress with a warlock?"

The jock sat up in his chair. "A warlock creates a connection to the Abyss, and invokes the black arts. It's what makes them so dangerous."

Christians believed in Hell. Witches believed in the Abyss. The only difference was that we could actually prove ours existed. The Abyss was some sort of portal, or world, or dimension that was basically a giant, living pit, and that pit was full of dark power. It was called Maleficia, and it was a devastating alternative to magic.

If magic was a language and a voice, Maleficia was a glass-shattering shriek. You didn't cast spells with Maleficia, you released its power from the Abyss—and it sowed chaos and destruction wherever it spread. Even the tiniest invocation of the black arts could create devastating weapons that would continue for hours.

"Maleficia was the power that gave Moonset the edge in the war," I said, interrupting. Mrs. Crawford thought to shame me by reminding me what our parents had done, but all of us had come to terms with it a long time ago. "They would strike in secret, unleash their black arts, and by the time the Congress could mount a defense, they were too busy trying to contain the Maleficia to fight back."

"You will speak when called upon, Mr. Daggett," Mrs. Crawford snapped. "Continue, Kevin."

"Well, he's right," Kevin said uncomfortably. "A warlock is someone who becomes connected to the Abyss, and it makes them irrational. Insane. It's the reason most people believe that Moonset was beaten in the end. Because their minds were compromised."

"You can't tell someone is a warlock just by looking at

them," Maddy chimed in. "Which is why—" she cut off abruptly, but not before she glanced my way.

So it's not entirely a secret. Things were starting to become a little more clear. "You want it to be me who drew that on the board," I said slowly, "because you don't want to think about who else it could have been." Better the Moonset bastard than the warlock that was walking free around Carrow Mill.

"That is *enough*, Mr. Daggett."

"How long has he been active? Why haven't they caught him yet?" I demanded. "I mean, we *are* talking about a warlock here in town, right?"

The room went so quiet I could almost hear the steam coming out of Mrs. Crawford's ears. "We are not discussing this," she hissed. "If you disrupt my classroom one more time, you will be removed from it."

I sat back in my chair, my thoughts racing. So the witches in town knew. But what were any of them doing? Why hadn't the Witchers caught and executed the warlock yet? And it still didn't explain what he wanted with us. Why bring us to Carrow Mill?

I tuned the class out for several minutes, only picking back up when I heard the word "Maleficia" crop up again.

"Talk to me about the Black Scare," Mrs. Crawford said, looking down at Maddy.

"The Black Scare was a period during the fifties when witches grew paranoid over the idea that any of their neighbors or friends could secretly be experimenting with the dark arts. Invoking Maleficia."

"How many years?" Her question was like a whip crack the moment Maddy had stopped to take a breath. The girl fumbled, her mouth opening and closing several times but the answer would just not come out.

"Two and a half years," Kevin piped up. "From '54 to just before Christmas of '56."

"Our illustrious wide receiver with the save," the teacher commented. "But I would expect nothing less of *you*, Kevin. Your grandfather played a part in quelling that very hysteria, didn't he?"

"He did," the guy nodded.

"So continue on, Kevin. Tell us what you know about those years."

"It started as a political ploy between rival covens. Accusing someone of invoking the black arts permanently scarred their reputation."

Behind the podium, she nodded. "So what happened?"

"It continued to spread until it became a class issue. Covens started banding together, accusing Solitaries that were in positions of power or authority. Positions they wanted for themselves. Tensions between the Covens and the Solitaries continued to get worse, and it became a hysteria."

There had always two kinds of witches—the covens that made the majority of the rules, and those who were solitary—who didn't have a coven of their own. Since the coven bond could not be forced, or faked, it was looked at by some as a kind of divine providence. Coven witches were stronger, could access more complicated magicks, could pool their powers in ways that a group of solitaries could not.

Mrs. Crawford held up her hand to stop him. "A handful of men and women stirred up a firestorm of paranoia and panic. We saw the same thing happen only a few years later with the Red Scare and Communism. What lessons can we glean from the past?" She swept across the room as she spoke, her words as animated as her body. "Luca?"

He lifted his head from the desk, lines creased into his skin. Were his eyes red, or was that just a trick of the light? It was hard to tell. There was enough of a pause that it seemed like he hadn't heard anything but his name, but eventually he answered. "We hate too easily?"

"Are you kidding? " Maddy didn't wait to be called on, nor could she hold her tongue. "It's not *hate* to want to be vigilant. Maybe if people had been more concerned with rooting out evil instead of wringing their hands about violating witch's rights, Moonset never would have happened." Her eyes found mine. "They would have been put down like dogs, right from the start."

Maddy's opinion didn't surprise me. People talked about killing Moonset the same way they talked about killing Hitler. Sacrificing one to save thousands. It was hard to say whether or not they were wrong, since the only advantage I could come up with to Moonset's existence was that it led to my own.

"But who gets to decide who lives and who dies?" I found myself speaking up.

"There's a reason that the Congress is overseen by some of the Great Covens," she said stiffly in reply. "It's harder for a coven to succumb to the lure of Maleficia." But when they did, the result was so much worse. See: Moonset.

The taint of Maleficia took over after a while, and warlocks became essentially brainwashed puppets with the Abyss's agenda as their only direction. Supposedly, the Coven bond made witches resistant to Maleficia's influence.

"So you believe in an oligarchy? A police state ruled by the Covens? You're not in a coven. That makes you a second-class citizen."

"He's right. That would make him better than us." Kevin had turned in his seat, but he lacked Maddy's malice.

Mrs. Crawford swept in front of Maddy's desk. Her smile was disturbing. "We're having such excellent debates today." The pit in my stomach dug a little deeper. "Maddy, Mr. Daggett," she continued. "Let's have you both come to the front."

Mrs. Crawford pulled a second podium from its place against the wall and dragged it forward. "Maddy, you can stand over here," she said, putting Maddy on the side of the room closer to where she'd been sitting. "And you can take my podium," she said to me. I stepped behind it, resting my hands on the sides.

Mrs. Crawford walked to the back of the room. "Let's move forward in time," she said. A knot formed in my stomach. Before she said anything else, I knew what we were going to discuss, and that it was going to blow up in my face.

"Let's discuss the political climate leading up to the Moonset War," Mrs. Crawford said, her hands carefully clasped in front of her. Kevin and Luca both started to stir. "Madeline, take the perspective of the status quo, the Covens and their oversight over the magical community. Justin, take the perspective of the dissidents. How do we resolve this issue? Let's debate."

"I don't think this is appropriate," Kevin started.

The teacher's eyes were feverish, her smile forced. "I didn't ask for comments, Kevin. Keep your opinions to yourself. This is the perfect opportunity to discuss our history."

Even Maddy knew this was a bad idea. The only difference was that she *also* thought it was a fantastic one. I'm sure she thought the debate was a slam dunk—after all, was I really going to defend the actions of terrorists?

There was a pad of paper in front of the teacher now, and a pen in her hand. "You each have thirty seconds to make an opening statement. Maddy?"

She cleared her throat, shot me a smug look, and opened her mouth. "I think the magical community is doing almost everything right," she began. "But I think we can all agree that more strict guidelines need to be in place to oversee who's learning what kinds of magic."

"Why is that? Why can we all agree?" Mrs. Crawford interjected.

Maddy fumbled for a moment. "I think the past speaks for itself," she said carefully, "and if we've learned anything from the Black Scare, it's that we need to marry vigilance and wisdom together, rather than waver too far in one direction." *Marry vigilance?* The sinking feeling got worse. Crawford hadn't just pitted us against each other because Maddy didn't like me. Maddy clearly had a history on the debate team.

"Nicely said. And for the rebuttal, Mr. Daggett."

The only problem with this scenario was that she wasn't

the only one who'd spent some time on a debate team. And I was *good*. If you counted the four aborted runs on various debate teams, I was technically undefeated. A lifetime of pulling defenses out of my ass translated well to debate. But this ... this wasn't just some debate about capital punishment. I was supposed to take the side of the people who were upset at the status quo. The witches that we now called insurgents. Warlocks. Traitors. Spurred on by Moonset.

There had always been tension between the Covens, who felt like they had been chosen to lead by some supernatural providence, and the Solitaires, the witches who were never swept up into a Coven bond. Moonset had appealed to the disenfranchised, and turned their discomfort and frustration into insurrection.

I ran my fingers along the edges of the podium, choosing my words just as carefully as Maddy had. "My opponent talks about vigilance, but what she means is wedging the divide between the Haves and the Have Nots even further. Where does the power in our world rest? Are we all equal? Or does an arrogant minority decide who lives in peace?" The fact that I could relate to this so easily wasn't lost on me.

"The most powerful Covens had been the ones in charge for hundreds of years. Solitaires simply weren't taken as seriously because they had no status in the eyes of anyone else. The Covens had access to resources, strength, and even magic that they didn't share with their solo-brethren. Since no one understood how, or why, the Coven bond formed, it only worsened the divide between the two. Covens felt their right to rule was almost a birthright." I took a breath, pausing in case I was going to be cross-examined as well, but Mrs. Crawford didn't say anything. So I went on. "The fact of the matter is that we're not all equal. Some of us lord ourselves over the rest. A two-class structure can never be equal, and she has made it clear she doesn't want it to be. By vigilance, what she means is the strong suppressing the weak, and by wisdom she means following only what those in power—"

"Time," Mrs. Crawford said firmly.

But my point was made. I saw it in the widened eyes of Kevin and Luca, and the almost dumbfounded expression on Maddy's face. If she'd thought I would stand up here and stammer how she was right, clearly she'd picked the wrong target.

"I think Justin has hit upon the crux of the issue. The Haves versus the Have Nots. That is, after all, one of the deciding factors that led to the rise of Moonset's popularity with the disaffected Solitaire movement." Mrs. Crawford was writing something on her pad of paper, but once she was done she looked up again. "Maddy, refine your view to a more proactive stance. You're coasting."

"I don't know what that means," Maddy said, still a little dazed.

"She means stop assuming you're right because history makes you right. And start thinking about your side of the argument," Kevin said, before anyone else could say anything. "But this is still a bad idea," he said, turning around to face the teacher. "Are you even allowed to do this? It's harassment."

"Enough," Mrs. Crawford said with a flamboyant roll of her eyes. "While Madeline gathers her thoughts and tries to put together a coherent argument, let's let Justin begin. Explain exactly *why* the establishment is wrong. How are you proposing to change things?"

I looked at Kevin, who was shaking his head. *He's right. This is a mistake. But was this some kind of test? Or was she setting me up?* She was asking me to defend my parents—to stand against everything I was raised to be. Was I supposed to back down and concede? I couldn't do that. "Well, if I was going to tell the Covens to shove it, I'd probably start by gathering the Solitaries together and making sure the movement was behind us."

"History isn't defined by the complacent, Mr. Daggett. You need action. You need passion." She coughed, covering her mouth with her hand. Her eyes were locked on mine, and for a moment I couldn't look away. The room shifted like the stop and start of a car. My face grew warm, then my hands and legs. I shifted, suddenly unable to get comfortable. "How about you just blow up a building?" Maddy remarked snidely. "That seems to work wonders."

Suddenly things became very serious again. The temperature in the room had gone up at least ten degrees in as many seconds. Even my heart lurched to keep the immediate silence that blanketed the room. No one breathed for a moment. The pit in my stomach burned hot, becoming wildfire racing up my spine. "How's that any different from advocating assassinations?" I demanded. "You suggested it earlier."

"If killing a dozen people saves the lives of thousands, I think that's an acceptable risk," she snapped back.

My mouth moved faster than the words could form in

my brain. It was funny—I didn't *feel* angry, but my words were heated all the same. "And who decides who lives and who dies? One of the Covens? What happens when they start abusing that power?"

Her eyes narrowed. "There's no reason to even think that would happen. I'm talking about carefully removing the threats from the rest of us before someone gets hurt."

"No reason?" I laughed. "Power corrupts. Or have you never cracked a history book? If you give a man too much power, he *will* abuse it. Men with power become despots, people like you who think they're better than everyone else."

"Who are you better than, Justin? You're broken-down white trash with warlock blood in your veins. You think you'll ever have a place in this world? They should just lock you up and save us the trouble."

"And who are you? Some small-town fish who thinks the world has some great destiny in store for her?" I snorted. "You're just another vapid Mean Girl clone who'll peak in high school. It probably kills you that you'll never find a Coven. People like *you* are the reason people like me stop taking it anymore."

All focus on a debate, or even on anyone else in the room, was long past. We were nearly screaming at each other. Even if someone had tried to interject, I don't know if I would have heard them. My pulse was pounding so loudly in my ears I could barely hear the sound of my own voice. The room was washed out in pulses of red and black, the only thing I could see was the girl across from me.

"So what are you going to do? Start another war? Recruit

for your terrorist cell? How about you read *your* history. The last time that happened? Wicked old Illana Bryer hacked off your Mommy's head."

YOU CANNOT HIT A GIRL. My vision wasn't flashes of red and black anymore. It was just red. Solid, painful red.

The things that happened next were hazy. I remember shoving the podium out from in front of me. Screaming something about terrorists. Then I remembered Kevin was suddenly in between the two of us, and I was snarling incoherent things.

Things were happening fast, but the blood pumping through my veins was so loud I couldn't concentrate. There were loud noises, I was being moved, but I couldn't get control of my tongue. I was still shouting, screaming, and it didn't even matter that it didn't make sense.

And then I wasn't in the classroom anymore.

I was in the hallway, sucking in huge lungfuls of air, with Kevin standing in front of me with his arms held out, as if at any moment I might try to shove my way back into the classroom.

It was like the air in the hallway was somehow cleaner than the classroom. My head started to clear immediately, and I came back to myself. I didn't know what had happened . . . but I didn't like it. No one had put that rage deep inside me—I'd already had all that. Just waiting for an outlet.

Somehow Maddy was able to tap into it. Even at my worst with Jenna and the others, I'd never lost control like that.

I sank down onto the steps, putting my head in my hands. I didn't trust myself to speak.

EIGHTEEN

"No one knew how to react. Do you grieve?
Or do you mobilize? We were attacked, our
governing body martyred. It was an act of
terrorism, plain and simple. But no one
claimed responsibility. Not at first..."

Robert Cooper (C: Eventide)
Interview for *Moonset: A Dark Legacy*

Twenty minutes later, I was waiting in the hallway directly between the principal's office on my left and a conference room on my right.

"Someone will deal with you eventually," the secretary had said. Mrs. Crawford had come to the door, handed my bag to Kevin, and directed me to the office. Kevin had walked to the office with me—escorting me or making sure I actually went.

I'd never lost my temper like that before. So why now? Shouting, throwing things. Everything from the last few minutes of class was hazy, like it had been something that happened to someone else. None of that was *me*. I didn't lose control like that.

" … Daggett doesn't know?" My ears caught my name, and I looked up. It was coming from my left, from the principal's office. The door was still open a crack, and whispers of private conversation filtered through.

"I know what I told you," the first voice said. Illana Bryer. Her voice was encoded in my brain.

"Then how do you explain it? Threatening other students, losing his temper? Illana, you assured me that bringing them here would *solve* our problems. Not create new ones."

"Justin is not your concern," Illana said in an icy tone. "I think you should be more concerned with what Marisol was thinking. Using spells like that on a student? Not to mention on *him*?"

"I … " the other woman trailed off helplessly. I could almost hear her stiffening. "I will handle Marisol. She'll be reported. But the *boy*?" Marisol? Were they talking about Mrs. Crawford? She'd used a spell on me? She'd provoked me? *Why?*

"The children are doing exactly what we need them to be doing," Illana replied. "Being visible. Focusing the attention upon themselves. This is crucial to the stratagem."

"And you're sure everything else will stop?"

"We're working on it," she confirmed.

The next thing I knew one of the secretaries was standing in front of me. And she was repeating something.

"I said, go into the conference room, and they'll be with you shortly," she said, raising her voice.

The conference room was not like the rest of the school. It was huge. A large rectangular table set in the center was surrounded by those ritzy-looking office chairs with wheeled legs and plush cushions. Thirty people could easily have sat around the perimeter, with another fifty filling in the sides and corners of the room.

I was still standing there, trying to figure where to sit when I heard the clack of heels behind me.

"Have a seat, Mr. Daggett."

Illana Bryer stalked around the table, taking a seat in the center, directly across from where I was standing now.

"Or stand if you wish," she add. "Fantastic impression you've made. How proud are you? Tired of letting your sister take the spotlight?"

Was she trying to be funny? "I know she used magic on me. I heard you."

"You are no idiot," Illana confirmed. "But how you could walk into a situation like that and let your guard down is beyond me. The woman drew out every scrap of anger lingering in that sullen little brain of yours, and you didn't even try to stop her."

"She was supposed to be my teacher." I wasn't making an excuse or defending myself. It was a statement of fact. "It's not my fault she provoked me."

"Wasn't it?" she drawled. "You should have known from the moment you met her that Marisol Crawford was no friend to you. Do you really think that just because someone is a teacher means they were never a daughter? A friend?"

She was saying Moonset took someone from Mrs. Crawford. Again, not the first time I've ever been in that situation. I dropped my head. "I should have been paying more attention," I admitted. "What happens now?

The door opened behind me, and a woman not quite as old as Illana appeared. Illana stood up, gestured next to her. "Justin Daggett, meet your head principal, Miss Villanova."

"Not the twin I thought I'd be spending my afternoon with," Miss Villanova said. "Have you gone over everything already?"

"We've only just started," Illana said.

Miss Villanova didn't looked like she smiled much. "The school board maintains a low tolerance for violent outbursts, Mr. Daggett. Now, I understand that most schools bend the rules for you and your … family." Her mouth twisted, just saying the word.

Bending the rules? Had they even read Jenna's file? The principal continued. "But we set our standards a bit higher. Alternative arrangements will be made for your Independent Study classes. I can't have my other students put in jeopardy. In the meantime, I think a two-day suspension will give you enough time to reconsider your behavior in my school."

The room was suddenly frigid. "What?"

"You're suspended." Illana didn't beat around the bush.

She was blunt, forceful, and without regret. "Use your time wisely. Learn to pay more attention."

This couldn't be happening.

There was a knee-jerk reaction where I was filled with relief that the word she used was "suspended" not "expulsion." However, there were much bigger problems with that statement. I wasn't the one who was supposed to be suspended. I wasn't the one who got expelled. I was the good twin.

"But you know I was set up," I said. I had to fix this. Somehow. "She did…something. She wanted me to freak out like that."

"Which you did," Illana agreed. "Regardless of how it happened, you still violated school policy."

The principal cleared her throat. "Your guardian has already been called," she said to me. Her expression said everything she wouldn't say out loud. Disgusted and dismissive. "You can wait out by the secretary."

I hesitated only long enough for her to snap an additional, "Go!" Then I was up and out of the chair so fast it kept rolling back even as I was turning the doorknob. I waited in the front part of the office.

People came and left, most throwing curious glances my way, but I kept my eyes focused on the ground. I couldn't believe this was happening.

"I know what it's like."

I looked up to see Luca slouched in front of me. He fidgeted, shifting his weight from one foot to the other, never quite meeting my eyes.

"Know what it's like?"

"Being put down by people like Maddy. It's not just you." For a second, he looked like he wanted to say something else, but the secretary dropped her phone, and the sound bulleted through the office. Luca flinched so hard he probably had whiplash, and scurried for the door.

Five minutes later Quinn showed up, the muscles in his jaw clenched. Five seconds after that, we were leaving.

We made it four blocks before he said anything. The heaters were going full blast, filling the car with warmth and tension.

"This is a joke, right? Tell me this is a joke."

"I get it," I responded quietly. "But she used magic on me. What was I supposed to do?"

"Do you have—" he cut himself off, frustration strangling his voice. Despite the obvious tension in the car, Quinn was a model driver. He slowed for school zones, came to complete stops, and let me dwell for whole streets at a time before continuing. "If you don't want people to connect you with your parents, you can't lash out like that."

"She used *magic*." The "it wasn't my fault" should have been more clear than it was.

"Do you think anyone's going to tell that part of the story? No, they're going to remember the son of Sherrod Daggett spewing hate speech and threats. In a week, no one will even remember that the teacher was fired for abusing her power. They'll say she lost control of her classroom and put the other students in danger."

"But that's not what happened!" How was logic failing me all of a sudden? I'd always been the levelheaded one, the one who could cut through the heightened emotions and reach some kind of common ground.

"That's all anyone will care to remember," Quinn replied. "It makes a better story than the truth."

"I should have expected something," I said after a moment. "I saw the way she looked at me last night."

"Last night?" Quinn's voice was suddenly sharp.

"She was there. Outside … y'know," I waved my hand around, rather than say the words. "She was glaring at me, like I was something she'd stepped in. Or like she blamed me."

"But she was in the crowd," he persisted. "Before you got there? Why didn't you tell me that sooner?"

"Why would it matter?" I asked as we turned onto our street. "There were a lot of people standing outside last night. You guys interrogated them all, remember?"

"Not all of them," Quinn murmured. "You're sure it was her?"

I nodded.

We pulled into the driveway, and Quinn turned off the engine. There was a moment where I thought he was going to confide in me—tell me what was *really* going on in Carrow Mill. But as usual, the truth was skipped when gruff ignorance would suffice.

"You have to be better than even they expect you to be. If you can't prove them wrong about who you are, they'll eat you alive."

He opened his door and went into the house, leaving me in the passenger seat. "I don't even know who I am," I said slowly, to absolutely no one.

It took me a while to make it inside. Part of me still didn't trust Quinn. But his advice was sound. It always was. But he still hadn't told us the truth about anything. His allegiance was to his grandmother and the Congress, no matter what advice he gave.

That wasn't enough.

He was in the kitchen looking over a small stack of papers. Were they about me? *I might actually get expelled before Jenna this time.* I picked up the manila folder he'd dropped on the table before I lost my nerve. I walked over to the coffee maker, and the jar of pens and markers next to it. Quinn didn't say anything, but I could feel him watching.

As carefully as possible, I began to draw the Moonset symbol in permanent marker on the file folder. First the circle, then outlining the crescent moon and coloring in the rest. Then the tentacles, one at the top, one at the bottom, and two on either side.

"There's a warlock in Carrow Mill," I said as calmly as I could, even though it felt like some kind of betrayal to confide in Quinn without checking in with the others. Jenna would be furious, of course, and Cole and Bailey could hold a grudge almost as long. "I thought he was stalking us with this symbol, but he's been using it longer than that, hasn't he?"

Quinn's eyes locked on the drawing, but the rest of him was frozen.

"He's been spreading this symbol around town, and somehow, you figured out it was a request. He wanted us brought here, and the Congress thought it made brilliant sense. You thought you could draw him out. So you brought us here, and you've been waiting for him to make his move." I picked up the folder and waved it in his face. "Stop me when I'm wrong."

"You're not wrong," he said. "But I'm not supposed to talk about that with you. My grandparents would have my head." He considered that for a moment. "Maybe literally."

"You've been putting us all in danger ever since we got here. It's not like you're with us every hour of every day— what if something happened? What if he came after us when we were out at the mall that day, or at school?"

"Do you really think we just brought you here and left you unsupervised?" Quinn asked, smirking a little. "Justin, there are more Witchers in the five miles surrounding Carrow Mill than almost anywhere else in the world right now. Not one, but two of the Great Covens have relocated here. My grandmother basically wrote the book on how to deal with warlocks. And I'm no slouch, if I do say so myself."

"That doesn't change the fact that you've been using us. I'm not bait, Quinn. None of us are. And it's bullshit that you all get to decide otherwise."

"I understand why you feel that way," Quinn said carefully.

"Screw that," I shouted. Now that I was really being honest, and saying all the things I'd been thinking for weeks, it was hard to rein it in. "Don't placate me because you think it's what I want to hear. It's bad enough that they treat us like we're *tainted* most of the time. But now they're telling us that we're expendable? That it's cool if a warlock kills us in the line of fire?"

I expected Quinn to tell me to calm down, or to breathe. That's what adults always said, when they wanted you to shut up. "Go on," he said instead.

"God, Jenna's right. You never had any intention of teaching us to defend ourselves, yet you're throwing us into situations that could get us killed. First, you left us in Kentucky when you *knew* a wraith was coming—"

"That was Meghan's call," he interrupted, but I kept talking anyway.

"—and now you brought us here like you don't even give a shit what happens to us."

For as far back as I could remember, I'd been the one to play by the rules. Mal was the model kid—barely got into trouble and way too mature for his age, but I was the one who'd always followed the rules. I cleaned up after Jenna when I had to, but even before that I tried to keep everyone on the same path. The *right* path.

But what was the point? The Congress was never going to see us as anything other than what we were now: five mistakes that were occasionally useful in drawing out the Congress's enemies.

"Was this even the first time?" I asked, somehow suddenly shocked. "Or are the places we end up less random than we thought? Do you make sure we go places where we can stir up your enemies?"

"I'm not the Congress," Quinn said, in the same way he'd have said "I'm not your enemy."

But I believed one as little as I would have believed the other.

"Your grandparents *are* the Congress," I pointed out. Illana Bryer, the war hero of Fallingbrook, and Robert Cooper of Eventide. There hadn't been a more celebrated match in history. "And blood is thicker than water."

Quinn leaned against the countertop. "There *is* a warlock in Carrow Mill," he confirmed. "But you're under a better guard than you seem to think."

I crossed my arms in front of me. "If there are so many Witchers around, how is he still walking around? Why haven't you caught him yet?"

"Because we can't find him, obviously," Quinn said, and the fact that he actually *told me* rather than left it unsaid caught me off guard. My irritation and anger faltered. "Whoever he is, he's flying just enough under the radar that we can't figure out what he's doing or what he wants."

"Except us."

"Except you," he agreed.

"But there's only so many witches in town. It can't be that hard to keep track of what they're all doing."

"You'd think that," Quinn said, "but can you even say with certainty where Jenna is at any given moment? If a witch wants to disappear, they disappear. And people who know they're being watched don't tend to do things that are illegal."

"He killed that man yesterday, didn't he? The Harbinger?"

"Or the Maleficia did," Quinn said. "Sometimes, they're

one in the same, and sometimes one acts independently of the other."

"How is that possible?" I asked. Everything we were taught told us that Maleficia was a force—like the stuff that made a bomb a bomb. "I thought the warlock opened a conduit to the Abyss, and the Maleficia came out and destroyed everything it came into contact with."

"If only it was that easy," Quinn muttered. "Maleficia *wants* to destroy—it's like the base desire for destruction. But how it gets expressed depends on the environment. It can adapt to cause the most damage it can, almost like a cancer."

"So it's not just a source of power?"

He hesitated. "Yes and no. Some people will tell you that magic is a living force—that's why we can't control who gets bound into a coven; because there's something greater at work. But you can't reason with magic. Maleficia is the same—it's corrosive, but not exactly alive. Most of the time, it's a symbiote. It latches onto a host, and it becomes as smart as that person is or isn't."

Most of the time. What was that supposed to mean? He was leaving something out. "But?" I said, prompting him to keep going.

"But that isn't the sum total of what lives in the Abyss. Some people believe that the Abyss is just a cauldron, brewing up dark magic. There is that, but there's also more. But we can only guess at what it's really like. There are stories of creatures . . . *things* that live there. Things like the Princes."

"Hell has Princes?" I sounded as skeptical as Jenna. It wasn't that I was trying to mock him, but Quinn sounded so *serious*. The idea that there was some kind of infernal monarchy was crazy.

He sighed. "Children's stories meant to keep bad kids in line. They say that if you travel down deep enough, you come to the court of the Princes of the Abyss."

"And those are?"

Things in the house had suddenly gotten too quiet. It was like all the clocks had stopped ticking, the wind had died down, and the pipes and floorboards had gone deaf. Even my question was hushed.

"Once upon a time, there was a war between the forces of the Abyss and the forces of Chaos. Demons and Faeries. Only the Faeries aren't like the kind in any Disney movie. They fed on souls and wore the skin of humans like it was an accessory. When the Faeries lost, the Abyss set a price— they would feed it a soul every seven years. If they failed, a Faerie would take its place."

"And these souls become the Princes?"

"No," he said softly. "Every so often, the Fae can't pull themselves away from their pleasures, and they are taken. Drafted, you could say, against their will. And just like the Maleficia taints those who summon it, the Abyss tainted those Fae. Broke them and reshaped them into something different. We call them Abyssal Princes. No one knows how many there are, or what they want, but even one of them is the kind of monster that the world hasn't seen in five or six hundred years, back when magic was plentiful. And Maleficia makes them even more powerful. Because that's what Maleficia is: power and destruction."

"It's a power that Moonset tapped into," I said. "So why isn't it destroying more?"

"Because . . ." Then he stopped. "We're not really sure," Quinn admitted. "If the warlock wanted to just blow a hole in the side of the world, he could. That would make sense. After a while, that's all they want anyway. But this one is different. All his attacks are small. Weak. It's like he's playing with us."

I got the impression that he wasn't supposed to be telling me all this. There was a difference between admitting the truth about the Congress's plans, and then there was admitting the places where the Congress was weak.

A car door slammed outside. Jenna and the others were home, finally.

"I won't ask you not to say anything," Quinn said as he pushed himself off the counter. "But just be careful what you say. You *are* under guard, Justin. Whatever the actual intent was to bring you here, I can promise you that you're safe."

I wanted to believe him. I nodded, let him walk away as I waited at the table for the inevitable crowing that would come with Jenna's arrival.

Safe. From what, I had to wonder. The warlock? Maybe. But was he really the biggest threat to us? What about the Congress? What would they do if it came down to a fight? Would they save us, or would they wait until the warlock was done and then swoop in to save the day?

Their track record spoke almost as loudly as Jenna's did.

NINETEEN

"Now is the time for sacrifice. There is blood in the water. And it isn't ours."

....

Sherrod Daggett
From a speech to his disciples

It wasn't Jenna who came inside, though. Malcolm came in like the head of a parade. Cole was right behind him, and behind *them* were the boys from magic class, Kevin and Luca. It had barely been an hour since I'd seen them, but I was still caught off guard. Unfamiliar people in our *house*. We never invited people back to the house.

Luca. Seeing him and Malcolm in the same room was even more disorienting than seeing him at school. Mrs. Crawford had been right, they had the same *look*. The same eyes, the same hair color, but Luca was much shorter—only a little taller than Cole. My eyes flashed to Mal. "You...he..."

"Yeah, we figured that part out already," he said. He glanced over his shoulder, but I saw the way his eyes skidded over Luca's head. There was a strange pit in my stomach that lightened when I saw the stiff lines of Malcolm's shoulders. Knowing he was tense and uncomfortable made me feel better. Part of me didn't want to admit it, but knowing Mal had blood relatives freaked me out. We were only a family because we had no other options. Mal, who always had one foot out the door anyway, now *had* options. So to find out that the reunion wasn't a thing of instant harmony relaxed me.

"They look like brothers," Cole chimed in, ever helpful. "Even more than we do."

"That's because they're actually related," Kevin said, hands tucked into his jacket. It didn't sound like he was trying to be mean, just stating a fact. Kevin seemed like kind of a dick, but at least he was really polite about it. "Sort of."

"Whatever," Luca said, scuffing his feet. "I don't even know why we're here." He wouldn't actually look at any of us, instead focusing his attention on the decorations sparsely spread around the room, as if they were absolutely more fascinating than any of the people. I eyed him, still mulling over what he'd said to me in the office.

"We wanted to see how you were doing," Kevin said, turning towards me. "Everything got totally out of control in there. Even Maddy felt a little bad about it afterwards."

Maddy felt bad? She hadn't bothered to hide the fact that she didn't like me very much. "Really?"

Kevin's lips quirked. "I said a little," he admitted. "There's a much bigger part that's happy that she basically won the debate and proved you were a danger to the rest of us."

"I thought you were going to deck me for a minute," I admitted.

"I was," he said. "Don't get me wrong, what Mrs. C did was messed up, and Maddy didn't help matters any, but I thought you were going to hurt someone. You were all red-faced and spitting. You looked insane."

"I wasn't insane," I said.

"You looked like it," Kevin said. Luca made a noise of agreement. "And if it came down to defending the crazy guy or the people I've known all my life, well … you know how it was going to end."

That I did.

"Maddy doesn't know we're here," Luca put in quickly. "She'd probably be really pissed if she did."

"I thought she was friends with Jenna," Cole chimed in, hopping up on the kitchen counter.

"Jenna doesn't have friends," I said automatically.

Kevin smirked. "I was going to say the same thing about Maddy."

"None of us have friends," Cole said, pulling one of his knees up and resting his chin on it. Oh great, maudlin Cole. It didn't happen very often, but when it did, Cole was even worse than normal. I glanced at Malcolm, but he was too busy ignoring Luca to pay attention to me.

"We move around a lot," I explained.

"Well, yeah," Kevin responded. "Makes a lot of sense.

It can't be easy to keep the Moonset kids under the radar, right? And now you're here, and ... "

" ... and there's a warlock already here looking for us," I interrupted. Malcolm and Luca both stiffened, and again the resemblance was too strong to miss. "Do they tell you guys anything?"

Kevin shook his head. "Not much more than you, I bet. We get a lot of 'Don't do dark magic' PSAs, though. And every time he attacks, we have a curfew for about a week after. Like after last night and then the drawing in the classroom today, they're not taking any chances."

"Not that it does any good," Luca pointed out. "They can't figure out what he's doing."

"What happened last night?" Mal asked, grabbing an apple out of the bowl.

Kevin shrugged, looking to me.

I sighed. "The guy we saw in the diner? The crazy one? He killed himself last night. They think the warlock might have had something to do with it." There hadn't been any time to talk to Mal and catch him up with what had happened since yesterday. Suddenly, the tension in his shoulders wasn't just about his cousin being in my house.

It was hard enough trying to keep everything straight, but harder still to remember what I'd told him or what I'd told Jenna. I'd become too good at holding things back, and every tiny oversight was a huge drama.

"Don't worry," Cole said, correctly interpreting the sudden shift in tension, "Justin doesn't tell me anything, either. He doesn't tell anyone."

"Cole," Mal said, his voice a warning.

"What? It's true. Everyone lies to us lately."

"That's enough!" Mal snapped.

"How long are you out for?" Kevin asked, trying to steer the conversation back to something less personal.

"A few days." I grabbed one of the apples, too, but instead of devouring it the way Mal was, I tossed it nervously back and forth between my hands. Just to give them something to do. Cole huffed and hopped down off the counter. He crossed the room and headed into the hallway, Luca following after a few moments later.

"He's not a bad kid." Kevin watched me as I watched them. "Luca's got a rough deal. His dad never could cope with what his brother did. I don't think he ever intended to have kids, either. Luca was an accident."

So it wasn't any easier being from the "good" half of the Denton line. Malcolm was watching them, too, but I wondered if he watched for Cole, or for Luca.

"So if you guys are still around in the fall, you should try out for football," Kevin said to Mal. That started a whole conversation about school sports and college teams, and my head couldn't take it anymore. There was aspirin in the cupboard by the microwave, and I shook a couple into my hand and dry swallowed them as Kevin's sports talk got a more energetic tone out of Malcolm than I'd heard in days.

"Who's having the best day ever?" Jenna announced when she swept in a moment later. "Really, though, Justin. A murder threat?" She laughed, and added in a conspiratorial tone, "It's much better if they don't see it coming."

I sunk down onto the kitchen table. Gloating Jenna wasn't helping the pounding in my head. "Get it all out now," I said, dropping my head onto the table's surface. *Cold*, I thought in relief, the wood like a balm against my head.

"What are the Odd Couple doing here?"

I shrugged, but since my head was currently resting against the table, I imagined the effect was wasted. "Don't know."

"So you threaten unholy murder and carnage, and that gets you a visit from the welcome wagon?" Jenna rapped her fingers against the table, knowing full well it would aggravate me. It did. "Maddy really must not be in the running for Miss Congeniality."

"The teacher went psycho and used magic on me."

"I heard," she snorted. "It's not turning out the way she expected, I'm sure. His grandfather is another big deal. They probably should have warned us that this place was preppy central. Everyone's got a relative who was some sort of mystical war hero or Moonset veteran."

Which was something else to worry about. Why now? Why put us in a room with people who had every right to hate us? Moonset had targeted the magical elite, the witches with the most knowledge and political power. "Wait, what do you mean it's not turning out the way she expected?"

Jenna looked surprise. "Baby brother's the victim, haven't you heard?" Her smirk widened into something that would have been a smile on anyone else. Jenna's smiles were few and far between. "She wanted to make you look unstable, and instead, she made you look sympathetic. People are talking about how poor little Justin was taken advantage by someone he was supposed to trust."

"They're saying that?"

She nodded in the direction of Kevin and Mal. "That's what he told his grandfather, at least. Even Maddy mentioned that it wasn't entirely your fault. But then, she's also claiming that you forfeited the debate, so there you go."

Maybe things were looking up. If we weren't the scapegoats that everyone always tried to make us out to be. Even Jenna seemed halfway composed today—and we'd already made it through the first few days of school without her setting something on fire or staging a mutiny.

Luca slunk back into the kitchen, one hand stuffed inside his jacket.

"Where's Cole?" I asked, lifting my head at his approach.

He shrugged, turning until he was facing Kevin. "We should go. I have to be home before my dad comes back," he said softly. "He won't be happy if he knows I was here."

"I told you," Kevin said, sounding like he'd repeated this several times already, "no one's going to find out, okay? Besides, it's not that big of a deal. If he finds out, just tell him we were forced to come by the school."

Luca shifted his weight from one foot to the other. "Whatever," he sighed. "Can we go now?

"We're going," Kevin said, annoyed now. *What was Luca's problem, anyway?* He'd been fine when he left the room with Cole.

Cole, I sighed. "He didn't say anything to piss you off, did he? Cole doesn't always think before he talks. He doesn't mean anything by it."

"I'm still here!" a voice shouts from the other room, his irritation audible.

Jenna sighed, standing from the table. "I'll deal with him. But you should probably get them out of here anyway." She strode from the room, and I could hear muted voices from the front of the house. Then the front door opened and slammed shut. *Cole storming out.* An audible huff. Then the door opened and closed again. *Jenna went after him.* At least there was that. If anyone could wrangle Cole, it was Jenna. It was just that Jenna usually was wrangling him for nefarious purposes like school riots. Cole's exuberance only braked for mischief.

"Yeah, we're going," Kevin said, grinning. "Think about what I said about the team, man," he added to Malcolm.

Mal shrugged easily. "We probably won't be here in the fall, and I'm not much for team sports anyway."

"Yeah, I get that," he responded. "Easier to pick up and move when no one else is relying on you."

"Something like that," Mal deferred.

"Look, I get that it can't be easy for you guys. Being here," Kevin said as the four of us approached the door, Mal and me in the rear. "Especially for you guys. With both of your dads being here and everything. But maybe it's the smart choice. Where better to start over than where it all started in the first place?"

Luca looked startled, maybe at the reminder that he, too, was related to a terrorist. But I was caught up in thinking about our fathers: Mal's and mine. Sherrod and Cyrus had reportedly been the best of friends all their lives. We knew they'd grown up here. But no one had really talked to us about them before.

Well, one person had. The old man at the curio shop. He'd taken one look at me and recognized my father. Maybe there was more of an opportunity here than I'd thought. But Kevin's suggestion also brought up another thought. Why would the warlock want us here, exactly? Why Carrow Mill? Because that was where Moonset had started?

A chill settled in as I wondered. Was he hoping that lightning would strike twice?

TWENTY

"You have to understand. One day, everything was fine. People were recovering and we were trying to heal. The next, we were at war. (Moonset) had mobilized a cult under everyone's noses. They struck at every faction of power that remained, and eliminated anyone that could have challenged them."

....

Adele Roman
Moonset Historian: From a college
lecture series about Moonset

The next morning, the first of my suspension, started with a lot of rampaging downstairs. I think Jenna wore her loudest heels just so the sound they made against the hardwood floors would pierce through any attempts I made at sleeping in.

By the time I finally made my way downstairs, the house was empty except for Quinn. He glared at the coffee maker like it was about to come to life and begin the cyborg apocalypse. "I have to head downtown to take care of some errands. And get some coffee," he added under his breath.

"Coffee sounds good," I said, suddenly perking up at even the *mention* of caffeine.

"Pretty sure the common punishment for getting suspended is grounded. I mean, it's been awhile, and I of course was a model teenager."

"Of course you were," I muttered.

"But if I take you out for coffee, that's almost like a reward."

"I'm just asking to tag along when you go downtown. All I want is some coffee. Supervised coffee, even! It's like a field trip!" I said, suddenly inspired. "Schools have field trips all the time!"

"Fine," he said after a long pause. He threw on a leather jacket and grabbed his keys. "Get your coat."

I looked towards the ceiling and thanked the invisible heavens. Getting out of the house, even if it was only for a few minutes, was like some sort of reprieve. I grabbed my jacket and met him at the car, shivering in the January air. New York was *cold*. Every time I thought I understood just how cold, the weather made a point of showing me something colder. Once we got in the car, Quinn turned on the radio, clicking through the presets until he found a classic rock station.

The ride through town was short. He took the most direct way to the coffee shop—the same route I'd walked only a couple of days ago when I'd met up with Ash. Other than a brief encounter in the hallway yesterday, I hadn't talked to her since that night. I wondered what the story going around school was. Was I the emotionally disturbed jackass who'd picked a fight? Had anyone heard me making threats? The witches all knew what had really happened, but what about the regular kids? I was nervous about what they were saying. The fact that I was nervous even caught me by surprise. When was the last time I'd cared what anyone else thought about us?

By the time Quinn found a parking spot on the street, the car was only fractionally warmer. The only open spot had been equidistant between the coffee and curio shops.

"I've got to run to the bank and then drop something off," Quinn said, cutting the ignition. "Shouldn't take me longer than fifteen minutes. Don't wander off. And holler if anything happens."

"Like what?"

Quinn stared at me impassively. "Just yell if something happens."

I peered across the street, shielding my eyes with my hand. The sun was out and shining off of all the storefront windows, making it almost impossible to see. It took a few minutes for my eyes to adjust and for the traffic to break up so that I could cross the street without getting hit by a car. I was pretty sure that wasn't the kind of "anything" that Quinn was referring to. While I was waiting, I saw the curio shop owner leaving the coffee shop with a cup in hand. *Ethan,* I remembered, more because I could still hear the gruff rasp of his father shouting throughout the store.

I looked between the coffee and curio shops, debating. *His dad talked about Sherrod. He's the only one who has since we came here.* It was like the thoughts were sparks and my brain the tinder—as soon as I started wondering about Sherrod before Moonset, I couldn't shake it. I squirmed in place.

I was in and out of the coffee shop—with a turtle mocha—faster than I think was humanly possible. That still gave me at least ten minutes before Quinn would be back to the car and looking for me. I charged across the street during a lull in traffic, nearly bumping into a minivan, and jogged the half block to my destination.

"Sorry, sorry, give me a minute," the man's voice called out as I opened the door and a chime went off. There was a ladder propped up against one wall near the back of the store, and he was pulling pictures down. I waited until he'd climbed down and moved back to the counter.

"How can I help you?" he asked as he turned, wiping his hands on the legs of his pants.

"Hey...I was in here the other day?"

There was no recognition in the man's eyes. "Oh? See something you liked?"

"Not exactly." This was going to be awkward. "I was in here when your dad..."

"Oh!" The man's eyes suddenly seemed to find mine, like he'd come out of some sort of fugue state. "Of course I remember you. I was thinking about you and your brother just the other day."

"Really?"

He hurried behind the counter, favoring one knee as he moved. Maybe bad legs ran in the family. "Well, I mean I'm sorry my dad went and frightened you boys off, but he's harmless most of the time. Just has his moments, y'know?"

"Well, it's nice that you're still taking care of him," I replied, unsure of what to say in a situation like this.

"Oh, right, right. Can't go turning our backs on our parents," the man said. "It's just unconscionable."

I shifted in place, turning my attention to the things he was pulling off the wall. "Dusting everything? Or just putting different things up?"

"A little of both," the man admitted. "Making some room for a new collection I picked up in an estate sale—the rest we'll try and sell at the flea market. People around here will pay a nice bit of change for antiques."

"Really?"

He nodded. "But that's not why I was thinking of you boys. Well, you remember my dad was rambling on about some boogeyman?"

I nodded, feeling my heart trying to bust its way out of my rib cage. Any minute Quinn was going to throw open the door and lay into me for being here. Any second.

"I found that old book he was talking about," he confided, leaning over the counter. "It's a whole bunch of gibberish, but you can see that name he mentioned right inside the cover."

"Really?" My heartbeat pounded in my ears, and an electric sort of panic was screaming up my spine. *Go now.*

Leave now. You know this isn't going to end well. How could I have been cold earlier? The room was an inferno and I was sweating through my clothes.

He rummaged around on the desk tucked in the corner, finally pulling out a small journal. It was ordinary enough—the kind of journal mass-produced and sold in chain stores. I expected something … more. The kind of book that implied danger by its very design. Or something hauntingly familiar, calling me to it. But it was just a notebook. It could have belonged to anyone.

"See?" He flipped the cover open, turning to a random page. Each one was lined with painstaking rows of chicken scratch. Magic was a language, and most languages had a written equivalent, but written spells were still spells. Great care had to be taken that the words were so evenly divided up that the spell was still readable, but it took some work.

It was like the drawing guides in school when kids first learn how to write their letters. Each line is taken separately, one at a time. Spellbooks did the same. The added bonus was that normal people never realized what, exactly, they held in their hands.

Right in front of me, the curio shop guy was showing me a spellbook filled with what looked like dozens of new spells. I didn't trust myself to hold it, but I stared at the words, translating in my head.

"Crazy looking, right? But I guess I can see how Dad saw something in this book, y'know? It's just a bunch of doodles, but it almost looks like a real language. See? There's spaces between the words." He pointed to a particular page where there were indeed spaces, but I didn't feel like explaining that those weren't separate words, but simply beats between syllables.

"Yeah," I said, only half-convincingly. I forced myself to look away—there was something that looked like a beacon spell—to find your way to something that wasn't there anymore. "That's crazy." I turned away, forcing myself to stare at one of the paintings—one of a woman seated primly on a bench surrounded by a garden exploding into spring.

Sherrod Daggett's spellbook. Just the idea of it was crazy. If the Congress had known something like this existed, they would have snatched it up and destroyed it in a heartbeat. If they knew I had seen it—and hadn't reported it—there was no telling what they'd do. If they found me with it, that might be enough to force their hands. A fatal move to be sure.

He was a traitor—a warlock and a terrorist. All true. Sherrod Daggett was everything the books said and worse. But people who met him—even those who hated him with a passion—still spoke of him with reverence. Like even in Hell, he still knew who was talking behind his back.

But was he evil in high school? Or was he like me? The thought soothed as much as it terrified. I remembered that night in the hotel room on our way to Carrow Mill, telling Jenna with certainty, "We could never be like them."

If it was just a normal grimoire, it wasn't illegal to have. But it was *where* the spellbook came from that was the problem. Just because they wouldn't teach us anything but the most basic magic didn't mean we weren't *allowed* to learn it.

They got to decide what scraps to teach us, because we didn't have any other alternative.

This might be one. Jenna was right when she said we needed to defend ourselves better. Our protection was up to us because there was no guarantee Quinn or anyone else was going to be around.

There was a clatter further on in the building. "Oh Dad," the man muttered. "I'll be right back."

He left, and I glanced at the book. Really stared at it. *Do it. Take it.* My hand trembled. It was the first spell-book I'd ever actually seen—live and in person. The owner didn't have a clue what it was. All I knew was that I had to have the book. It *belonged* to me, or it would have, in a different world.

But this wasn't something the man had out on the shelves—it was his father's. The irony wasn't lost on me. *Just take it.* It was like a growing compulsion in me, something hot and hungry that needed to be satiated.

"Oh Dad, what did you do?" I heard faintly over the sound of a television talking head discussing POWs.

You wouldn't be starving for knowledge anymore. If there's anything bad, you can just get rid of the book. If Sherrod really was bad from the beginning, it'll be obvious. The call to darkness will be there.

Almost before realizing I was doing anything, I was heading for the door. The book slid perfectly into my jacket's inside pocket. I threw a twenty-dollar bill on the counter, and ran out into the cold winter morning and crossed the street, trying to duck down and stay out of sight.

I stayed slunk down in the passenger seat, my eyes glued to the side mirror and the door of the curio shop (which never opened) when Quinn threw open the driver's side door and scared the crap out of me. My head nearly hit the roof.

"You look guilty," he said.

My blood froze in my veins, and I could feel the book burning against my chest. I'd checked my reflection once I'd gotten into the car, but you couldn't even tell it was there.

"No, I don't," I said automatically, speaking almost too fast. Which only made me sound more guilty.

Quinn just looked at me. He tossed a bag over the back of his seat and climbed into the car. "Okay, then."

Whatever weird thing I was on today, he clearly didn't want any part. "Yeah. Okay."

"How about no more caffeine for you? What'd you get, extra shots of espresso?"

The tension drained out of my body. I mustered up a fake smile. "Two."

As we pulled off Main Street, I glanced in the mirror and instantly froze. Meghan Virago was crossing the street, arms linked with Mrs. Crawford. *What were* they *doing together?* I knew Meghan hated us, but was she really friends with the teacher? Or had they bonded over my outburst? They were coming from the same direction Quinn had gone. I couldn't tell for sure, but it looked like they were smiling.

"So how was the bank?" I asked lightly, while my thoughts ran and tried to come up with explanations. I had to keep it together, to show that everything was okay.

"Fine," he said, his words clipped. "Long line."

"Ahh," I said, although I had no idea what I was ahh'ing over. He took the long way back to the house, driving through one residential neighborhood after another. I didn't enjoy the drive much, barely listening to Quinn chatter about small towns—he'd been born and raised in the big city—and how it was a nice change of pace.

Now that I'd actually done it—actually stolen the book— I couldn't believe myself. I wasn't a thief. *You left money*, I reasoned, but it still didn't change the fact. The worst part was that, underneath it all, I felt a rush of satisfaction. For once, I'd been the one to break the rules and get away with it.

"I said, what do you think about a magic lesson today?" Quinn's voice was louder, interrupting my train of thought as we passed yet another church, Saint Anna's, which had a giant steeple poised over the church building.

"What? Seriously?"

"Yeah," Quinn said, leaning back in his seat and resting his head against the back of his seat. "Besides, maybe it'll do you some good to have something new to focus on for a while."

The icy knot in my stomach was only getting stronger. It was like Quinn knew something—like he was just stringing me along and messing with my head. He probably knew everything—the old man in the shop must have called him as soon as I'd left.

You're being crazy. He doesn't know anything. I forced myself to look at him, just a quick glance as I started to shift in my seat. He wasn't paying any attention to me at all, his attention was solely on the road.

It wasn't much longer until we were turning onto our street, and I could see our houses in the distance. "Sounds good," I said, trying to sound more even and relaxed. *Remember, it's okay to be excited.* "I'm always up for learning something new." Apparently, I was also up for a round of grand-theft spellbook.

TWENTY-ONE

"There is no war. There's only the slaughter.
Every time we try to regroup, they push us
even harder than before. There is no opposition.
We have no leaders. They've won before
we could even strike back."

....

Report from the Field
Attributed to Clay Ewell

I was out of the car and walking up into the garage before I panicked. *What would Quinn do if he found the book on me?* There were Witchers coming and going in our house all the time. Any one of them could be going through my things, right?

"I'll be right there," I said to Quinn as he headed inside. I fumbled with the pocket of my coat, walking towards the garbage can in the corner like I needed to throw something away. Since the holiday season was over, Quinn and the other guardians had gone to town one Sunday pulling down all the decorations that had plagued our house. There were so many boxes that they took up the majority of our garage space.

Tucked against the wall next to the garbage, for instance, was one of the giant plastic Santas that had a hole at the bottom to stick the pole with the light bulb attached inside. The hole was so big that Cole could probably have squeezed his way inside the Santa, but all I was wanting to do was find a place to hide the book.

Once the door had closed behind Quinn, I slid the spellbook out of my pocket and into the Santa's foot hole. The black-painted boots on the exterior made it hard to see that there was anything inside. Unless you were looking for it, or for some reason started moving around all the decorations, no one would know what was inside.

I dropped my still half-full coffee in the can and went in the house. "Is this going to be some lame 'show me all the spells you know' thing?" I asked, unusually loud. My heart was still hammering in my chest, and the small smile I was wearing was more at breaking the rules than about the idea of a magic lesson. But no one else needed to know that.

"Relax," Quinn said. "It's not going to be anything super exciting, but it's something you've never done before."

"What are you going through?" I nodded at the papers he was sorting on the table.

"Just some papers for work."

"You work?"

He looked up, annoyed. "Aside from the fact that I don't just crawl out of bed looking this fantastic," he said dryly, "there's more to my job than wiping your noses and setting curfews. Which your sister insists on ignoring, much to my irritation."

"Jenna's never met a rule she didn't like to bend to an inch of its life." I tried not to smirk. There was something else, though. Quinn always did that. Whenever I asked him something, he deflected, either with a quip or a question. "Ever notice you don't like answering questions?" I tried to subtly read the papers, even though they were upside down.

"Why would you think that?" he replied, a maddening smile forming.

"Because half the time you answer with another question."

"What makes you think you deserve to know all my secrets, Justin?"

"Maybe it's the fact that you know all of ours. A little reciprocation goes a long way."

"I doubt I know *all* your secrets," he said, and for one solid heartbeat I thought he knew something. It was like he'd struck some sort of tuner—my whole body thrummed out one solid note of panic. "Just the ones in your file," he finished.

I exhaled. He didn't know anything. I was being paranoid.

"Almost done," he said, straightening the piles.

"So they're important?" I still wasn't able to read anything except one word. *Loose.* I don't know what was loose, or how loose it was.

"Moderately so."

"You never mentioned what it is you do when you're not…wiping our noses and setting curfews."

"You're right," he said, sliding a large rubber band around the thicker pile, and a paper clip over the second. "I didn't."

He headed up to his room—the master bedroom—and this time I followed him. We'd never done more than poked our heads into Quinn's room. It wasn't like we respected his privacy, exactly; it was more like we had a healthy respect for our own necks. Several of the guardians they'd sent us to live with before had very insane notions about privacy, and so much as stepping foot into their bedrooms was nearly a declaration of war.

"C'mon, being a Witcher can't be as boring as you make it out to be. I mean, you don't do anything but hide out in your room or skulk around the house looking for reasons to yell at us."

"You think I skulk?"

I shrugged. "There's definitely a skulking-like quality to what you do."

He frowned at me, but didn't shut his door as he crossed the room. His bedroom was only partly what I expected. The bed and the computer desk were normal, but the big workstation desk looked like someone had pulled it out of a woodshop room. There was a stack of folded laundry on the hope chest at the foot of the bed and a dresser on the far wall, but there wasn't so much as a picture or anything personal anywhere. It was very literally a room where Quinn didn't do anything but work or sleep.

He set the two groups of papers on the desk, then slid open a drawer and pulled out his athame.

"Is that one of the Witcher blades?" People talked about a Witcher athame like it was the Ginsu of magic knives, but no one ever explained exactly why.

"My personal one, yes," he answered. "I've got a couple of extras just in case. You never know when something's going to happen and you're going to need them. First thing they teach you? Always be prepared for the most unlikely situations," Quinn said, gesturing carefully with the knife. "Do you know why most warlocks get caught within a few weeks of their first invocation to the Abyss?"

I shook my head.

"Because in situations like this, power is *literally* a drug. Maleficia enters their system, and anything is possible. They have the kind of power that can destroy anything in their way. That's where the high comes in. It would make a junkie out of anyone."

I thought I understood what he was getting at. "So be ready for anything, because someone on a high is unpredictable."

I expected some sort of acknowledgment or praise, but he just nodded sharply. "I thought I'd show you a little bit about why using an athame is so important." He looked down at the blade, bending it in the light before he looked up at me. "Especially for someone like you."

"Someone like me?" My mood soured. "Because I'm a child of Moonset?"

He looked at me evenly. "Because you wanted to know how to protect yourself, remember?" Hearing my words thrown back at me, not even an hour after they justified my stealing the spellbook, made me shiver.

He might take it easy on you, if you just admit what you did. I *wanted* to trust Quinn, but there were just so many lies and half-truths. He didn't make himself out to be someone who could be trusted. His loyalty was to the Congress, and the only honesty we'd gotten out of him was what we'd found out already for ourselves.

No, I couldn't give up Sherrod's grimoire. At least not until I'd looked through it.

"Using an athame is easy," Quinn continued. "You focus on the spells you're casting, and you draw them one by one. You have to be very precise, though, because of how particular the language is."

But I knew all this already. "And you use a knife because it represents cutting through things," I repeated the lesson I'd learned in sixth grade. "Athames have to be used to call on spellforms, and used to invoke the darkness, too."

Spellforms were primal magic—the most powerful kinds of spells out there. Most magic is about specifics—choosing the target of the spell, saying what is going to happen, and limiting how that power is channeled. That's why pronunciation was so important—saying a word wrong changed the limits of the spell.

Sometimes, especially with us, spells had a little more natural "juice." No matter the limits we put into the spell, the effects were amped up as there was too much power to be channeled into such a tiny effect.

Spellforms were on the opposite end of the spectrum. They were the most basic words, covering powerful concepts that could cause immense destruction. A spellform for *fire* was the literal embodiment of fire—and could cause a sweeping firestorm that would destroy hundreds of acres or cause an explosion that would take out a small town.

In the aftermath of Moonset, the people who were taught spellforms were very strictly monitored. No one I'd ever met had known one, and teaching someone else without permission was a criminal act.

Quinn nodded slowly, and then began whipping the knife in front of him in a complicated pattern. One, two, three spells took shape before I even had them all counted. They hovered in the air, glowing blue symbols. "If this was a fight, what'd I just do? And how would you counteract it?"

The first was a version of *cor*, which was a base form for spells dealing with communication. The tip of it bled to the right, tying into the first stroke of the symbol, *eresh*, which had something to do with spirits, or illusions. "It's some kind of telephone spell? Like holograms?"

"Not quite," Quinn said, passing the knife over the top of the third symbol. "The third ties them all together." I knew this one—*Geonous*, it dealt with travel. Once the spell was complete, the blue turned incandescent, like the filament of a light bulb.

"And that's helpful how?" But I looked a little closer, and then I saw it—saw the way the spell's words worked together, they way they tangled up in each other, a machine of many parts. Astral projection. You could use it to spy on people without anyone knowing—and all the while your body is safe at home. Even worse, the people you spied on would never know.

"Do you—have you been using this on us?" I asked, the momentary thrill of breaking the rules snuffed out by an overwhelming, poisonous terror. *He knew. He knew all along. It was a test and I failed and he brought me back here knowing what I did.* He'd seen the book, he knew it had belonged to Sherrod, and rather than confront me, he was playing it casual. Hiding condemnation underneath a lesson.

I couldn't breathe.

"Relax," Quinn said soothingly, hands raised like a white flag. "It's not like that." There was something in his dark eyes I didn't like, though. Speculation. Awareness. "No one's spying on you. That's not it at all."

"Then what is it?" Panic was making me reckless, speaking and acting without thinking. "Why are you showing this to me?"

"Just because I can't teach you to fight," he said, "doesn't mean I can't show you how to keep yourselves safe."

"How is *spying* going to keep me safe?"

"Haven't you ever heard the expression 'work smarter, not harder?'" Quinn dropped the knife, and the phosphorescent image of the spell started to fade. "You may not know as much as you could, and you definitely don't know everything you should. But like it or not, the five of you are a coven, and you're stronger together."

"What are you talking about?" Quinn wasn't even making sense anymore. How did a spying spell have anything to do with what we did or didn't know?

He raised the athame again, and, quicker this time, slashed three symbols into the air. None were exactly the same, they were reversed, and the middle one was more elevated. *Geonous* was the only one that was still identical, while *cor* was more elaborate this time. But all three featured sharp, block-like lines at their edges, creating something like a border at the edges of the spell.

This isn't another projection spell, I realized. *It's a ward.* Finally, I started to understand. I crept closer to the spell as it shifted from blue to white, trying to memorize the flow of the lines. My hand itched, wanting to trace my own version of the spell and see it flare into existence.

"No one's spying on us," I said slowly. "But they could. Or they're going to start." Quinn wasn't showing me how to spy on someone else; he was trying to show me how to protect ourselves. How to keep other Witchers, or maybe even the Congress, from taking even our small semblances of privacy away from us.

"That's crazy talk," Quinn replied, but his flat tone suggested otherwise. "Either way, this was just a hypothetical situation, and it's moot anyway. You don't have your own athame."

I tried not to smile. "Lucky you have some spares."

"I don't know what you're talking about." He dropped his

hand again and the spell disappeared. "I've got some work to finish, so I'm going to put this away." He hefted the athame. "I can't tell you where the spares are hidden, but stay out of the hope chest in my room, all right?"

My forehead knitted up in confusion. "Why are you telling me all this?"

"I'm not telling you anything. I'm certainly not violating about a dozen specific warnings and straddling a couple of laws concerning treason. Teaching you spells that haven't been approved and arming you with an athame—if something happened, it would be political suicide."

He left the room, and this time I didn't follow. I couldn't get a read on Quinn. Half the time he seemed like he wanted to help, and the rest of the time he seemed like he was only making the situation worse. But if he was telling the truth, and it *was* illegal to be helping us, then why had he done it?

I thought of the spellbook in the garage and felt even worse. *I have to get rid of it,* I decided suddenly. *As soon as he leaves the next time, I'll take it and throw it in a fireplace or a trash can or something.*

The air still felt warm where Quinn's spell hung. I stayed close to it, trying to ward off the chill.

———

I changed my mind. Quinn was such an asshole.

Just before dinner, he came downstairs with a trio of very old, very dusty books. "Tomorrow's project—I want a thousand-word essay on the Coven Wars at the turn of the last century and how that impacted modern coven policies."

"You're kidding." I stared at him, and the books he dropped down onto the table, with nothing short of shock. I sneezed, then kept on sneezing. Homework … while I was home? This was absurd.

"Definitely not kidding," he said.

"I don't even know anything about the Coven Wars," I argued, already knowing how this was going to end.

He flashed a smile. "Lucky for you I've got all these books. They'll tell you everything you need to know."

"What is it you expect me to write about?"

"There's a wealth of information," Quinn said. "Talk about how women weren't allowed to lead a coven for two hundred years. How magical law grew around the coven bond and took it into consideration. How due process was affected by coven-on-coven violence. The Coven Wars are a fascinating part of our history."

I looked at just how much history was dusted over the covers of the books. "Obviously."

Quinn left the room as Jenna appeared, looking from the stack of books to the pasta I was cooking on the stove. "How's it feel to be incarcerated at such a young age?" she asked. "Thinking about getting a prison tat? Maybe a butterfly on your shoulder?"

"You're enjoying this way too much," I said, for about the thousandth time.

"You could put flames around it," she grinned. "Make it look a little more badass."

"I think that's too much detail for a prison tattoo."

Jenna shrugged. "Sure, ruin my fun. What are you cooking?"

"Spaghetti and meat sauce." I pointed to the package of ground beef on the counter.

She squinted. "Shouldn't you have cooked that first? Noodles will be done before it."

I grunted. Cooking was hard. And annoying. But Quinn was the proactive sort, and he kept insisting on teaching us how to cook. Neither Jenna or I had any right to be in the kitchen. I was just lucky that I hadn't caught the pot of water on fire.

"Saw your girlfriend today," Jenna added a few minutes later, when I was stirring the meat waiting for it to cook.

"I don't have a girlfriend," I said automatically.

Jenna shrugged. "Fine. Then I saw the pretentious little rich bitch who's not good enough for my brother today." She didn't miss a beat.

Curiosity won out over playing it cool. Jenna already knew what I thought about Ash. Pretending otherwise was pointless. "Where was that?"

"She went into that shop with all the weird stuff. You know, across from the coffee shop? It has *costume jewelry* hanging in the window." She tinged the word with an appropriate amount of disgust.

"So maybe she was looking for something retro." *Ash had gone to the curio shop? Why?*

I looked away, knowing full well Jenna would be turning

her glare on me any moment. "Besides," I added, "you don't even know her well enough to say that she's got money."

"I know I don't trust her."

"You don't trust anyone," I countered. "That's not saying much."

"That's why I'm never disappointed," she replied in satisfaction. At this point, we both knew the conversation would just start going in circles, with Jenna inevitably claiming victory. I'd point out that she was always disappointed about *something;* she would counter that she was never disappointed in people, unlike the rest of us who kept getting hurt.

After dinner, I took Quinn's homework up to my room and tried to start making headway on tomorrow's project. I wasn't even a chapter in before the technical jargon started, and I had to read each page three times before it started to make sense. Falling asleep was a relief.

I didn't remember dreaming, but I remembered a lot of thrashing. When I woke up, the covers had come off the bed, and I was all tangled in them. And I was abnormally hot—I could feel the dampness of sweat all over my body, soaking into the sheets.

"You remember this?" Jenna leaned against my dresser, barely visible against the dark. I squinted, trying to figure out what she was talking about. Night had started to fall sometime while I slept. The only thing I kept on my dresser was a picture of the five of us that we'd taken the summer before. It had been tucked up into the side of the mirror, but now it was in her hands.

We'd been in a resort town, the kind that was mostly

invisible from fall to spring. Cole had found a shopping cart about two miles from any stores that even *had* shopping carts. Mal and I had picked him up and stuffed him in the basket. For some reason, we all crowded around and took a picture, laughing around Cole's flailing indignation.

It was the closest thing to a vacation we'd ever had. Cole had to go to summer school that year after skipping two straight months of English. The rest of us had walked around on eggshells the whole time—he thought every comment was about him. There could have been a book written about it. *Summer of My Emo Brother.*

"Yeah," I said, my throat feeling raw, like I'd been screaming.

"I tried talking to Cole today," she said.

"How'd that go?" The inside of my mouth tasted funny. Like gravel and something sour.

"Not so good. He blew me off." I saw the flash of pain, but I don't think Jenna realized she'd let it show. She could be heartless and relentless, but she could be hurt just like the rest of us. "Has he talked to you lately?"

"Should he?"

Jenna squirmed. "It's just … he's been acting weird lately. Funny, y'know? But he won't talk to me about it. And he talks about *everything*." She was pointedly quiet for a few seconds before she switched gears. "C'mon," she said, holding out her hand to me. "Something's going on."

I took her hand, confused, as she helped me up and out of bed. "What kind of something?" I followed her out of my room and down the stairs.

"Not sure. But Quinn just got a call and flew out the front door. Told me not to leave the house, that it was life or death."

"Was there another attack?" I was having a hard time pulling myself out of the sleep fog I'd been in. There was something I was missing. *Something with teeth.*

My stomach sank and I didn't know why. Jenna went to the front door, peering out one of the windows on either side of it. The porch lights were on at Mal's house, and at Bailey and Cole's.

Farther down the street, standing in the street itself and positioned perfectly under one of the streetlights, Quinn and the other two guardians were huddled together. Mal's guardian Nick, and Kelly, the sorority guardian.

All three of them were clutching their athames, prepared to use them at a moment's notice. A car turned onto our street and slowed as it approached the trio. Nick opened the driver's door and Meghan stepped out.

"What's she doing here?" I don't know why I was whispering.

Jenna looked at me, an eyebrow raised. "If we knew we wouldn't be spying, would we?"

Nick was getting in the car now, and he closed the door once he was behind the wheel. Then, like nothing had happened, he continued driving, turning towards downtown.

"You feel that?" I looked over at Jenna, and saw the most peculiar look on her face. Like she could almost make something out, but it still didn't make any sense.

"Feel what?"

She shook her head, and focused back on the adults in the street. "Nothing. Never mind. Just one of those 'someone walking over your grave' feelings."

Maybe they know about the book. The thought struck me at all once. Maybe. It looked serious enough.

My coat was still tossed over the railing post at the bottom of the stairs. I grabbed it, figuring I could be outside and back in just a minute or two. Sneak into the garage and see if the book was still there. If it was, I'd grab it and hide it somewhere else.

Two minutes, tops. *If they find it, they might punish one of the others. It's no one's fault but mine. If anyone should take the blame, it should be me.*

"Where are you going?" Jenna's voice rose.

"I'll be right back," I said, opening the door before I could give her a chance to respond. Everything was fine as I first stepped off the landing and down onto the concrete porch. It was when my second leg left the safety of the house that something went wrong.

It was like that moment when you're somewhere between being awake and asleep, but you're still kind of dreaming. Everything is fine until you trip in the dream, and then you're suddenly awake as your body jerks itself in compensation.

That was what this was like, except it was almost exactly opposite. I stepped down onto the porch, but some dream-part of me missed the step. I kept falling, like there were two of me. One on the porch, and one that was hurtling somewhere else.

There were a thousand pairs of hands, and they were all grabbing for me, each pulling me further and further down. There was a glimmer of light so far in the distance I thought I must be imagining it.

The farther they dragged me, the worse the pain. At first it was like every muscle in my body was clenching at the same time. But every few feet, it was like more and more of those muscles were being torn off my body, ripped from where they were supposed to be.

I was there, but I was also on the porch. Jenna had been standing next to me, but now she was towering over me like some sort of wild and terrified Amazon. She hadn't stepped down onto the porch yet. I don't know why I noticed that, but I did.

I tried to say something to calm her, but there was a tunnel between my mouth and my voice. It was like looking at a slide from the bottom up. Such a long way back.

They're here. Now they're here. Finally. Whispers chittering against my skin. Their voices were legion; hot and icy against my skin, fetid and honey against all the things on the inside.

Part of me could still see Jenna, framed by the porch light. I was sinking faster, or she was floating higher. Either way, the distances kept growing.

Her mouth moved, but the words were unintelligible. All I could hear was the Others. *Here now. Finally here. They've come. Everything you've ever clawed for in nightmares. Here for you, crackling open your bones and biting down on your rage. You know what we need.* A thousand voices, all talking in the same tongue. Something that wasn't English, and wasn't the language of magic. Something else.

Blood rushed to my skin, but it bounced down the tunnel all the way down to me before I felt the slap. Jenna's face, blocking my vision. She'd grabbed me. Dragged me back towards the door. Slapped me.

She did it again, and I floated between two worlds. The hands released, though they struggled to regain their grip.

A third and final slap. Long enough for a single moment of clarity. This was not my sister. Jenna's makeup never smeared, her eyes were never that wild. Her skin never flushed like that. Her breathing was never so erratic.

This was not my sister. She would never ask for help.

Jenna had never in her life screamed the way she did. "Quinn!" It was a howl, fearful and breaking apart at the seams. If I kept watching, I was sure I would see things spilling out the side of her as she came undone.

One of the voices crept close, a whisper-burn against my spirit. *You know what we need. We only need one. We only need one. We only need one.*

That was the last thing I remembered, before the hands pulled me back down. It was almost like sleep. Almost exactly opposite.

TWENTY-TWO

"People thought it was a sick joke at first. Moonset hadn't even graduated from college yet. How could they be behind this? The reports said that their magic had been amplified by the Abyss—they'd willingly become warlocks and turned their black arts on the rest of us."

....

Elizabeth Holden-Carmichael (C: Risenleaf)
Personal Interview

There were snatches of conversation as I floated back towards my body. Fearful words, some accusations, and the sound of tears. Whatever had happened, it wasn't pretty.

" … fixing … "

" … never so quick … "

" … damnit, tell me … "

"He's awake."

Everything was blurry. My eyes burned at the harsh light. There was a bulb hanging from the open ceiling, the long chain swaying back and forth. Everything smelled musty and sour.

Basement. This was our basement. Why had they taken me down here?

Jenna's face swallowed my vision. She'd wiped off her makeup and tied her hair back. Then she was pulling away, and Quinn was there, looking concerned. Standing on the stairs, looking over his shoulder, Meghan tapped away on her computer.

"Can you talk?" Quinn crouched down on his haunches, watching me.

Meghan looked up "He wasn't in a coma, Quinn. Of course he can talk."

"He had some sort of seizure," Jenna snapped.

I had?

My throat was on fire, like something had reached inside and left huge gouges on its way back out. "Why the basement?" Even my voice sounded burned out.

"Best place for you," Quinn said, stepping back. "Closest to the warding spells." He looked over his shoulder, "Shouldn't you be hovering over my grandmother, Meghan? There's no one's ass to kiss down here."

I tried to sit up, but there was a problem. I could feel all my limbs, but I wasn't having much luck moving them. My head wouldn't even lift off the pillow. The next thing I knew, there were footsteps coming down the stairs. Even though

I couldn't see who it was that descended, I saw the way the new person's arrival stiffened Quinn's spine and caused Meghan to suck in a nervous breath. It had to be Illana.

"How is he?" Illana asked.

"The boy is stable," Meghan said crisply. "He doesn't seem to have a concussion, and there aren't any lingering side effects from his episode. Psychological deviations have yet to be determined."

"Deviations?" Jenna said, making it sound like something vulgar. "You're the last person to talk about being deviated."

I could hear it in her voice—she was getting close to losing it. I tried to force my arms to move again, to prop me up. I could barely twitch on command.

"Relax, young one," Illana murmured, sweeping down next to me. She dabbed a towel against my forehead. "The darkness can act like a paralytic."

"What?"

"She means it can paralyze you," Quinn said. "Like getting hit with a taser. So don't panic."

"Someone ... used Maleficia?"

"Yes," Meghan said, her voice heavy and dramatic. "A warlock right under our noses. *Quelle surprise.*"

"You're not helping," Quinn said under his breath.

"Meghan." Quinn's grandmother called out her name and waited. The room grew silent as everyone waited to see what she'd say. "Next time let's try for an evaluation that is actually comprehensive. The boy can't move. I'd qualify that as a side effect."

"Yes, Mrs. Bryer."

I opened my eyes to see Meghan hovering on the stairs, her eyes wide. She kept doing some sort of twitch, like she couldn't decide if she was going up the stairs or coming down them.

"That will be all," Illana said coolly. A moment later, the girl vanished up the stairway. "Honestly," the older woman exhaled.

I laughed weakly. "She's *that girl.*"

"What girl?" Quinn asked. Even Illana was looking down at me with curiosity. Only Jenna knew what I meant. We shared a private grin.

"The girl whose father has to make a phone call to get her into college," Jenna explained. "Never quite measures up, and has to kiss ass and beg favors to get ahead."

"Meghan was top of her class," Illana chided, although she did so absently, proving how little she cared about the girl.

"Meghan was *second,*" Quinn corrected smugly. He came down quite clearly on the "Meghan is a raving beyotch" side of the argument.

"Yes, yes," Illana murmured. "We all know you were precocious. Don't gloat; it's a sign of poor breeding. Now then. Justin? What do you remember?"

Even blinking my eyes felt like it was some sort of process. "There were voices," I rasped.

"Yes," Illana drawled, sounding like she was humoring me and nothing more. "I'm sure there were."

"They said, 'They're here.'" I looked to Quinn, who grimaced but didn't immediately reply. "What's here? Is something coming?"

"You're here, Justin," he said, his tone growing softer. "The five children of Moonset."

"Do you remember anything else?" Quinn asked, staring down at me.

"They were talking to someone," I said slowly, thinking back to the voices and the cold that had slipped inside me. Just remembering it was enough to make me start shivering again. "It was a conversation."

"Did you get a name?" Quinn pushed. "Hear his voice? Anything?"

"Hey, lay off him. He's not——" Jenna said, before cutting off abruptly. "Did you *let* this happen? Did you know something was going to happen to Justin?"

"Oh, do be serious," Illana muttered with irritation. "How would Quinn have known that Justin would leave the house? Don't be foolish. He thought the two of you smarter than you obviously were."

"Why did you leave, Justin?" Quinn asked, leaning in. "I told Jenna you needed to stay inside. This is exactly the kind of thing we've been trying to protect you from."

"Great job there," Jenna said. "A rousing success."

We only need one. "I thought the warlock wanted us here?"

"He does." Quinn narrowed his eyes. "Why?"

Because they don't need all of us. I looked over his shoulder, at the woman who'd moved us here like a bold chess move. I couldn't speak freely in front of Illana. Even if I *really* trusted Quinn, I still didn't trust his grandmother. She looked like she could garrote any one of us and not lose a night's sleep over it.

"Because I'm still alive. I thought you said Maleficia

liked to destroy things." I looked down at my body. "It looks like I'm still in one piece."

Quinn shifted, a guilty look in his eyes. "That's because—"

"Quinn!" I couldn't see Illana anymore, but the whip crack demand in her voice left no doubt. She didn't want him answering.

"The warlock tried to kill him tonight," Quinn said, getting heated. "They need to know."

"I'm not so certain that they did," Illana replied. "It's entirely possible that they wanted something else from him."

I couldn't feel a lot, but there was a sudden pressure on my leg. Right by where Jenna was standing. "I don't like what you're implying about my brother," she said tightly.

Implying? It took my brain a second to put things in perspective. What else would a warlock want from me? *Recruitment. Moonset 2.0. A new generation of darkness.* But had Illana implied it? Or was Jenna jumping ahead like she always did, reading people too well and determining the undercurrent?

Illana huffed out a breath. "Relax, child. It isn't like this is a formal accusation."

"Then there's no reason to continue keeping secrets from them," Quinn announced. "If you're convinced they're not part of the problem, then they need to know."

I heard a sigh, and then caught a glimpse of Illana and her flowing skirt heading for the stairs. "Then do as you think is best, Quinn," she said. "I'm going to look in on the other children. I dare to hope they are better mannered."

"Everyone's okay?" I asked, my voice still a groan. Quinn nodded.

Tingles started running up my hands. Just little bursts, running down my fingers, then up the wrist, and then again at the elbow. Everything in between was still numb and senseless.

Once Illana was gone, the front door slamming ominously behind her, Quinn started helping me back upstairs. Except when he tried to sit me up, my body was still foreign and wasted. *I can still feel shame at least,* as the rash of heat crept up my body. My face was about a thousand degrees.

Quinn had to carry me up the stairs, and even though he tried to make light of the situation, no one laughed. I kept my eyes closed, not wanting to see either of their looks of pity. I was supposed to take care of *them.* Not the other way around.

He set me down on the living room couch. Jenna hovered at the edge of the room. I looked around Quinn and listened. "Are we the only ones here?"

He looked curious, but nodded.

I settled my hands into my lap. I still couldn't bend my fingers properly, but at least I could move my arms around. "Is anyone listening?"

Quinn stared at me for a moment, chewing on his lower lip.

"What's going on, Justin?"

"One second, Jenna," Quinn said. He pulled the athame out of a holster that I hadn't noticed before, tucked against the side of his jeans. As quickly as he had earlier, he slashed at the air. But this time, it wasn't the simple astral ward he'd showed me. It was spell after spell, almost a dozen of them. He waited until the blue fire burned white before turning back to me.

"'We only need one,'" I said shakily. "You wanted to know what the Harbinger said to me that night."

"Justin!" Jenna's alarm was more shocked than acerbic, which only proved how traumatized she'd been tonight.

"We have to tell someone," I said, slumping down in my seat. "And we need answers."

"And you think *he's* going to give them?"

I would have nodded, but I wasn't sure I would be able to lift my head back up if it dropped. "Check his wards. He's not making this conversation private for his health." I didn't have to see the symbols burning in the air to know what they were. I thought I had some understanding of what drove Quinn now. If we could help him stop the warlock, he might not break faith with the Congress, but he would skirt the line as much as possible.

"Why do you think the warlock doesn't want you here?" Quinn asked. "Downstairs, you sounded confused."

"Not the warlock," I said, "something else. There weren't just two voices I heard. There were a *lot*. I knew they were talking to someone, but he didn't say anything back. It wasn't a conversation."

Jenna's eyes widened. "They were instructions."

I would have nodded if I could. "They've kept saying, 'They only need one.' One of us. One of Moonset's children." I turned my head as much as I could and looked at Quinn. "Why only one? Everyone knows we're a package deal. We can't be split up. It doesn't make any sense."

The curse that was bound up between all of us meant we couldn't be ripped away from one another, but the voices sounded like that was exactly what they wanted. *It can't be that easy. If it was, all we would have to do is wait, and the curse would eliminate the warlock and whoever was pulling his strings.*

"The Coven bond protects you," Quinn said slowly, "but that protection comes with a cost."

Jenna crossed her arms in front of her. "What kind of cost?"

He held up one finger. "It's easier for the Abyss to gain a foothold into a solitary witch because there's only one mind to contend with." He then held up both hands, and linked his fingers together. "A coven, on the other hand, has a bond that links them. It's harder to infect a Coven witch, because a group is stronger than just one."

Jenna and I looked at each other.

"But there are weaknesses, too," he continued. "If the Abyss can single out just one witch, and overcome him even despite the Coven bond, it gains an advantage in taking the rest of the Coven. With each member it claims, that control gets stronger until the Coven succumbs entirely."

"So you think that's what happened tonight? The warlock sent some Maleficia out to try and take control of one of us?" Jenna asked.

"It would certainly fit," he said. "But we still don't know what, exactly, the warlock wants. The Congress hoped that bringing you here would at least make that much clear. If we knew what he wanted, we could plan to stop him. But ever since you arrived, he's been erratic. Confused. We think the Maleficia may have broken him. And now it seeks a new host."

"One of us," I whispered.

"*All* of us," Jenna clarified.

I meant to ask more, to find out more about what the Congress had in store for us, but I could barely keep my eyes open.

"Sleep," Quinn said. "We'll wait, and figure this out in the morning."

———————

Only there wasn't anything to figure out in the morning. In fact, the rest of my suspension was a blur of books and boredom. Quinn warned me that I'd be sore for a day or two, lethargic and worn down because of the Maleficia attack. But he still expected his stupid essays.

Last night's attack led to some changes, one of which was that while the other four were still allowed to go to school (there'd been some debate on whether or not it was safe), they had to arrive and leave together. In addition, all of us had to be home and indoors before nightfall, when the Maleficia was believed to be strongest. In the event of another attack, the Witchers wanted to make sure we were as protected as well as possible.

Which meant that my day was filled with constant inter-ruptions as groups of Witchers in twos and threes walked through the house, examining weak points and bolstering the house wards. Maleficia wasn't supposed to be able to cross a house's threshold, but they didn't want to take any chances.

I stayed on the couch, because half the time I could barely keep my eyes open and I didn't think sleeping at the kitchen table would end well. Gravity was a bitch, and the floors were hardwood.

I finished the first paper about the Coven Wars by the skin of my teeth, but as soon as I emailed the document to him, he came downstairs with another stack of books and my next assignment. If possible, these books were even dustier than the first ones. "I want you to write a report on how a warlock is brought to trial. How is a charge of invoking the black arts proven? Talk about the trial, the investigations, and everything up until a guilty verdict. And then you can talk about how the process has changed in the last twenty years."

I was waiting for a word count, but Quinn didn't say anything further. "How long?" I'd max out on a thousand words before even covering half of what he was asking for.

"As long as it takes," he said. "Be succinct. You should be able to wrap it up in … five or six thousand words."

Quinn wanted the Never-ending Paper. Five thousand words was huge—that would take me at least a month! But I was too drained to argue. But surprisingly, the books he'd given me weren't nearly as dry as the ones for the first assignment. Maybe the writing style was more modern, or maybe it was because the subject matter hit closer to home.

Coven trials were cruel, devastating processes that always ended badly. In comparison, the Salem witch trials and the witch hysteria that gripped the world were passive, calm affairs.

Now trials were public affairs, open to any witch who wished to attend. An emphasis was placed on "innocent until proven guilty" and other modern conceits—with one main exception. Moonset, the book explained, had been tried "in absentia" and thus their sentence had been carried out almost immediately upon capture.

It made sense, though. If there had been a trial, it would have been a circus. Sherrod Daggett was charismatic and enticing. Putting him on the stand would have only done harm by giving him yet another platform.

The last day of my suspension, I felt a little better. I only slept about half of the day, and while I was still tired, I wasn't as bone-weary as I'd been the day before. I worked on the paper at the kitchen table, spreading the research out.

Tucked in the middle of Quinn's stack of books, I found one book that wasn't dusty and unused. It was a copy of *Moonset: A Dark Legacy*—the definitive encyclopedia of the lives of our parents, from beginning to execution. It was full of personal letters, interviews, and trial transcripts that covered every aspect of their lives.

All of us had read the book cover to cover. Well, all except Bailey, I think. Jenna, Mal, and I had read it when we were still in middle school, sneaking copies out of our guardians' houses. We wanted to know more about who our parents had been. As soon as we were done, we all wished we'd never read it.

"How goes the slave labor?" Jenna asked as she came

inside, dropping her school bag on the papers filled with notes I had spread all over the kitchen table.

"Not as bad as I thought." I stretched, using the motion to shove her bag forward, away from my things. Yawning, I pulled the loose sheets back into a pile and stuck it next to the laptop I was working on. "How was school?"

"Monotonous. Until further notice—meaning until they hire a new sucker to take over the magic class—we're all reading biographies of important historical witches. What's the point of having magic if you can't ever *use* it?" *Sherrod's spellbook was still in the garage.* I couldn't get it now, not with all the Witchers sniffing around the house. And I certainly couldn't trust Jenna to take care of it. She'd take it for herself and abuse the hell out of everything she learned. I had to get rid of it somehow. The Maleficia attack hadn't happened until I brought the book home. I needed to get rid of it.

But what if there's something useful in there? What if you could use Sherrod's magic for good? Wouldn't it be worth it?

I shook my head, trying to shake the thoughts free. That was what had gotten me into this mess in the first place. Second guessing myself, and *wanting* to believe that there was something that our legacy could do to redeem itself.

"Justin? You okay?" Jenna had been more concerned lately, ever since the attack. Concern for others wasn't a good look on her.

"I wish people would stop asking me that," I said in annoyance. The sooner Jenna stopped acting like I was a fragile flower, the better. "Where are the others, anyway?"

"Mal went to the gym. Cole and Bailey are hanging out with the runt of the litter."

"Who?"

She rolled her eyes and huffed. "Luca. You realize it loses the humor when I have to keep explaining things to you."

"How was I supposed to know he's the runt of the litter. That's not even accurate. There's no litter!"

"You must be feeling better. You're back to being tedious."

I yawned. The words on the computer screen were starting to blur. I was halfway through a section talking about how Covens were charged as a single entity. If one Coven member was believed to be a warlock, they were all guilty of his crimes.

Did that happen with Moonset? Were some of them just caught up in Sherrod's crimes? The Moonset biography didn't seem to think so. It made a point of singling out all six of the members and breaking down each of their crimes.

"Have fun with that," Jenna announced. "It's back to school for you tomorrow. Who wants to bet the science wing blows up before noon?"

TWENTY-THREE

"The tide turned when two of the remaining 'Great Covens' aligned and commandeered control of the resistance. Illana Bryer, a new grandmother, transformed into the most capable general any of the Covens had ever seen. Within a month, she'd beaten back Moonset on three separate fronts, and given the resistance the momentum it desperately needed."

Moonset: A Dark Legacy

The science wing didn't blow up. Neither did the main hallway, the gymnasium, or the auditorium. Everything was actually normal my first day back. The only change was that my last period was now a study hall spent in the library, since I couldn't be trusted around the other witch kids. Quinn told me to keep working on his research paper, that for now it was the best use of my time.

I was so busy trying to catch up on what I'd missed and preparing for midterms that I barely got to talk to anyone all day. I only caught sight of Ash once in the halls, but the bell rang before I could track her down.

The weekend passed by so slowly I thought for a minute that time was going backwards. It wasn't until Monday that our house had quieted down enough to sneak the spellbook out in the morning, tucking it into my book bag.

In lieu of any better ideas, I hid it in a locker at school. I asked for a hall pass to use the restroom, that way the halls would be mostly empty when I hid it. Only about seven hundred kids attended the high school, but there were enough lockers to support twice that. All the unused lockers had locks on them, but lucky for me that was one of the few spells I knew.

The unlocking spell only worked on certain locks— specifically the kind that kept school lockers closed. Each of the lockers in the school was numbered. Locker 666 would have been too obvious—that would have been Jenna's choice for sure. I chose 999 instead, hiding the book in the bottom corner of the locker, and replacing the lock when I was done. With the book hidden, I felt like I could breathe again.

On some level, I think all of us were waiting for the other shoe to drop—for the warlock to make his next move. Only he didn't. For a week, Carrow Mill was completely normal.

"You've been avoiding me," Ash said, appearing at my locker before the first bell on Friday.

"Not avoiding. Drowning. Missing most of last week totally threw me off." I closed my locker door, and by unspoken agreement we started walking towards the stairs.

"Well, that's what happens when you get suspended," she said lightly.

"Maybe I'm just a rebel."

Ash laughed. "Mr. French Vanilla is suddenly feeling rebellious?"

"Hey, I ordered a turtle mocha all on my own."

Her eyes widened, and she fanned herself. "Stop, please. We're in public. You'll embarrass me."

A week's worth of waiting on the warlock's next move had me feeling stir-crazy and reckless all at once. "Do you like movies? Like, watching movies? Maybe, I mean, tonight? With me?" *Oh God, what is happening to me?* My mouth couldn't trip over the words fast enough. I took a breath. *She's smiling, that's a good sign, right? Or maybe she's going to laugh?* "I mean, would you want to go to the movies with me? Sometime?"

She was still smiling. "Like a date?" As if she were suddenly the coy ingénue. "Yeah, that would be okay. You could use a little spice in your life, doll face."

"Doll face?" She shrugged in apology. "Does that mean I can call you a moll?"

Her eyebrows rose, and she half shrugged. "Hope you

like scary movies," she said with a wink. She turned back the way we'd come, and headed back down the hall. "They're my favorite," she called back.

I walked around in a stupor after that, unable to wipe the smile off my face.

"What's with you?" Mal asked in Economics.

"I've got a date," I said, unable to hide the smug tone in my voice.

"About time."

I grabbed my Econ book out of my bag. I was actually caught up in this class, which was something of a relief. "With Ash," I added, as if that needed clarification.

"I figured," Mal said, his tone dry. "Where are you taking her? I assume she's driving?"

"We hadn't talked about that," I said. I didn't have my license, so that meant I'd have to ask for a ride. I turned around and faced Mal, giving him my best look of desperation. "We're going to the movies tonight. Something scary, she said."

Mal threw back his head and laughed. "That's perfect."

Uh oh. "Why is that perfect?"

He shook his head, and before I could press him further, class started. I spent the entire class trying to figure out what he meant by "that's perfect." What did he know that I didn't? But no matter how many times I tried to turn and catch his eye or how many times I wrote on the back of my notebook, he ignored me.

Forty minutes later, when class was finally over, I turned around to finish interrogating Malcolm, only to find his seat empty and Mal halfway to the door. I struggled to shove everything back into my bag and chased after him.

Malcolm and Jenna were congregated around her locker, speaking in low tones. *Since when do they get along?* Somehow, I was getting screwed over. I just didn't know how yet. What did Mal have in store? And why was he punishing me? What did I ever do to him?

Bailey came running up at the same time that I approached them. "Are you serious?"

"Someone needs to tell me what's going on," I said. "This is getting annoying. How does me taking Ash to a movie have anything to do with the rest of you? No offense or anything."

Jenna and Mal shared a look, and I wanted to smack the both of them. *Stop collaborating. That is not how this is supposed to work. You're supposed to be at each other's throats!* Jenna gestured for Mal to explain, which he did.

"Bailey has this group date thing she wants to go on. The adults said it was fine as long as one of us goes along to keep an eye on her. They don't want any of us out alone, but things have been quiet so they're willing to allow us a little freedom. Since you're going to the movies, too..." Mal trailed off.

"Wait, that means I can go?" Bailey squealed, then jumped up and down and grabbed Mal around the waist, squeezing him.

"I didn't agree—" Before I could finish, Bailey released Malcolm and then grabbed me, too, hugging the daylights out of me.

"Oof! We don't even know that we're seeing the same

movie," I sighed, already accepting defeat. Too much information was being processed at once. "And wait, group date?"

"It's not a date," Bailey said quickly. "It's just a bunch of the girls on the freshman cheer squad. Mal keeps calling it a date because there's going to be a few boys there."

I crossed my arms. "How *many* boys?"

Jenna slid her arm around Bailey's shoulder. "Just a couple of guys. It's nothing to freak out about."

"Normally, I'd say Bailey's too young to date," Mal said with a grin, "but I'm not the chaperone. So I'll leave it all up to Justin."

"Please, Justin?" Bailey grabbed at my sleeve. She did puppy dog eyes and everything. "I promise, it's just a movie. You don't want people to think I'm a freak because I'm never allowed to hang out with them, do you?"

"You can still go out on your date," Jenna added in a sweet tone. "I'm sure Ash won't mind."

The three of them had teamed up against me. How was this even fair? "What were you planning to see?"

Bailey's smile could have powered all of Carrow Mill. "*Santa Claws 2—Bloody Christmas*. It's a sequel to *Santa Claws*—you know, the one where Santa gets possessed by the demons…"

"Yeah," I said, holding up my hand in the hopes of stopping her. "I remember. You really want to go see that? Wouldn't you rather go see something…I dunno, a little more appropriate?"

Bailey went from excited to frosty in an instant. "What's

that supposed to mean?" she asked. "You think I should go watch some stupid kiddie movie? I'm fifteen, Justin. God!"

She stormed off, and Mal and Jenna both looked at me with something like glee. "You really stepped in it that time," Mal offered.

"Shut up," I glowered, walking away from the pair of them. Date-ruiners. That's what they were. Awful, selfish, date-ruiners.

———————

When I went over to Malcolm's house later that evening, Cole was perched on the front steps. His hair was down in his eyes, and he looked like he'd worked himself up to an intense brood. *This could last for hours.* Cole didn't get into bad moods often, but when he did, it was always a struggle for the rest of us.

"Hey buddy, how's it going?" I sat down next to him.

Cole snorted, looking at me from underneath his fringe. "Like you care. All you care about is Ash now."

Okay, wow. "That's not true. C'mon, you know me better than that."

"I thought I did," he muttered. "All you care about is going out with her tonight."

"That's not *all* I care about." How was I supposed to fix this before Cole went haywire and started goth-ing it up again? "Why don't you come with us tonight? Bailey's going with a group of friends. We could make a thing of it."

Another snort. "Don't worry, I've made actual friends here. You don't have to pity me."

"I don't pity you," I said slowly. "Where is all this coming from? This isn't you, Cole."

"How would you know?"

"Okay," I said, trying another tactic. "Things have been weird since we got here. I get it. It hasn't been like any of the other times. But that doesn't mean I'm going anywhere." I nudged his side. "You're kind of stuck with us. We're a package deal, remember."

He leapt to his feet and stomped away without another word.

"Look at my babies, all grown up," Mal said with a mock sniffle as we pulled up in front of the theater. It was at the same outdoor mall we'd gone to our first week in town, in the next city over from Carrow Mill. I let Bailey take the front seat, allowing me to lounge in the back and worry. *What if I keep talking stupid? What if she thinks I'm boring and that's why I wanted to go to a movie. What if she decides I'm lame?*

I'd been fine up until this point with Ash. She was strange and bizarre and utterly fascinating, but I'd always thought I liked that. But now, ever since I'd used the D-word, it was like all I could do was panic. I second-guessed every conversation we'd ever had, overanalyzed every laugh and smile. She was friends with Maddy, and Maddy disliked me for obvious reasons. What if that rubbed off on her?

I wiped my palms on my jeans for about the thousandth time, and swallowed my gum. *What if my breath is awful?* I pulled the pack of gum out of my pocket and slid another stick in my mouth.

"Is Cole going to be all right?" Bailey asked from the front.

"He's going to be fine," Mal assured her. "You know how he gets."

"He hasn't had much luck making friends," she said, looking down at her hands. "I mean, Luca's been cool, but I don't think people here get Cole's sense of humor."

"He just takes a little bit to warm up to," I said.

"Maybe," she said. "But everyone's been so busy, so he probably feels like you guys are all moving on, too."

"No one's going anywhere," Mal insisted. "We've just been busy. And things have been a little crazy. They'll settle down soon."

"I hope so." Bailey glanced back at me. "You can't walk in with me."

Mal reached back and grabbed my hand up in his. "But we want to introduce ourselves to your young gentleman."

I snatched my hand back, laughing. "Speak for yourself. Go be someone else's gay parent."

"Just be careful, okay? Weird stuff's been going on and all," Mal said. We still hadn't talked to Cole or Bailey about what was going on. They only knew what we'd told them on the first week.

"We'll be fine." Part of the agreement with Quinn had been about an escort. Not just me being there to escort

Bailey, but a Witcher escort. There were supposed to be two of them somewhere in the theater, just in case something happened.

We got out of the car and climbed up onto the sidewalk. It was only six, but the sun had already set. Luckily, the theater believed in a hefty light bill, because there were streetlights and blazing spotlights everywhere.

The window rolled down. "You have protection, just in case?" Mal called out, peeking his head out the window.

Bailey looked no more mortified than I did. But only barely.

She saw her friends and ran off, and I hovered near the doors for a few minutes, wishing I'd been smart enough to pick a better spot to wait at. But I didn't have to wait long.

"Hey there, hot stuff. Don't you look nice?" Ash appeared at my side, wrapped up in a black coat. Her hair was crimped and curled tonight, and the lights brought out all its different shades of red.

"Oh," I said, looking down at myself. "Thanks. I mean, it was nothing." Nothing for me at least. I'd made Mal pick me out something to wear, which he insisted was offensive and playing into stereotypes. But he did it, criticizing my taste as he went along.

"You had Malcolm dress you, didn't you?"

I laughed. "That obvious?"

She shrugged. "It's a gift. I admit I have a keen awareness when a boy suddenly develops a radical shift in style." She linked her arm with mine and started pulling me towards the theater doors. "Plus, I might have texted him while you were, and this is a direct quote, 'throwing the biggest fit he's ever seen,' about ironing your shirt."

I…he…oh. Malcolm was so dead! "I'm afraid I'm going to have to ask you to delete his number," I managed. "Especially since I'm going to break his thumbs to make sure this doesn't happen again."

"Oh, it's all in good fun," Ash said. "Now open the door for me like a gentleman." I did so, and she dipped her head as she swept past me. "Thank you, kind sir."

The whole "Mal texting" scenario had me distracted, and I nearly walked straight into Santa Claus. "What the—"

Ash returned to my side, slipping her gloved hand into mine. "Wicked, isn't it?" she said in a breathless, excited voice.

"Wicked," I agreed. This Santa was no ordinary Christmas elf. It was a life-sized mannequin, dressed up like one of the demonic Santas in the movie we were about to go see.

"I love when theaters do the cool promo stuff like this," Ash said. "They've got Santas all over the place." She tapped one—boop!—right on the nose.

I looked around the lobby. "This movie is really that big?"

"Of course. Christmastime plus horror? Every kid at school has probably gone to see this movie twice. The holidays make us all want to engage in a little patricide, don't you think?"

"Wouldn't know," I said absently.

"Oh, shit, I forgot," Ash said, ducking her head down. "Sorry," she said quietly, squeezing my hand. Neither one of us said anything for a long moment, and the silence hung between us even in the noisy theater lobby. I didn't know what to say to hijack the conversation away from my parents, and the dead elephant in the room.

We passed another pair of Santas on our way to the box office. I paid for our tickets, and we skipped the insane lines at the concession stand to head directly into our theater. It had been awhile since I'd been to a megaplex—the downside to small-town living was that the movie theaters usually only had one screen.

"Hold up," I said, trying to pretend my brain hadn't skipped on account of Moonset. *Ash didn't mean anything by it,* I told myself. "I'm not supposed to walk in with her," I said, nodding to Bailey and her friends, who were still in line for the concessions.

"It's really sweet that you look out for her," Ash said, glancing up at me for only a moment before she looked away. She pulled a pink lip balm pot out of her purse, unscrewed the cap, and ran her ring finger over the surface of the balm before transferring it to her lips. It was enough of a distraction that I forgot about my parents entirely.

"Look," I said, trying to ease some of the sudden awkwardness between us. "It's not a big deal. People slip up about my parents all the time. Don't worry about it. You don't have to walk on eggshells around me."

"Yeah, but it's tactless," Ash said. She slipped her hand out of mine, the sudden cold startling me. "Guess I'm just a little nervous."

"You, nervous?" I laughed. "I doubt it."

"I like you, Justin," she said quietly. "Maybe at first it was just a game, but you're sweet."

I didn't know what to say to that, so I didn't say anything. We waited near one of the benches until Bailey and her group of freshmen sauntered past, barely looking at us. I noticed Luca in the group. "I didn't know he was a freshman," I said to Ash.

"He's not," she said, watching the group thoughtfully. "But Maddy's cousin is, and he basically chauffeurs the both of them around whenever they want. Sara's a lot nicer about it than Maddy is, though."

"So he's just like ... on call all the time? That kind of sucks."

"He doesn't seem to mind," Ash said absently, like she'd never given it much thought. "You ready?"

I nodded. We headed into the theater and waited near the door, until our eyes adjusted to the change in lighting. The previews had already started. "Come on," Ash said, grabbing my arm and dragging me up the stairs. She chose seats a few rows up from Bailey's group, for which I was eternally grateful. I looked them over as we passed, Bailey making every effort to act like she didn't know me. There were only a couple of guys, and Luca on the end. I nodded to him as we passed.

"So, since we're chaperoning, how much trouble are we allowed to get into?" Ash pulled off her jacket, and set it on the seat next to her. The gloves she pulled off a finger at a time.

"Yeah, you're not exactly chaperone material, I'm afraid."

She gasped. "Are you telling me I'm a bad influence?"

"I'd give you examples, but you know I'm not supposed

to talk about your criminal charges until the jury comes back with a verdict."

"Touché, Mr. Daggett," she laughed, grabbing my hand again. The movie started soon after that, and I was quickly caught up in holiday cheer and dismemberment. The premise was fairly simple: evil Santa. It wasn't highbrow by any means. About halfway through, just as the heroine and her love interest were finally getting close for the first time, I turned to see Ash watching me, not the movie.

"What?" I said, dropping my voice so it wouldn't carry. "Is there something on my face?"

"You're not anything like I thought you'd be," she said, her tongue darting out to lick her lips.

"Fi-first impressions aren't what they used to be," I said, transfixed. I wasn't sweating now, but my skin was flushed. Hot. I couldn't stop staring at her lips, and wondering what her lip balm tasted like.

"Definitely not," she whispered, leaning in.

Just before our lips would have touched, our first kiss, I happened to look down past her nose, and pulled up short. "What is he *doing*?" I demanded.

Ash pulled back in surprise. "What?" It took her a second to follow my line of sight. There had been some seat changes in the freshman group, and now instead of having a girl on either side, Bailey was on one of the ends, and talking to a blond-haired kid with a bowl cut. He kept leaning in to her, showing her something on his forearm.

"Relax," she chuckled. "At least they're not making out."

Making out? I almost jumped out of my seat. But Ash

grabbed my hand, stopping me. "Relax, it's just a movie. They're just talking."

"That's not the point!"

"God," she said softly. "You really do think of her as your little sister."

"Of course I do," I said, suddenly confused.

But before I could push the issue any further, sirens wailed in our ears.

TWENTY-FOUR

"The alliance between Illana Bryer and
Robert Cooper gave us a fighting chance.
But for three years, we stayed at a stalemate.
Moonset went to ground, and continued to
direct the war front from the shadows.
We thought they'd never be found."

....

Adele Roman
Moonset Historian, From a college
lecture series about Moonset

The movie kept playing, but the lights rose in the theater. Emergency sirens continued to blare from the hallway—they weren't the ringing bell of a fire alarm, more the whoop-whoop of a tornado alarm.

"What's going on?" a girl cried from behind us.

"Trying to watch the movie," someone bellowed from down below.

Bailey twisted in her seat, her eyes meeting mine for the first time tonight. She looked afraid. But more than that, she looked *aware*. Like she knew something the rest of us didn't. "Oh no," I muttered, getting to my feet. *Not now.*

Ash looked up at me. "Justin?"

One by one, like items being checked off a list, each one of the light bulbs exploded with a paff. Darkness was gradual, but by the time the last one popped, the only light was from the projector. People screamed, and there was movement all around me.

"Justin," Bailey called warningly.

I spun around, looking for the source. If this was a Maleficia attack, there would be a *feeling*. A sense in the air where nothing was visible, but something was definitely there. "Please be wrong, please be wrong," I whispered.

"What the hell?"

The shout came from the floor, and I whipped around immediately. Someone had come into the theater while I was distracted. The emergency lights flicked on, spotlights that did little more than create an ominous amber glow.

"We ... we ... we ... we ... " The movie began to skip, cutting the same moment of an earnest blonde dropping a cell phone onto a table. Over and over again, that same two-second clip. I took my eyes from the floor, from the new arrival, and that was long enough for chaos to break out.

Another shout, pained this time, as a body went flying

through the air. From beside me, Ash's shock was palpable. "Santa?"

She was right. It *was* Santa. More specifically, one of the zombie Santa mannequins that had been set up all over the megaplex. And he was heading directly for my sister.

I leapt over the chairs in front of me in an instant, already shouting for her. Bailey took one look at her friends, and then a longer look at the Maleficia-possessed spirit of Christmas, and started backing away down her aisle.

"Only … only … only … only … " The movie jerked again, cutting to a totally different scene. The man's voice was hoarse and full of rage.

More Santas surged into the theater, their movements jerky and awkward. As people tried to run, the Santas grabbed them in mitted hands. Most they pushed aside, but a few they threw. Quickly, the crowd of theatergoers realized that running for the door was not an option. The crowd, however, was evenly divided on an alternative route. Half ran down the stairs on the far side, heading for the emergency exit that led outside. The other half ran for the top of the theater … and no route of escape.

"What's going on?" Bailey grabbed my arm, squeezing for dear life. "What's happening?"

"It's going to be okay," I lied. The first row of seats had a pipe railing over it and open space for wheelchairs. Since the stairs were occupied, I pushed Bailey under the railing and climbed up after her.

One of the Santas lunged for us, but tripped over his own feet and clattered to the ground.

"Eed … eed … eed … eed … "

"We have to get everyone out of here," I said, trying to think. With a row and a railing between the advancing army of Santas, they couldn't come directly at us. *At Bailey. They were going after her first.* It was just a theory, but I wasn't about to test it out.

We ran to the end of the row. Most of the kids who were making for the theater's exit had already passed us, but they were cut off from the exit by one of the Santas. I looked towards the place we'd entered from, and Santas were guarding it, too. *They're cutting off escape routes.* But how was that possible? Maleficia was supposed to destroy things. Break them down. Not play puppetmaster.

"They're not hurting anyone," Bailey said at my side. "Just the ones who get in their way." And then a moment later, "They're after us, aren't they?"

"One … one … one … one … "

"Yes," I said, keeping my voice short. "Stay away from them," I shouted to the one or two kids who still thought going up against the Santas was a smart move. The majority of the red-suit pack kept heading towards us.

The Santas by the emergency exit couldn't be toppled by any of the kids rushing for the door. Time and again, they shoved back anyone who attempted to run away. Eventually the crowd panicked and ran for the stairs, though the rest of the people were still hiding on the top row.

A shift seemed to come over the monsters then. It was like Bailey's first question had reminded the Santas that they were supposed to be the demon-filled patriarchs of a bloody Christmas, because where they'd been content to push people out of there way a moment ago, now the violence was escalating. Their movements stopped being as jerky, and they kept their balance better. Mouths that had been painted closed now opened, revealing bloody teeth.

It's like they're becoming more alive. But I didn't know what that meant. Or how it could help me.

One of them shoved a boy to the ground below us, crawled on top of him, and started punching. Bailey gasped. "Jesse!" She dropped her hand and bolted down the step towards the Santa.

"Bay!" I yelled profanities, jumping under the railing and trying to cut her off. The Santa raised its fist like it was going to punch her, and I threw myself between them. "Bailey, run!" *There's the curse to think about. Come on, hit me.* When the curse had activated before, it had been like being covered in something heavy, right before it had cut through the wraith that had attacked me. Hopefully, history would repeat itself. I turned my neck, giving the creature a perfect target to hit.

The Santa raised its fist … and then it hesitated.

"Hit me! C'mon, hit me!" I shoved it, but the Santa wouldn't complete the act. It took the shove, then turned its head to look down at Bailey.

"Hit me!" I shoved it again, and this time it toppled backwards. Jesse, the hair-swooping boy that had been sitting next to Bailey, struggled to his feet, Bailey at his side.

They know what happens when we're threatened. Everything Quinn told me was wrong. Maleficia wasn't stupid at all. It was smart. Really smart. I raised my voice into a yell. "You want us to go with you?"

"Justin, no!" Bailey looked up from the boy, shaking.

"You only need one?" I continued, raising my hand to point at them. "Take me. But you leave my sister alone." I looked around the theater, pretending it was so I could look at each of the Santas, one by one, as if I really were speaking to them and not whatever was pulling their strings. But the truth was I had to figure out a way to keep thirty people safe from creatures that were about to be really, *really,* pissed off.

I'd seen enough creepy things in my life. The wraith, the Harbinger, the Moonset symbol. But all of those were trumped by a legion of devil Santas all cocking their heads to the side, as if they were contemplating something.

I dropped my voice, and spoke out of the corner of my mouth, moving my lips as little as possible. "Bailey, remember that thing I made you promise to never, ever do again?"

She looked startled. "What?" Then recognition hit her, and her face knotted up. "You said *never.* Not even if it was an emergency."

I looked at the army of zombie Santas. "We're a step past emergency."

I backed up and took a step down the aisle, moving toward the screen and never once turning my back on the Santas. I kept my hand raised, finger pointed. They seemed to follow it with their eyes. I grabbed Bailey by the shoulder, and once she was behind me started to back up again, only this time I was heading for the emergency exit.

The few who were still there by the door backed away

from us—a few of them Bailey's friends from the group, I noticed.

The guards couldn't be moved. They were like statues. But I was willing to bet that those rules didn't apply to me, either. "You can't hurt me," I said to the pair of them. "And you can't stop me either. Can you?" I shoved first one, then the other, and both tumbled away from the door like they were nothing.

Above us the screen started skipping again, a blurring of images and sounds as each second of the movie was extrapolated and thrown out of order. Until it finally settled on the words it was looking for.

"*They…die. They…die. They…die.*"

My eyes widened. Even as I'd opened up an escape route, the Santas had turned on the crowd, and were now heading up the stairs, single file. A boy in a white T-shirt was collapsed on the ground, unconscious. One of the Santas approached, settling his black boot over the boy's neck.

"No!"

I stepped forward, throwing out my hand the way I'd seen Quinn do against the wraith. What was the *spell*? "*Les divlock.*" Nothing. "*Lex davlock.*" Nothing. Shit, what was it?!

Ash appeared at my side, punching her fist forward. "*Lex divok!*"

The Santa went flying back, spinning up in the air like a top. My brain went spinning in much the same direction. *Ash just used a spell. Ash just used magic.*

I opened my mouth, expecting to confront her about

being a witch, but what came out instead was, "You knew who I was all along?"

She looked guilty, but determined. "Justin, we've got to get them out of here. I'll explain later."

"The hell you will," Bailey muttered, a suddenly fierce expression crossing her face. "Now, Justin?"

I shook my head, trying to regain my focus. "Yeah," I said, my mouth dry.

When people thought about which of us was the most dangerous, they always picked Jenna. Occasionally Cole. Rarely me. But never Malcolm or Bailey. But Bailey had the talent for evocations, and an inability to understand the difference between when to use her powers and when not to.

Bailey dropped her head, whispering words to herself.

Fascinations were brainwashing spells, in which the subject is literally fascinated into believing whatever the witch wants them to. Witchers were basically the reigning lords of fascination magic—they used it the most frequently, and they limited who they taught it to. But Bailey's gift was self-taught, something innate she was born already knowing how to do.

The night of the Harbinger's suicide, the Witchers had split the crowds up into fours and fives because that was the limit that most people could influence at one time.

Bailey looked up, and near on thirty pairs of eyes stared at her blankly, awaiting orders.

"Tell them to avoid the Santas, to help each other, and to head for the emergency door," I said.

Bailey nodded, concentrating. She didn't have to say the words out loud.

"You can't let them go outside," Ash said. "*Lex divok!*" She turned her palm towards the Santa at the top of the chain on the stairs, and *pulled*. Instead of flying forward, the Santa went tumbling back, and like a stack of dominos he knocked down every Santa below him until the entire line was off their feet.

"Why not?" I demanded. "We have to get them out of here. Did you miss the big warning?" I gestured towards the screen. "They'll kill everyone."

"And if this is just a trap to get you out in the open?" she snapped back. This was not a side of Ash I'd seen before. Confident and in control, yes, but never angry and harsh. Even knowing she'd been lying to me since the beginning, I was fascinated.

"Do you have a better idea?"

It turned out that she did. "Clear a path to the main door. Get everyone out into the lobby. The Witchers are probably on their way already."

Right. Witchers. "They're already here."

"And if they're not in here, that means they're neutralizing whatever else is going on. Distractions to keep the Witchers busy while the warlock came after you."

"*Lex divok!*" I shouted, sweeping my hand from left to right. The Santas I'd pushed from the door had climbed to their feet, only I knocked them back down again, sending them sliding against the concrete floor towards the other wall.

"Bay, change of plan," I said. "Make them go for the lobby exit. We'll clear a path."

Bailey didn't say anything, but there was a brief jut of her chin that I took for understanding. She was sweating. I wondered how long she could keep the spell going before it overwhelmed her. Mind magic was a lot of things, but easy wasn't one of them.

As hard as it was to admit, Ash and I worked well together. She kept the demon Clauses on the stairs tumbling down, and I knocked the ones that had blocked the exit toward them. Between the two of us, we kept most of them down at all times. Bailey stayed behind and between us, head down and hands balled up into fists.

She's not going to be able to do much more. About half of the kids were in the hallway, moving orderly but a bit slow. But the way everyone was moving, I didn't think Bailey would be able to hold out until we all out of the theater.

"Can you set off the sprinkler system?" I asked, looking over Bailey's head at Ash … who wasn't in much better shape. Constantly using the knock-down spell was taking a toll on her, too. I was barely winded, but she looked like she was in the middle of a marathon.

"What?" Ash squinted up at the ceiling. "Why?"

"Can you do it or not? I would, but I don't know the right spell."

"I think so," she said. "When?"

"When I tell you." I leaned over, put my arm around Bailey's back. "Bay, when I tell you, you're going to drop the spell, okay?"

"But everyone's still—" she tried to protest, her voice flimsy and weak.

"I'll get everyone out, okay? You did good." I rubbed her back, then nodded my head at Ash, who concentrated on the ceiling. Fifty feet above us, tiny fires sparked to life, in tune with the spells coming out of Ash's mouth. One by one they circled, until each of them targeted one of the sprinkler heads. Just as the first drop of water struck my head, thirty people regained awareness and my sister started to drop.

I scooped her up immediately, having expected exactly this. "Fire!" I shouted. "Fire!" One side effect of fascination was the period of disorientation after the spell ended. Minds were jumbled around, and it took a minute for the brain to reboot itself. Unless, of course, you provided people with a shock. Like a fire in a movie theater.

There were screams and shrieks, but since everyone was already in the process of leaving the theater, they kept at it, only faster. Ash and I were the last two in line, and before we even reached the doors, a man and a woman in black suits appeared. The Witchers. Finally.

"In there," I said, gesturing backwards with my head. "The mannequins."

"Get them out of here," the man said to his partner. She took one look at Bailey and nodded sharply.

"We're fine," I insisted. "Bailey just used too much magic. Is there anything else out there?"

"We banished the rest," the woman said. "We've been checking theater by theater to make sure we got it all."

"Big mess in there, then. Might take both of you."

"I'll keep an eye on him," Ash said quietly from my side.

Whoever she really was, they seemed to know her. "Make sure they stay in the lobby. No one's being allowed to leave until the mess is cleaned up."

Once out of the theater, we saw people milling around in groups near the lobby, but the theater hallways were clear.

"You have an in with the Witchers," I said as we headed for the concession stand. There was an argument going on between two of the groups, trying to decide what had happened. One side thought fire, the other suggested a gas leak, but neither could explain why the building hadn't been evacuated yet.

Ash was subdued. Quiet. "I've been training with them since I was a freshman."

"Of course you have." I shifted my grip on Bailey, and Ash looked up immediately.

"I can help," she offered, but I shook my head.

"She's my responsibility."

"Justin..." but she couldn't follow it up with anything. What could she even say? *Sorry I lied to you? Sorry I knew all along who you were? Sorry you thought I was normal and bizarre and sweet?*

It was almost ten minutes before the Witchers emerged, declaring the threat banished. The Santas had dropped almost as soon as we broke for the doors, but Maleficia could have been lingering in the shadows and corners of the theater. Backup, in the form of a half-dozen plainclothes twenty-somethings with a military way of moving, arrived not soon after.

It only took another ten minutes to turn a potential attack into something less stable than a dream. The Witchers worked quickly, wiping memories and replacing fears with a sense of calm. Under their direction, kids with footage on their phone deleted the evidence, and the theater's security cameras were erased. I looked around while all this was going on, not sure what I was looking for exactly, but knowing I didn't find it. *Something's not right.*

They decided to blame it on a gas leak, exacerbated by someone, probably a teenager, pulling one of the fire alarms and setting off the sprinkler system.

Quinn arrived with the reinforcements and grabbed Bailey out of my hands after I stumbled.

"I've got her!"

He shook his head. "You need to take a minute. Catch your breath. Stretch."

"I can take care of my sister," I snapped, reaching for her.

"You already did," Quinn said in a soothing tone. "You kept her from getting hurt. But now we need to take care of both of you and make sure you're both okay."

I didn't like what he was implying. "We're fine."

"Maybe it looks that way ... "

I reached out and grabbed for Bailey. Quinn only resisted for a moment before he helped shift her weight over to me. "We're fine. We kept the warlock from hurting as many people as we could. And now you're just going to imply that there's something *wrong* with us?" My stomach turned. "We saved people tonight. And you're still looking at us like we're the bad guys."

"Justin, that's not what he's saying." But I didn't want to hear what Ash had to say either.

I moved for the exit. Righteous indignation or not, carrying Bailey was a struggle. I wasn't born in a gym like Mal—my arms only had so much strength. I might have moved a bit quicker than necessary, but they'd blame it on the anger.

There was a car out front, and I slid Bailey into the back, laying her head carefully down on the seat. She started to stir as soon as I pulled away. "Jus...?"

"You're okay," I said, swallowing. "You did really good, Bails. Saved the day."

"Not yet," she murmured, shifting until she found a more comfortable position. She was out again almost instantly.

Quinn wasn't one of the Witchers who drove us back to the house, and the two who rode with us didn't try to say anything or interfere at all. I carried Bailey up into her room, passing Cole's shut door and hearing the bass of his music rattling the walls. He didn't even open the door to see what was going on.

Jenna appeared at the top of the steps when I walked into the house. "Quinn called. Told me what happened. Are you okay?" She looked like she was about to fly down the stairs, and that was a remarkably un-Jenna like thing to see.

"I'm fine. We're both fine. Bailey wore herself out. She's sleeping it off. I'm about to do the same." While I'd been fine slinging magic around at the time, now that the adrenaline had started to disappear, exhaustion crept in and took its place.

"Right," she said quietly. "Everyone's meeting over here tomorrow. They want us to stay inside again for a couple of days. Totally ruins my plans for the weekend." She didn't sound too broken up about it.

"Have you noticed how every time there's a problem, they try to pull us off the streets?" I wondered, grabbing the railing post at the bottom of the stairs. "I thought we were supposed to be bait."

Jenna shrugged. "I think they don't know *what* they want us to be. For what it's worth, Quinn was arguing on the phone with someone about pulling us out of here. And that was before the attack." She came down the stairs slowly, her mouth pursed in thought. "Not saying he's our new best friend, but maybe he's not a total pawn."

"Maybe," I agreed, licking my lips. I wanted something to drink, but the kitchen was too far. I'd just grab some water in the bathroom. Or maybe there was still a bottle left in my room from earlier.

I started climbing the stairs, almost at the top when she asked, "Other than the warlock interruptus, how was the date? Everything you ever dreamed?"

Everything I should have expected, more like. I wasn't ready to tell Jenna about Ash. I wasn't ready to tell *anyone.* "It was fine. I'm going to bed."

Jenna watched me from the bottom of the stairs. "Night, Justin."

All thoughts of sleep evaporated when I walked into my room. There, carefully laid out on the edge of my bed, was my father's spellbook. The one that I'd locked up in the school a week ago.

TWENTY-FIVE

(On being asked why she followed Moonset)
"We changed the world. Who wouldn't want that?
They never acted superior to us. But they were."
(pause) "They had plans for all of us."

Lucinda Dale (S)
Personal Interview

What was it doing here? It had been almost a week since I'd deposited the book inside a locker at school until I could figure out some other way to get rid of it. The book was dangerous. Maybe not physically dangerous, the way the Santa mannequins had been tonight, but dangerous on so many other levels. The amount of trouble I could get into if someone knew I had Sherrod Daggett's spellbook *in my bedroom*.

There was something poking out of the top. A paper that

I definitely hadn't seen before. Something new. I flipped the book open, and a postcard fell out. Well, half of a postcard. It had been torn right down the middle. Turning it over in my hand, I saw the Golden Gate Bridge in half of its glory. I turned it back around, and the message that had been written in red pen.

Happy reading. CB.

CB. Cullen Bridger. Like the bridge on the postcard hadn't been obvious enough. He'd been here? In my house? He was here in Carrow Mill?

I went to the door, about to shout for someone—Jenna, Quinn, anyone—but reality stopped me. I couldn't show anyone. Not *anyone.* Jenna would want to know where the spellbook had come from. Quinn would turn me over to the Witchers and the Congress. Mal would just get pissed.

He's been in my house. There's been Witchers all over the place for weeks and he just strolled in here like it was no big deal. I sank down onto the bed, wondering what I'd gotten myself into. Why did I even steal it? What was wrong with me?

Bridger knew I'd found Sherrod's book. But why would he want me to have it? Unless there was something in the book he wanted me to find. All the more reason to get rid of the book again.

But the Maleficia attack tonight only reinforced how little I knew on my own. If it hadn't been for Ash, the mannequins would have taken one of us. Or both. Maybe there were spells in the book that would help me protect the others.

I kept going back and forth, seeing both the pros and the

cons. But a knock at the door tore the thoughts from my head and sent a fresh wave of panic rushing through my chest.

"Just a second," I managed to say, shoving the book between the mattresses and pulling the comforter down over the top. It wasn't the most ingenious hiding place ever, but it would do for a minute. I looked around the room, concerned that anything else might be out of place. At a casual glance, everything *looked* the same, but appearances were deceiving. A warlock had been in my room. Who knows what else he'd done in here.

I couldn't worry about that now. I looked towards my door. Jenna wouldn't knock. Quinn must have gotten home. But when I opened the door, it was Ash standing there, not Quinn.

"Jenna let me in," she said, not meeting my eyes.

"I'm really tired," I lied.

She came into the room and closed the door behind her. "I'm not staying long." It was like all the fight had drained out of her, and it made her almost unrecognizable. Ash was chaos and flirtation. This melancholy girl was like a pale imitation. *But maybe you never knew the real her. It would make sense, wouldn't it?*

"Was any of it true?" I asked. Even though I didn't want to, I had to know. I had to be able to prepare myself, so that this never happened again.

"Do you know who Robert Cooper is?" she asked in lieu of answering.

I shrugged. Everyone knew who he was. He was the

closest thing the witch world had to a president. "Head of the Congress, Coven Leader of Eventide."

"Your guardian's grandfather, and Illana's husband. He's been watching you ever since you came to Carrow Mill. He's the *reason* you're here." She ran her fingers through her hair, trying to smooth it down. "He's the reason I'm here, too."

There it was. The truth. Finally. "So you're a spy. Watch what I say and do, and report back. But why me? Why not one of the others? What made me so special?"

"You told me once that all you had was each other," Ash said as she moved toward my window. As she passed my bed, my heart froze in panic, but she passed by without noticing the hidden tome between my sheets. Most kids hide *Playboys* between their mattresses. Not me.

"But it's more than that," she continued. "All you have is them, and all they have is you. You're the one they listen to, the one that keeps order as best you can. All the files say it: if you want to learn about the children of Moonset, you go to Justin."

"So you *were* spying on me." Hearing it all laid out so clinically didn't make me feel any better. It made me sick to my stomach, thinking about the hours people must have put into assessing us, speculating about our lives.

"At first," she admitted. "Justin, I wasn't lying when I said I like you. You're not what I expected. But it's not that easy to tell Robert Cooper that you're giving up on the job he gave you. He was the one that recruited me into the Witchers in the first place—I mean, for now it's just training but after I graduate—"

I couldn't believe I was hearing this. She was so *calm*! "Do you get how messed up this is? I was starting to trust you! Do you have any idea how many people I actually confide in like that?" It was a short list. Four names.

Ash looked up at me, and met my eyes. "I know," she said. "I studied your file. You asked me if it was all an act earlier. I never lied to you, not really. They picked me because I fit the profile of what they thought you'd like."

They know me pretty well. The thought crossed my mind unbidden, and only served to make me more angry. This was a game to all of them. The Congress thought they could throw us here, dangle us in front of the warlock, and play with our lives. *Was this what they did to our parents? Were they just as manipulative back then?* Because if the answer was yes, I could see why my parents started a rebellion.

"I think you should go," I said, trying desperately to stay calm and keep my voice level. If I started screaming at Ash, I might lose control again. And this time, I wouldn't have the excuse of some teacher working magic against me as a defense.

"Justin, that's not the only reason I'm here. You need to be careful. Cooper wants you all handed to the warlock on a silver platter. He had me watching you to see how you'd react. How long it would take before the warlock either took you out—or recruited you to his side. He wants the warlock dead, and he's just hoping the five of you will be collateral damage."

The spellbook. My eyes moved towards the bed, and I had to physically force myself to look up at the ceiling. Cullen Bridger was taunting us. He had been all along.

"The Congress is split, though. Illana wants the warlock caught, but she's not willing to sacrifice you and the others."

"Illana hates us almost as much as everyone else does. She's just too classy not to say it to our faces," I said.

"I don't think it's like that. Honestly, I think she wants to keep you guys safe. That's why she moved here. Why she's been so involved. But you haven't exactly made it easy."

The idea that I hadn't made life easy for the sixty-something battle-hardened woman almost made me smile.

She walked over towards me, her hands reaching out and then pulling back before she actually touched me. She looked almost scared. "I know you can't trust me anymore, and I get it. I'm sorry I lied to you, but I'm not sorry I got to know you. People could have gotten really hurt tonight. *You* stopped them. I won't ever forget that."

"We stopped them," I muttered.

"Yeah," she said, like I said something incredibly sweet, "we did."

"You probably could have taken them on by yourself," I said, unable to help myself. Bitterness clouded my words. "The only reason I was any help at all was because you taught me the spell. I mean, if Bailey and I hadn't been there..." I trailed off suddenly. I had been about to say that Ash wasn't the only witch in that theater.

"What is it?"

I thought back to the lobby after the attack. Looking for something I couldn't place. Now I remembered what that was. "Have you heard from Luca? He got out okay, right?" I hadn't thought about him at the time, but in hindsight, I had to wonder. Mal would probably be upset if the only living relative he had died accidentally and no one noticed.

She looked at me in surprise. "He must have slipped out before the attack. Probably got scared when he saw all the Santas on parade."

"But you saw him?"

"I mean, for a minute," she said, eyes distant. "After it was all over, he was there with us when the cleanup crew was finally leaving. Why?"

I shook my head. "I just wanted to make sure." I cleared my throat. "You should probably go."

"Yeah, I'm pretty tired," she said, shifting her weight and biting the corner of her lip. "I meant what I said. I'm sorry."

"Yeah," I said, tersely, moving to the door and pulling it open. "I heard."

———

Sleep never came. I laid on my bed and stared at the ceiling. With every minute that passed, I imagined I could feel the weight of the spellbook up against the mattress more and more, until it was an unavoidable lump under my leg. No matter how much I shifted, or how I rearranged myself, I could still feel the book underneath me.

After about an hour of tossing and turning, I gave up. The spellbook was almost like a siren's song, calling me to read it. It was the middle of the night. No one was awake. But just to be sure I locked my door and moved my desk chair underneath the knob, creating a barrier if anyone tried forcing their way in.

I turned on all the lights. I don't know why, but it made me feel better. Then I pulled the book out from between the mattresses, and set it on my lap. This was it. I could just take a little peek. Just enough to see how bad the contents were. If Sherrod was the monster I expected, I'd stop right there.

I flipped to a random page.

There is something about her, a light in her eyes that only I see.

What? I leaned closer, as if I could learn more of the book through osmosis. I held my finger on that page and continued flipping through. Page after page was lined with shorthand—spells and their explanations, all written in a tight, clear hand. And then there was the English—thoughts and anecdotes of people I didn't know and stories I'd never heard.

It really was a journal.

Emily likes to be chased—all chicks do. She spellcasts with such finesse—so unlike Diana. One could end a drought with just enough rain, the other would unleash a hurricane to show off her power. So vastly different—they should hate each other on sight, but there is some sort of… understanding between them. I do NOT understand women.

I almost dropped the book. He was writing about my mother. And… Jenna's. The fact that he called them "chicks" was too unbelievable to even process, so I pretended I hadn't seen it. I'd never understood how either woman continued to stand by him, knowing that he'd gotten both of them pregnant—one his wife, one his mistress.

Yet they'd both stayed with him, for the sake of their Coven and all their plans. Their wars.

This is your chance to find out what made him tick. The thought didn't ease my conscience. Jenna would take the offer of new spells without question, without caring what strings came attached to that power. But I wasn't so short-sighted. This book was dangerous.

I flipped to the one of the pages lined with spells— Sherrod was meticulous about breaking everything down for later. It took only a minute or two to translate the written.

It said: "to avoid the thought police."

I looked over the lines of the spell, pieced them together in my head. Most verbal spells were only a few words long— but to write it out, and do it safely, you had to break each piece down into several lines worth of longhand. There were forms of "connection," "thought," and "channel."

A telepathy spell? I perked up, more intrigued than I was a moment ago. This didn't have the staccato rhythm of a traditional spell—was it something Sherrod had invented himself? It sounded as though the spell could open a link between two minds, although I wasn't sure what the name meant by the "thought police."

I continued paging through the book, stopping every so often to translate the title of spells. Sherrod was a fan of obscure names, ones that didn't always explain what the spell actually did so much as some anecdote of his life I wasn't privy to. Or maybe he just liked to be pretentious. Some of his spells had the ring of bad poetry. "Crows nesting on my heart." "Forever the blanket of silence." "The empty night sours."

There were mentions of my mother, and Jenna's, but it wasn't a traditional journal. More like random thoughts and observations that he needed to get out, and the spellbook was there. Before I even realized I was doing it, I started copying some of the spells in my English notebook, tucked between notes I'd taken about the themes of *Macbeth*. I followed each entry with my guess as to what the spell did.

The problem was in the details. Some of the spells were self-explanatory—Sherrod had written out a whole section of spells that made his school life inconsequential. Spells to enhance memory and eloquence, ones that made him more persuasive—something he didn't need—and spells to make people receptive to his ideas.

It was the other spells that had caught my interest, though. No one had ever mentioned that Sherrod was something of a maverick when it came to learning magic. He preferred the spells he created with his own hands, rather than those he'd been taught. The same points were repeated constantly in the journaled sections—magic should constantly be evolving, but it was witches who forced it to stagnate. He thought the practice of handing down spellbooks was deplorable.

There were also whole passages that read like an opus to his ego. Emily continued to elude him, and Diana made it clear she wouldn't play second fiddle. It was hard to reconcile the teen I was reading about—who clearly wanted both girls—with the man who was technically my father.

The other part that was troubling me was that there was nothing that suggested Sherrod Daggett was drawn to the darkness. He wasn't the outcast student, secretly thinking of how he'd get his revenge. There was only an occasional sense of his growing awareness of politics—of the Covens and their role in administrating our world. If anything, he sounded like a revolutionary. He had grand ideas, and thought outside the box.

If I didn't know who he'd become, I could have almost admired him. At least his ideas—Sherrod as a teenager sounded like a douchebag. I might be the same age now as he was when he wrote some of these entries, and I didn't have an ounce of his self-awareness or his activism. And I hoped I wasn't half the douche he was.

Then, somewhere around the last third of the book, the personal entries stopped. There were no more hints about how torn he was between the girls or how everyone should be involved in their government. The last section of the book was devoted to Coven spells, spells that utilized the bond between the witches. There was no explanation for what had changed—had Moonset changed him right from the start?

The next time I looked up from the book, my room looked different. Bright. I looked out the window, and realized the sun had risen already. I was tired—not exhausted like I'd stayed up all night reading—but the kind of tired that came from studying for too many hours at once. My mind was snapping with ideas and thoughts, but my body was struggling to keep up.

I needed coffee. I tucked the book back under the

mattress and put my English notebook back in my bag. A quick review of my room didn't show anything else out of the ordinary. At least not yet.

Bailey was already in our kitchen when I walked in. She sat at the island, her arms resting on the counter and her head resting on top of her wrists. She barely looked up when I approached.

"Hey, Bay," I said softly. "You feeling okay?"

She shrugged, and I went to make a fresh pot of coffee while she slouched there. It was too early for anyone else to be up, so it was surprising that Bailey was not only up but had already come back over from her own house.

When Quinn came in a few minutes later, followed by Mal, I reconsidered what I thought of as "too early."

"Did anyone get any sleep last night?"

Mal studied me, his eyes thoughtful. "Did you?"

"I'm making coffee," I said, turning back to it while avoiding the question. "If anyone wants."

"Yes, please," Quinn said tiredly.

Mal took up the seat next to Bailey, eyes smudged dark just like hers.

"You two look like the walking dead," I said, trying to pry a smile out of them. Hell, I would have settled for one of them. But Bailey was sleep-deprived and grumpy, and Mal looked a step beyond grumpy. Crabby?

"I stayed on the couch at Bailey's house," Mal added. There was something off about his voice. It was flat. Almost robotic? "Someone had to."

The dig knocked me sideways. Was he saying I hadn't

done enough? I'd done everything I could to keep both Bailey and I safe!

He's probably just sleep-deprived. Give him some time, and he'll calm down. A weird squirming feeling in my gut said that this was more than just a rough night talking.

Were Mal and I fighting now? I knew we hadn't talked much lately, but I had figured he was off doing his own thing. He was so against anything to do with the magic anyway. I just assumed he'd prefer it that way.

"Where's Cole?" Quinn asked, looking down at Bailey.

It took her a minute to raise her head. "Sleeping," she said, her expression unusually hostile.

"Hey, enough of that," I said easily. "Don't take it out on Quinn. Why don't you go into the living room and curl up on the couch? Take a little nap or something."

Without another word, Bailey got up from the kitchen island and headed into the living room. Mal shrugged and followed her. When they were both gone, I looked in Quinn's direction. "I guess it's been a rough night for everyone."

"Keep an eye on them," he said, watching the direction they'd disappeared in. "Just in case."

"Just in case of what?" I could feel last night's frustration rearing up again. Quinn kept trying to take over, to edge me out of the way. But it wasn't his job. He wasn't the one who'd still be here in six months, looking after Bailey and the rest. I had to do it.

He held up his hands. "Just … in case. Let me know if anything's off."

"We're. Fine." I said, and that was the end of that.

Cole trudged over about an hour later, around the same time that Jenna graced us with her presence. Jenna and I were the only ones in any semblance of a good mood, although mine was more coffee based than anything else.

The five of us watched television in the living room for a few hours, Mal dozing in one of the recliners. Jenna tried on several occasions to start up a conversation with Bailey, but Bay was having none of it.

"So we're just supposed to stay in the house all day?" Jenna asked, turning towards me after the latest attempt to talk to Bailey failed. *What's with her?* she mouthed.

I had no idea what to tell her about Bailey, so I just looked away. "Yeah, for a couple days maybe. They've got extra Witchers coming into the city I guess, and they want us to stay out of the way."

"I've left the house lots of times," she said thoughtfully. "And I haven't had half the problems you have. Why's he so focused on you?"

Ash had summed it up perfectly earlier. *If you want to get to the others, you go through Justin.* Maybe that meant he'd read our files. Or he'd been closer than we thought all along. *Someone* had brought that spellbook into the house, and with the amount of Witchers in the neighborhood, someone would have noticed a stranger.

Was Bridger hiding in plain sight?

"I'm just extra annoying," I offered, and Jenna made a noise of agreement.

No one seemed very active. We all just kind of dozed in

front of the television. I curled up in one of the arm chairs, Cole sprawled around my feet. It was late afternoon by the time my yawning became uncontrollable, and I went for a coffee refill. *Just need more caffeine.* I don't know *why* I was so insistent on staying up, but I wasn't going down without a fight.

Jenna followed me into the kitchen. "You should get some sleep. Just an hour or two. You look terrible."

"I'll be fine," I said. "I'm not even tired." I think I was a step beyond tired. Exhaustion had passed me by entirely and now I was running on nothing but coffee and stubbornness.

Bailey craned around in her seat. "You should sleep, Justin."

"I don't need to sleep," I insisted.

There was a weird tension in the room. Jenna watched me, looking like she was trying to make up her mind about something. Finally she nodded, then shifted her weight from one foot to the other. "At least take a shower. Five minutes. You look like hell." She grabbed down a bowl, a box of cereal, and the milk out of the fridge, setting it up on the counter like some sort of self-serve station.

"Would you guys just stop? Seriously." Part of me was worried about leaving them in the house with Sherrod's book in my room. Did I give it away somehow? Did they know?

"You stink," Cole said flatly, from his spot spread out on the floor. A chorus of agreements (or grunts in Mal's case) followed.

"Fine, I'll take a shower," I snapped.

Once I was under the spray, and I could feel the tension

of the last twenty-four hours draining out of me, I had to admit that maybe it was a good idea. I was still only in there for about ten minutes, but it was enough time to pull myself together, and figure out what to do next.

I came out of the bathroom, dried and dressed even if I was still a little damp. I got as far as my room before I realized just how quiet the house had gotten.

"Jenna? Bay? What are you guys doing?" I called down the stairs. The house was silent. Still.

Oh no. Oh no oh no oh no. I dropped my towel and dirty clothes and flew down the stairs. *No no no no no.* I went through the living room, the dining room, and finally the kitchen. The chairs were still pulled out, but each of them was empty. "Quinn!"

The milk was on the countertop, turned on its side. Most of it had already spilled out, and trickled down onto the floor, but there was still a steady *plop plop plop*. "Quinn!" I shouted, as my eyes fixed on the edge of the table. Lined up like toy soldiers or a stack of dominoes were four cell phones. *Their* four cell phones.

Quinn came thundering down the stairs. "What's wrong?"

I turned in a circle. "I—I just left for a minute. I just went to take a shower. Five minutes, max."

"Justin?"

The others were gone. And it was all my fault.

TWENTY-SIX

*"We knew it was coming. They made us promise
not to avenge them. To lay down our arms.
Even on the last day, knowing they were
embracing death, they were so tragically
beautiful. I wish I could have gone with them."*

....

Lucinda Dale
Interview about the day Moonset surrendered

After that, the house was a whirlwind of activity.

"Someone disabled the guards," Quinn said when he
came back inside. There'd been two Witchers sitting out in
front of the house, unconscious when he'd gone to check. No
one had seen anything, coming or going.

"He got into the house somehow," I said. "He made
them go with him."

Quinn didn't immediately agree with me, and the expression on his face suggested he thought the answer was something else.

"They wouldn't have gone with him," I insisted. "Not by choice."

"I didn't say anything."

"I know what you all think. That we're just like Moonset, just waiting to turn evil and bring down the establishment. But we're not! Jenna and the others wouldn't do that!"

"Okay," Quinn said, his voice calming. "Relax. We're going to find them."

There was a sick feeling in my stomach, and it was only getting worse by the moment. Something was wrong. *Really* wrong. It was more than a hunch; it was like there was an intangible part of me inside, and it was all knotted up. Like my spirit was cramping.

I spent two hours pacing the downstairs waiting for news. Quinn left with one of the search groups, but each one came back later without news. Finally, I couldn't stand it anymore.

Last night I was half convinced that I would never talk to Ash again. But now she was my only option.

"Justin?"

"I need your help," I said, trying to push down the hurt I still felt at the sound of her voice. "I need to break out of my house."

She laughed, sharp and brief, immediately followed by a long pause. "You're serious?" It wasn't a question.

"You owe me," I said, and hung up the phone.

After that, I was very busy. The sun was setting, and night

would be here before long. My earlier exhaustion was a distant memory. Now my body was wired, running on fear and a weird kind of anticipation. *This is what we've been waiting on.* I didn't know where the thought came from, but I knew it was right. *This* was the warlock's plan. Finally.

If Bridger thinks we're going down without a fight, he's an idiot. I don't know how he managed to get the others out of the house—and I refused to think about any other alternative—but I would find them. Somehow.

I emptied my school bag of all but two of my notebooks, and then I tucked Sherrod's spellbook in between them. Moving very carefully, I crept through the halls, pausing at every minor creak and groan of the floorboards. The downstairs was full of Witchers, but none of them was up here.

I didn't turn on the lights in Quinn's room, just in case someone downstairs noticed. He kept his tools in the cedar chest at the foot of his bed. I needed one of his athames. Just in case. I misjudged the distance right off the bat, slamming my toe into the side of the chest, and making a sound I was sure could be heard all the way downstairs.

I froze in place, and started counting to fifty. Any minute, someone was going to slip up the stairs and find me in Quinn's room, rummaging through his stuff.

But no one came. I got to fifty, waited a few extra seconds, and then found the chest. With the spare knife in hand, I slipped back out of the room, and dropped it in my book bag. I wasn't sure if we were going to need it, but better safe than sorry.

"It's getting pretty rough down there," Ash said, materializing in my doorway. "What happened?"

"Everyone disappeared. Witchers think they've all gone rogue. Trying to convince them it's the warlock is pointless. They'll just keep letting Bridger do whatever he wants until he collects all of us."

"Whoa," Ash said, eyes widening. "Slow down. Reverse. Start over. Bridger? As in *Bridger*?"

Crap. I looked at her helplessly. Begging her to forget what she heard wouldn't work. I might have been running on nerves, but my brain was still a little slow. I sighed. "He came after us at our last school."

"I thought you got attacked by a wraith?"

"A wraith working for Bridger," I said. "And now he's here. He left me a note yesterday. And it makes sense. The warlock's been doing stupid little attacks, trying to get the Congress to bring us here. Why would someone like Cullen Bridger care about burning down a building? He'd burn the whole town."

"So how can you be sure it's him?"

I showed her the postcard of the Golden Gate bridge, and the note on the back.

"Okay . . . " Ash took a moment, then nodded. "Okay. Why doesn't Quinn know about this? They still think the warlock is a local."

"Because I can't tell them how I got it."

"How did you—no, never mind. I don't think I want to know." She looked around the room, her eyes considering. She looked up, and met my gaze. "It's a lot tamer than I would have thought. I expected a poster of Carissa the underwear model over your bed or something."

"Sorry," I said, zipping up my bag. "Any idea how to get us out of here?"

Ash very carefully closed the door behind her. "Start walking around."

"What?"

She twisted the little lock on the side of the handle and spun around. "Walk around."

I paced out of surprise, walked to the side of the bed and then back to the closet. Meanwhile, she sauntered over towards my bed, whispering words under her breath. And then she fell back, bouncing off my mattress with a laugh.

"Come here," she murmured, eyes full of mischief.

Was she kidding? "Ash, I can't. We need to focus."

"Come. Here." She even crooked her finger at me, a challenging smile on her face.

I crossed to the bed, set one knee on it, and hesitated. But that wasn't good enough for Ash. She leaned forward, grabbed me by the shirt, and pulled me forward. On top of her.

"There," she said breathlessly once we were nose to nose. Her eyes were dark. Fathomless. There was a moment where my breath caught hers, where we were staring into each other. Where I started to lean forward.

Then she pushed me back off. "That should do it," she said brusquely, leaping to her feet.

I sat back, dazed. "Do what?"

"*Araic infious*," she murmured. Suddenly I heard the sounds of movement on the floor, despite the fact that neither of us were moving. Bedsprings groaned, there was laughter. Every sound that had happened over the last thirty seconds. As the sounds and the shuffling repeated over again, I got it. It was an illusion, but a realistic one. As far as anyone else in the house was concerned, we were still just hanging out in my room. And they'd be too busy to worry about the girl in my room.

"It'll buy us some time," she said, heading for the window. "But they're going to find out you're gone quick." She pulled the window open and had one leg out onto the roof when she looked back at me still on the bed. "Well?"

I followed her onto the roof, moving carefully while Ash seemed to bounce from step to step. We crossed the front of the house and over the garage towards the backyard. "Hope you're not scared of heights, Ace," she grinned. She whispered "*aerous*" and leapt down into the backyard.

"Come on," she called up, the sound of her voice muted by the storm. I looked down. At least a ten-foot drop. But Ash seemed to be fine. *Ash was also trained by Witchers*, I reminded myself. But I jumped anyway.

I knew enough about physics to know that when you jump from the roof it's supposed to hurt. But landing on the ground was about as painful as jumping off the last step of a staircase.

Ash saw the look on my face and waggled her fingers. "Magic." Then she turned around and started cutting through the backyard. I rushed to follow. "I parked on Carnegie Street. I figured there's no way they'd notice my car over there."

"You're good at this," I said in surprise.

"Of course," Ash said, her face going serious. "Now tell me what's going on. Where did you get that postcard?"

"I found one of Sherrod's spellbooks from when he was in high school," I said. "But I got rid of it," I said hurriedly, "after I had some time to think. Bridger dropped it off at the house for me last night. He was *in* our house."

"Are you sure it was him?" she asked.

"You don't have to go with me," I said. "This isn't your fight."

"Yeah, but if we save the day, maybe you'll forgive me," she said, offering me a weak grin.

She might have been right. The fact that she'd come when I called and still helped me sneak out went a long way. "Come on," I said, hurrying towards her car.

"You don't even know where we're going yet," Ash said.

We cut through one of my neighbor's backyards, slipping around a covered up above-ground pool. As we crossed the house and into the front yard, the so-far silent night was interrupted.

"Do you hear that?" Ash asked, stopping and cocking her head to one side.

I didn't at first, but a few seconds later, I picked up on it. "Sirens," I whispered. They grew louder and louder until they were nearly deafening. Half a block away, two fire trucks and I don't know how many other flashing vehicles started surging past, heading towards downtown.

"What do you think's going on?" I asked, my voice hushed.

Ash looked severe. "Distractions," she said. "Now, how are you planning to find the others?"

I patted my bag and explained about one of the spells I'd read that morning. Ash didn't turn on the radio when we got into the car. We drove away from the direction all the emergency crews were heading. If she was right, and it was a distraction, Bridger wouldn't be setting up anywhere near there. So we drove to the parking lot of a Walgreens and parked near the back. Ash put the car in park but left the engine running.

"You're sure this is going to work?"

I pulled my father's spellbook into my lap. "I don't have the slightest."

I kept flipping, searching for one of the first spells I'd managed to translate. I studied it for almost a full minute, piecing together the words that were so carefully lettered in the book and trying to form the cadence of the spell.

To cast the spell wrong might not do anything. Or it might make my brain explode. At this point, brain-explodey Justin was still looking like he'd have a better future.

"*Igneus terrous itie,*" I said, the words sounding thick on my tongue.

Just like that, and it felt like my vision was clearing. Like I could see in a way that people rarely did, and if they understood, they would want to be like this all the time. I continued flipping through the book, careful not to spend too long on any one page.

"And this spell just lets you ... memorize anything you read?"

I nodded, my focus still on the words on the page.

"Your dad was wicked smart," she said, and it almost sounded like a compliment.

It took time to translate the shorthand-like writing into words, and then to figure out what they meant, but eventually I found the section I was looking for—the one with every spell relating to the Coven bond that Sherrod Daggett had known in high school.

It took five minutes for me to read, comprehend, and store away every spell in that section, and half the spells in the beginning of the book. I sensed Ash moving around while I studied, blocking out the streetlights for moments here or there as she shifted, but my focus was totally on the book.

Each spell I translated and remembered felt like it was being slotted into my brain. It would have been better to know what they all were meant to do, because "Raven in the noontime" wasn't exactly the kind of name I would have given to a spell. It didn't take nearly as long as I thought, and I went back and looked over several of the spells I'd already translated. The more practice I got, the faster I could figure out the next spell.

Once I was done, I closed my eyes and took a deep breath. As soon as I thought about the book, I remembered the spells perfectly, like I was still reading them from the page. Instant memories. They'd fade eventually, but maybe they would help tonight.

"You okay?"

I had to blink a few times to clear my eyes. "I think so, yeah."

"Good," she said, sliding a much thicker journal out of her bag. "Now this."

"Your spellbook?" I reached out a hand, but then held back. That wasn't what I was using Sherrod's book for—to randomly learn as much magic as possible. The desire was there, definitely so, but this wasn't the way to do it.

"No," I said, pulling back and turning towards my window.

"Justin, you're planning to go find your family. And odds are, they're in the middle of a black magic war zone. If he's summoning more Maleficia, you need to be prepared."

I pulled Quinn's knife out of my pocket. "I'm prepared."

"Beautiful," she said, her tone dry, "you're bringing a knife to an Apocalypse. Do you even know how to use that thing?"

"It's a knife."

"It's an athame," she corrected. "Have you ever used an athame in a fight?"

"Have you?"

"Well, no. You're supposed to be eighteen before they'll teach you." She shifted the car into drive and started pulling out of the parking lot. "Do we have a general direction to go on, or are we just going to guess?" The spell I'd been thinking of—the one that prompted the entire night's insanity—didn't have a flashy name like all of the others. Maybe Sherrod had been sick that day. Or maybe it didn't do what I thought it did. But a spell called

The Beacon seemed rather appropriate for tracking down lost Coven mates.

I focused on the knife in my hand, in the feel of it in my grip. And I pictured Jenna in my head—the way she'd casually toss back her hair and laugh when she was feeling particularly superior. The look she got in her eyes when someone pissed her off.

"*Invenio van culum*," I whispered, tasting magic on my tongue, the thrill of casting a spell for the first time. Then I waited.

And waited.

And waited.

"I'm sure that happens to lots of guys," Ash said quietly.

Then the car died, at the same time as the city lights of Carrow Mill winked out all at once. The city didn't fall into darkness. It jumped headfirst.

TWENTY-SEVEN

"There were reports of children, of course,
but we discounted them. Why would a terrorist
cell like Moonset endanger everything by
choosing the middle of a war to procreate?"

....

Robert Cooper
Transcript from the Moonset Trial

"Shut up," I said immediately. "I did *not* do that."

Ash sounded like she was struggling not to laugh. "I didn't say anything."

"You were going to say something."

"I was not. Why would you even think that?"

"Because you exhale sarcasm." I glanced at the window, even leaning towards the glass like it would give me more visibility. "The timing's a little suspicious, I'll admit."

Ash paused. I should have started counting down, because I knew *something* was coming.

"Hey, Houdini. You abracadabra'd and made all the lights disappear."

The street was suddenly awash in light.

"See? The streetlamps are all back on again."

Ash was peering out above the steering wheel. "Streetlights aren't usually blue."

Then we were both looking out the windows, studying the lights. The streetlights were only lit on Ash's side, and only for a couple of blocks. Everything else was still...darkness.

"The spell?"

Ash looked at me, then shrugged. "Unless you've got a better suggestion."

We followed the lights for the two blocks, and at the intersection Ash hesitated again. The path of lights continued to the left, turning even farther from the main downtown area.

"Can we trust it?"

I wiped my hands on my jeans. "Maybe this is how the spell works. Let's go with it."

Wherever the spell was taking us, it certainly wasn't the fast route. The minute we were off one of the main roads, it was a circuitous path through every side road in the city. We'd reached the outskirts of the town and were now circling its perimeter.

"The lights are out here, too," she said, keeping a slow and steady pace.

As I was jostled and bumped around my seat, I kept looking for some sort of guide. Some idea of where we were going.

Just as I was starting to get comfortable, Ash slowed the car and pulled off to the side of the road. "No more lights," she said quietly.

"Is that a church?" I squinted.

"Oh," she said, sitting back in her seat. She sounded . . . I wasn't sure. Surprised? Resigned? It was hard to say.

"Ash?"

Her hand moved, pointing towards the building. "It's not a church. It's a farmhouse. At least it used to be."

"Used to be?"

She hesitated. "It used to be the Denton farm—Luca's dad grew up there until the explosion. After that, I guess they just left it to rot. They've lived in town ever since."

"There was an *explosion*? Did it have something to do with Moonset?" If Mal's dad had grown up there, it was a possibility.

"There was a party," she said simply. "Something happened, but no one can agree on what. Just that it was bad, and then something blew up and the house was unlivable."

"This happened when they were in high school?"

"Yeah."

"So it could have been a Moonset thing? Experimenting with Maleficia, maybe?" So why would Bridger come back here? Why to this particular place?

"It wasn't just them, though. *Everyone* was at this party. All the kids they went to school with. All the other witches. Whatever happened, happened to all of them."

She looked over at the building, her hands clenched on the steering wheel. "Are you sure this is where she is? That they're all here?"

"I don't know." My knuckles were white, my grip on the door handle should have dented the metal. "All I know is that Jenna's in there."

"And what if you find her? I know you don't want to hear this, but … what if she wants to be there? Quinn said they could have left by choice."

"You talked to Quinn about this?" I demanded. "He doesn't know anything. He doesn't know *us*. Jenna's a lot of things, but she'd die before she ever became like them."

I hated these questions, the uncertainty they raised. My plan was simple. Find them. Bring them home. Easy. So easy it couldn't fail. As long as I didn't stop to worry about what it all *could* mean.

But logic wasn't always easy. And it was a lot more insidious.

"Okay," she said. "Forget I said it. But if we're going to go, we should hurry. God only knows what's happening in there."

Ash had gotten me this far—but she was right. I opened my mouth, planning to tell her to wait here, but she bulldozed right over me.

"Don't do that," she warned, a sharpness to her words. "Don't do the boy thing. I'm not waiting in the car, I'm not running away, and I'm not leaving you by yourself so I can go find help." She threw her door open, and nearly leapt out of the car. I hustled to catch up to her.

"Besides," she snapped, now pointing her athame at me from over the hood of the car. "Someone has to make sure you make it out of this in one piece. You're not going to sacrifice yourself for nothing."

Was she some sort of crazy person? "This is serious! You could get hurt."

There was just a hint of crescent moon in the sky, but more than enough to throw just a twinge of light across her face, illuminating a look I'd almost call viperish. "Now might be a completely inappropriate time to say this, but I've *always* wanted to punch your sister in the face. Just once." She paused, looking up towards the sky wistfully. "Just saying."

This was the last thing I needed. I stared at Ash, proving herself to be the insane girl I've always known she was.

"God, I hope that's not your idea of a pep talk," I said.

The moment ended, we looked at each other, and began walking the dirt path to the farmhouse. The closer we got, the easier it was to tell that the farmhouse had seen better days. The building had wood siding, nearly peeled completely off. The windows in the front of the house were all broken, and weeds had begun growing up at the corners, feeding off the building like a parasite.

In short, it looked like something out of *Children of the Corn*, or any other rural horror movie.

I'm such an idiot for doing this on my own. I glanced at Ash. Almost *on my own.* I'd managed to shove every scrap of nerves down underneath the fact that I didn't have a choice. I had to do this. The Witchers wanted to believe that Jenna and the others had left willingly. Whatever happened, they'd look at them as suspects, not victims.

That was what kept me going as we approached. And then the darkness settled in, grew limbs, and squeezed us tight.

It *was* still the middle of winter; it was always freezing at night. Maybe that's why I didn't notice it at first, the way the cold crept inside. My jaw clenched, my body grew slick with sweat, and my legs trembled a little. *This is normal,* I told myself.

"You feel that?" Ash whispered, sounding...uncertain. Nervous. Two things I didn't expect to ever hear from her.

I stopped, noticing that as I did Ash stopped immediately too, and listened. Silence. And then, once I allowed myself to focus on the things around me, I felt it. A feeling like being watched, only not by just one pair of eyes. Hundreds.

Half of me wanted nothing more than to freeze in place, and wait for it to move along. This wasn't any normal predator—this was something that the core of my being feared. "We know we're in the right place, then," I said, keeping my voice pitched low. We were almost at the front door.

"What is it?"

"Maybe it's the Maleficia. Maybe he's already started invoking it." Maybe it recognizes me. "Keep breathing," I cautioned.

"Easy for you to say," she muttered.

"Come on," I said. "I think it'll be better in the house."

I didn't allow myself to think as I leapt forward, jumped the stairs on the porch, and threw open the half-hanging screen door. Only one hinge was still attached, making the bottom swing around haphazardly.

I twisted the knob of the front door and crossed the broken threshold. The moment I was inside, all the fear and nerves I was feeling melted away. There was nothing of the dark feeling inside—if anything, things inside were calm.

Too calm.

The front rooms were empty, except for leftover tools from half-finished renovation projects. One wall near the side of the house had been ripped down to the studs, and bundles of wires had literally been pulled through drywall and left exposed.

I led the way, like I'd in some way be the one doing the protecting if push came to shove. Middle school witches knew more magic than I did. My only saving grace was the athame—if it came down to it, I could seriously mess up whatever Bridger was doing here.

Ash and I didn't talk, and we moved slowly, but neither one of us was making much effort to be quiet. The overwhelming, soul-crushing pressure outside meant that they were waiting for us. I kept in front of her, in case something came at the two of us. She kept pace with me, moving carefully through the house.

We didn't have much further to look. The first open doorway we found—which looked like it had once boasted double doors—opened up into the rest of the house.

There were a few dividing walls in the house, but everything else had been demolished. The doorway opened into one large room—what must have once been a kitchen, dining room, and at least one, if not several, living areas. The far corner from us was covered in thick tarps, rustling against the night wind and leaking in a draft I could feel all the way over here.

Now it was some sort of makeshift chapel. Row after row of church pews had been set up in the room, facing a fireplace. Along the walls were dozens of candles and piles of wax spilled all down the wall and onto the floor.

"I'm here," I called out. "I know you've been waiting. But I'm here now."

Directly in front of us was the oldest fireplace I'd ever seen. It was made from bricks that had seen better days and mortar that had been chipped away decades ago. There was a distinct jaggedness to the shape, and it even leaned to the left. A man stood in front of it, and I steeled myself for my first meeting with Moonset's only surviving protégé.

But the warlock standing in front of me wasn't Cullen Bridger, a man almost old enough to be my own father. It was a kid, even younger than me.

It was Luca.

TWENTY-EIGHT

"I don't know why they surrendered, nor do I care to speculate. At this time, all we know is that Moonset has been apprehended, their cult dismantled, and the war ended."

Illana Bryer
On the voluntary surrender of Moonset

"Luca?" Ash's voice was barely a whisper.

I expected some kind of attack, or at the very least, gloating. But Luca looked like he wasn't even aware of our presence. His was hugging himself, and he looked lost. At the sound of his name, he dropped to the floor, legs tucked under him, and began rocking back and forth.

Framing him on either side, with their backs to us, sat my family. They were seated in the first row of pews, with

Malcolm and Jenna to the left, and Bailey and Cole slumped on the right.

All four of them faced Luca, but he didn't seem to notice. He continued rocking. That's when I noticed the way Jenna was slumped against Mal's shoulder, and Cole's hand was dangling lifelessly from the arm of the bench.

I don't know what I'd been expecting, but it wasn't some sort of demonic Bible study. "What the fuck," I breathed.

Luca didn't even notice us. His head was craned awkwardly to the side, looking more like an extra in *The Exorcist* than a high school boy. He finally looked towards us, though his eyes never actually left the ceiling. "Who are you?"

"It's Justin," I finally said, keeping my hands upright at my side, trying not to look like a threat. Luca was the warlock? Luca had been the one to summon us to Carrow Mill? But he acted like he hated us. I didn't understand.

He cocked his head to the side suddenly, and I flinched. Luca didn't notice, his ear was towards the fire. Then he started nodding. "I remember now. You're one of them." He cupped his hand and made a beckoning motion.

A burst of air swept forward from behind me, like a giant fan that had just been turned on. It stank, smelling like burnt plastic and Cole's dirty gym socks. At first I thought the room was darkening, but then I realized it was the wind. It was just like the presence I'd felt when the Harbinger had killed himself, with faint traces of awareness like we'd felt outside. *Maleficia isn't supposed to be aware. This is something else.* The shadowy wind, like diluted black smoke, swept over the fire and caught fire: smoky air igniting into green fire.

The flames sailed across the room, swirling around Luca. *Into* him. He flinched, his body seizing up for a moment as he absorbed…whatever it was. Maleficia?

Luca raised his head, nodded once, and Bailey turned in her seat. Her eyes glowed with the same shade of green as the fire that had just disappeared inside Luca. She squinted at me, eyes sightless and vacant. Next to me, Ash exhaled and then collapsed onto the ground.

"Ash!" I dropped down next to her, feeling her neck and praying for a pulse. Why was Bailey doing this?

We only need one. At the theater, Bailey collapsed after using too much magic. She'd been weak. Something must have slipped inside. That had been what Quinn was worried about. But even above my arguments, he wouldn't have ignored the signs. They would have checked her out to make sure she was okay. So whatever was inside of her had been able to fool the Witchers.

Ash drew in a breath. Slow. She was still alive, but unconscious. Bailey settled back in her seat, looking straight ahead. *They needed one, and they took Bailey. She could make the others do whatever she wanted.* Ash shifted next to me, murmured something nonsensical. She wasn't dead. Bailey hadn't killed somebody.

"Don't be angry," Luca said, faintly. "They slip through the cracks, and you'll never know they're there."

"Is that what happened to you?"

Luca tapped his temple. "I have to keep them safe. They need us. We're *chosen.*"

We only need one. We. I looked at Jenna and the others. "Are they…"

"…sleeping," Luca finished. His voice was hoarse and he was drenched in sweat. Sitting so close to the fireplace couldn't have been helping. More than hoarse, his voice sounded raw. As if he'd spent the last hours screaming.

Luca had aged twenty years in just a day. His skin was sallow, hanging off of his bones. He'd already been skinny, but now he looked almost emaciated, his eyes sunken in and huge. "They said that you must come together. I had to prepare the way."

"Who said?"

His head rotated towards me, like a creepy doll's head. "The ones in the fire." Our eyes didn't meet, he was looking somewhere above me. At *something* above me.

"Luca? Were they the ones who taught you how to invoke the darkness?" Ash's voice was thick but gentle. She braced herself against the back of one of the pews. Whatever happened to her, she'd recovered somewhat.

He started laughing then. It wasn't the crazy laugh, but something that was half guffaw and half throat-clearing. "I'm not crazy," he announced, as if we would believe him. "I just… can't think while they're here. But now you're here. They'll let me go, now that you're here." "Right," I said to him. "I'm here now. All five of us are here. That's what you were trying to do, right?"

His eyes dropped again, his head shifted. He was looking at Bailey and Cole, limp and empty on their bench.

No, he was looking at Bailey. "He didn't tell me. Not anything." His head shot up. "I didn't know. I promise."

"You didn't know what, Luca?"

Their were tears in his eyes. "They get inside your head. Crawl around like serpents. Leak out your sockets and nibble on your feelings. They won't leave. Won't leave. Don't even know they're there unless they take a little bite." He flinched, his whole body convulsing in one single spasm, and then his head was craning to the left. There was a shimmer in the air around him, like the air was bending around something that sunk into the fireplace. It was gone almost as quickly as it had appeared.

"Will they leave now? Now that you've brought us here, Luca?" I kept using his name, I wasn't sure why, but I felt like it was important.

Just like that, the boy snapped. I don't know what it was I said, or what he heard in my words. His eyes were suddenly hot and his face flushed red. "You don't know me! They told me to bring you here, and I did! They told me the truth! No one tells the truth anymore!"

Ash stepped up, touching my shoulder and stepping to my right and holding out her arms. Drawing his attention away, I realized. Whatever it was I'd said, maybe he wouldn't see it in Ash. He knew her, after all.

"Just talk to us, Luca," she said. "Say whatever it is you need to say."

"You'd like that, wouldn't you?" But with Ash, his voice wasn't angry. It was just tired. "*Now* you have time for me. *Now* you know I'm alive." He flinched, and then again, like something in his head was causing him pain. Again, there was that moment of bending air, like a mirage that wasn't fully formed.

"They're coming," he said woodenly.

The bottom dropped out of my stomach. I couldn't stop myself from asking. "Who's coming?"

"The Abyssals."

"Is that what you've been doing?" Ash asked, her face pale. "Trying to open a door for them to come through? Is that what tonight was about? Bringing them out?"

He looked at us like we were crazy. "They're not coming *here*."

My mouth had gone dry. "Then where?"

He shifted to the side, and his left arm pointed towards the fire. "There. They want to remember what warmth feels like. It's so cold there."

"I remember," I whispered. Ash shot me a surprised look, but I didn't explain. Not only was now not the time, but I didn't think I could talk about that night. Just thinking about touching the Abyss and remembering how it felt like it was devouring everything that was good and happy inside me.

He flinched again and started rolling his neck. I couldn't hear the sounds, but he sighed in relief after a few rotations. "It... gets easier when they leave," he said, as if that made any difference.

"And they... talk to you?" I asked.

Luca started to stand, stretching as he did. "Sometimes. Sometimes it's not... words, exactly. Sometimes it's like they're rooting around in my brain, and I can feel their fingers digging through all my memories."

"How did this happen, Luca? How could you do this?" Ash sounded afraid, even if it didn't show on her face.

"I didn't have much of a choice," he snapped. "I didn't know the spells were opening a pathway. I'm not an idiot." His look said he dared Ash to challenge him. "I thought it was something forgotten. Something Moonset hadn't destroyed. He didn't know what he was selling me, but I saw it for what it was. I was going to show everyone that I was more than this."

His coloring had even improved. It was like whatever had been ravaging him a few minutes ago was ebbing away more and more the longer we were here. "And you thought you could finally step out of our shadows," Ash finished for him, understanding dawning on her face.

"It wasn't like that. I just thought . . . I could stand out. Stop being the one everyone forgets about. My parents. You. Maddy. Even *them*," he said, glancing at my brothers and sisters. "They looked at me and saw him." He reached forward and grabbed Malcolm by the hair, pulling his head forward.

"Hey!" I stepped forward, holding out the athame.

Unfortunately, this was the wrong approach. The next thing I knew there was a knife in Luca's hand too, and it was pointing at Mal. There was no way I could cross the room and push him out of the way before he attacked— maybe killed—my brother.

The curse. But Luca must have known about it, too, because he dropped the knife. "She'll do anything I want," he said, nodding to Bailey. "She knows I'd never hurt her.

And she'll scramble their brains and leave them nothing but vegetables if I tell her to."

"Okay," I said, dropping my hand. "I'm sorry. You're in control."

"Do you want to know why you're here, Daggett? Haven't you wondered? Why Carrow Mill?"

"Because you wanted us here," I said. "You wanted us here, and we came."

"No," he said, with a smile that suggested darkness. "*This* is where it all started. It's where the blood was spilt, and everything changed."

But in this case, he was dead wrong. "Moonset started here," I said evenly. "My father and the others were students here. I know."

He didn't like that. He took a step back, releasing Mal and pointing his athame at me. "You knew? *You knew?* And still you're kissing up to Fallingbrook like they're going to save you?"

"What's Fallingbrook have to do with this?"

"Fallingbrook killed your parents. How can you even *think* about trusting them?"

"Luca, I know this," I said, tucking the knife in my back pocket and returning my hands to the surrender position. "Everyone does. We're taught it in school, remember? We talked about it my first day."

"You know the lie," he said, the knife cutting imaginary lines in the air. "But you don't know the truth."

"What truth?" I said, growing impatient. "My parents

embraced the black arts, turned to terrorism, and started a war. *Everyone* knows this story."

"Because that's what Fallingbrook tells them to believe," he crowed. "They don't know the truth. History's written by the victors, Justin. Moonset wasn't a cult. They didn't start out as terrorists."

"What are you talking about?" Ash's voice was trembling.

Luca shook his head, all traces of his earlier weakness were now completely gone. In fact, he looked better than I'd ever seen him. A new kind of life surged in him, replacing his earlier weakness with vigor. In the halls at school, even with Bailey, there was always a kind of greasy, slouching going on with him. For the first time, he was standing straight, and he'd never more resembled his cousin.

"Covens form for a reason. Moonset was no different. They weren't monsters. They were heroes. Destiny brought them here ... to turn back the tide. And they were feared, after all the good they did. The Congress *turned* on them. Tried to destroy them from the inside. They couldn't make heroes out of them. That would threaten the Congress's power. So they tried to destroy Moonset ... and created an enemy they couldn't defeat."

"That's not true," I said. Everyone knew what Moonset had stood for.

"It is," he said. "*They* told me. Moonset never embraced the darkness. They weren't warlocks."

"Stop lying, Luca!" Ash turned to me. "He's just trying to trick you. Toying with your emotions. You can't believe him."

"I know," I said, but my voice was quiet. Couldn't I?

What if the story had been wrong all these years? What if Moonset weren't the villains everyone thought they were? What if there was another side to the story?

"They'll be here soon," he said, stepping away from the fireplace, and away from the church benches. "They can *show* you the truth."

Ash's voice broke in, warningly. "Justin... the fireplace."

The bricks inside the fireplace had started glowing. Spellscripts had been written all around the fireplace, and they were moving, streaming from brick to brick like some sort of ticker tape. Row after row, glowing scarlet against the bricks.

"To the... downward... silence... habits..." The symbols were moving too fast for me to decipher, washing out the closer they got to the fire, and then reappearing on the other side.

The wind had picked up; the tarp against the back corner of the house started whipping against the wood siding.

"They made me do it," Luca suddenly whispered, losing some of that shine and bravado, and reminding me of the kid I'd met on my first day. The one who wanted nothing more than to lay his head down on his book bag and pretend that none of this was happening. "They made me."

"People could have died. You invoked Maleficia. You're no better than them," Ash said, suddenly harsh. Though I'd put my knife away, she hadn't. But it didn't look like she was going to be flinging around magic with hers. More like flinging that knife into his chest. I grabbed her by the shoulder. She tugged against me, but I kept holding on.

"But when they get in your head," Luca snarled, "you

don't have a choice. Disobedience isn't an option. They were in control. They killed that man. Not me."

"You opened the door, Luca! You can't possibly think you're innocent."

"Ash…maybe now's not the time," I muttered. Something was going on in the fire. A normal hearth fire was all sorts of healthy oranges and reds and even a little blue. The fire in the fireplace, though, was changing. The blue gained more prominence, and the hissing of the burning wood started growing louder, sounding more like a acetylene torch.

And it was growing darker, giving off less light.

The blues split into tongues of blue and green, each a sickly, unhealthy kind of shade. The room was suddenly cast into something much like moonlight.

And then the fire spoke.

"Child of Moonset," the fire crackled.

Ash had already started backing away when the fire began to change. She moved to my side, and then her hand was in mine. There wasn't anything visible in the flames—not like the inhabitants of the Abyss had faces—but there was that same predatory presence. Like the Devil had personally turned all his attention on just the two of us.

If it came down to a choice, I preferred the preternatural presence outside that made me feel like prey over the monster in the fire pit. Monsters shouldn't speak.

"I brought them, just as you demanded." In contrast to us, Luca had actually gotten closer to the fireplace—and the thing inhabiting it.

"Yesssss," the thing hissed, cracks and pops punctuating its words. The fire grew larger, darker and larger. Each tongue of flame that stretched out seemed to do so with purpose, like hands straining against a cage. One extended out, reaching towards Luca with a caress. He leaned forward, and the fire brushed his skin but didn't seem to hurt him.

The air was thick with something profane—a presence that was so vast it dwarfed the rest of the room and made the oxygen taste strange and sulfurous. My grip tightened on Ash's hand, and almost like we were one we both took another step backwards.

"Scion of Daggett." The fire shifted, sending a veil of sparks up the chute. "Know usssss."

"No," I replied.

"So ssseditious. Like your maker."

"I'm nothing like my father," I snapped. Ash's grip tightened.

"Ssstanding there wearing his face," a second voice—this one more feminine—said, sending up another shower of shimmering sparks. "Human irony."

"Justin, we need to do something," Ash whispered.

I nodded, but my focus was on the fire. They'd been summoned into the fire. Maybe there was something to that.

"You brought us here, didn't you? *You* were the ones who wanted us to come here. Why?" My words were all bravado, but I was hoping the things peering through the fire couldn't know that.

In the aftermath of the fire's touch, Luca had grown silent, glassy eyed and drooling. Sleeping, just like the others, only his eyes weren't closed.

"Yessss. Feel. Let it burn inssside you."

"They want you angry?" Ash was talking, but it was half to herself. And then, more forcefully, "What do you want with him? With all of them?"

"Moonssset trespassed against us," the female seethed. "*You* shall be the tithe that balances the scales."

"You can't have him!" Ash called out, extending her knife once again. She stepped forward, leaving me behind. She pointed her knife at Luca, but it was more than that. I recognized the quick flicks of her wrist, the way her hand looped around at the sides.

She was drawing something.

The fireplace erupted, just like it would have if someone had thrown a bucket of gasoline on it. Where there had been only a pair of voices before, suddenly there were dozens. Some seared with rage, others with lust, but most were impatient moans. "OURS!!!"

"I don't think they liked that very much," I said, edging forward.

"Their blood bindssss us," came the voice from the flames. This one was different than the others. Dry. Cold-blooded. "Your blood releasesss."

My blood? "I won't free you," I said.

"You will. So it will come to passsss. Hisss blood is not enough."

I looked down at Luca, saw the cut down his arm. I don't know how I didn't see it before. The cut was old, crusted and clotted, but it still looked serious. "Was Luca telling the truth? Was Moonset innocent?"

Sparks surged upward, and for a moment they had a face. "Villainsss. Monsterssss."

I wanted that sinking feeling in my stomach not to exist. I *wouldn't* feel disappointment. Moonset had made their beds a long time ago. There was no sense trying to change the sheets fifteen years later.

"Ssstriking down one of our own as they did," the fire hissed. "Who were they to pronounce such a fate upon her?"

"Kore," a second voice moaned. "Sister mine."

Ash hesitated, looking at me over her shoulder. "I know that name. But Moonset didn't kill her," she said, her voice less certain. "Robert Cooper did."

The fire voices had seemed to forget us. It shrank a little, now little more than three separate tongues each striving upwards in a different direction.

"So shall she be avenged," the female said.

"And she shall walk into the world, fettered and forgotten, her blood shall sow seeds of vexation," recited the dry one.

"Kore," again moaned the third.

Ash was shaking now. I moved to her, the two of us now standing in a line with the benches. If I reached to my left, I could tuck back a stray lock of Bailey's hair. Just sleeping. All of them looking so peaceful.

"The female works against ussss."

Just like that, the fire erupted into motion. It became not just a fire, but also a creature with three fire-born tentacles. One moment we were standing there, the next one of those tentacle arms was flying towards us. "*Aere dis,*" I shouted, using one of the spells from Sherrod's book, but the wind it called didn't slow the tentacles down. I did the only thing I could think of: I grabbed Ash and pulled the two of us down.

Quick, but not quick enough.

"Agh!"

I had smacked my shoulder against the side of the church bench, but when I looked up at Ash's cry, it was to see her hand almost in my face, and the blue-green tentacle wrapped around her wrist. Her athame clattered to the ground, and just as quickly as it had flown our way, the tentacle unwrapped itself and slithered back towards the fire.

I was grabbing her arm a moment later. "Are you okay?"

But a closer inspection revealed only a hint of redness on her skin. No burn.

"Cold," she whispered through her teeth. "Numb." One whole side of her face had gone slack, the skin sinking downwards like a stroke victim. "Have to get out of here..."

I turned back towards the fireplace. "Why do all this? Why? Luca, and everything you put him through. My *family*. WHY?"

"Ripen and rot, Child of Moonset. Touchstone of all those bound to you." The dry voice whispered, crackled really, like a viper. "Ripen and rot, for this night they have condemned you to us, a plague to send to the Abyss itself. Swear unto usss."

"To usss."

"We will bless you, vessels of our essence. Free usss, let usss in, and we will crush those who persssecute you. Our powers are legion. We can teach you to channel the Abyss. To live forever, with usss. In usss. As usss. Swear!"

"That's not going to happen."

"They will spill your blood where you ssstand," the viper hissed. "Swear, and your hour of vengeance will be had. Sssuch power we will bestow upon you."

I could feel it in the air, the symbol that Ash had been drawing. It hung there, half-finished and pulsing with magic that could quite possibly rip me to shreds. Rip any of us to shreds. I could feel it—this wasn't just another spell, it was something more. It was almost finished—it was *begging* to be finished.

"Swear!" the viper demanded. The fire began to rage again, the three prongs losing cohesion as the fireplace was consumed in one giant ball of cold fire.

"Swear!" repeated the female.

"Swear," moaned the other.

The knife was still in my back pocket. My hand slid around the pommel like the blade had been crafted just for me. It was hot against my skin, warmth the fire couldn't provide.

They asked for it.

"Fuck you," I snapped, bringing the knife down in a slash that ripped through and completed the symbol that Ash had started.

Aerous. The symbol glowed so bright that it dimmed the Abyssal fire. It was a familiar symbol, but still one that I had never quite seen before. But I knew what it was, now. Aerous. The primal wind. A spellform. I didn't have time to wonder how Ash had known a spellform, or how I'd known how to complete it.

A tornado exploded in front of me, throwing me backwards. For a moment, I sailed in the air, my eyes drawn to the sickly blue green of the fireplace. I saw the fire wrap itself around Luca like a cocoon; heard a dozen inhuman shrieks; and felt a whirlpool pulling us down, down, down into the darkness.

Then the roof collapsed.

TWENTY-NINE

*"When we found them, they had been
lined up in a row of cribs. The twins were
together in one, of course. It was almost a month
before we found evidence that Baby Girl
Daggett had a different mother."*

....

Adele Roman
Moonset Historian Official Witness Statement,
From the raiding of the Moonset compound

I don't know how any of us made it out of there in one piece.
A magical SWAT team had descended upon the farmhouse
property. Adults were *everywhere*, searching the grounds, talking in hushed circles. Spotlights blazed on the remains of the
farmhouse.

I was awake for a long time before I was actually conscious. For the longest time, I watched Witchers hustling to and fro, and others farther away, combating the weather magic.

"Someone really huffed and puffed all over that house, didn't they?" a familiar voice drawled from next to me.

Jenna was leaning against a tire. I craned my neck around, realizing that we'd both been propped up against the side of an SUV. "Are you okay?"

Her hair was a mess, and both of us were covered in dirt and grime, but she nodded slowly. "Think so. Last thing I remember is leaving the house with Malcolm."

"They've got Witchers all over the place trying to maintain control," Jenna said. "I heard them talking earlier. They're spread thin, trying to cover up what was happening in town, and contain all the shit Luca stirred up."

"You idiot." There was suddenly a voice and a presence in front of us, blocking out the light. My stomach tightened, thinking for a moment that the ... demons, or whatever they were, had come back.

It was Quinn. "Do you have any idea what could have happened to you tonight? What did you think you were doing?"

"We ran out of Thin Mints?" Jenna asked, assuring me that she really was okay. If she could crack jokes so quickly after a house caved in on her, she was going to be all right. "You wouldn't believe how hard it was to track down a Girl Scout at this hour."

"Do you know what's going on out there? How could

you be so stupid?" he demanded, his voice oddly whispered. Like he was afraid someone was going to overhear him. Come to think of it, he was facing us at a strange angle, more like he was looking towards the back of the house than talking to us.

"It was Luca," I said. "I thought...I thought it was someone else. But he released more of the darkness. I know. It *talked* to me."

Quinn's self-possession got the best of him, and he spent the next several moments like a gaping fish in front of us. Mouth opened. Mouth closed. Opened. Closed. "Now you listen to me you little asshole," he managed to get out, though his voice was strangled. "You don't remember anything. *Anything.* Any of you."

I went to argue, to say something, but Jenna caught my eye and shook her head. It became an elaborately silent conversation, with complex thoughts expressed only through our looks.

I have to tell them what happened. They need to know.

She tugged at her hair, trying to create some order out of the chaos. *No they don't. But you'll tell me later.*

Of course I will. Don't be stupid. I scratched at my forehead, my fingernails coming back dark with dried blood. My second attempt was much softer, more uncertain. There wasn't any wound I could feel, no sensitivity, but nevertheless there was a whole section of my hair that was plastered against my scalp, congealed with that same brownish red.

Is everyone okay? Jenna's head didn't move, but her eyes moved around quickly and anxiously. She didn't have to say anything. I read the question on her face.

I shrugged. That in itself said everything I knew.

"Ahh, it's about time they began to awake," Illana Bryer was suddenly above us. Her outfit was some sort of strange mesh of skintight slacks with a black shawl hanging nearly down to her ankles wrapped around her.

"So helpful of you to keep an eye on the two of them, Quinn," she continued, staring down at us. I met her eyes only for a moment, enough time to see the calculating coldness in them, before I turned and scooted closer towards Jenna. "But someone will be around shortly to take care of them."

"Take care of us?" Jenna's voice was acid. "Considering something attacked us, and my brother looks like someone beat the shit out of him, you'd think a little medical care wouldn't be out of the question."

Illana's lips thinned. "Yes, well that was before the five of you were found cavorting with a known warlock."

"Who?"

She didn't seem to like my question. Or maybe she didn't like the challenge in my voice. "Luca Denton, obviously."

Jenna, God bless her, started to laugh. The kind of Mean Girl laugh that said she enjoyed other people's misery just a little too much. "Luca?" She glanced at me, amused deception in her eyes. "This is some kind of joke, right? Or some sort of test?"

"I assure you this is a matter of the utmost gravity," Illana said.

"I'm sure," Jenna laughed, throwing her head back a little. "Luca invoked the black arts without screwing it up? He's

Maddy's little lapdog. If he'd even *had* an original thought in his life—and I seriously doubt that's the case—then I can't even picture him doing it right in the first place! He's a loser."

"That's enough, Jenna," Quinn said.

"You're awfully silent," Illana murmured, and I looked up to find her homing in on me with her laser eyes. "No reaction? No protests of innocence?"

"I remember something," I said, fully ignoring the advice of Quinn, whose posture tensed immediately. Even Jenna was sitting straighter now.

"I thought *you* might," she said, her emphasis on the "you" sounding much like I was the only one she expected would. Her tone was hungry for it, her expression wolfish. "Tell me."

"We know about Kore," I said, my tongue stumbling over the name. "Who really killed her."

Illana stared at me, her expression cool, her eyes searching mine. I don't know what she saw there, but after a few moments, her lips parted and her eyes widened.

I watched as the effect of the name took its hold over her. At first, there was shock. Then uncertainty. For the first time, perhaps ever, Illana Bryer dropped her gaze and turned away.

"Where did you ... " she whispered, her voice trailing off. And then, as if she realized that she'd forgotten herself, all of the arrogance and prestige of being Illana Bryer came flowing back into her. "Quinn, with me," she suddenly snapped. "Evanson and ... you with the hair, come here." Two adults, a man and a woman, were suddenly in front of us as well. "No one is to speak to them," Illana announced, glancing over her shoulder down on us, and then over to Quinn. "No one at all, until I send for them. The others are gathering as we speak."

Once she was gone, Jenna leaned into me. "What was that?" she whispered. "What did you do?"

I shook my head and shrugged. I really didn't know.

Despite what Illana had dictated, they didn't keep us in the field for much longer. Jenna and I were bundled up, blankets thrown around us, and taken away by Evanson and ... the one with the hair a short while later.

But they didn't take us home.

———

The storm had finished passing over us, and already the temperature was starting to rise slightly. The driver seemed to have no trouble on the roads.

Entering the high school in the middle of the night wasn't my idea of a good time. By this point, I'd long since been picturing my bed, and planning a long, long recovery from everything that had been going on.

We entered from the rear parking lot, walking through one building after another as we headed towards the front of the school.

"I want to know where the rest of my family is," Jenna demanded of Evanson. "We haven't seen my brothers or my sister since we woke up outside that ... *farmhouse.*" Somehow, she made farmhouse sound like it something reprehensible.

Evanson didn't say anything, however. Neither did the redhead who walked behind us.

"It's just like the drivers," I explained to her.

"They're not going to talk, no matter how much we try."

"If Maddy would have taught me that spell to set his boxers on fire, I'm sure he'd say *something*," she sniped. I thought I caught a glimpse of a smile on Evanson's face.

As we approached the main building, there was more activity in the halls. Men and women, stationed at every intersection. The closer we got to the front of the school, the more guards we saw. All in all, we probably passed thirty to fifty, and that was just down the main thoroughfare of the school. Every single one of them stopped what they were doing long enough to watch us pass. No one said a word.

Our guards led us towards the main office, a place that was quickly becoming my home away from home. From there they led us back into the conference room where I'd been spending so much time lately. Only this time, there weren't only one or two people inside. There was a full-on dozen. The long rectangular table was full on three sides, with Illana Bryer in the dead center of one of the long sides. Across from her, the entire side of the table was empty, except for two empty chairs clearly left for us.

"Oh no," Jenna whispered, as Evanson held the door for the two of us. One look at all the closed, emotionless faces in the room and I think we both knew that this wasn't just a simple expulsion.

"Thank you, Aaron. That will be all," Illana said formally. Once we were in the room, Evanson nodded once and closed the door from the outside. I watched him disappear down the hallway through the slats in the blinds.

"That's Robert Cooper," Jenna whispered at my side, nodding to a white-haired man who was so sour he looked like he had lemon juice running through his veins.

"This is a troubling night for all of us," Illana spoke first, but she was speaking to her gathered comrades, not to us. We were the only two in the room under the age of fifty—although with witches you could never really tell. Some could have been close to one hundred. "For the past several months, we've all heard the whispers and scandal that has been plaguing this town."

"Excuse me. But before you convene the lynch mob, the *polite* thing to do would be to introduce yourselves." It was the standard Jenna response. However, it wasn't Jenna who was speaking. I was.

Illana Bryer stared at me in shock. Twice in one night, I'd caught her by surprise. But I didn't stop there. "And before you start with *anything*, the least you could do is inform us how our family is."

"Absurd!" Robert Cooper glared at us from Illana's right. "I don't answer to you, *Moonset*."

In the corner of the room, where I hadn't noticed him before, Quinn pushed himself off of the wall. "Grandfather..."

"And I've heard more than enough out of *you*," the man continued with a brief look to his left, his voice dripping with contempt. "You're lucky you aren't seated next to the warlocks."

Conversation began to spring up between different groups around the table. Two women to my left were murmuring about how it was "so upsetting." A group of men who looked like they should have been at a sports bar were grunting about "mistake letting them come here."

Jenna had taken her seat, but I didn't. For once, I wasn't going to be the one trying to placate everyone, and make things better. Besides, this wasn't a fire we were just going to walk away from.

Screw the good twin.

"Excuse me!" My voice rang throughout the room, and all movement stopped. Quinn's grandfather looked like he'd swallowed his tongue. "Are they okay? Where are they?" I kept my voice loud, and controlled. I thought I caught a glimpse of approval on Quinn's face, but with him it was so hard to tell.

"Your family is fine, dear boy," Illana said, her voice smooth and uncompromised. "As is the girl, I can assure you." She, too, looked less murderous than some of the others around the table, but her tone wasn't entirely respectful either. "They've shown no adverse effects to their… trials this evening."

"Where are they?"

"Safe," Illana said.

"They were not deemed a threat," Robert snapped.

"He has a right to know what's going on," Quinn fired back.

There was a moment's pause before Illana stepped in.

"Justin Daggett. Jenna Bellamont. We've been gathered tonight after accusations that you have been known associates with a warlock."

"That's ridiculous," I said, feeling fire in my veins. "Jenna wasn't even involved. She was as much a victim as the others."

"Nevertheless," Illana continued, as if I hadn't said anything of value, "those are the accusations in play."

"We're the only ones they're scared of," Jenna murmured quietly, looking up at me. "They don't care about the others."

Robert Cooper cleared his throat. "And that's all you need to know. Now then—"

"I am not bait." I took a deep breath, and looked at the members of the Congress. None of them, save Illana, looked particularly intimidating. "And this is the last time you'll use any of us like that." Someone had to stand up. Someone had to put this to an end.

They'd brought us here, hoping we'd draw out their warlock. Hoping that maybe, just maybe, the warlock would take care of the Moonset problem for them. And if not, well, we could both be painted with the same brush. The whispers once again picked up around the table, from smug whispers of "how inappropriate" to more scandalized "of course it was *them*." Everyone around the table had an opinion, it seemed. That's when I knew for certain.

The Invisible Congress. Made up of the leaders of the Great Covens and a few token Solitaires. They pulled at our strings and toyed with our lives. I looked down at Jenna, who was looking back up at me like we'd never seen each other before.

"Young man, should you choose to interrupt *me* again, I will have you bound and gagged," Quinn's grandfather said, taking to his feet. We stood across the table from each other. I swallowed. "We're all well aware of your need for dramatics," he said, waving his hand in a way that included the two of us. "And I won't tolerate it this evening. You lost your rights the moment you consorted with the Abyss."

"Calm yourself, Robert," Illana said, placing her hand on his arm. "Remember, we're not at war any longer."

The rotund, sweating man seated on the other side of Robert cleared his throat. "Are we sure that both of them are involved with the Denton boy? Their files indicate the girl is a risk, but hardly the boy."

Robert looked to his left, pitching his voice for his grandson. "Bring the girl in."

I followed Quinn with my eyes until he went to the door, and then I turned to watch as he disappeared across the hall. A few moments later he returned with Ash following behind.

There was soot covering her face. I could see rips in her shirt underneath the too-large jacket she was wearing, and her hair was a mess, but she looked otherwise unhurt.

"You can stand with Quinn," Illana said, not altogether unkindly to her. But Ash didn't move.

Jenna's fingernails clawed into my wrist all of a sudden. I jumped, trying to pull my arm away, but she held fast. Her attention never left Robert. Her point was obvious— *stare at your girlfriend later.*

"The evidence is clear," Robert continued. "The Moonset children may not have initiated the influx of dark magic into our world these last few months, but their involvement cannot be denied. If Ashen Farrer hadn't invoked the spellform that saved their lives, who knows what would have happened?"

I glanced at Ash, who was still standing near the door, her eyes uncertainly moving around the table. *She realizes there's more to this, too.*

"How *did* she learn a spellform at such a young age?" one of the ladies across the table asked, leaning forward in her seat. "There have been no applications on file with her name on them."

Ash opened her mouth, but as it turned out, no one really cared to hear what she had to say.

The sweating man shifted in his seat, his hands steepled in front of him. "I could not presume," he said loftily. "My boys would never violate the law like that."

"You handle the training of spellforms," the woman accused the sweating man. "How else would she have learned if not from one of your trainers?"

"Ash didn't invoke that spell," I interjected. "At least not by herself. I was the one who finished it. Not her." In that moment, our eyes met, and Ash took a step forward. A step towards Jenna and I.

"You weren't brought here to speak," Robert said, coming to his feet again. "And I will not tolerate it any longer."

"Point of order," Quinn interjected, stepping forward again. "But the law states that Coven leaders have the right to speak before the Congress."

"Oh, you can't mean," Robert sputtered. "That's preposterous."

"It's well documented that the children are bound into a coven," Illana murmured. "Although they are still Moonset's offspring." Her lips twisted in distaste.

"They are *infants*," Robert argued. "Neophytes."

"The law is the law," I said slowly. It was something that I'd believed in wholly before tonight, and the one thing our parents had never believed. To them, the world demanded revolution. "I am a coven leader, the same as many of you. And if we're to be charged with aiding a warlock, then I lay the same charge."

The room erupted into loud chatter, but I raised my voice and pointed. "At Robert Cooper."

THIRTY

"There was something disturbing about the five of them. They would look at you with these eyes... like they knew what we'd done. And then there were the spells. Simple magics went haywire around them. Miranda Abbot suggested euthanasia, and was struck down by some sort of seizure. Those babies... those children of Moonset... they're a threat."

....

Nicholas Stone (C: Eventide)
Official Report

This meeting, or trial, or whatever it was, was a farce. Cooper wanted us out of the way—and he'd break the law to do it. But thanks to all the reading I'd done for Quinn, I knew that a charge of invoking the black arts couldn't be ignored. So long as it was made by a coven leader. *Now all those papers make sense. He wanted me to be prepared.*

All conversation died. Every pair of eyes in the room was locked onto me, and not a single one of them was anything less than dumbfounded. Especially not my target.

"This is preposterous," he sputtered. "We don't have to listen to this."

"Yes, you do." I realized what they must see when they looked at me—the spitting image of Sherrod Daggett, calling them to account. "You brought us here, hoping that a myth named Cullen Bridger would come after us. He came close to catching us once. I made the same mistake you did—I assumed Bridger was the warlock here, but it was just a kid that no one cared about."

Robert's eyes narrowed. "Who are you, to make such baseless accusations?"

I didn't back down. I raised my chin, and met his glare with one of my own. "I am the son of Sherrod Daggett." Gasps around the table.

Over a dozen faces were staring up at me, most of them in fear. The room had grown so quiet I could almost hear a bead of sweat dripping down the sweating man's temple. I looked to Quinn, but his dark eyes were impassive. Even Illana's face gave away nothing.

"But I am not my father. *We* are not our parents."

The sentence hung in the air, and no one wanted to hear it. One by one they looked away from me, stopped meeting my eyes.

"You can't keep punishing us for the things our parents

did. And you can't keep manipulating us in hopes that we'll commit a crime more to your liking. In America, that's called entrapment."

"What does this have to do with your charge against Eventide?" one of the woman asked.

"I will not continue to be slandered like this," Robert spat from the other side of the table. "We will not humor your outbursts any further."

"I think we will, darling," Illana said coolly from his side. She turned and addressed the sweating man. "Alexander?"

"I, for one, would like to hear what the boy has to say," Alexander said. "And I want to know where they learned the spellform they used tonight."

Ash sank down in her seat a bit. I had a feeling that no matter what happened tonight, they weren't just going to forget that she knew spells that she hadn't been legally authorized to know.

"I . . ." And then I faltered. This wasn't like trying to convince a principal not to expel us. This was worse. "We can't be held accountable for something we didn't do, unless you hold *him* accountable for the things he did."

"And what is that?" Alexander asked.

"He kept the children in their last home and waited until a wraith attacked before he pulled them out. He's shown a consistent disregard for their lives and health, and each one of you already know it. My grandfather spearheaded the campaign to bring the children here, all under the excuse of seeing what the warlock would do," Quinn said, both his hands behind his back. "That's a violation of the law."

"Bringing us here set into motion whatever Luca was planning," I added. "The Harbinger that died did so because of the Maleficia. Isn't he responsible if he makes choices that cost others their lives?"

Quinn didn't volunteer anything else, and everyone stared at me, waiting.

"Is that everything?" Alexander asked, his fingers steepled in front of him.

I swallowed. "I know that you've been lying. All of you. Moonset stopped one of the Abyssals here once, and you covered it up. It's name was Kore, and everything that Luca did was because the other Abyssals wanted revenge. Which they might have gotten since you brought my family and me here."

The earlier silence exploded outward, as a dozen of the most powerful witches left in the world were united in a growing din of questions, condemnations, and dismissals. What was most telling, however, was that not one of them was silent.

"ENOUGH!" Robert's thundering voice boomed across the table, and cut through the commentary like a knife. "Enough," he repeated, his voice growing quiet but still just as firm. His eyes beaded up from across the table, his earlier contempt replaced with a newly stoked rage. "You know *nothing*," he spat.

Illana stood up, her back like a steel spike. "The Prince led Moonset down the path to darkness," she said stiffly.

"Then why does everyone say Robert Cooper and Eventide were the ones to kill her?" Ash demanded.

"Who told you all this?" Robert trumpeted in a moment of quiet. He looked strangely smug all of a sudden.

"Luca," I replied automatically, my guard up. "Before he died."

"Convenient," he replied, dragging out the word. "Although the boy hasn't died," he said, clapping his hands together. There was an implicit "yet" at the end of his words.

"What? But you said—"

"We said that your family and the girl were unharmed," Illana provided. "But Luca Denton's condition is a bit more ... contentious."

"Another tragedy for that poor family," one of the women near Illana said under her breath, pressing a handkerchief against her lips.

"I think we've heard enough," Illana said. "It's clear what must be done, for the safety of our families."

"Finally, you come to your senses," Robert muttered. I don't think he meant for anyone else to hear him, but we all did. "Once we move past the boy's baseless accusation, we can decide how to proceed with their sentencing."

"Are you mad?" Illana was taller than her husband, I realized. It was also clear that their marriage wasn't full of sunshine and crossword puzzles. "You cannot bulldoze this through as you might once have, Robert."

I started to smile. "The law is the law."

He didn't like that very much. "*We* are the law," he replied coldly. "*You* are an inconvenience."

"But the law protects me. A coven leader has the right, or rather the *obligation*, to lay a charge of Maleficia if he knows it has merit." Thank god I read all those books while I was under suspension. "And the charge can't be dropped just because you don't like me."

"Laws can be changed," he said, his eyes growing more narrow by the moment.

"That's enough, Robert," Illana said, sounding exhausted. "The boy is right." And then I was on the receiving end of that patented Illana Bryer death stare. "Completely inappropriate though he may be, he is also *right*. You cannot charge him without proving your own guilt. Any crimes he committed only occurred because he was brought to this town, and into contact with these people."

"What say you?" Alexander asked, looking around the table. "Eventide arranged for the children to be brought here, hoping to draw the warlock out. Which they did, and with minimal casualties. Like it or not, they helped stop the warlock." And then he waited, but no one else spoke up, no one offering a protest. "I think that's your answer, Robert."

Robert Cooper didn't say anything.

"Then if we're done here," Quinn announced, "I'm taking my charges back home. If you plan to interrogate them, you can send someone to the house." After a moment's consideration, he added, "Tomorrow. After noon."

"I'm not done yet."

Quinn gave me a death glare of his own. "Justin."

"No. They need to hear this." I turned from him to address the rest of the Coven leaders. "We're not *them*. And you need to stop treating us like we are. Things need to change. We're not Moonset the next generation."

Illana cleared her throat. "We'll take that under advisement. Now then, if that will be all," she said as she indicated the door.

Quinn led us out of the office, but before I could follow after the others, a hand on my shoulder stopped me. I turned, facing Illana.

"You don't tease the hornet's nest as much as you destroy it, do you?"

My forehead knotted up, and I glanced back into the conference room to see him staring at the two of us. "I can see why Quinn thinks your husband's a dick."

There was choked laughter coming from behind me, but Illana's face remained smooth. "Robert may not be the most ... impartial viewpoint where you all are concerned," she said, choosing each word carefully, "but he acts as he does out of precaution."

"We didn't do anything wrong," I said, exhaustion starting to settle in. I don't know why I thought I could convince Illana, but part of me did.

Her lips thinned. "Don't overestimate yourselves. You won two victories tonight. But along the way you broke so many rules, violated trusts, and acted completely inappropriately. In my day, children would *never* speak to their elders like that."

"Maybe we'll teach him some manners," Quinn interjected. "We've got all the time in the world."

Illana stared at me, one of those hard stares that made it impossible to look away. "Just remember something," she said softly. "Your parents did great deeds once, too."

THIRTY-ONE

"You piteous wastes did not take my life. I gave it."

....

Sherrod Daggett
Final Words

"It's going to take me at least an hour to wash out my hair," Jenna said, hand on her hip. The five of us had reunited at the front of the school, staring out the glass doors. Mal's hair was limp and hanging down over his eyes, and both Cole and Bailey looked wiped out. Bailey had been crying, and even Cole's eyes were a little red.

But they were together. All four of my siblings. Something inside me loosened, finally seeing for myself that everyone was okay. I looked to my left, and saw that Quinn and

Ash had wandered farther down the hall, giving us a moment of privacy.

"I think things are going to be different now," I said.

Cole looked up from under his bangs. "No more secrets?"

Mal straightened. "I can't believe I'm saying this, but maybe Cole's got a point. Remember, we've got to be in this together."

Jenna shrugged, sighing. "Do we really have to get all sentimental and in touch with our emotions?"

"I think it's a good idea," Bailey laughed.

There was just a moment, where we were all smiling and looking at each other. Then just like that, it was over, and everyone followed in Quinn's wake. "We'll see," I said.

Bailey hung back, grabbing my arm. She was worried, but serious. "It's not over," she said.

"What's not over? We stopped him, Bay. Everything's going to be okay."

She bit her lower lip. "I know it's my fault." I tried to argue, but for once she didn't back down. "It snuck inside me, and most of the time it was like I was sleeping, but every once and awhile I'd wake up. I could *see,* but I couldn't do anything. But I saw Luca cut himself. I saw him offer the blood. One of them escaped. He's *here* now."

"Who is?"

Her eyes got wide. "The Prince."

One of the Abyssals had escaped? My heart thudded once—hard—and dropped like there was a sudden influx of gravity. "Are you sure?"

But Bailey didn't have time to answer. Ash suddenly

appeared, and linked her arm through mine. "Come on, hero, I'll give you a ride home."

We caught up with the others, who were waiting at the side entrance of the school. Quinn eyed the pair of us, focusing on our entwined arms. "Follow right behind me."

Ash rolled her eyes. "Right, like I'd kidnap him looking like *this*. Have you met me? I could do so much better." Ash dragged me away, heading towards the side entrance while Quinn and Jenna headed for the rear. She dropped her arm the moment we stepped back outside.

"Get rid of it," she said, turning on me before the door had even finished closing. "Throw it on the roof, in the garbage, I don't care."

"Get rid of what?"

She stared up at me. "You know what. I don't know when you found time to get it out of my car, but if they find it on you, you won't get to bluff your way out of what they do to you."

The spellbook. Of course. "I left it in your car," I said, starting to panic. "I didn't get a chance to sneak it away. They had someone watching us the minute we woke up." She bit her lower lip, shaking her head. "That's not funny, Justin. The book isn't in there. I *checked.*"

"Then you made a mistake," I said, moving for the parking lot. Before we even crossed into the actual lot, Quinn's black SUV approached.

He waited just ahead of us while we got into the car, and though I tried to circumspectly look for the spellbook even with him sitting right in front of us, I didn't see any sign of it. And I couldn't start digging under the seat until he pulled away.

"Just drive," I said, squirming down in my seat and feeling in all the gaps between the seat and the console.

But the book wasn't there. Neither was the bag I'd brought along with us. All of my stuff was gone. Even Quinn's athame. "So what happened to it?" Ash said, her voice low as if Quinn would be able to hear her from fifty feet in front of us.

My fingers brushed against something, in the spot where the spellbook had been. Thin, like paper, but harder. I trapped it between two of my fingers and pulled it up. The postcard that had been left in the book.

Something about it didn't look right. It was still the Golden Gate Bridge, with a glimpse of San Francisco in the background. *But it's not the half of the postcard I had before.* I flipped it back over. Two words were written on this half.

Well played.

Another wave of cold swept up my spine. The spellbook was gone. Bailey believed one of the Abyssal Princes had escaped. Sooner or later Robert Cooper was going to pop back up wanting revenge. And Cullen Bridger, the last living link to Moonset, was sending me congratulations.

I glanced across the car at Ash, whose face was screwed up in concentration and exhaustion. It had been a long night, and tomorrow might be longer still.

"I think you owe me a makeup date," I said.

THE END

About the Author

Scott Tracey (Avon Lake, Ohio) lived on a Greyhound bus for a month, wrote his illustrated autobiography at the age of six, and barely survived Catholic school. His gifts can be used for good or evil, and he strives for both for his own amusement. *Witch Eyes* was his debut YA novel.